THE TRUTH ABOUT HER

Jacqueline Maley is an award-winning journalist and columnist with the *Sydney Morning Herald* and *The Age*. She lives in Sydney. This is her first book.

THE TRUTH ABOUT HER

JACQUELINE
MALEY

THE BOROUGH PRESS

The Borough Press
An imprint of HarperCollins*Publishers* Ltd
1 London Bridge Street
London SE1 9GF

www.harpercollins.co.uk

HarperCollins*Publishers*
1st Floor, Watermarque Building, Ringsend Road
Dublin 4, Ireland

This hardback edition 2022
1

First published in Great Britain by
HarperCollins*Publishers* 2021

First published in Australia in 2021 by
HarperCollins*Publishers* Australia Pty Limited

A catalogue record for this book is available from the British Library

HB ISBN: 978-0-00-852017-5
TPB ISBN: 978-0-00-852373-2

Printed and bound in the UK using 100% Renewable Electricity
by CPI Group (UK) Ltd

for Evelyn

You are my one, and I have not another;
Sleep soft, my darling, my trouble and treasure.

– Christina Rossetti,
'Crying, my little one, footsore and weary'

PART ONE

CHAPTER ONE

The summer after I wrote the story that killed Tracey Doran, I had just stopped sleeping with two very different men, following involvement in what some people on the internet called a 'sex scandal', although when it was described that way it didn't seem like the kind of thing that happened to me. It seemed like something that happened to the people I wrote about, who were a different sort of people altogether. That summer I was living in a tumbledown terrace in Glebe with my small daughter Maddy, who was the centre of everything. The house was old, and it stood under the firm guardianship of a giant Moreton Bay fig which was even older than it. The fig was huge and occasionally menacing, like a cross between a giant pterodactyl and a piece of ancient fauna that belonged in the business end of a fairytale. It was always threatening to overwhelm the house, but I had other things to worry about then. The fig I lived with, the house I loved. It stood across the road from a park that was stitched into the foreshore, and it boasted harbour glimpses, if you stood on the lip of the bath and threw up the sash of the window above the toilet. I often stood on the lip of the bath, not to glimpse the harbour, but because it was the only way you could get a survey of your entire outfit, there being no full-length mirror in the house. Since moving in, I had been meaning to buy one, and fix it to the back of a door, but that had been over two years ago. There never seemed to be any time for this project, and I had become used to regarding my body in segments – face, décolletage, a pair of floating legs. As I moved through the city for my job, every now and then I came upon myself reflected in a full-length mirror in an office bathroom or a boutique. *Here I am*, I would think. *There I go*. It was a fresh surprise every time, this vision of my whole self.

The lack of a large reflective surface was not the house's only fault. It had rising damp and crumbling plasterwork. The backyard was carpeted with spiky sweet gum pods and its French doors swelled when it rained. Still, it was the kind of uniquely Sydney prize that caused real estate agents to slime their business cards through the letterbox on a near-daily basis, and even, once, to sidle up to me at Maddy's preschool Christmas concert (she played an unconvincing sheep) and ask if I was thinking of selling, the market being what it was. I would never have thought of selling, not least because the house wasn't mine. It belonged to my Uncle Sam, who had bought it for $20,000 in 1970, a fact which caused people to gasp when he relayed it at dinner parties.

Maddy and I had lived there since she was two years old and I had left her father, following The Incident. Or Charlie had left me, I still wasn't sure which. All I knew was the idyll of early motherhood, of milk stains and night feeds, of worries and firsts – first smile, first finger-clench, first step, first supermarket tantrum, first haemorrhoid (mine), first pang of gut-clenching guilt – had come to a crashing end for me. Later, when I discovered how hard it was to care for a child alone, Charlie decided that it was me who had done the leaving. He settled on that position and could not be moved from it. He taunted me, reviling me, saying I chose to go, so what did I expect? But I wasn't sure how much choice really came into it.

At first the Ruby Street terrace was meant to be a temporary arrangement, but Uncle Sam had been so charmed by Maddy – a delectable toddler who threw out smiles like confetti – that we ended up staying. Eventually it was Uncle Sam who moved out, after he had a fall in the bathroom and broke his hip while Maddy and I were on holiday in Queensland. He went to a Potts Point retirement facility where he was visited by a plump and efficient nurse, and where he could walk the harbour at Beare Park, or at least hobble the harbour at Beare Park. It was his favourite stretch of Port Jackson, he said, and it was where he wanted to die. Uncle Sam talked about his death quite openly, as though it was a trip he was planning, a sort of long service leave he would soon be taking up.

I didn't mean to kill Tracey Doran, and as the summer began, I would never have dreamed it would be defined by her death. She was just another story.

*

It being Sydney, the summer started actually sometime in September, when the bottlebrush trees bloomed and the magpies began to warble and swoop with murderous intent – a double act that represented the Australian bush: its beauty was only offered in a context of danger. That year a magpie actually did kill someone, a cyclist, by swooping him so viciously he veered off the cycleway and into the path of an accelerating Mack truck. How to prove mens rea in a bird? I had half a law degree but I didn't know. Whether it was murder or manslaughter was between the magpie and his god, said my colleague Victor as we read this story in horror, sat at our desks and scrolling through the news. Or *her* god, I said, because since Maddy had been born I had been trying to eliminate all forms of sexist language in my speech. This was a goal that was certainly doomed because, despite living in a progressive middle-class milieu, and being mothered solely by a single mother (me) who did literally everything for her, Maddy was a strong enforcer of gender norms. She refused to believe that any child with long hair could be male – something that proved embarrassing in playgrounds full of bountifully tressed boys named things like Leaf and Miro. Maddy also corrected me laughingly when I told her the prime minister could be a girl, too. 'No it can't, Mummy!' she chortled, and I had to admit that the evidence I had for my case was scant. Maddy wore pink clothing as though it had been mandated by a higher power than me, and she had somehow absorbed the holy trifecta of girlish interests – fairies, princesses and unicorns – despite my attempts to push on her books about inspirational female trailblazers, and other blatant early feminist propaganda, like a picture book entitled *Mummy Goes to Work!*

I hoped she kept these opinions to herself at her preschool, where she was looked after beautifully by a tribe of kind but firm women, far more patient than me in their ministrations to her. Every morning before I went to work, I conveyed Maddy into their arms, like they were simply the next link in the maternal daisy-chain, the women who worked so that women like me could work. Who looked after their children while they worked? It was a Russian doll trick that feminism had no answer for. I tried not to feel too guilty about them, or to feel guilty about the fact that Maddy was in childcare full time, while most of the other children were only there a few days a week, like they were in a job-share arrangement, or just indulging a hobby. The mothers of the part-time children had careers but also the ability and financial freedom to take a few days a week to absorb the fleetingness of their children's early years. This was a fleetingness of which I was achingly aware, never more so than when I dropped Maddy off in the mornings and left her dabbing at a bowl of cereal, the fleshy column of her arm dimpling where it met the crease of her wrist in a way that made me want to hold her close, to fit her back into me like a puzzle piece. Despite the mess she found herself born into, I thanked god I had her. Or I would have thanked him, had I believed in him (or her).

On these mornings I would be rushing to work while also wishing myself into my parallel life, the one that had been tagging me like a persistent shadow since The Incident. In this life, Charlie and I were still together, and happy in the kind of way that meant he still kissed my neck. In this parallel life I would have a boutique yet successful career I could dabble in a few days a week, allowing me to use my brain and participate in the right kind of dinner party conversations, but which would also allow me to have days with my child. Days would be spent at the park, and going to storytime at the library, and making shopping trips to Kmart, trips which started off ironic but quickly became something I looked forward to because they broke the tedium. This was true motherhood, as it seemed represented to me by the women I knew. There would be days and days in full mummy-mode, attending indoor play centres and inquiring about the best swimming classes, packing well-balanced lunches into Tupperware that came with special compartments so as to minimise plastic waste, and paying good money for babycinos, which, my colleague Vic had roughly calculated, had a higher profit margin than a blood diamond. These days would give me entrée into another type of dinner party conversation, the kind that occurred in the kitchen, among the women, as they helped the hostess clear up. That conversation was a mixture of podcast recommendations and tips for good parenting books, and was edged with judgement of other mothers who were not in the room, judgement which was couched as concern for their children. In reality, I avoided those dinner party conversations, and stayed with the men at the table, to talk about subjects that I was interested in, and that were sufficiently distant from me, like politics or media industry gossip. I suspected I wasn't invited to a lot of those kinds of dinner parties, anyway. After that summer I was probably the one being gossiped about, something which necessitated my absence.

One day in early November, I shepherded Maddy through the door of our Ruby Street house and closed it behind us. I helped Maddy negotiate the roots of the fig, which were surging through the pathway, and opened the rusted iron gate. It let out a quiet scream. Maddy was four years old, and she was a slow walker. Our speeds were always mismatched on the walk to preschool, because Maddy liked to trail her fingers along fences and pick up things she found on the ground, like bottle tops, and important rocks. I held her hand and checked my phone for emails, and the time. After I dropped her into the arms of one of the demigods, I walked to take the bus to the office of the newspaper where I worked. I still called it a newspaper, even though writing for the newspaper was increasingly less important than writing for the website and foraging for what was called reader engagement. I had 50,000 Twitter followers and nearly 10,000 on Facebook, and I also had an open Instagram account on which I posted vignettes from the stories I was researching – a prime ministerial press conference, a shot of a kerbside media scrum, or a trayful of sweet tea and almond biscuits laid out by a family of refugees who had fled certain death.

That day I was running early, which was unusual, and I decided to walk into the office instead of taking the bus. The jacaranda season was at its full height, and the streets were full of purple clouds which rained flowers onto the pavement. They were sticky balloons underfoot. The air was still cool but it was edged with the promise of later warmth. I was listening to *News Agenda* through my headphones, when the phone rang. It was my news editor, Curtis. Curtis was sort of a news editor cliché – excitable, a smoker, recently divorced. I told her I was on my way in.

'So you haven't heard?' she asked.

The question irritated me. All journalists fear people knowing things before them, as it is our job to know things before other people. My dealings with Charlie had made this instinct even more acute. My psychologist had told me that the cohort of people who had been gravely deceived could be divided into two types: the need-to-know people and I-don't-want-to-know people. I was a need-to-know person, something which had caused me pain. This need-to-knowness meant I had numerous unwelcome images indelibly scored on my temporal lobe, images the brain stubbornly held onto against my will. My chronic, long-term sleep deprivation caused me to forget all sorts of things, from my PIN number to, once, my own mother's name. But the images stayed, and sometimes they were so vivid they were more present and real to me than my own reflection.

'Haven't heard what?' I asked. Possibilities fled through my mind – news events that were big enough for my editor to call me at 7.50 am. Terrorist attack? Political assassination? Perhaps I had been nominated for an award.

'Oh god, Suze,' said Curtis. 'There's no easy way to say this.' She paused.

'No easy way to say what?'

'Tracey Doran has died. She died last night. She. Ah. Listen, Suze …' Curtis mumbled herself to a halt. 'She killed herself.'

I stopped walking. Saliva vanished from my throat, like seawater sucked from a blowhole. My legs grew unreliable. I moved to sit down on the stone wall of a garden I was passing. There was a yellow rose bush there, in fierce bloom.

'I spoke to her just last night,' I said. 'So I don't think so. She was alive last night.'

'We saw it out on police wires early this morning,' Curtis said. 'Then one of Kate's guys confirmed on background it was her.'

Kate was a police reporter. She was prone to breathlessness in her copy, but never mistakes.

'Fuck.'

'I know,' said Curtis. 'But listen to me now. She was troubled, right? So I don't think we should go blaming ourselves here. This is not your fault. Your story was accurate.'

Technically, that was true.

'How did she do it?'

There was a pause. I could hear Curtis breathing into the phone, heavily, like a sex pest, or a toddler.

'Curtis.'

'Do you really want to know?'

My heart beat like it was angry. 'Yes,' I said.

'Pills. She drugged herself. Alcohol and pills.'

That stood in the air for a while, mingling with jacarandas and the mildness of the morning, and the yellow cheer of the roses. I wondered where Tracey was, physically, when she died. Was she in her bed, Marilyn-style? Or in her claw-foot bath, floating on a fragrant sea of petals and essential oils, like an Instagram Ophelia? Perhaps she had laid herself out like a sacrifice on her white linen couch. All of these possible suicide locations I had seen on her social media accounts. Just last week she had posted an Insta story tagging the manufacturers of the couch. They were French. Tracey called them 'cotton providores'.

Curtis breathed out again into the phone. I realised she was smoking as she was talking to me. Whenever I smoked, I liked to do it alone, in contemplation, like a form of cancer-causing meditation. Curtis's habit was more like breathing – she did it as an accompaniment to all other activities.

'Why don't you take the day?' she said. 'Go spend it with your daughter. Take her to the beach or something. It's pretty much beach weather already.' She paused. 'Water might be a bit cold still.'

'How will we report it?' I asked. 'Will we report it?' The protocol for reporting suicides was strict, in order to prevent copycats. I had a ghastly thought about how Tracey was what they called a social media influencer.

'We'll work out how to cover it,' Curtis said. 'You don't need to be involved. Just stay home today. Take a bath. Take a walk. Do … those things.'

In other circumstances I would have laughed at how flimsy was Curtis's grasp of what people did in their downtime. Curtis herself didn't have downtime, only time when she was either working or sleeping, or segueing between those pursuits I couldn't think of anything worse than taking a walk or a bath, or spending the day with Maddy – her innocence, her sweetness, the bloom of her would seem like an insult in light of this news. So I told Curtis I would see her soon. I walked down the sandstone steps to the harbour path that wound around cliffs and past boatyards to the office. I watched the sunlight spark the water. A jogger passed, her ponytail twitching like a hand puppet. Seagulls sat in a row on the wharf, like pensioners at a matinee. Early summer days like this were my favourite kind of day. They were a warm-up, the heat was still gentle, the sunshine still dappled, the humidity no big deal. They were a tickle before the gut punch of summer. I walked on, into work, and as I walked, I tried to gauge the weight of what had just descended.

*

Curtis was at the news desk, chewing nicotine gum and scrolling Twitter with frantic energy. She chewed the gum to tide her over to the next cigarette, not because she was trying to quit. Sometimes I wondered about her blood chemistry. She closed down the screen as she saw me approach.

'Ben really wanted you to stay home today,' she said, looking up.

Ben was the newspaper's CEO. He managed public relations, budgets and staffing, and mostly stayed out of editorial matters. He was bear-like, but not in a cuddly way. He was one of those people who commanded power through silence, and the threat he might only break the silence with something you didn't want to hear.

'I'll take it easy,' I said. 'I'll keep a low profile.'

I took the papers and my coffee to my desk, just as I did every morning. On my desk was a photo of Maddy from her babyhood, smiling broadly and toothlessly, her hair tufted up in a way that always stunned my heart with love. The photo was my only personal effect. It stood on a pile of notepads and stacks of paper – reports, freedom of information requests, and other documents. Post-it notes bloomed out from the paper stack like algae. I had some statuettes from the awards I had won, which I kept on my desk only because it seemed too pretentious to take them home and display them there – for what? For whom? Coffee cups studded the mess, hosting puddles of curdled milk. The newsroom was quiet, as though pretending for a moment it was an august place, like a library, or courtroom. I loved being there when it was still, before the whomp of the daily news cycle began. It was like being in a theatre before the crowds filed in and the curtain was raised. I liked to walk past the empty desks of my fellow reporters, which looked like they had been ransacked overnight – few journalists were neat in their personal habits. I liked the newspaper stacks with the latest editions laid freshly on them, like new sheets on a bed. I liked to drink my first coffee while I read the morning papers in hard copy, relishing the brief pause between the delectation of yesterday's news and the writing up of today's. I didn't see why this morning should be any different. Mostly, I didn't want to be alone in the gawping, early too bright day that was waiting for me outside, blankly, without work to fill it up.

It was not my fault.

After I finished with the papers, I fired up my computer and opened my Twitter, took a look, and logged straight back out again. I opened my email instead. There were various media notifications from ministers about their activities for the day. E-newsletters from the overseas newspapers I subscribed to. An email from a former evangelical pastor I was working with about a story on a sexual abuse cover-up within his church. My eyes lit on an email from Tom, the guy I was involved with (sexually, not romantically, never romantically). The email had nothing in the body of it except a weblink to an obscure art show. I clicked on the link. The exhibition seemed to consist of dismembered televisions. It was called *Disruption*. The subject heading of Tom's email said, simply: 'Wanna go?'

I most certainly did not. In the years since The Incident, I had gone to bed with many men but had never woken up with any of them. I was not looking for love, or companionship, or anything approximating it. I didn't even bother making excuses to myself about this anymore, although occasionally I had to make them to other people – single mothers (possibly single fathers too, I had no idea) became accustomed to the earnest pity of their acquaintances, the people who said *I don't know how you do it*. I saw fear in the eyes of these people. They worried that what happened to me was contagious somehow.

But the flipside of the pity was even worse. It was the go-girlism of being asked how your love life was, and if you had been on any dates lately, the perky questions about whether you were on apps or websites, questions asked with curiosity so naked it gave you no alternative but to suspect, hopefully, there was some deep bed of dissatisfaction within the marriage of your interrogator. To those people I made excuses about why I wasn't 'dating' (since when had we accepted this Americanism so gladly into our lexicon?). I had so little time! I was focused on Maddy. I was focusing on my career. Babysitting was expensive. I was taking a break.

Tom was different, because he had just sort of floated into my life like a benevolent cloud. He was a local barista who worked at a café where I often took Maddy. I patronised this café because it gave out babycinos free with adult coffees. Our fling had begun with Tom dropping at our table extra pink marshmallows for Maddy, a sort of inverse version of the Marshmallow Test, which Maddy passed admirably by eating up every one, and then turning her milk-pudding face to Tom to ask for more. It started with the marshmallows, and culminated in my ad hoc visits to his share house, just up the hill from us, on Glebe Point Road. Tom was black-haired, bearded and tall, but in a furtive, loping way, as though his height was something he forgot about until he went to move himself through the world. He was expert and efficient in bed. He was, I believed, both involved in some sort of attempt at an artistic career, and far too young for me. I wasn't sure exactly how far, because I was afraid to ask.

I was about to turn 40, and although I had an ideological commitment to never hiding my age, or being ashamed of it, that commitment was faltering as I neared the birthday. At times I had the vertiginous feeling I was inching towards the invisibility zone middle-aged women talked about, which felt more like a drop-pit. Beautiful women had a preternatural fear of the drop-pit, I had noticed, as though they had lived their lives on credit and now their debts were being called in. I supposed that included me. I was tall and long-legged. Men had admired my eyes. My hair, which I grew long, was a pleasing auburn, but the colour was borrowed – more and more of it belonged to the hairdresser every week, while my real hair turned grey as rain clouds. I had begun to suspect my eyebrows were on the march to invisibility, sidling out the door slowly, so as not to alert attention. One day I would whirl around and they would be gone. Some of my pubic hairs had lost pigment, while other parts of me sprouted unauthorised hair.

Tom restored something to me. One afternoon, soon after we began seeing each other, I smoked a cigarette as I lay stretched and naked on his provisional bed. He had foraged the mattress from the street, a fact I wished he had never told me. He lay in opposite formation to me, with his feet up near my head. His head was framed by a square of sunlight projected from the window above him. He raised his head to look at me, and he told me: 'You know what you are? You're *lithe*.' I kissed his ankle and said nothing, but silently I took the compliment and put it in my pocket to inspect later. It was something to turn over in my hand and examine for its truth. For now, at least, with my hair endowed by the hairdresser, and under Tom's gaze, I stayed visible, and I was grateful for that. But that could not translate to public displays. There would be no art shows or introductions to friends. I resolved to politely ignore Tom's email, although it occurred to me that there was no way for Tom to understand the polite part of me ignoring him. Perhaps I would text him later, or even drop over. I knew, from long experience, that sex was my best chance at avoiding questions.

Scanning my inbox, my eye was caught by an email from a name I didn't recognise – Patrick Allen. I opened it. I learned that Patrick Allen had associates. I learned that Patrick Allen was a lawyer. I learned that Patrick Allen was a lawyer representing a now-retired mogul I had passingly referred to in a story I wrote a couple of weeks back. I learned that I was being sued.

*

It had run on page two, an unimportant page where stories went to die, or at least to rest for a minute or two before vanishing. They had buried it online, and for once I had not been bothered. It was short, a harmless 400 words, covering the state funeral of a former deputy prime minister. That morning I had dropped Maddy at preschool, ignoring the reddening skin around her mouth, while at the same time telling myself it was just saliva rash – an unheard-of medical diagnosis I invented as I rushed to make the funeral, which was at Town Hall at 9 am. I made it with minutes to spare. There were swathes of flowers and mourners in black. There was a string quartet and a haze of words about the great man. There was a widow, bowed and bent.

The deputy prime minister was known for his role in the reformation of the tax system, for advocating unpopular cuts to university funding, and for being one of the most shameless sleazes Canberra had ever seen. He wasn't just handsy, according to the stories. He also used his eyes to grope ('I believe it's called an eye-rape,' one older colleague of mine had noted to me, drily) and he used his arms to turn hugs into hostage situations. His female staff were on notice, and the older ones used to guard the younger ones, never leaving them alone with him, although sometimes even that was not enough, because there were stories which had him detaching foot from shoe during meetings, and working a socked toe up the leg of a young female neighbour.

All great detail, none of it publishable, at least not on the day the great man was buried. Sometimes truth is in the silences, in the gaps, but gaps are hard to report. So I had written a fairly bland story about the funeral and the names who had turned up to it. One of those was Bruce Rydell, who, in the 1980s, had been the owner of a commercial television network. He was rumoured to keep a pistol in his desk drawer. He was often described as 'colourful', which meant he was a prick. Rydell had wanted to own a newspaper as well as a television company, but media ownership laws prevented him, so he went to war with the government over the laws. The deputy prime minister, who also had the media and communications portfolio, was his chief point of contact, and of conflict. There was an old story, which had been reported before, about the two men clashing during a meeting in the deputy prime minister's office. The language had been allegedly colourful. Threats had been allegedly made. I had placed asterisks in all the offending words and included this anecdote at the bottom of my story, a sort of historical footnote to liven things up. As I went to file it, a thought streaked across my mind: *I should probably get this legalled.*

But then a call had come in from Maddy's preschool. The red spots around her mouth had been confirmed as hand, foot and mouth disease, a fresh bacterial horror which managed to sound both agricultural and medieval. The preschool manager, a woman well practised in disease control, told me Maddy's temperature was 39.5 and said I had to collect her immediately. I experienced a swirl of guilt so vivid it wrong-footed me for a moment, and I had a flash of the parallel life. In this life, Maddy would not be the last child standing at daycare when her mother raced in, heels skidding, at two minutes to 6 pm, a little soldier with the buttons on her cardigan done up wrong. In the parallel life, there would have been no constellation of mouth sores, no confusing hours spent in the preschool isolation room. There would have been days at home with colouring in

17

and cookies. There would have been calm, and a proper family GP, not the array of 24-hour doctors Maddy had to see because I could never quite escape work in time. There would have been order, and fewer meals consisting of 2 Minute Noodles, and less worry about what trans fats did to four-year-olds. In the parallel life, there would have been someone to hand me a glass of wine after Maddy's lights-out, someone to rub my shoulders and offer small ministrations, like *How was your day?* and *Dinner's ready!* and (love's greatest act!) *You stay there, I'll go.* But that life was a ghost and this, here now, was the flesh, covered in sores though it was. The true life.

So: I had filed the piece in haste and raced to collect my daughter, who was too sick to even cry. She flopped mutely as I took her home, and I spent much of the night making sure the rise and fall of her chest stayed reliable: just in case, just in case. It was a mother's first duty, what it all came down to: the continuation of breath. All thoughts of legalling had been lost. No lawyer had scanned the story. It appeared in the Saturday paper, apparently blameless, although I didn't notice because I spent much of that day agonising over whether to take Maddy to the hospital. It seemed a stark choice between being the mother who overreacted to a simple infection, and being the mother who didn't take her child to hospital even when her temperature was edging 40 and her forehead was aflame and she seemed too tired or sad to talk and *what on earth was the woman thinking.* Finally, I bundled Maddy into a taxi and took her to casualty, where the nurses were so nice I could have hugged them, or wept, and in the end I did both. Maddy's symptoms subsided once she had ibuprofen and an ice block. After we came home from the hospital, safe, Maddy went to sleep on the couch in a nest of cushions, clutching her blanky and the ringless ring finger of my left hand. I spent the next four days at home with her. I waited for the sores to change from volcanoes to crusts, so I could return my girl to preschool and myself to work.

*

'I hope you're not on the internet. Twitter is a sewer today. Like, even more than usual.'

Victor greeted me as he slid into his desk. Vic was an investigative reporter who specialised in underworld stuff. I kept to myself at work, and many of the journalists I once knew had taken redundancy, so now Vic was my only real friend in the office. He spent his days quite mysteriously, sometimes reappearing right before deadline with the knees of his trousers dirtied, or once, a grazed hand. 'Oh, I had to crawl under something,' he would say. Or, 'It was just a bikie thing.' He had a puff of hair which he coloured lavender. He was softly plump and could easily, from the back, have been taken for the kind of lady who judged sponge cake at the Easter Show. Vic was from a small town in northern New South Wales. The town had a jacaranda festival and, from the snippets Vic had told me of his childhood, a widespread distaste for effeminate boys. His early suspicions about himself had been confirmed by his own father, who had pulled him aside when he was playing with his sisters' dolls, aged six, and told him that only faggots played with girl toys.

Ah, Vic thought. *That's what I am.*

I swivelled in my chair to face him. He was wearing a button-up shirt covered in zebras. This shirt was one of his favourites. He said it was a witty play on 'zebra print'.

'So you've heard?'

'It's all over the internet,' Vic said. 'Are you okay? You know it's not –'

'What are people saying?' I asked. 'I want to know what they're saying. I'm too afraid to look.'

Vic had turned on his computer and I glanced at the screen, which was open to our website. Tracey Doran's face, with its wholesome cheeks, looked directly at me. Her death was the top story. She was holding an emerald-coloured smoothie and smiling. Her teeth gleamed with health.

'Okay. Well,' said Vic. 'Here's what I've read. It seems that after your story broke yesterday, Tracey's fans turned on her, many of them. They started bullying her online. Fake bitch, I hope you die, why don't you just kill yourself, that sort of thing.'

I closed my eyes for a moment.

'Are you okay?' Vic asked.

'I'm fine,' I said. 'Go on.'

'And so the reaction to her death seems, mostly, to be turning into an anti-bullying kind of thing,' he said. 'You know – people talking about the insidious nature of internet trolling. Mental health. That sort of thing.'

'What are people saying about me?'

'Just stay off the internet for a bit.'

'Sure,' I said. 'The internet is easy to avoid.'

We were interrupted by Curtis, who told me the CEO wanted to see me. She led me into one of the glass-walled meeting rooms which edged the newsroom. The reporters called these glass boxes 'crying rooms', but if you wanted to weep unnoticed in one of them you had to crouch in a corner like a ninja, or shield your face with a phone. I knew this – in the dark days after The Incident, I had cried at work a lot.

Ben and Curtis sat across the table from me. Ben's barrel-chest jutted out over the table top in a way that made me lean back in my chair. I could see the dark mat of his chest hair under his white shirt. Ben was a person who was mostly silent. But his silence somehow helped him fill up more space, not less. He explained that management wished to protect me and keep me out of the spotlight for a while. He said he would be taking me off news duties and I could continue to work on features with longer lead-times. He said it was for my own good. As he spoke, Curtis fidgeted, seemingly uncontrollably. When Ben finished talking, the only sound in the room was the noise of Curtis's pen, which she was repeatedly rapping on the table with the rhythm of a metronome set to fast. He turned to look at Curtis's fingers and the rapping stopped.

'So,' I said. 'I'm in trouble. I'm, like, in some sort of disgrace here.'

'Not at all,' said Curtis, jiggling. 'This is not that. It's to protect you.' She ran her hand through her hair.

As Curtis spoke I remembered the words of a criminal psychologist I had once interviewed: *If you want to catch the lie, watch the hands.* He had told me that lying people almost always felt the need to move their hands, to exorcise their anxiety through some sort of movement. Through long observation of Maddy's father, I had concluded this was true.

'Protect me from what?' I asked. I looked at Ben, who had no trouble meeting my eye.

'From what people are saying, mostly,' Ben said.

'But what if what people are saying isn't true?' I asked.

'That doesn't matter.'

Ben turned his watch on his wrist and looked at it. The watch was an expensive gold thing that looked nautical, as though he might be called upon at any moment to check his coordinates. His gesture was minute and meaningful. It said: *We are done here.*

*

Tracey Doran was a wellness expert, organic food fancier and a social media influencer who had pretended to have bone cancer, and then pretended to cure her own bone cancer with an organic vegan diet. She had documented her 'journey' (nobody had stories anymore, only journeys) on her well-subscribed Instagram account, building a huge social media following. She posted pictures of herself, bright of cheek and shiny of hair, drinking green juice in a pastel kitchen. She curated salads of kale and rocket, on which boutique vegetables and ancient grains were laid like jewels. Her pets became part of the spectacle – a ginger cat and a slurry-coloured mutt who had a disconsolate air, like he was the only one sceptical about the enterprise. The cat and the dog were photographed and posted, with Tracey at their centre, the sun to their sunflowers. After a while, Tracey got a book deal. Six figures for recipes and wellness tips, interlaced with snippets of memoir. The deal was written up in trade journals and on business pages, as one of the early examples of crossover, of traditional media being led by disruptive media, by social media. But to Tracey, the book was merely a flirtation with legacy media, necessary to boost her profile for the main game: the wellspring of the internet, where fame could be tracked in real time and mountains of money could be made from taps and swipes, the distracted semi-attentions of her fellow millennials. There was also a podcast, on which she hosted various wellness industry guests. Nearly all the money, she said, bar running costs and a small salary for her, was going to charities. She named which ones, tagging them on social media, and received effusive thanks in return. That was her brand – wholesome, selfless, unthreateningly spiritual. A few weeks previously, the Sunday lifestyle lift-out of *The Tribune* had run a story about Tracey, and the next day I received an email. I read it as I ate a packet of cheese twists at my desk.

Hello, it read.

I hope you read this. I am a Queensland housewife and a fan of your work. I enjoyed your story on the foster care system. Why are politicians so hopeless! Yesterday I read a story in your newspaper called 'The Wellness Warrior: How one woman conquered cancer through diet and mindfulness.' The subject of that article was Tracey Doran. I have known Tracey all her life. She attended Newgate High with my daughter, graduating in 2008. She is 28, not 23 as the article claims. I know because I was at her 18th birthday party. I worry she is a pathological liar. She has never had cancer. Her own mother does not believe her lies. It is one thing for Tracey to lie to her family but it is another to lie to Australia. What if other people who are really fighting cancer fall for her lies? You MUST investigate this. Sincerely, Concerned Reader.

I licked cheese dust off my fingers. Sceptical, I did some casual Googling. Then I made a few calls. Once I had a high school, I could find alumni (they had their own Facebook group) and from there, it took not much more than a fortnight of phone interviews and internet research to unravel Tracey Doran's organic life. I quickly found that most people close to Tracey did not believe her claims. It was only when she began to disseminate them on social media that they took on the solidity of truth. If a story was retweeted enough times, it hardened into fact. My exposé was legalled okay, and I waited until the last possible moment to contact my subject for comment. I didn't want to risk Tracey cruelling the story by posting a spoiler to her online 'community', as she called them. I gave Tracey a day to respond to a long list of questions. She came back with a bizarre and rambling email in which she reiterated her philanthropy, alluded to 'dark forces which threaten authenticities of the soul and heart' and attached a spreadsheet documenting her alleged donations to charity. There were no receipts and some of the charities she named did not seem to exist. Rarely had a story fallen so neatly into my lap – something which only served to exacerbate my guilt later on. It was almost too easy. The newspaper splashed with the story. It went viral: 100,000 unique page impressions by noon. Camera crews arrived at Tracey's Brisbane home that afternoon. In the evening, as I ate what was left of Maddy's fishfinger dinner, I took a call from Tracey threatening a lawsuit. She sounded drunk. And now it was morning, and she was dead. It seemed too short a cycle. It didn't seem real. It didn't seem true.

*

I spent the rest of the morning making desultory phone calls for a feature I was uninterested in writing, a profile of a female politician, and fending off thoughts of Tracey. I hoped it hadn't been the bath. For some reason it was important to me she had died on the couch, as though her death could be softened by organic French linen, and so, too, could the consequences of it. About three o'clock, my phone rang, startling me. The ring tone was the first few bars of 'Gimme Shelter' – this was something Tom had done, somehow, as part of an argument we were having about which was the best Rolling Stones song. I hadn't worked out how to remove it. The call was from an unknown number. I picked up. There was a pause, and then a voice talked into the phone – it was a female voice, spry but earnest, and it took me a moment to realise it was Tracey Doran's. It took me another moment still to realise she was not alive. The voice was not speaking to me, but rather, it was being played to me. It was audio from one of her podcasts.

'Hey guys, it's Tracey here. Today we are going to talk about *courageous participation* in your own truth. And how that *speaks to* your wellness goals,' said the voice. 'And how energy blockages –'

'Hello?' I said into the phone. 'Who's there?'

'– can interrupt your path to growth –'

24

I put the phone down. I looked around me, feeling as though someone might be watching me. My phone pinged with a text message – again, this had been made into a ridiculous sound, courtesy of Tom. Now it was the noise of a bass guitar being plucked, with the effect that every text sounded like an incoming porn movie soundtrack. The message was not from a number but from an email address I didn't recognise. It said: *I hope you're proud, you fucking bitch. You killed her.*

I decided to leave work early. I went to pick up Maddy.

*

Maddy's preschool was an early childhood utopia laid out to stimulate different developmental outcomes. There was a 'home corner', where dolls lay in shoebox cots, all crammed together as in an unregulated orphanage. There was a science corner, where insects sat sullenly in tanks, peered at by toddlers. Occasionally they were brought out to be prodded by them too. There was a free play centre where the children slashed at felt canvases like small expressionists. I could not say my daughter had an aptitude for drawing, or art. Her works were on the lazy side of impressionistic. I punched in the security code to enter, and scanned the yard for Maddy. One of the teachers saw me and greeted me. This woman's name was Indira. She often put Maddy's hair into braids, crowns of plaited hair that had her looking like an escapee from a children's book set in Switzerland. Maddy adored her.

'She's in the reading room,' Indira told me. As she spoke, a child gouged her ear with a straw. I often wondered how these women coped. Was it because they worked in shifts? Perhaps everything was bearable if you could count down towards its end. I walked back inside to the reading room, a womb-like space with low lighting and cushions on the floor, a place which resembled nothing so much as the chill-out rooms of the illegal warehouse raves of my teenage years. It even had a lava lamp. I looked through the pane on the door and spied Maddy. She lay with her head on a cushion, listening to a story being read. Her face was framed by her dark hair, the sharp lines of the haircut at odds with the round proportions of her features. I could have written a sonnet to my daughter's cheeks. She was my clearest line to joy, the closest access to delight I had ever had.

Following The Incident, sorrow had leaked out of me like droplets of condensation. But even at my lowest, the pleasure I took in Maddy was never spoiled. Maddy was the steady cliff from which the light shone.

One day when Maddy was around three, about six months after Charlie left our lives, apparently for good, I left her drinking milk on the couch in front of her cartoons, as was the custom after she came home from preschool. I slipped outside to the laundry to put on a load of washing. The backyard was a possum playground. They were pests – they threw masticated figs around like rice at a wedding, and the fig morsels stuck under my sandals as I sorted darks from lights. As I walked back across the yard, a neighbour attracted my attention. We chatted for a few minutes over the fence, until I heard, faintly, the constricted wail of Maddy's distress, muffled but unmistakable. I ran to the back door and opened it, and found Maddy cantering hysterical laps of the house, a terrified pony, her panic as animal as a scent. She had wanted me, looked for me, and, not finding me, she had believed herself deserted. I calmed her and made her a silent vow: *I will love you even more fiercely. I will love you more than double. My one will be better than two.*

I opened the door, casting an isosceles of light into the warm dark of the toddler cave.

Maddy lifted her head from the cushion, and squinted up at the doorway. 'Mummy!' she cried.

*

It was Maddy's firm belief that mice, a class of animal with which she was obsessed, lived in trees. This belief didn't come from nowhere. It was the result of a misleading picture book I often read to her, in which the mouse-family lived in a treehouse – an elaborate, beautifully furnished house with turrets and winding staircases and little mouse-sized runners along the corridors. These tree-mice were one of the main sources of conversation between Maddy and me, although we also discussed Maddy's dolls, Maddy's friends at preschool, what we were going to have for breakfast, lunch and dinner, what we were doing on the weekend, and, lately, what colour people's eyes were. The discussions were completely distinct from our arguments, which were chiefly about what Maddy would wear, and things she didn't want to do at any given time – eat dinner, leave the place where we were, brush her teeth or hair. There are many things no one tells you before you become a parent. At the top of the list is how hard it is to brush the teeth of another person. I found these arguments frustrating, and there were times when I had to walk out of the room and go to my own bedroom and shut the door to breathe myself back into calm. I would sit on the blue counterpane and look through the French doors which gave out to the balcony, and think: *I have become enraged by the refusal of another person to wear socks.* And it really was rage – an uplifted pulse, a temptation to say something irrevocable, a loosening of the tongue in readiness for shouting.

But the rages came and went. Our discussions were lasting and satisfying – often meandering in unexpected directions, like inquiries into what are bones from and where is the sun gone and do we only have one coat of skin and once, terrifyingly, *where are people made?*

'Babies grow in their mummy's tummy,' I said, briskly, and Maddy accepted that, although she seemed to sense it was only part of the truth.

We discussed mice as I walked Maddy down the street after picking her up. I took her to Tom's café for a shake-milk, which is what Maddy called milkshakes. She also said 'cockporn' instead of popcorn, which was embarrassing at kids' parties. The café was one of those ones that had chalkboard-black walls and signs advertising the origin of the coffee they were serving that day. Today's was from the Galapagos Islands and had notes of brown sugar and green apples. I ordered a cup of it, and a banana milkshake for Maddy. She wriggled out of her chair to go play with the miniature kitchen they had set up for children in the corner. It was sufficiently Scandinavian in its design to blend into the café's aesthetic. She liked to make me tea and bring me slices of cake made from blond wood. I looked around for Tom but remembered he had mentioned it was his day off. I wondered briefly what he did in his free time. It wasn't something we talked about. Sometimes we talked about the books Tom had strewn around his room, many of which I had read before I dropped out of university.

A young, pretty waitress delivered my coffee. She had a tattoo which advanced like a vine from her neck to her breasts. The breasts were lovely. I thought about how many times a day Tom must glance at them, just a quick shot of the eyes, downwards briefly and back up to the face. Most men seemed to be able to accomplish this glancing quickly, although others seemed incapable. I wondered why Tom was sleeping with me when he could be sleeping with this young woman, or any number of others who had interesting tattoos and a self-assurance I had long grown out of, if I ever had it. My own breasts were defeated, as though they were the only part of me that had truly absorbed the sorrows of the past few years. The rest of me had held up quite well, I thought, at least physically. But my breasts – disc-like, uninterested – had sponged up the tragedy and become tragicomic themselves.

As I watched Maddy play, the sounds of a bass guitar emanated from my phone. I looked down to see a text from a number I didn't have saved in my phone, but which I knew well. *I'm around tomorrow. Are you?*

The tattooed waitress swung over to us bearing the milkshake. I called Maddy over, and she sat on her stool and drank the milkshake earnestly, occasionally pausing to push her hair out of her eyes in a gesture that seemed adult. Her head tipped down and her cheeks plumed outwards, perfectly spherical, like balls of ice cream. I looked at my daughter and felt the same commingling of responsibility and love that had awed me when her father left (or when I left him). The first time it happened, it was frightening – this overwhelming realisation, arriving suddenly, that I would be wholly responsible for keeping this baby alive, that it was on me to feed her and to read to her, to make sure I had the right clothes for her, to make sure those clothes were clean, to earn enough money to buy a house where we could one day live (because I knew the Ruby Street idyll could not last forever), to cut her fingernails, to teach her manners, to teach her how to talk, read, drive, love, be; to explain to her *where are people made*. I had to support her belief that mice lived in turreted tree-manors until it became undeniably obvious that they didn't. This responsibility oppressed me. There was no point pretending it didn't, except I did pretend, all the time. I left it out of conversations, and sat with it alone, sometimes in the middle of the night when I worried, absurdly, about some goalpost that was far off – who would teach Maddy how to change the oil in a car? Among all the responsibilities, I tried hard to hack out some space for myself. The main space I had was work, and so work was how I stayed visible. Work was how I kept my head above the waves. It was the oxygen I gulped.

When you are left to care for a small child alone, your choices contract like a frightened creature. Your personal liberty shrinks to a pinpoint. Small envelopes of time – a train ride alone, the few hours between her bedtime and yours – become more valuable to you than your own teeth. Developmental milestones are blunted by hurt. Time becomes leaden and the afternoons – especially the afternoons – are long. The defection sparks anger, a tsunami of righteous aggrievement – how can it not? It sparks anger so titanic it threatens to swallow you. You learn that if you are to make a life, you must keep your head clear of it. You must find your oxygen. So you exercise your only choice: you decide how you will bear it – because you have no choice but to bear it, a fact unacknowledged by the *I don't know how you do-its* you meet at dinner parties and in the park. Nobody likes an angry woman. A bitter woman – a mutterer, a denouncer, a seeker of vengeance – she makes people uncomfortable, and that is intolerable. Repellent, even. Nobody asks themselves how it is possible to bear abandonment politely, with grace and ease. Certainly, nobody tells you how to do that. People like the saintliness side of the single mother thing. They're not so hot on the anger, the struggle, the unholy mess of it. I made my decision early on. I chose not to be angry, which is to say, I decided to govern and police my anger, even though often it felt utterly ungovernable – wild, rogue and fearful as an animal escaped from captivity, charging down main street, villagers fleeing. As Tracey Doran would have said, you have to manage your brand. If I couldn't abolish my anger, I would ignore it. I would be a high-roader.

Maddy trotted over, wearing a mini-apron. 'Mummy, would you like sugar, madam?'

'Yes, two sugars please, café lady.'

'It's only attending, Mummy.'
She meant pretending.
'Okay. Can I have some attend sugar?'
'I don't have any attend sugar.'
'Oh right. Milk then.'
'Say please, Mummy.'
'Please.'

CHAPTER TWO

He chose the hotel. In all the time we had been meeting, he never took me to the kinds of hotels he stayed in while travelling for work – the expensive, elegant ones with views over parks or harbours or rivers, the ones with complimentary slippers and doors that made no sound when they closed behind you. He said those hotel rooms were just as lonely as all the others, and he was the expert. Instead, I met him in middling hotels, hotels which awarded themselves a few stars for being clean and commodious, but made you pay extra for wi-fi and breakfast. In those hotels he was unlikely to run into anyone he knew. I often observed the other guests at these indifferent places and wondered who they were. Middle managers, tourists, perhaps other adulterers. The hotels were always part of a chain, and the chain always had a name like Allure or Azure or once, Entice.

The hotel that day was in North Sydney, a place with as little romance as you would expect from the secondary commercial centre of a major city. We were not about romance. As I drove across the Harbour Bridge, the water flashing at me, I had a vision of the parallel life, of driving this way with Maddy in the back and Maddy's dad in the front, heading up to Palm Beach, or somewhere north where the traffic would thin out and the shadows would grow long with the afternoon, somewhere we could watch Maddy chase waves into the sea like a puppy. I waited for the image to pass. They always did. I parked and found the hotel. It was wedged in a snarl of roads right under the Harbour Bridge, but with no view of it. He was already checked in, he had texted me while I was driving: *Hurry up.* He liked economy. I walked past reception and took the lift up to the room, along the corridor, past a maid tugging a vacuum cleaner cord like the leash of an unruly dog. I smiled at her thinly, and followed the chemical scent of the air freshener. That was another crucial difference between the middling hotel and the five-star: the five-star hotels were scentless. The mid-budget hotel always had a pungent, cloying scent distributed soundlessly through the air vents, or somewhere, a scent that was meant to make you forget what it was trying to cover up: the smell of people.

I knocked on the door. He swung it open and nodded to me, holding his finger to his lips. He was speaking on his phone.

'It's room service,' he said. 'I'm having lunch at the hotel. Yep. Nup. Yes, I will. Okay then, Beano.'

It was his wife. He called her Beano. He said they hadn't had sex in three years.

'I think so. No, I'll take a cab. See you then.'

He pressed his thumb on the phone to end the call, and I caught a glimpse of his wife's picture as it faded from the screen. Sensible bob, glasses, a pretty mouth. The kind of decent married woman I might have become, had events taken a different turn. He looked at me, but only barely, and roped his arm around my waist, pulling me to him, with his face in my neck.

'She thinks I'm in Melbourne,' he said. 'I have a meeting at three.'

'That's fine,' I said, and put a hand to his belt.

He worked his head into the neckline of my dress and told me to shut up. This was the way it was with us. Our intimacy revealed itself in the lack of niceties. He turned me around and leaned me against the walnut-veneer desk, and I lost my gaze in the notepaper with its hotel-branded letterhead, and the cheap biros resting on the ink blotter; and the hotel phone with its carefully inscribed buttons: *concierge, room service, outside line.*

The sex was quiet, like it always was, but respectful, in the sense that he always made sure I got what I needed. When it finished, he left me abruptly and walked into the bathroom, shutting the door. There was no cuddling or physical lingering. That would have been beside the point. I was in it for his blatant need of me, the need that kept him returning despite the risk involved, and despite the obvious shame he carried over deceiving his wife. I heard the sound of water running. He emerged in a new shirt and I stepped forward to help him with his tie, a wifely act, but one so small it felt like playing.

'What will you do tonight?' I asked.

'Hmm?'

His mind was already elsewhere.

'Tonight. Your wife thinks you're in Melbourne. So you have a free night. Don't tell me you have another lover?'

'I'm only two-thirds stupid,' he said stiffly.

'So what then? I bet you're a member of a gentleman's club or something.'

'I like time to myself.'

'Do you sneak off to movies? Or maybe you have a truly revolting habit, like playing Bridge,' I said. 'Tell me.'

I finished his tie, drew my hand over it to straighten it, and looked up into his face. His eyes were edged with something sad, and I had a quick realisation of how lonely he was, this man I met for sex and knew nearly nothing about, not really. I had always assumed he no longer loved his wife, but now I thought that maybe the opposite was true, and that's why he sought me out, why he drank me in the way he did, meeting me in a four-star hotel where he could fuck me quickly, then compartmentalise it; leaving his need in North Sydney for a week or three, until our next meeting, when he would face it again.

'I dance,' he said.

I laughed, thinking he couldn't be serious.

'You dance?'

'I do. I like to go salsa dancing. Beano – Jenny – she hates it. Always has. She is too self-conscious. Of course, at the places I go, it doesn't matter how good you are, but she still won't come,' he said.

'I would have put money on Bridge, or – I don't know – jujitsu, before salsa.'

'I did a year at Berkeley as an undergrad. Dated a Cuban. She used to take me to salsa clubs in San Francisco. I broke up with the girl but kept the dancing. As much as I could.'

'And you go to these places alone? Can you do that?'

'Oh yes, there are always unpartnered women looking for men.'

'No doubt.'

'You misunderstand if you think it's like that. It's really not like that.'

He looked wounded. He was very prim, in his way.

'I'm only teasing. I'm impressed.'

'Perhaps you could come along one time.'

He looked at me now, and took a stray piece of my hair and tucked it behind my ear, a small gesture of solicitude that almost undid me.

'Maybe I will.'

I knew I never would.

I broke away from him and moved around the room collecting my things, kneeling on the floor to search under the bed for a lost earring. I found it, one half of a set of sapphire studs Charlie had given me, a guilt-gift I had not recognised as such at the time.

'Will you go back into the office this afternoon?' I asked him.

'Yes,' he said. 'I have news conference. And a meeting with marketing. The new website is launching next week.'

'Oh yes, that's right,' I said. I speared the earring into my lobe.

'Do we need to talk about what happened yesterday?' he asked. He didn't look at me – he was checking his phone for emails.

'We agreed to keep everything church and state,' I said.

'We did. But for the record, I really did make the decision in your best interests.'

'It wasn't my fault Tracey Doran died.'

'Nobody thinks it was. It's not punishment. It's protection.'

My face burned, and I had a sharp stab of feeling, a nauseous swirl of regret for all the small decisions that had brought me to this hotel in North Sydney with its branded notepads and its overwhelming smell of pine forest.

'Anyway. Church and state,' I said, and picked up my bag. 'You're church and I'm state. I think.'

He glanced down at his nautical watch. 'Bye,' he said. 'I'll see you in at work.'

'Bye, Ben.'

*

It was not, I knew, best practice. Women who slept with their married bosses were in a special category, and it was not a socially acceptable one. They probably had their own place in hell: the place for women who don't help other women, the place for boyfriend-snatchers and murderesses, and bolters who abandon their kids. Women like me betrayed the sisterhood twice over – once by screwing someone else's husband, and again by confirming a thousand negative stereotypes about how women get ahead in the workplace.

I had tested out a few feminist loopholes which might at least allow such conduct, even if they couldn't render it correct – empowerment, liberation, the far spectrum-end of personal choice? But ultimately I concluded there was no rationalisation that could make this appropriate. I could argue to myself it was not aiding my career, but that was an argument with myself, and so it didn't really matter how convincing it was, or how well formed. As soon as Ben and I were exposed, it would fall apart.

Why was it that the risk felt so hypothetical? Particularly, notably: why did Ben's wife, poor dear Beano, feel far off, so far away as to be imaginary, a construct? Actually, it was me and Ben – not that there was truly any me-and-Ben, only the encounters we had, the sex we had – who were the unreal ones. Give Beano the dignity of solidity, of realness, of existing on the wide-open plain of shared bank accounts and school concerts and the family calendar and common sense. That was Beano's terrain. I roamed the netherland of Ben's life, a place on the edges that only existed in our memories and in various charges to his credit card, a credit card I supposed he kept secret. The netherland was shadowy and deniable, at least to oneself.

It was not best practice, sure, but it was not real either. This was not real life.

*

I had forgotten to bring snacks. It was a few days after Tracey's death, and I had picked Maddy up from preschool and taken her down to the park across the road from our house. We called it Tree Park, in honour of the Moreton Bay figs. I loved it at dusk, when it was veiled in gold light, and populated loosely with children and dog walkers and a few contented sitters. On good days, Tree Park felt like the seat of happiness, and I didn't wish my past away, because it didn't exist, and I didn't wish for the parallel life, because the one I had now – with Maddy playing in front of me, and me watching her, seemed like the one true life, small but perfectly formed.

Maddy had taken full advantage of the slippery dip, the swing, and the dreadful giant roundabout which made me so nauseous I could not even watch it turning from a distance. Now Maddy was hungry, and as usual I was unprepared. Snacks – their quantity, their quality – were one of the markers of maternal prowess. This was something I had learned through bitter experience. Fury was really at its purest in a toddler with low blood sugar. There had been tantrums in cars and parks and, worst of all, supermarkets, before I had really put this together, and realised that it was the mother's duty to stave off hunger, not just to sate it. Still, snacks were one of the things that dropped out of my brain through sleep-deprivation memory loss. I often forgot the snacks, or I failed to bring enough. Once or twice I had offered Maddy a peppermint from my handbag as a last resort. I nearly always forgot to bring a water bottle like the good park mothers, who offered their offspring designer sippy cups made of reclaimed plastic, with anti-spill mechanisms and eco-friendly straws, vessels with special handles that could be clipped efficiently onto the straps of prams, all forming part of the orderly child-infrastructure that signified good motherhood in the middle class.

As a consequence of my forgetfulness, Maddy often begged snacks from her friends at the park, edging close to them like a pushy seagull, her eyes bulging as their mothers drew cornucopias from their sensible handbags: organic sweet potato chips, sugarless crackers, cut fruit folded into Tupperware like origami. We were with one such mother this afternoon, Minh, who was mother to Maddy's friend Annie. Minh was married to a man called Stan, who worked in finance and was often in Hong Kong. They lived up the street from us, in a Victorian manor renovated by an interior designer whose work had featured in *Vogue Living* (I knew this because my mother had a subscription). Minh was smooth-skinned and compact in a way I found intimidating, and she was minimalistically stylish in her mummyness. That day I was wearing a shirtdress that had a fallen hem, something I had only noticed once I was at work and had access to a full-length mirror. Minh was wearing linen shorts and a pristine white T-shirt, together with sandals that wound decoratively around her pretty feet. She reached into her canvas bag, and produced a thoughtfully compiled snack-box for her daughter. She opened it like a treasure chest. It contained squares of soft wholemeal-bread sandwich (crusts off), some organic crackers, a sugar-free yoghurt, and grapes cut in half. Maddy eyed it off.

'I'm hungry, Mummy,' she said to me. 'I need snacks.'

I watched as Minh brought out wet-wipes, and then – this did seem like showing off – a napkin embroidered with a Bunnykins design. She tucked it into little Annie's collar to catch spills while she ate.

'Mummy will go to the kiosk to get you something,' I told Maddy. 'Do you want a muffin?'

'I want a ham sandwich like Annie got,' said Maddy, traitorously.

'There's plenty for everyone,' said Minh. 'Here you are, Maddy.'

She proffered one of Annie's sandwich squares, causing her daughter to howl in outrage, and I couldn't blame her. Maddy

ate the perfect sandwich and asked for more. Minh distracted
Annie with a drink (from an enamelled sippy cup, its branding
discreet, yet not so discreet you couldn't see it was branded).

'I need milk too, Mummy,' said Maddy, looking plaintively
at Minh.

Minh looked over at me with apology on her face. 'Sorry,
we don't generally share drink bottles. We're really trying to
avoid getting sick right now.'

We: the casual signifier of the nuclear family.

'Oh gosh, of course, I totally understand,' I said. 'Maddy
and I had gastro last month. She vomited in bed. Twice! And
then she vomited in my bed.'

Minh looked disturbed by this anecdote. Not for the first
time, I reflected that while people often told single parents *I
don't know how you do it*, they almost never wanted to hear the
details of how it was, actually, done.

'Maddy, let's go to the bubbler,' I said, and took her padded
little hand in mine.

Maddy found bubblers exciting, and she perked right up at
this suggestion. We walked across the park together. I looked
down at my daughter's small, dear head, as she trotted along, her
hair studded with rainbow-coloured clips, and resolved to make
her veal schnitzel that night – her favourite – with a Panko crust,
and both butter and cream in the accompanying mashed potato.
I lifted Maddy up to the bubbler and tried to position her mouth
in front of the spout, while simultaneously pressing the button
which released the water supply. I was well practised at this
move, but still, I was rarely able to accomplish it without wetting
Maddy to an extent which would have occasioned a change
of clothing, had I remembered to bring a change of clothing.
I dangled Maddy in front of the tap and tried to balance her in a
way that allowed her to drink deeply but not waterboard herself.

'Can I help you with that?'

It was Tom – he was in shorts, and he was sweating, a basketball tucked under his arm. He was wearing sweatbands on his wrists, and high-top sneakers. He looked young.

'Hi!'

I eased Maddy down from the bubbler. She wiped her mouth with the back of her hand.

'I didn't know you came here. What are you – you shooting some hoops?'

Was that the correct term for casual basketball playing? I felt old.

'There's a bunch of us who play here on Wednesday afternoons,' Tom said. 'What are you guys up to?'

He looked down at Maddy, who was shaking herself like a wet dog.

'How's my number one homegirl?'

Maddy beamed up at him, and hiccuped.

'I think her water went down the wrong way,' I said. I patted her back.

'Did you get my email about that art show?' Tom asked.

'I did. I'm so sorry, I've been slammed at work,' I said.

'That's okay. Can you come? It's next Friday.'

I had forgotten about the dismembered televisions. I worked my brain fast.

'I would,' I said, 'but I have to get a babysitter, and Betty is studying a lot right now. The HSC.'

Betty was the teenager who lived next door, the daughter of my neighbour Felicity. She babysat for me a lot. She came from a big family in a crowded house. My place was a quiet spot to study.

'Isn't Betty in Year 11?'

I remembered that Betty worked occasional shifts at Tom's café. She knew him. She probably had a crush on him. If I had been a teenager, I certainly would have.

'Sorry, yes, you're right,' I said. 'Her mother mentioned exams.'

Tom fixed me with his eyes – green, their colour a ridiculously comely contrast with the darkness of his beard, which somehow managed to highlight his features instead of swamping them. Why was he doing this? What was the point of this dance?

'Do you want me to ask Betty? I think she's working at the café tomorrow.'

'Oh, well, babysitting gets so expensive. That's the real thing,' I said, lamely.

'Let me pay. I'd be happy to. Let me take you out.'

His kindness sparked irrational anger. Why was he so insistent that I come to look at an art show consisting of televisions with their innards pulled out onto the floor? Televisions that the gallery's website called 'vintage', but which were, actually, identical to the one I had grown up watching? Televisions with modest screens and bulbous backs, televisions that required their watchers to stand up and move if they wanted to change the channel. Since when was that vintage? It was my childhood.

Somewhere below us, around thigh height, Maddy hiccuped.

'Look, the truth is that it's a rough period at work, and I just … I'm not really an art person anyway.'

I hoped this last statement would draw a line under things. An artist, even an aspiring one, could not possibly want to make a girlfriend of a non-art person.

'That's okay,' he said, smiling at me. 'I'm not really a news person but I still read the newspaper sometimes.'

As we spoke, Maddy swivelled her small head to watch each of us, in turn, as though she were a spectator at Wimbledon. She hiccuped again, her small chest jerking outwards as she did so. She giggled.

'I thought that no one under 30 read newspapers anymore,' I said.

'Maybe they don't. I'm 31.'

I tried to remember what I had been doing at 31. Working. On a break from Charlie. In a brief relationship with a ministerial staffer. We had gone on a holiday to Ireland together, and cycled the Ring of Kerry in the rain.

'So you're a millennial?'

'Yes. I suppose I am.'

'Well I'm gen X. Or Y. I can never be sure. There seems to be no central definition of it. But I'm older,' I said.

'I figured.' He reached a hand up to his forehead to wipe his brow. Sweat droplets slunk down onto his Roman nose. He looked like he should be rendered in bust form and displayed in a private museum.

'Mummy, why does Tom got black stuff under his arm?' asked Maddy, with genuine curiosity.

'Sometimes men have hair under their arms, darling,' I said, and then checked myself. 'And ladies do too. Women,' I added.

'Does *my* daddy have that too?' Maddy asked, with a hiccup.

'Yes, yes he does.'

'Hey listen,' said Tom. 'I have to get back to the game, but lemme know about Friday, okay?'

I said I would.

'Bye, Mad. You come and visit me soon, yeah? I'm keeping some marshmallows for you.'

He turned and jogged off in the direction of his game. His friends greeted him with hoots and taunts, wide grins on their faces. I looked down at Maddy, who had now hiccuped a portion of her ham sandwich – Annie's ham sandwich – onto the front of her pinafore, where it smeared together with the dampness from the bubbler water, forming a hammy paste. I glanced over at Minh, who was watching on with open interest. Women like Minh loved to hear the details of my sex life, or my love life, as they called it. It always felt like an asymmetrical exchange, this deep dive into details. It was never available to me to ask them how their sex lives were going, not that I wanted to know. I fished in my pocket for a tissue and tried to remove the chunkier parts of the regurgitated sandwich from Maddy's chest.

'Are you all right, darling? Do you feel sick?'

'Oh I'm fine, Mummy. Thank you, I'm fine,' said Maddy.

Occasionally she interpolated her speech with perfectly formed adult sentences.

'Are you all right?' she asked me.

She often asked me if I was all right, and other times she asked me if I was happy, which seemed like something no four-year-old should ever ask her mother. I did not have an honest answer for her anyway.

'I'm all right,' I said.

We walked back over towards Minh and Annie.

'Mummy?' said Maddy.

'Yes, darling?'

'Where do hedgehogs go in the night?' She pronounced 'the' softly, as 'dee'. 'Is hedgehogs octurnal? Do they like night-time or daytime?'

The previous night, we had been discussing owls, which led to a broader conversation about nocturnal animals. I had mentioned possums, foxes. I told Maddy I wasn't sure about hedgehogs. I would have to make inquiries.

*

Not true, not entirely true: I knew a little about hedgehogs. I knew they lived in Sicily, because I had seen one there, a sighting as rare as a glimpse of a platypus in an Australian creek.

Five years ago I had travelled through Europe with Maddy's father. We conceived Maddy in a Parisian attic room, a room which belonged to a friend of a friend who was a professional clown. In France, clowning was taken seriously as an artistic form. The clowning friend of a friend, Elodie, was in Berlin for the summer, attending a mime workshop, so Charlie and I sublet her attic room, in a grand 19th-century manor-cum-share house in north-west Paris, near the pho shops of the Boulevard de Belleville and the Parc des Buttes-Chaumont and the laughing French boys who jumped the gates at the metro but paused to hold them open, afterwards, for pretty girls to pass through. Maddy had been made during the dry heat and long empty days of August, when we had Paris to ourselves, and not much to do except enjoy each other, back in the days when we still could. Maddy's creation occurred in an alcove bed surrounded by built-in bookshelves, which would have been charming had they not been crowded with clown wigs, red noses, and caked-over jars of stage makeup. Long afterwards, the smell of a damp pancake sponge elicited in me a strange, faraway feeling that was partly erotic and mostly sad.

After Paris, with the beginnings of Maddy buried deep within me, we had travelled south to Greece, where we fought, and then on to Sicily, where we made up. In Taormina, on Sicily's east coast, we mingled with just-off-the-yacht Eurotrash, American tourists and perma-tanned oligarchs. Taormina was ancient and patrician, sprawling high on cliffs above the Ionian Sea. We rented a small condo set back in the stony hills that overlooked it. The place belonged to a doctor, a slim, handsome man who wore uncrumpled linens, and looked, to me, like he should be advertising some high-end product aimed at the elegant older gentleman market: cigars, perhaps, or whiskey. His name was Silvio. Every morning he brought us blood oranges from his garden. He lived alone, and seemed weighted with some sort of sadness that had him hang around at our place longer than he needed to. One morning, I made him coffee from the coffee pot he owned, and served it in porcelain demitasse cups which gleamed a Sicilian orange in the sunlight on the balcony. Silvio informed us, heavily, that the cups belonged to his wife.

'*Lei e morta*,' he said, and then, when we looked confused, he explained in heavily accented English: 'My wife is passing to the sky.'

He gestured above him, and I said: 'I'm so sorry, Silvio. *Apologia. Scuse*,' before realising that wasn't quite right. He nodded in a serious way and was silent for a moment before changing the subject.

'When do you … *matrimonio*?' he asked us.

Charlie had an enviable ability to leave silences hanging in conversations. Spaces didn't seem to trouble him at all. As is often the case in relationships, I became the opposite to him, moving myself to balance him out. So I always rushed to fill silences up. The more awkward they were, the more unseemly was my haste to do so.

'Oh no!' I told Silvio, with a light laugh. 'We are not … *no matrimonio*.'

Silvio looked grave. '*Matrimonio* is good. You should *matrimonio*,' he said.

How to explain to this kind, grief-maimed man the Ionian Sea of resentment, awkwardness and need that surged between me and Charlie on that very topic? To Silvio it was so simple – you loved someone, you married her. She died, you grieved her. He finished his coffee and pointed to Mount Etna, which puffed in the distance like dirty exhaust.

'Volcano is *attivo*. You cannot go there,' he told us, and left.

With Mount Etna scratched from the itinerary, we had little to do except take the funicular to the crowded, black-pebble beach, read books, sleep, make love and eat. I ate prosciutto crudo and lemon granita. Charlie ate every fish he could find. One afternoon, when Charlie wasn't talking to me, for reasons which were obscure, I tied my feet into runners, and set out from our condo to hike up to Castelmola, a village built into rocks even higher up than Taormina. I left Charlie with his book on the balcony – he was reading *The Patrick Melrose Novels*. That was the year everyone was reading *The Patrick Melrose Novels*. I gasped my way up to the village, a cobblestone terrace-town wrapped around the ruins of a Romanesque castle. I heaved through side streets, and wound my way up to the castle. As I was picking through the ramparts, peppered with graffiti, I looked down to my feet and saw I was about to tread on something. A hedgehog. It was small and nearly black, shining like a pinecone among the worn stones. Its spines were neatly shuffled around its body, a spiky cloak. It was attempting to amble somewhere, its little nose protruding from the spike-cloak like a stamen on a flower. I didn't know where it was going or what it thought it was doing, but I worried it wouldn't get there. I squatted on my haunches to look at it, but when I got close, it contracted in fear and folded itself into a spiny ball. I tried, gingerly, to use my foot to move it out of the main thoroughfare. I could see it getting trampled, its spines snapping like twigs under the foot of a tourist or a graffiti artist. But it was hard to roll, and after a while, attempts to make it unfurl itself and walk to a safer place seemed like cruelty. So I left the hedgehog and lolloped back down the hill to Charlie. I found him asleep on a sun lounger, his book collapsed on his chest. The next day, when the handsome doctor came to visit, I told him about the hedgehog. I had to look up the Italian word. It was *riccio*, from the word for sea urchin.

'*Riccio* are very *raro* in Italy!' Silvio told us, excitedly. 'In Sicily, we have very dark colour *riccio*.'

After he left, trailing his sadness, I lounged on the couch, reading a guidebook, while Charlie washed up the coffee cups, humming to himself. When he finished, he leapt upon me affectionately.

'*Riccio* are *raro*. *Ricc-i-o* are very *raro!*' he recited.

He kissed me. Charlie's moods were as inscrutable to me as the workings of Mount Etna. I only knew I had to sit out the storm cycle, wait for the weather to change. Now, perversely, I felt an urge to ruin his sunny mood somehow, to puncture it.

'When are you going to ask me to marry you?' I said.

But it didn't work. He only smiled at me, kissed my nose, and said: 'Soon, my hedgehog. Soon.'

CHAPTER THREE

@SuzeHamilton You fucking journo bitch

@SuzeHamilton Keep washing but the blood is on your hands

4 good she was a bright sole you killed her with your words of bullshit

@SuzeHamilton You are fak news

@SuzeHamilton I hope your happy now she is dead

@SuzeHamilton You should die instead of her

Vic was right, Twitter was a sewer. After a few days of avoiding social media, I thought I would make a clean breast of things by checking my accounts, mopping them up as best as possible, blocking whomever it was necessary to block, and moving swiftly on. I had considered putting out some sort of social media message about Tracey Doran's death, and had even gone so far as drafting one. But what could I say? *It was with deep sadness I learned of Tracey Doran's death*: insincere. *I take no responsibility for Tracey Doran's death*: defensive. *Every single one of you can get fucked*: aggressive, off-brand. I logged on to Facebook – my work account, not my real account. On my real account I did nothing, posted nothing and barely commented on anything. Occasionally, I lightly stalked a man I was having sex with, or a man I was interested in having sex with. That was what the vast pro-social social media project boiled down to, in the end, wasn't it? That and the creation of space for abuse in realms where discretion, if not silence, had previously ruled.

My work Facebook account, I saw, was also flecked in bile, some of it in the comments section of the Tracey Doran exposé, which I had posted on my account and forgotten to remove after her death. My Facebook message inbox bulged, and that wasn't pretty either. It was a choicer, fruitier version of the Twitter comments, but more laden with sexual slurs and some threats of violence (both implicit and explicit). The beauty of Facebook was that trolls operated with even more impunity there. On Twitter, most people posting truly vile stuff hid their identity by using anonymous accounts. On Facebook, probably because it was too much bother – and nothing, in the Internetocene, should ever be too much bother – people didn't tend to set up fake trolling accounts. They just masqueraded as themselves. This led to the comical situation in which you would get a rape threat (as I did that day) from someone whose profile depicted him as a happy, balding, family man who had his picture, complete with kids, right there in the open digital daylight. His preferred football team, the high school he attended, and even his music taste (Dire Straits, later Paul Simon) were all accessible to me, as was the picture of his daughter's seventh birthday party. She had a *Frozen* cake. I toyed briefly with the idea of exposing him to his wife, whose profile was linked to his, their relationship signified with a love heart icon. The wife worked as a nurse at a hospital in Sydney's south, and on her page she had shared a stream of inspirational quotes. The memes, which said things like 'You can't start the next chapter of your life if you keep rereading the old one'; and 'If Plan A doesn't work, the alphabet still has 25 more letters!', were a way for some women to work

out their quiet desperation in the environment of the internet.
I looked the wife over – netball player, member of a local boot-
scooting club – and decided to leave her unmolested. I blocked
her rapey husband. But Facebook wasn't just a site for words.
It also hosted pictures, and as I clicked my way through the
messages in my inbox I came upon a picture sent from a person
I assumed was a male correspondent, a picture of a penis. It
looked like an engorged slug.

'Oh my god!' I said. This was new. I wasn't sure what to do.

Victor strode past me and plopped himself into his desk,
next to mine. His hair had moved from lavender to pink. It was
iridescent and gleaming, like the mane of one of Maddy's My
Little Ponies.

'What's up, babe?' He looked over my shoulder onto my
screen. 'Oh,' he said. 'Oh.'

Vic signalled for me to move aside. 'I've got this,' he said.
'Dick pics are my *milieu*.'

He tapped around for a few moments and then gave me
back my seat. 'There you go, babe. The bad man is gone. He
won't bother you again.'

'You're my white knight,' I said. 'I thank you.'

'Namaste,' said Victor. 'How are you? Things seemed to
have calmed down online? Now everyone is outraged about
that TV host guy who went dressed as an immigration officer
to his Christmas party.'

I knew the presenter in question. I had written a profile of
him, years ago, for our weekend magazine.

'A fresh outrage is always guaranteed,' said Vic. 'That's the
cycle of internet life.'

'I can't believe it's nearly Christmas already,' I said.

*

Once the dick pic had been disappeared, I knew I had to face the legally fraught music of the defamation threat from Bruce Rydell. I forwarded to the in-house lawyer the letter from Patrick Allen and his associates. I hoped she would tell me we should ignore it, that Rydell was a crank who threatened to sue people all the time and that no one ever took him seriously. All I knew about Rydell was that he was retired, and spent most of his time on his mega-yacht, cruising the Mediterranean and bothering women in the nightclubs of Capri.

I felt like a cop who had been pulled off the beat and put on desk duties. I could discreetly follow a few story leads I had — there was a petty corruption yarn, a city councillor who had been awarding contracts to companies connected to his wife. There was a solid tip about the previous domestic violence conviction of a gun lobbyist with friends in government. But none of it was available to me, according to Ben's edict.

I had glimpsed Ben earlier that day, as he entered the lift and I left it, and I felt a wave of shame wash over me. I never knew what to say when I encountered him in the office, and I always felt awkward during our interactions, as though others must be watching, and parsing our words for indications of romance. As a boss, Ben treated me gruffly, which was fine, because he treated everyone that way. He was respected, and slightly feared, because he was so economical in his conversation. His inscrutability was why I liked having sex with him. Or why I allowed him to have sex with me. I wasn't sure I liked it. It had been going on for about a year, but our contact was very intermittent, and we went through months when we didn't meet up, and I would be relieved and think that it was over, and then I would get a message with a request to turn up at a middling hotel, and something would always compel me to go.

It had started after an awards night. I had been nominated for a series I had done on the illegal labour at Sydney's fine dining restaurants. Some of the restaurants I exposed had advertising partnerships with the paper, and they had threatened to pull ads, but Ben had argued for the story against the commercial director. We sat next to each other at the awards night. It was black tie, and I noticed Ben as a man for the first time, a man who looked good in a suit, not because he was elegant in any way, but because the suit's elegance contrasted with his brutishness, and the result was he looked hyper-masculine and terrifically desirable. I didn't articulate any of this to myself at the time, but Victor, who was sitting next to me, did.

'Fuck, the boss looks fuckable tonight,' he whispered in my ear.

Victor had skirted the black-tie dress code by turning up in what he said was a kilt, but which looked a lot like a plaid skirt. He teamed it with a purse slung around his waist, which he pretended was a sporran.

'You're a wordsmith,' I replied.

'They should nominate me for a prize.'

In fact, Victor was up for a prize too, and he and I both won in our categories. I had genuinely not expected to win, so the announcement of my name was a thrill that lay somewhere between an unwelcome shock and a nice surprise. I walked to the stage, my blood surging unexpectedly with adrenaline. I found myself washed with unbidden thoughts about Charlie and how he might have, in the parallel life, been proud of me. He might even have been with me that very night, watching from the table as I collected my award, clapping and whistling and twinkling with proprietorial happiness. Of course, he probably would have done no such thing. He probably would have announced that he hated black tie, and was not in the mood for bosses and small talk, and stayed at home. That was the problem with the parallel life – it was un-disprovable. Everything that happened in it was theoretically true. There was no way of knowing, so it was unassailable. It was a fantasy, but unlike other fantasies, it offered no comfort and zero hope. I carried it with me always, like a heavy cloak. And there it was, laid across my shoulders that night, as I walked to the stage in my backless dress, my earrings glinting under the lights, and there it was as I shook the proffered hand and took the heavy statuette and I looked out into the sea of the crowd. It shadowed me as I was shuffled off the stage – they had to move things along, they had a schedule to keep – and a camera was flashed in my face as I arranged my teeth into a smile and stood next to the corporate sponsor who said *Congratulations, Ms Hamilton, so well deserved* and then released me without looking at me, and I had a moment of complete existential nothingness when I realised that this thing I had wanted, this award, this thing I thought would comfort me, offered no comfort at all. As I walked back to my table, my colleagues all stood to greet me; they were proud of me, and the men hooted and the women kissed me and I put on my face a mask of modest happiness, and I looked up at Ben as he held out my chair for me, and I saw his eyes and the firm knowledge of his desire flashed between us. *He wants me*, I thought. And there was, at last, some comfort in that.

Nothing happened until after the petits fours. By the time the waiters brought them out, I had drunk a gallon of white wine, and my edges had smudged nicely. All night I was acutely aware of Ben – where he was, who he was talking to. Looking back, it was like watching a slow-motion fall. As though our movements had been plotted in advance. We knew we would come together soon enough, so there was no rush. After the main course was cleared and the award announcements finished, everyone vacated their seats and fanned out, stalking the room to praise the winners and to network with the bosses. I remained at the table, alone, quietly eating a strawberry fondant. I had missed my main course while I was up on stage accepting my award. Ben sat down next to me, heavily – he was drunk – and asked the waitress for coffee.

'How's our star reporter?' he asked me.

'Hungry, actually. They cleared my dinner away before I got to eat it.'

'We can't have that,' he said. He gestured to the waiter and asked him for bread. The waiter brought a dinner roll and a butter dish.

'Let me butter it for you,' Ben said. 'There is nothing better than fresh, well-buttered bread. It would be my last meal if I was on death row.'

'And what would you be on death row for?' I asked.

'Oh, murder, undoubtedly,' Ben said. 'I am moved to contemplate murder several times a day. It's only a matter of time before I commit one.'

'I had no idea,' I replied. 'Your surface is so unruffled. Would it be, like, a crime of passion kind of thing? Or more random?'

'Random. Well, to a degree. I might take out the guy who keeps stealing my paper in the morning. It would be worth it, just to catch him.'

'Your paper is getting stolen? That seems especially cruel.'

'Tell me about it,' Ben replied. 'Doesn't he know who I am?'

He looked down at the roll. He was applying the butter to every corner of it.

'How do you know it's a he?' I asked. 'If you have never seen the person.'

'Yes. You're right,' he said. 'Never assume.'

He placed the buttered roll before me, a small offering.

'Assumption is the enemy of truth,' I said, and I ate the roll, tearing it with my teeth.

*

Later, there was a bar in the city, a dark place with booths and lanterns on every table. Our colleagues stood in a clutch around us, chattering in merriment, circles darkening under their eyes as it got later and later. Eye makeup smeared and ties were loosened. Ben ordered cocktails on the company credit card. Victor drew a packet of cigarettes from his sporran-purse and led expeditions outside to smoke. People left, one by one. Victor got so drunk he had to be folded into the cab like an invalid. Then it was just me and Ben, and we wandered down an empty Macquarie Street, past the State Library and past Parliament, and somewhere around the Barracks we fell towards each other, and he led me to Hyde Park and we had sex, hastily, riskily, beneath a Moreton Bay fig, amid a bed of cyclamen. Afterwards, Ben put me into a cab, and I had trouble believing it had happened. That was the first time.

*

I was going through the tedious business of making background calls for my feature, beginning with parliamentary colleagues, who said only nice things on the record, and made only criticisms off it. The subject of my profile, an up-and-coming politician called Rita Delruca, was dedicated, intelligent, had a firm grasp of policy. She was a dirty factional player, she was a policy lightweight, she had only been promoted so quickly because she was a woman, but you can't say that out loud these days. This was why I preferred writing news to profiles. In news stories you gathered the facts, you sought responses from all parties involved, and you let the reader decide. But writing a profile was different. It involved nuance and emphasis. It meant shaping your information into a narrative even when it didn't naturally cohere to one. It meant trying to convey character through the words of other people, and other people always had biases that were opaque. How do you sum up a person in 3000 words? Since The Incident, I had been firmly of the belief that other people were essentially unknowable, and not in a pleasantly surprising way.

I made about five phone calls before lunch and wrote up some notes. The newsroom whirred around me, and Victor strode in, bringing news of his latest scoop. He'd found out that a man charged with the murder of his wife and kid had been on an intelligence watchlist for his involvement with white supremacist politics. He was pink-cheeked and pleased with himself, and he sat down to file. Vic was a picture of dedication when he wrote, working the keys of his computer like he was playing a sonata. I envied him silently as I took call after unrevealing call from Labor backbenchers. I hit my limit at about 2 pm, stood up, stretched and offered to do a coffee run.

'How well you anticipate my needs,' Victor said, his eyes fixed on his computer screen. 'I should have married you. Want some money?'

I said no, and caught the lift to the ground floor, where I ordered a couple of coffees from Marisa, the company barista. I scrolled my phone as I waited, my attention atomised by the ticker-tape parade of social media. Ben rounded the corner, saw me and walked over, his face serious.

'Have you got a minute?' he asked me.

'Always,' I said.

He frowned at the over familiarity. 'What happened with this Bruce Rydell story?'

'What do you mean?'

'The lawyer rang me. Well, actually, Colin Preston rang me.'

Colin Preston was the chairman of the board.

I asked why.

'Rydell called him. They know each other. They belong to the same ski lodge or something. Rydell is really pissed off. Says you should never have repeated something that was hearsay. Says the conversation with the deputy PM never happened that way.'

'Well – I –'

'Did you put in a call, Suzy?'

'It had been reported before. That story is old. Everyone in the press gallery repeats it.'

'Repeating a defamation is still a defamation.'

'It's not a defamation if it's true.'

'Yes, it is. It can be. Besides, who says it's true? The only person who could vouch its veracity is a dead man.'

'Skim flat white! Almond latte!' said Marisa. She beamed at me as though she was announcing a prize.

Ben looked at me. His face was closed over. 'It's not me you have to worry about,' he said, and he walked away.

*

Back up on the newsfloor, Victor was putting the final touches on his front-page story, checking facts with his intelligence contact, battling with Curtis over the lead of the story. Curtis always wanted to introduce the conflict in a news story right up there in the first par. But like many journalists, Vic harboured some Capote-ish dreams for himself, so he liked to go for more of a slow build. I deposited Vic's latte on his desk and sat down. There was a large envelope on my desk, addressed to me, in looped cursive script. I flipped it over: no name, and no return address. I opened it and unfolded the one-page note inside. The back of the paper was dimpled from the pressure of the biro used to write the note.

Dear Ms Hamilton, it read. *I thought this might interest you.*

The handwriting was expansive, rendered in blue ink. Enclosed with the note was a small booklet. I turned it over to see the full, young face of Tracey Doran, with her name written in sombre type across the bottom page, along with numbers indicating her date of birth and her date of death. It was the order of service for her funeral.

*

After work, I snuck in a beer with Victor. My mother picked up Maddy early on Thursdays, and took her back to her own place to cosset her and feed her what she called 'proper food'. We went to the pub around the corner from the office, which was attractive in its proximity to work, but in no other respect. It had been refurbished in the 1990s, at the precise point when the 1990s had been at their ugliest, design-wise, and had not been touched since. It was a museum to chrome tables and primary colours. Vic was adrenalised from his front-page story. Sometimes it was hard to calm down after a big story. I believed this was probably one of the reasons journalists drank so much, to release the nervous energy of racing to meet a deadline, and also because of the constant low-level anxiety that you might get something wrong and be sued, or disgraced, or both. Certainly, that was why I was drinking.

'So it was just the booklet thing from her funeral?' asked Victor. 'No address on the back? Who do you think sent it?'

'Someone who was at her funeral?' I replied.

'What hymns did she have?' he asked.

'I don't know,' I said. 'How is that relevant?'

'You can tell a lot about a person from the hymns they have at their funeral.'

'No you can't,' I said. 'You can tell a lot about what the person organising the funeral wants to project about the dead person. But not much else.'

'Well, okay, fair enough,' Vic said. 'But my question stands. What hymns did she have?'

'I don't know. I didn't look at the order of service. It's sick.'

Victor considered this for a moment as he took a swig of his beer. He drank draft bitter, in large quantities, like he was in invisible competition with the beef-faced country boys who had tortured him at high school.

'You didn't cause Tracey's death,' he said. He had a foam moustache.

'Sure,' I replied.

*

Later, I took the bus to my mother's house to pick up Maddy. I had stayed for too many drinks. Beverley had a hawkish instinct for even the slightest amount of alcohol consumption, and I would have to explain myself to her. As the bus sighed its way up the hill at Vaucluse, I opened my handbag and flipped through the booklet. No hymns had been sung at Tracey Doran's funeral. Instead, they had played the Beach Boys: 'I Just Wasn't Made for These Times'.

*

Charlie liked the Beach Boys. He had wanted to play them at our wedding, which followed his eventual proposal, which followed our return from the Europe trip and my discovery of my pregnancy. I knew he had taken a while to work himself up to it, and so when he finally asked me, I felt more relief than joy. We didn't have much money, or not money we wanted to spend on a wedding, so we had a registry ceremony with just close family as witnesses, followed by a cocktail party at Uncle Sam's Glebe terrace, which was still just his home at that point, with no hint that it would later become a refuge for me and the contents of my flourishing stomach. We had our first dance in the backyard, which was strewn with lilies and lit by fairy lights. The yard was overlooked by a precarious deck that had been tacked onto the back of the house. The guests piled out onto it, to watch us as we danced, or shuffled, to Al Green. Charlie had wanted 'God Only Knows' by the Beach Boys, but I hadn't, and I won the argument. I was, by then, six months pregnant, and the dress I ordered from a tailor on the internet had been too tight around my rear, and, as a final humiliation, too loose in the bodice. I had hoped much of my weight gain was water retention, but who retained water in their arse? I ended up getting married in a flowing cotton maxi-dress with spaghetti straps and no waist. It was all I could do not to wear thongs. Victor threaded flowers in my hair and told me I looked beautiful, but I didn't believe him. My belly made the first dance awkward, the antithesis of everything Al Green would have wanted his music to inspire, I felt sure. We circled the yard looking at each other, as all our friends and family watched on, and I had no access, even in my imagination, to what Charlie was thinking. I was wondering if it was supposed to feel this way.

A few years later, I stood in the same backyard, alone, with my toddler sleep in the house behind me, and with Charlie I knew not where. I paced the yard where I had once danced. I wore my hair tucked under a shower cap, and I had kitchen gloves on my hands. I looked like an unhappy dishwasher, or a meth cook. I smoked cigarette after cigarette. I looked up at the little white ghosts in the frangipani tree, and turned the Hills Hoist with my hand, making it creak in the dark. I wondered what I was going to do now.

CHAPTER FOUR

'She's asleep.'

When I hopped off the bus at the top of the hill at Vaucluse, I tried to gauge how drunk I was. Sometimes if you're very drunk, you can kid yourself you are thinking clearly. I did not think I was that drunk. I walked in a straight line to the front door of my mother's house – a modest Californian bungalow she shared with my dad, although my mother took up so much space he often seemed incidental. I made an attempt to fix up my hair, tested my breath, popped a mint in my mouth and chewed it quickly. Beverley swung the door open, and her silhouette hovered impressively in the doorway for a moment. She looked like she was going to demand papers before allowing entry.

'Yes, I'm a little late,' I said. 'Hello, Beverley.'

I kissed her on the cheek. At the age of about 15, I had started calling my mother by her first name, as a sort of experiment. I continued the practice when I saw how much it irritated her. Beverley stepped aside and we walked through to the kitchen. I called out to my father, who was on his easy chair in his study, his glasses slung on his head and the crossword on his lap. The television burbled the late news.

'Hello, darling!' he called.

'Suzy is late, Simon,' Beverley said.

'Should we fine her?'

'Very funny, dear.'

We walked past him and into the kitchen. Beverley said I looked like I needed a cup of tea, and I couldn't deny the truth of that.

'I'm sorry,' I said. 'I had a late deadline and then I got too comfortable at the pub.'

Half of that statement was correct – in fact I hadn't filed anything that day. I hadn't had a byline all week and it made me itch with anxiety.

'Have you got a story coming out? You haven't had a byline in a week,' Beverley said. She read everything I wrote, sometimes phoning in errors or inconsistencies.

'I'm working on a feature for the magazine,' I said. 'It won't be out for another month or so.'

'I see.'

Beverley pulled out an elegant canister and doled tea leaves into a Marimekko teapot. She thought teabags were common, or something. Sometimes it felt like my mother did everything correctly in order to emphasise how incorrectly I did everything. I was their only child. There had been attempts at another, I gathered, but ultimately they had given up and settled their hopes on me. Beverley had wanted her daughter to be a solicitor or, better still, a barrister. She had been deeply disappointed when I dropped out of my law degree to take up a journalism cadetship. She had pointed out that, as a cadet, I would earn less than 50 per cent of the salary of a law graduate. The pay gap would only widen as time marched on, she said. I had scoffed at the time. Now, I often thought about the marching pay gap, particularly when the amount I earned as a journalist only narrowly justified the amount I paid for childcare. Beverley eventually adjusted to my choice of career, but she sometimes joked, in a way that wasn't really a joke, about how they would leave Maddy enough in their will to set herself up in chambers. I tried to picture Maddy, who could put her own shoes on, but almost never on the correct feet, as a barrister. Perhaps a horsehair wig would suit her.

'I'm just going to go and say goodnight,' I said.

'Don't you go waking her,' my mother called after me, causing me a flash of irritation. Was it always this way when your parents became grandparents? Beverley had always felt, in some primal way, that she owned me, so it made sense she felt she owned the things that belonged to me. And Maddy definitely belonged to me. She was asleep in the spare room, which had been converted into her own room, through the liberal application of pink pillows and unicorn toys and the magnificent structure of a Victorian-style doll's house, complete with bay windows and a tiled roof, which took pride of place next to the bed. I could see that Maddy had arranged various dolls around the dinner table, a (faux?) mahogany piece of miniature furniture with carved legs and matching, turned-wood chairs. Often, when I inquired about the dolls, or the tiny bunnies, or the little mice, that Maddy was playing with, asking their names and how they were related to each other, Maddy would say, 'Dair mummy is at work.' Even her toys were latchkey kids.

Maddy's cheek bloomed on the pillow. She clutched her blanky and was sucking her thumb in her sleep, creating a faint slurp-and-suction noise which was as familiar to me as my own breathing. I leaned over and kissed her and nuzzled her softly. There was no greater contentment than to watch your child sleep. My mother's shadow crossed the door and I backed out of the room. Beverley shepherded me back to the kitchen, where two teacups stood on the bench, perfectly spaced. They matched the teapot.

'It took me an hour to get her down,' Beverley said. 'I had to read her six storybooks. She wanted to know where you were.'

'She knows Mummy has to go to work,' I replied. 'She knows I always come back.'

Beverley let that statement hang for a minute. She wasn't one to offer undue reassurance. She took the milk bottle from the fridge and poured a few glugs into a small china jug.

'My contribution to gracious living,' she said as she set it down, and she poured out our tea. She stirred milk into her cup. The teaspoon made a dink-dink-dink noise which took up most of the room. We sat for a moment without speaking as we sipped. The silence was more silent than it was companionable.

'Heard anything from Charlie?' she asked me.

'Nope.'

'Do you ever wonder what's keeping him so busy?'

'Nope.'

That was a lie. I wondered about that all the time.

My mother drained her tea and opened another canister. From it she drew a single cigarette. She smoked one a day, no more and no less, and always in the evening. She said she couldn't stand the way smoking had become a moral issue, like climate change, or using plastic straws. I leaned across the kitchen island, took the book of matches that was laid there, and lit one for my mother.

'Thank you, darling,' she said. She drew on the cigarette like it was medicine.

'Do me a favour?' she said, her voice high as she sucked in the smoke. 'Go and see Uncle Sam. I think he's getting a little lonely. His girlfriend died last week.'

Sam was actually my dad's uncle, and he represented the only extended family we had left, seeing as Beverley's were either too dead or too distant. But my mother concerned herself with Sam more than my dad did. Dad wasn't so good at looking after other people. Beverley, on the other hand, was preoccupied with other people.

'Gina?' I said. 'That's terrible.' Gina lived in the same building as Uncle Sam and they often had dinner together. Gina called it 'supper'. She had arthritis and fairy-floss hair which she had set into a wave every week at an Elizabeth Bay hairdresser. She had not been Uncle Sam's girlfriend. I knew this because I was pretty sure Sam was gay. He had never married, and about six months after Maddy and I had moved into his house, and Sam had moved out, I found a startling collection of pornographic videotapes in a downstairs cabinet. I had watched them, one by one, and confirmed they were thoroughly homosexual in nature. I looked upon Sam with renewed admiration after that.

'Gina is not his girlfriend,' I said, and then switched to the past tense. 'They were just good friends.'

'Just go and see him,' Beverley said. She stubbed out her cigarette and said it was time for bed. It was not discussed, but it was assumed that I would stay the night. I dislodged my snoozing father from his chair, pulled out the sofabed in his study and made up a bed on it. I woke to Maddy's nose, about a centimetre from my own.

'Mummy,' she said gravely. 'Here I am.'

*

Sydney continued its lurch towards summer. Humidity crept into the mornings. All the plants that were going to bloom, bloomed, as though seizing their day before the real heat claimed them. The jacarandas lost their purple clothes. The sorrowful basil plant I kept on our kitchen ledge, my sole nod to cooking from scratch, came back to life, making me feel I could stake a greater claim to domesticity than I had earned.

I started putting basil on Maddy's meals – the fishfingers and the spaghetti bolognaise – as a garnish. Maddy called the basil 'leaves' and rejected it.

'Don't want leaves, Mummy,' she said, and complained until they were removed from her plate. Still, I kept putting them there. I had read on the internet that a kid had to be offered something a hundred times before they would try it.

A few days after Tracey Doran's funeral order of service turned up on my desk, I received another letter, in the same looped handwriting. This one contained a similar note: *Dear Ms Hamilton, this might be of interest.* Inside the envelope was a school report of Tracey Doran's. She had been a competent maths student. She received faint praise in geography and was much admired by her English teacher for her 'imaginative written expression'. A few days after that, it was a vaccination certificate for a pet, a dog who had the same surname as Tracey. I supposed it was the melancholy dog that appeared in some of her social media posts. Did the fact that someone had his vaccination certificate mean he was being looked after? I had not considered the orphaned pets.

Then came a bigger envelope, containing something soft and bulky, which turned out to be two crochet hooks attached to a just-commenced piece of crochet. It was done in pink thread, and looked like it was the beginnings of a baby's hat, or perhaps a piece of clothing for a small dog. *Tracey was working on this when she died*, read the note, and after that parcel, I had left the office to take a long walk around the curve of harbour near the building. I stood next to the water, my face turned up, my skin just beginning to burn under the late-morning sun, and I listened to the faint nicker of the cranes which lifted steel beams onto a construction site across the bay. More apartments. Sydney was sprouting them everywhere. I took some breaths and walked back into work. I threw the crochet into a box. I didn't want to touch something the dead woman had touched.

*

There were many reasons I was glad I had not become a lawyer. Chiefly, because I knew I would have been a very bad one. I had come to this conclusion while working as a legal clerk, in a big downtown firm, while still a student. My mother had helped me get this job, through Frederick van Steen, the husband of one of her tennis friends. Frederick was a partner, and whenever he passed me in the halls, he gave me a small captain's salute and said 'Keeping you busy, are we?' in a voice that was too loud. I wasn't sure if I was being kept busy – I found the work I was given totally incomprehensible. I was assigned to a litigation matter involving a big fast-food company that was embroiled in a dispute with its franchisees. It entailed a lot of document management, scanning contracts for possible breaches, and the deft application of meaningful Post-it notes next to particularly damning clauses. I had no idea, really, what I did all day, it all seemed so removed from reality, so wrapped in verbiage and legal cladding that it couldn't possibly relate to actual people who moved through the world like I did, people who attended work and fed families and stopped at traffic lights and threw out milk when it soured. The work, the fine-detail reading and the contract-combing, did, however, require enormous amounts of concentration, more than I had available to give.

I was dating a fellow law student that summer. He had a crooked smile and the limbs of an athlete, and my attempts at uninterrupted document-scanning were often spoilt by the intrusive sexual thoughts I had about him. The lights in the offices operated on a motion sensor and one day, as I passed a fellow legal clerk sitting in an office, solo, scanning documents, the lights went out on him. He had stayed stationary for so long that the motion sensor had thought the room empty. I watched as he paused reading, just for long enough to raise his arm sharply, vertically above him, an efficient gesture that served to activate the sensors and bring the lights back on, so he could return to his reading. I knew at that moment I could never be a lawyer. I would never have the powers of stillness necessary to deactivate motion sensors.

The firm was split over five floors of one of the city's most prestigious buildings. It had expensive designer stores nestled in its ground floor, and I used to browse in them at lunchtime. In my mind I was playing a game of chicken with the shop assistants, who surely knew I didn't have money to spend but were unable to do anything except trail me pointedly until I left. In one of those shops, during one miserable lunch hour, I saw a handbag bauble with a price tag of $725. For a handbag bauble! It was something I had not previously known existed. Now, I knew, it consisted of a spray of fur (real, I hoped, given the expense) stuck to a plaited leather cord, and fixed with a silver ball and a hook that attached it to the handbag proper. I turned over the tag several times to make sure the price just pertained to the handbag bauble, and not the handbag itself. It did. Anyone who had enough money for a handbag bauble had too much money, I thought, and the next day I responded to a newspaper notice advertising journalism cadetships.

I was reminded of all the reasons I had not become a lawyer when I entered a meeting with several of them in order to discuss the legal threat from Bruce Rydell. There was the company's in-house lawyer, Stefanie, and another lawyer from a specialist firm that had been retained to help with the matter. His name was Francis and he had something green stuck in his teeth, which it seemed that no one had told him about. Stefanie was compactly petite in a way that I found intimidating. Small women always made me feel overly large, as though my person was spilling out over the edges, even though I dieted to keep myself within what I deemed were the acceptable borders. Francis had brought along some kind of lawyerly hanger-on, perhaps his junior. The junior was not introduced and he spent the meeting typing notes into his laptop. Ben was also present. I made sure I sat several seats away from him, out of his sight line. Stefanie seemed to be chairing the meeting. She sat at the head of the table and shuffled some papers.

'Thank you all for coming,' she said. Her manner was crisp. 'I won't take up too much of your time. As we know, Bruce Rydell is claiming that the story, repeated in print by Suzy, regarding what was said in a meeting he had with the deputy prime minister in 1988, is false. He says comments attributed to him, particularly that he told the deputy prime minister to "prepare for fucking Armageddon" if he did not accede to proposed changes to cross-media ownership laws, were published maliciously.'

'I wrote *allegedly*,' I said. '*Allegedly* told the deputy prime minister he should prepare for fucking Armageddon.'

Stefanie looked down at her papers as I spoke, waiting for me to finish so she could continue.

'He is also claiming that he never said the words: "You cunts better prepare yourselves for a decade in opposition. We are going to kill you."'

'I never said he —'

'And he strongly denies ever telling the deputy prime minister he was a dingbat. Or a deadshit.' Stefanie paused.

Stefanie, Francis, the unnamed junior and Ben all swivelled their heads to look at me.

'I bowdlerised the swear words,' I said lamely.

Stefanie adjusted her glasses with a neat movement, and pressed on. 'The fundamental problem we have here is the unavailability of the truth defence,' she said. 'Given there were only two parties to the conversation, and one of them – the only person who could attest to the veracity of this anecdote – is dead ... well, we are hamstrung. Legally.'

I felt a surge of dislike for Stefanie. I wondered if she had ever bought a handbag bauble.

'Mr Rydell has also signalled his intention to sue for aggravated damages on the grounds of malice,' she said.

'My malice?' I asked.

'Yes.'

'How can he possibly say what my motivations were?'

'His lawyer would establish it – malice – through cross-examination and legal discovery. Your text messages, emails, that sort of thing.'

'They can subpoena text messages?' Ben asked.

'Yes,' Stefanie replied. 'They would most likely subpoena text messages between Suzy and her superiors, pertaining to the story.'

'What about messages sent on encrypted apps?'

'Not always so encrypted as you think,' she said.

I tried to remember what communications I'd had with Ben or Curtis over the story before I rushed off to collect Maddy. I thought of all the other communications I had shared with Ben over text message. I wondered how targeted such a discovery process would be.

Francis cleared his throat and spoke up. 'Were there any other people present at this meeting between Rydell and the deputy PM? Staff, perhaps? Or an employee from the relevant department?'

'We don't know. I don't think so ... I don't know,' I said. 'The anecdote has been reported multiple times previously. Can't we use that in our defence?'

'No,' said Stefanie.

71

'What do you recommend?' asked Ben, cutting across me.

'The publication of a full apology. An abject one. A correction printed in a prominent position in the paper. Payment of Rydell's legal costs and an ex gratia payment to him to settle the matter.'

'But he is a millionaire,' I said.

'Billionaire,' said Ben. 'Do it,' he told Stefanie.

And with that, the meeting was over. Ben fell into deep conversation with Stefanie and they left the room in tandem. The unnamed junior packed up his laptop. Francis gave me a sad smile as he loped out of the room. I saw that he still had the green thing in his teeth. I said nothing.

*

After I put Maddy to bed that night, reading her four stories, and fending off her attempts to make me read five, I left Betty the neighbouring teenager in charge, and walked up the street to see Tom. I took with me a bottle of wine and we sat on his balcony drinking it. I asked Tom about his work, his real work, and listened as he talked. He did mostly portraits, some landscape, but stylised. Sometimes he digitally manipulated his images to create trompe l'oeils. The series he was working on was called *Realist*, he told me. It involved recreating scenarios from the great Greek myths, using models he recruited mostly from his basketball team. He was currently doing a shoot using a Heracles who was a six-foot-tall centre named Dale.

'Maybe I'll shoot you,' he said to me, filling my glass.

We were drinking from mismatched tumblers which Tom had found on a bookshelf and washed out under the bathroom tap.

'Oh yes,' I said. 'Who will I be? Medusa?'

'Aphrodite, of course,' he said, and we went to bed soon after that.

Afterwards, Tom walked me home, through streets misted with early summer rain. We stopped off at a 7-Eleven so I could buy milk and bread for Maddy's breakfast. The attendant rang it up wordlessly, and slung the grocery bag over the counter like he was swinging a kettlebell. Tom picked it up and carried it for me.

'So tell me about Heracles,' I said as we walked.

'Well, you know, famously strong,' said Tom. 'But he had hidden depths. He had a tough life, actually.'

'How so?' I looped my arm through his.

'His troubles started young, when he was a baby. His father's wife sent two serpents to kill him in his cradle.'

'Oh,' I said. 'But the snakes didn't get him?'

'No, he killed them with his bare hands.'

'Boss move, Heracles.'

'Heracles was a boss.'

We reached my rusty gate and I pushed it open.

'Who was his mum, then?'

'Alcmene. Heracles' dad, Zeus, disguised himself as her husband to seduce her,' Tom said.

'So she committed adultery kind of inadvertently?'

'She was a mortal so she was easily fooled,' he said. 'The gods were always messing with the mortals.'

Tom handed me the groceries and kissed me goodnight.

'Come to the art show,' he said. 'It won't kill you. I can guarantee the alcohol will be of poor quality, but plentiful and free.'

'What if I don't understand the art?'

'The thing with art is you miss the point if you think there is a point to miss.'

'Okay,' I said. 'I'll come to the show.'

Inside, Betty was lying with legs akimbo on the couch, one arm hanging off its edge, slack. The light from the television danced on her sleep-fallen face.

*

I was in the city to meet a political contact who knew Rita Delruca, the subject of my profile. He had agreed to give me some details about the skulduggery Delruca had deployed to land preselection for her marginal seat. It was small beer but I needed to get out of the office. It was humid and as soon as I left the building and started walking into the city, my body filmed with sweat. The contact was a former Labor staffer-turned-consultant named Theo. He was still a party member and he brandished his ambitions completely openly. He was seeking his own preselection, but for a far safer seat, one in Sydney's south which he had been eyeing off since he had been a student politician, and announced, to his friends, that he would be prime minister one day. I had found this was common among politicians – they were perfectly blithe and unselfconscious in their self-confidence. They had no problem with the naked part of their ambition. I sometimes wondered what it must be like to walk around clothed in that kind of self-belief.

I met Theo in a coffee shop in the Queen Victoria Building. It was full of Christmas shoppers and as we drank our cappuccinos, a huge pine tree loomed over us, like we were children in a storyland forest. I had slept with Theo once, during a stint in Canberra, pre-Maddy. The combination of the bitterly cold winter and the drinking culture among the capital's political elite had led me to make some bad sexual choices during that period. Theo, at least, was funny. He lacked malice entirely, which was rare in a person, let alone a politician.

But did a lack of malice matter in someone so self-interested? I wasn't sure. Theo told me about how Delruca had branch-stacked, signing up lots of non-English-speaking migrants to her branch to vote for her. Possibly some dead people too. He said the preselection was the subject of an internal party investigation.

'Can you get me documents for that?' I asked. People would say anything, and it didn't count for much. Documents did.

'I can try. Give me a few days,' he said.

He took a swig of his cappuccino. 'The main thing is,' he said, 'is that Delruca is no angel. All this backstory about being raised poor, having it tough, you know, bringing up her kid as a single mum. It's a good Labor story, sure.'

He paused to wipe his mouth with the corner of a paper napkin. I had a stab of memory of kissing that mouth, with its narrow, flesh-poor lips. I recalled that Theo was the product of an expensive education. His father was CEO of a prominent listed company and he had probably been raised in a free-standing home with a pool, and someone who was paid to look after the pool. He was probably motivated by Labor backstory envy. That, and Delruca was in the wrong faction.

'So, sure, she's done it tough,' he continued. 'But she's no choirgirl. She gives as good as she gets. She knows how to handle herself.'

I was sure she did. I didn't think it remarkable that Delruca knew how to handle herself. I wondered why women with tough stories were expected, somehow, to be soft themselves, if they wanted understanding. If they wanted to be liked. But I didn't voice any of that. I just took notes, and when we were finished talking, I paid for our coffees.

*

What to wear to the opening of a conceptual art show? What clothes could help you look undone enough, without looking like you've tried to be undone? The one denominator of cool was lack of effort, I knew, but it was so hard to engineer. I strolled through Pitt Street Mall and browsed various shops. I watched covertly the fashionable twentysomethings as they hunted through racks. I believed there was some sort of nineties revival going on. I saw that jeans shapes had changed, all of a sudden, and there didn't seem to be any pants for sale that weren't cropped. Cropped trousers were always a problem for the tall – there was a risk you could end up looking like you were wearing knickerbockers, and that was not a risk I wanted to take. I tried on a black midi-dress, took a mirror selfie and texted it to Victor. He replied: *You look like a sad crow.* I settled on a pair of the new jeans, ankle-grazers, they were called. They were tight enough to excite some interest. I would wear them with flat shoes and a plain black T-shirt. If I could not look cool, I could at least be unobtrusive. I swam through the crowd and into a toy store to look for some members of the family of tree mice that Maddy so loved. They were called the Barnet Family Mice, and they had all sorts of buildings you could buy to house them in – a treehouse, obviously, a bungalow, and a cottage. They even had a ballet theatre, where the mice were affixed to small stands and stood, *en pointe*, as you turned a lever which rotated them, causing them to break into balletic dance. Maddy must have the dancing mice, but the store had sold out of the ballet theatre, so I asked them to order it in.

'Do you want the *Nutcracker* one or the *Swan Lake* one?' the assistant asked. 'The computer's telling me we only have *Swan Lake* left in the warehouse.'

'That's fine,' I said, and fished for my credit card in my bag. I saw my phone flash with a text message. I exited the store and stood for a moment, blinking, in the river of shoppers on the street. I opened the text up to read. It was from Ben, and my heart sank at the same time as my groin experienced a jolt. He had a hotel room, at the same place over the bridge, and he wanted me to go there. I found myself stepping into a cab.

*

Ben was there to tell me this had to end. He said this, almost sweetly, as he sat, his head hung low, on the bed in the mediocre hotel. The counterpane dented and rippled around his bulk. He said that the conversation with the lawyer had brought things home to him.

'The prospect of the text messages being found,' he said. 'It has focused my mind.'

My mind felt unfocused. I felt both relief and irritation – irritation that he had brought me here to sing me this song, the silliness of his feeling obliged to do things this way, to talk it out. We were not teenagers. We were not having a love affair. There was no requirement for chivalry. Ben might impose it on himself, but did he have to drag me into it? A phone call would have sufficed. After our meeting with the compact Stefanie, I had scrolled through my messages to Ben and deleted anything incriminating, but I had a vague feeling they might still be stored in the cloud. Where was the cloud? Over on the bed, Ben was talking about Beano, and his marriage, and the kids, and that's when I broke from my daze and told him no, no, no, we were not doing this.

'I owe you a conversation,' he said.

'You really don't,' I replied, and I meant it. I could shake Ben off. I could let him go quite simply, as easily as unclasping my fingers from the string of a helium balloon. I felt a surge of contempt for him, for the earnest face he had on, and I experienced an urge to mess with him somehow, to wrench back the power he had taken from me.

I reached for his hand and he gave it to me, and I moved to put my body on his. He hung his head at my breastbone and said my name softly.

'Why didn't you back me in that meeting?' I asked him.

'What?' His head was working its way into the ledge of my clavicle.

'You rolled over to those lawyers too easily.'

'I didn't think we had much of a choice,' he said. 'Ultimately, it's my call.'

He stood and moved away from me, adjusting the front of his pants. The counterpane held the dent of his bulk.

'It was a bullshit call,' I said.

'That's your opinion,' he said. 'It's time for me to go.'

He took a sharp glance at his watch, and shuttered his face. 'I'll leave first, shall I?'

'Go for it,' I said, and I listened as he closed the door and left, and I went to the window and watched, for a few minutes, the respectable business of the North Sydney street, its office girls and bicycle couriers, the Christmas cheer of its Santa-and-sleigh street decorations, and its tinselled telephone poles. I calmed myself with the thought that it was over at last, and the manner of the ending was unimportant. It was just another thing to fold up and pack away, and no one would ever know about it, except the two of us. I could work with Ben without ever having to meet his eye.

After a few minutes, I picked up my bag and went to go, and as I opened the door and walked into the corridor I heard voices raised, and as I lifted my gaze I saw Ben's back, and behind him, facing him, and facing me, was the face of Beano, Ben's wife, who wore a mask of anguish. The anguish ascended to fury when she saw me.

'I knew it!' she shrieked. '*I knew it!*'

Ben looked back at me. I had stopped dead with the horror of it, and his face was a portrait of shame that I knew would be added to my mental bank of indelible images, and he grasped his wife by her shoulders and spoke to her low and soft as she cried, while I did the only thing I could think to do – I turned the other way and left via the fire exit, my heart beating fast, like a mouse running from a cat, and eventually I was spilled onto the street, where the early summer sun lit me up, and I felt utterly unworthy of it.

It turned out there was an app you could download to track the GPS on someone else's phone, to see where they were. All of that information was available. It was in the cloud.

CHAPTER FIVE

I genuinely couldn't tell if the art was brilliant, or terrible, but after my second glass of white wine I began to see it didn't matter, and that the very classification of art was itself a bourgeois act, and therefore unnecessary. Tom was beside me as we looked at the televisions, which had been torn apart by the artist, and lay in pieces on the polished concrete floors. There were also some artfully destroyed radios, and a VCR video player, for which I felt a flash of nostalgia. When I was a kid my father used to bring home a new video tape from the store every Friday night. I would always hope for a new release movie, maybe something with Sally Field in it. I really did think Tom's generation were missing something, and it wasn't just the appreciation of rarity that was killed by everything being on-demand, from sex to television. They missed out on having to sit through things they didn't choose – songs, shows, people, even advertisements. They missed out on serendipitous discovery. They thought they knew best what they wanted. In my experience, people rarely did.

'Can I tempt you?'

We were standing in front of a late-nineties-model TV, from the early days of the flatscreen, but before they had become wafer-like. This set was solid and monstrous, with a bulbous back section that had been smashed out like a pumpkin. The television's screen, being also smashed, was not functioning, but a series of violent news images was being cast onto it, ghostily, from a projector set into a wall behind us. A baseball bat was chained to the wall with a small sign stuck on it. The sign read 'Try me', and one by one, people were coming forth to hit the television with the baseball bat. It was some sort of art-sanctioned violence.

'You first,' I told Tom.

He took the baseball bat and swung it lightly, athletically, into the jagged remains of the screen, creating a small rupture. He passed the baseball bat to me, and I found myself swinging it with some force, a force which had behind it a combination of cheap wine and the events of that afternoon.

'Easy there, tiger,' said Tom, taking the bat from me. 'Perhaps we'll make an art appreciator of you after all.'

'I am not sure I can claim to appreciate the art if I am smashing it.'

'Appreciation comes in many forms,' Tom replied. 'A lot of these people think art should be ephemeral anyway.'

He swung his handsome arms around him to indicate the crowd, which was comprised mostly of twentysomething hipsters. They fell broadly into two categories – the ones who dressed as mountain folk – the girls in old-fashioned dresses and solid boots, the boys in working trousers which were rolled at the ankles; and the ones who were dressed in cuter versions of the clothes I had worn as a teenager – high-waisted jeans, ripped tights, band T-shirts.

'I think I need another drink.'

Tom stopped a passing waiter and took a full wineglass for me. I passed back my empty one.

'The gimmick for this show is that after it's over, the artist is going to dump all the pieces in the tip, and film it, and that's going to form part of his next installation,' he said.

I sipped my wine. It tasted like metal and lemon.

'What if a wealthy collector should come along and beg to buy one of the pieces?' I asked him. 'You know, to have it on a plinth in his home, maybe next to his actual TV.'

'As a sort of memento mori?'

'Yes. A warning to the TV,' I said. 'Like, don't get too comfortable. You too will soon be obsolete.'

'Well, that would present a profound insult to his artistic integrity,' Tom said. 'The terrible prospect that he might make some money.'

'Who's making money?'

A young man approached us. He was short and redheaded, his hair shaped into a quiff, his skin pale. He would have looked like a 19th-century poet, and he certainly had the teeth of one, had he not been wearing leather shorts. There seemed to be a streak of obstinancy in this youthful art crowd, an aggressive rejection of anything that might make it look like they had dressed up for an occasion. Instead they just looked like they were in actual dress-ups. They were all groomed to look ungroomed. They wore ironic hats and some smelled of wet wool.

'Well, not you, I was just explaining to Suzy,' said Tom. 'Danton, this is Suzy Hamilton. Suzy, this is the artist, Danton. We know each other from art school.'

I shook Danton's hand limply. I had feared this moment would come. I had no idea what to say.

'Very interesting work,' I said. 'Congratulations.'

'Oh thank you. My usual work is street art, so this is a departure,' Danton replied lazily. His eyes roved the room behind me, scanning it. 'I like to build decay into my art. And what do you do, Suzy?'

'I'm a journalist.'

'Oh how wonderful. What is your surname?'

Tom had just told him that. I told him again.

'I know your byline,' Danton said, with nonchalance. 'I am an avid consumer of news. It's where I get most of my inspiration, actually. This whole show is about disruption. It's a physical depiction of the disruption of the media industry. The death of the dinosaurs.'

I never knew what to say when people, usually at parties, pontificated on the imminent death of newspapers. There were few polite responses.

'Far better to be in a growth industry, like conceptual art,' said Tom. He took my elbow and applied the faintest, comforting pressure. 'We won't keep you, mate. You should be off with the critics and the collectors.'

'What a bore!' cried Danton happily, and he stalked off to join another clutch of people.

'I worry about his knees,' said Tom, as he went. 'Exposed to the elements like that.'

I finished my wine. I was drinking ferociously. After this afternoon, after the hotel, and Beano's face of anguish-turned-fury, I had walked several blocks to find a patch of park wedged into the harbour between the mid-level office blocks and the suburban streets. I had waited there until the clutching at my chest eased, and then I hopped in a cab, not back to work – the office had become unthinkable, remote, hostile, as a result of what I had done. I went to collect Maddy, because as long as the earth still turned, Maddy would need bathing and fishfingers, and I would need the gentle pleasure of preparing her meal, selecting the bowl Maddy liked, and the mini-fork with which she speared at her food like a medieval king. Maddy needed me, but sooner or later, I knew, the pendulum would swing, and Maddy would reject me but expect me to still hang around, in the background, like a groupie, or a supplicant.

'Do you have a cigarette?' I asked Tom.

'I do, but you don't smoke,' he said.

'Sometimes I do. When I was younger I did,' I said, as though I had to convince him of my experience in this area.

We went outside, joining a small posse of people who held their ciggies dangled away from their bodies, like they were clutching the leash of an invisible dog. I thought about how much I smoked when Maddy was a toddler, after The Incident, when tobacco was the crutch which kept me from listing completely sideways. Tom leaned over with a lighter.

'How sweet the marriage between tobacco and alcohol,' I said.

'So why did you give up?' Tom asked. He breathed his smoke above him in a cloud, like he was sending it up to the gods.

'I didn't give up consciously, actually. I just got pregnant,' I said.

It was true – I had returned from Europe to find all wine tasted like it was corked. Cigarettes were sickly and I craved bananas with an urgency I had not previously felt for any fruit. I had wee'd on a stick, and then gone to the doctors for a blood test. My levels of the main pregnancy hormone were high, which meant a lower chance of miscarriage. Even as a zygote, Maddy surged with life.

'That's how I knew I was pregnant, actually,' I continued, taking a puff. 'I couldn't bear cigarettes, or wine.'

'I wish I had seen you pregnant. Or known you pregnant,' Tom said.

'It was not attractive,' I said. 'Every time I stood up, I made a noise like a grand slam tennis player hitting a forehand.'

I had always envied those women with husbands driven wild by their pregnant bodies. Was it the ripeness? Or just the need to take the body before it was overtaken by a greater force, a force they could never compete with? Whatever it was, Charlie hadn't felt it. He stopped wanting sex as soon as I started showing. My body became a secret, changing thing I shared only with the baby. My skin grew malt-scented and lush, a place of mutual experience with my unborn daughter.

'Sexy.'

'Oh yes.'

'Perhaps you can show me a picture,' Tom said. 'Of you pregnant.'

But I didn't have too many of those. Charlie, never an enthusiastic photographer, had barely taken any pictures during my pregnancy. I had felt too bovine to care, really, but every now and then, when I thought of it, I handed my phone to him and asked him to capture me. He always obliged, but it felt desperate, like I was begging him to notice me. Like Maddy would do to me, later, when she emerged and grew into herself. Maddy, on a swing at Tree Park, going higher than she had before, or executing her version of a *demi-plié*, or handing me a constellation of scribbles on a piece of butcher's paper, and announcing it as a portrait of something – a dog, a house, me. All these gestures, all this art, it all said the same thing: *Here I am. Look at me. See me.*

*

We went back inside, and I bothered the drinks waitress again, only to be told there was no more alcohol. The art crowd and I had drunk the gallery dry. People filtered out onto the street. Girls with hats said the show was amazing, and super-interesting, and super-innovative. One drunk girl with a ring through the cartilage of her ear said, too loudly, that the show was *super-derivative*. Everything was super, though, in some way. One of Tom's friends, Conal, to whom I'd been introduced earlier, said everyone was heading to the Marlborough, and we clopped down the street in a tribe, walking under the wash of the fluorescent lights, stopping at a petrol station for more cigarettes, and I fought the urge to buy milk for Maddy's breakfast. What, again, was I doing here with these young people who overused superlatives and behaved as though the world was waiting for their embrace? Then, the lit-up street again, the passing distress of a police siren, some difficulty walking and Tom's steady hand at my arm, again, and a 'You right?' and me assuring him that yes, I was all right. Then, inside the belly of the pub, lit with fairy lights and with a sad attempt at a Christmas tree that looked like a broken umbrella. Tom sitting me down and fetching me a glass of water, and me opening my mouth to protest but finding I didn't have the power of speech.

And then Tom went to the bathroom, and I took out my phone to check for any messages from Betty the babysitter – not that I was in a fit state to respond to possible crises. There was nothing, and I texted Betty to let her know I would be home by midnight. Mindlessly, reflexively, I opened my email app, which was connected with my work email. And there it was, right at the top of the email queue. It was an all-office email, and only a few people were authorised to send such messages. These emails reached all staff. The email was from Ben, one of the few people who had that authority. Except it wasn't written by Ben. It was written by his wife, the quiet, pretty-lipped Beano, who was ventriloquising through him the voice of her anguish and anger. She was writing to inform everyone – 'you all', she said, chummily, like it was a shoutout to join the office netball team – that her husband had been fucking Suzy Hamilton for months, 'maybe years', she said, really throwing open the timeline for maximum dramatic effect. And that she thought they should all know. She must have channelled her rage into breaking into her husband's computer.

It was the wife's prerogative to know all. Beano had stormed Ben's iCloud like one of the Furies. She was a Viking killing the villagers. She was hellbent. The email, which was short but packed with detail, just like a good piece of reportage, was time-stamped 11.10 pm, meaning it had just been sent. Tom returned and sat beside me, in the emphatic way he made all his movements, as though space was his to take up. Next to him, Conal was talking to a young woman with wine-red lipstick, who caught my eye and smiled at me, her mouth cracking open like a happy doll, and Tom was asking me, again, if I was all right, and I said, actually, I thought it was time for me to go home now.

PART TWO

CHAPTER SIX

No one wanted to work the New Year's Eve shift. Everyone who tended bar at the Little Friend wanted to be out, fighting crowds and taking drugs and ostentatiously eschewing the fireworks display. Sydneysiders were the only people in the world who could afford to be blasé about spectacular fireworks over their spectacular harbour. I had long been like this myself. The fireworks were too much bother, the harbour parks too packed, the waterfront parties too difficult to get home from. But I knew, too, that if you went to a party in the city's west, or any place with no view of the fireworks, that you would regret it at midnight, when you heard the crack and the boom of them, and the faded distant light of them was cast onto the face of the person you were talking to, in whatever earnest, non-harbour-facing backyard you were in. That noise, that feeling, was the sensation that life was happening elsewhere. It was the small and inconsequential sorrow of knowing you had missed something beautiful that was enjoyed by other people. That feeling was where all of life's sadness came from, wasn't it? I wouldn't see the fireworks this year. I wouldn't even attempt to. But I would get double time and a half. I needed the money.

In the weeks following Beano's all-office email, I had been placed on personal leave, communicating only with the Human

Resources department, and the lawyers who drafted the abject apology to Bruce Rydell. While on my forced leave, I had read the paper every day – stories of parliamentary fights over tax cuts and bikie murders and politicians who took commissions in paper bags from property developers. As time edged towards Christmas there was a lightness to the news, stories about what the Prime Minister would read on his summer break (the books always so judiciously chosen, a mix of national-prizewinners and important political biographies. No politicians ever said, '*The Cockroach*, actually', or, better still: 'Fuck all'.) There were stories about the Christmas lights in town, and the rush on the fish market on Christmas Eve. Vic had a great piece about a gropey Santa Claus in one of the department stores. Then, one day, it had appeared, in a prominent position, and large print, on page three.

On October 29 The Tribune *published a story, 'Foes and friends pay tribute at deputy PM's state funeral', recounting the story of a meeting in the 1980s between the then-deputy Prime Minister and businessman Bruce Rydell.* The Tribune *withdraws all suggestions of bullying, abuse or any untoward behaviour by Mr Rydell. The article was not intended to be understood in this way and* The Tribune *apologises to Mr Rydell for any hurt or embarrassment caused.*

So that was over, at least, and in the cocktail of my recent humiliations, it was barely a tasting note. Vic visited me at home. His only comment on the affair was: 'Look, no judgement. I can see why you went there.' He brought wine, and my mail, and we sat out on the balcony at my place, Maddy asleep upstairs, and drank his wine with dinner. I cooked pasta with homemade pesto. I had time on my hands, and the basil was thriving. Vic also brought news of work – Ben had resigned to spend time with his family. I winced at that. Curtis had quit smoking, for real this time, and so she was in a foul mood.

Victor was sure all the nicotine from the patches was affecting her news judgement.

I went through my mail, sifting out a couple of parcels with familiar handwriting.

'It's my friend,' I said.

'The crazy woman who sent you the crochet?'

'You don't know it's a woman,' I said. 'It might be a man.'

The first package contained a paperback book, dog-eared, lovingly grubbied-up. It was a copy of the best poems of Sylvia Plath. I loved these poems. Tracey Doran had too, according to the note that came with the book, written with the usual snarky politesse: *I thought this might interest you ...*

I opened another page, and saw it was marked with a thumbprint, its lines a small maze marking Tracey's identity. I shut the book and passed it to Vic.

'Well, this explains the suicide,' he said.

'It was Sylvia Plath's fault?'

'Depressive twentysomething girls love Sylvia Plath.'

The second package was smaller, and contained a lock of hair, flimsy, held together with an ordinary rubber band. It was a golden-brown colour, and it could have been anyone's. I had a similar lock in a box somewhere, from Maddy's first haircut. I had kept one for myself and sent one to Charlie, back when he had an address.

'That's just creepy,' Victor said.

'I don't know what to do with all this stuff,' I said.

'Burn it.'

'I think I'll keep it.'

Victor told me that the new CEO, Marsha Jenkins, wanted the paper to focus more on federal politics. Victor didn't like her, and seeing as I was inadvertently, or perhaps totally advertently, responsible for her appointment, this was another thing to feel guilty about. I added it to the load.

'The other day, she asked me to tell her the source of one of my stories,' Vic said. He waved his wineglass around in outrage. 'Can you believe that?'

I could not believe that. About a week after Vic came to dinner, I also came to dislike Marsha Jenkins. Marsha asked me into the office for a meeting. I had thought it would just be me and her, but there was also a representative from HR present, who issued me with a formal warning over the use of my work phone for personal purposes. Marsha Jenkins told me that she was recommending I take extended leave, and when I returned to work, we could have a conversation about a 'possible redeployment' of my 'skill base'.

Later, Vic told me that Marsha's backstory had included a cheating husband. He believed a professional ballerina was involved. I sat tight for a week, and then the story of the affair, and the reason for Ben's departure as CEO, was written up on the *Media Watchers* website, which everyone in the industry read. It stormed quickly across the various internet channels. I weathered a few days of extreme social media abuse, including a few more choice rape threats, and then, after a desperate week, several anguished drinking sessions with Vic, and a phone call from Marsha Jenkins urging me to 'consider' my position, I formally tendered my resignation, just half an hour after I filed my Rita Delruca feature.

I untethered myself from a decade of journalism, just like that. With an email. I felt weightless. I had reached such a high saturation point with change over the last few years, that this development was barely absorbed. I got a modest payout, just the small amount of leave owed me. I banked it. I harboured a wispy and probably unrealisable dream to one day buy my daughter a house she could grow up in. Or at least an apartment she could grow up in.

It was a terrible time of year to look for work, especially if you were recently disgraced in your industry, which (for Danton had not been wrong) was dying anyway. It didn't help that I had never finished my wretched law degree. (*As time marches on*, my mother had said, and it haunted me.) I took on some copywriting work, and one day, when I was visiting Uncle Sam at his nursing home in the eastern suburbs, I saw a note pinned to the noticeboard in the communal lounge, where ladies with silver-purple hair doddered about and there was always at least one man whose dementia had him convinced he was related to me. The note said: *Wanted: a professional writer, to assist with a self-published biography.* I rang the number supplied and I met one of Uncle Sam's fellow inmates (they called them 'clients'). His name was Jacob. He was a former captain of industry. He had an Order of Australia and a large ego, and he wanted his life story written for his family. Victor helped me set up a professional website for the copywriting work, and on the strength of my work with Jacob, I added 'ghostwriter' to my list of skills.

I did my writing work during the day, and at night I worked at the Little Friend, from 8 pm till midnight. I was an insomniac, and Maddy went to bed at 7.30 pm, so I figured it was a productive use of my time. Betty was happy to come and sit in my house and study while Maddy slept. I told myself the bar work was temporary, and in the new year I would think of a plan.

The Little Friend was owned by a middle-aged local guy called Trevor, who wore baseball caps that were too young for him. My paltry attempts to flirt with him were always met with good cheer but distant reserve. One evening I learned why, when Trevor's wife and children came in just before opening, and he kissed the wife, with genuine joy and on the lips. The other bar staff were mostly students at Sydney University, or they were vassals of the university in some way – teachers' aides or ageing wunderkinds who were hanging around hopefully for PhD funding, or to extend the life of the affair they were having with their supervisor, or whatever. I had completed a responsible service of alcohol certificate, online, and that had been almost fun, like the days of old, when I studied through the night for my Torts exam, or for Criminal Law and Evidence. In those days, I used to procrastinate by watching American police procedurals, late, on TV.

But when studying for the responsible service of alcohol certificate, there had been no time to procrastinate, because of Maddy, who seemed to sense a change in the atmosphere and was clingier than usual. One morning, I prepared her Weet-Bix, and Maddy sat at the table enacting a complex scenario with the tree mice, in which one was telling the other to 'Go to bed, *wight* now!' She paused her game, looked up at me and said, perfectly firmly: 'Daddy is coming home soon.'

'Is he, darling?' I said. Did Maddy know something I didn't?

'Yes. He will be home for my birthday.'

And she went back to the mice, while I poured milk on the Weet-Bix as my eyes filmed.

I found the bar work soothing. There was some art to pouring a beer, which I mastered, and pouring wine was something I was well practised at. I left the cocktails to my mixologist colleagues. From Thursday through to Sunday, the bar was always busy, busy enough to keep me on my feet and far from my thoughts, and if I worked the other nights, it was sometimes quiet enough that I could read a book. I was not reading any news at all now, and nor was I seeing any. I switched off the television when the nightly bulletins came on. Instead, I read books – everything from Nabokov to le Carré, Somerset Maugham and, even, over several blissful sittings, in the bath and slightly drunk, *Valley of the Dolls*. I avoided the radio and listened to podcasts instead. I learned about cold cases in Pittsburgh and riots in India. I listened to stories about cults and climate change and the troubles of distant strangers — people who had fallen in love, or got cancer, or had a baby they hated or a secret they needed to expunge. As long as I filled my eyes and ears with the stories of other people, I would have less energy to think about my own.

The copywriting consumed my days. Word got around at Sam's retirement home and I was engaged by a few families who wanted accounts of the lives of their parents or grandparents. I was also developing a mini-specialty in government agency work. Government agencies were always applying for grants, or trying to win intra-government agency awards, so they could justify their existence and stave off budget cuts. After years of being told, at parties, by people like Danton, that my industry was dying, I realised I did possess at least one skill. I could convey information clearly.

In the languorous days after Christmas, when the city was tapped out and the beaches were full and the CBD was a ghostland punctuated only by overheated Chinese tourists, I took the train to Museum, and walked through Hyde Park, past the cyclamen which were the scene of my original shame, and to the State Library, where I sat in the air conditioning and ghostwrote an application for Parks Australia to enter something called the Sustainability Awards. I took the dreadful prose the Parks Australia communications operative had given me, and I stripped it back, inserted plentiful full stops, and lightly peppered it with the phrases this crowd seemed to favour: core competencies and scalable initiatives and so forth. This work paid well but it was intermittent and difficult to predict, and that's what brought me to the bar, on New Year's Eve, when no one else wanted to work, but Trevor would make some money for his picturesque children and his kissable wife.

That night I was tending the bar alongside Jessica, who was plump and magnificent, and who wore her hair wrapped in a headscarf like the *We Can Do It!* woman from the advertisement for wartime jobs. Her arms were muralled with tattoos. Jessica had just broken up with her boyfriend. They had been living together and he moved out, suddenly, and she was struggling to pay his share of the rent. Jessica told me that when he left, he took all his belongings with him in one go. The last image Jessica had was of him walking off down the street, carrying a dumb-bell in one hand, and a long piece of plywood tucked under the other arm. Sticking out from the top of the backpack was a dustpan and broom, with the broom head standing high, like a meerkat on alert.

'Why did he have a piece of plywood?' I asked her.

'He reckoned he was going to make shelves,' Jessica said. 'He never did.'

Jessica was on cocktails and I was on general bar. Jessica wore a low-cut T-shirt with the acronym *ACAB* stretched across her wonderful breasts. It stood for 'All Cops Are Bastards'. Trevor was working too, supervising us and providing muscle, although he seemed like more of a negotiator than a puncher. Outside the bar's open windows, there was a wildness to the atmosphere. People shouted on the street. Tribes of teenagers walked past jabbering. Cops with drug dogs invaded the bar. They seemed oblivious to the insult Jessica had emblazoned on her bosom. The dogs strained at their leashes but found nothing. A police car stalked the kerb outside, low and flashing. We had live entertainment – a local guy who played a sort of synth-pop-rock hybrid, using an electric guitar, his voice and a synthesiser. He had dreadlocks which hung down his back like scratchy rope. His name was Pete. I liked how seriously he took his job, the earnestness with which he unpacked snake-coils of cords and plugged in equipment and readied his vocal cords with a martini and an exercise in which he sang 'Doe, a Deer' from *The Sound of Music*.

Pete performed mostly covers, but mixed them into strange concoctions. At the moment he was doing a reggae version of Beyoncé's 'Sorry', in which she tells everyone she's not sorry. I hummed along, under my breath, as I poured wine and doled out tap beer. The crowd was mostly the usual inner-city, designer sneaker crew, with some fortysomething couples, probably locals who had kids sleeping nearby in the generously renovated terrace houses which kissed the harbour. Houses like the one Maddy and I lived in, except beautifully restored, and owned by their occupiers. These middle-class professionals, with their mothers' groups and their double six-figure salaries and their desire for craft beer, were pricing the students and the poor people out of the suburb, so people said. But they drank liberally and tipped well, before leaving, I presumed, for parties, or home to kids for the 9 pm fireworks. The hipsters stayed, drinking whiskey in clutches, and bobbing their heads to the music. Pete warbled until 10 pm, when he took a break and inched up to the bar to ask for a drink. Trevor was refreshing the bowls of salted popcorn. That was one of Trevor's things – everyone who drank at his bar got a bowl of salted popcorn, decanted from a central barrel behind the bar. I ate it, clandestinely, throughout my every shift. When I got home I used floss to rid my teeth of the brown translucent shells the popcorn left lodged in them. Sometimes I took a cup of it home to Maddy, to whom popcorn meant parties.

Trevor put a bowl of it in front of Pete, who was wedged between two young women sitting up at the bar, with their backs turned to it. Pete asked for another martini, and Trevor said that seeing as it was New Year's Eve, we should all have a drink.

'A staff drink,' he said. 'Just keep one eye out for the cops or I'll lose my licence.'

Jessica poured herself a nip of whiskey, and I asked for a mojito, because, why not. Jessica mixed it expertly, and presented it to me, a small frosted sculpture fringed with greenery. There was a brief lull in service and the four of us – bar waitresses, owner and musician, clinked glasses.

'Happy New Year!' we cried, in unison.

Pete demolished his popcorn quickly and asked for more. I wondered if he relied on it as his evening meal. Possibly even the day's only meal. He looked undernourished and gnome-like, but that was the fashion among a lot of the local young men. Tom was an outlier among his peer group for being athletic and tall, for looking like he could loosen the lid of a jar for you. Tom was no longer speaking to me, although not in a dramatic way. After the news had broken of my sex-thing with Ben (I refused to call it an affair, although others did), Tom had simply withdrawn himself from me, neatly and without fuss. 'I think it's best we call it quits, don't you?' he had said, and he hadn't contacted me since. It had been a revelation, the way he had rejected me without histrionics or abuse. His self-respect was quiet and unshowy. I stopped taking Maddy to Tree Park, and when I walked down Glebe Point Road, I crossed the street to avoid walking past Tom's café.

'They're called old maids, you know,' said Pete, handing back his popcorn bowl.

'I'm sorry, what?' I asked him.

'The unpopped kernels. They're called old maids, in the popcorn industry,' he said. 'They don't have enough moisture to create steam for an explosion.'

'Are you fucking kidding me?' said Jessica. Her capacity for contempt was awe-inspiring. She loomed over Pete and took his martini glass away, even though he hadn't finished drinking it, a manoeuvre which made her breasts pulse angrily over the edge of her top. She looked like she could snap Pete over her knee, like a twig. I suspected he had a crush on her.

'*In the popcorn industry,*' Jessica mimicked, rolling her eyes. She dumped his glass out back.

Pete left his bar post and returned to his microphone stand, retuning his guitar as he munched the last of his popcorn. He had left the old maids uneaten in the bottom of the bowl. He welcomed back his audience and started singing 'In the Wee Small Hours of the Morning', which was one of my favourite songs. It reminded me of when I was a kid. Sometimes, rarely, my dad made me pancakes on a Sunday morning as he listened to music. Pete was doing a dub version of the song, which leached its pathos, somewhat.

Soon it was 11 pm, and he sped things up, lurching us all forward towards midnight, playing versions of David Bowie that were fast, jazzy even, and then some Beatles and Marvin Gaye. The older people in the bar sang along. I slugged wine into glass after glass, shiraz and chardonnay and French and Spanish varietals I took care to pronounce correctly, because I may have become a barmaid, but I still had an education, or half of one. The night reached a high-tide line, with the customers swaying and raising glasses and opening their faces up in drunk, happy smiles, all their features relaxing at the exact midpoint between pleasant tipsiness and grotesquerie. I was buzzed from my mojito – Jessica, in an act of sisterly solidarity, had waited until Trevor's back was turned before she poured in an extra shot of Bacardi, winking at me. Now the lights twinkled happily and Pete's strange music washed over me, a tide of sound, and it seemed to me we were all on a small jolly ship, sailing through the night. Tomorrow we would disembark in new country: the new year.

I took a trip to the back room to bring back a tray of freshly washed glasses, and the steam from them mingled with my sweat to flush me pink. When I returned to the bar, I saw a woman sitting up at it, seemingly alone, in the spot where Pete had eaten his popcorn dinner. She had short, thinning hair, and a large body which cascaded over her bar stool. Her face was plump, relatively unlined, and pretty. Her hair was heavily blonded and she wore an enormous, bedazzled leopard-print top which was cut low, to show off sun-damaged décolletage, before billowing outwards. The top had cut-outs across the tops of the sleeves, through which the woman's rounded, pinked shoulders peeked. She sat at the bar perfectly erect, with her diamante-encrusted purse laid before her. I noticed she had gel nails. Victor always joked about the women from his home town who had those nails.

'Can I help you?' I asked her. I took a small towel from the waistband of my apron and wiped the bar in front of the woman.

The woman lifted her purse to allow the sweep of the cloth. 'A Bacardi and Coke,' she said, and even though Jessica was the mixologist and I was the wine and beer guy, I got it for her. She looked so out of place. I wondered what she was doing there. Perhaps she had fought with her husband and gone wandering.

'Thanks, darl,' she said. 'You pulled the short straw, eh? Working New Year's.'

'Ah,' I said. 'I don't mind.'

The woman nodded as she tipped the drink into her mouth, which was decorated with a slash of crimson lipstick. 'Speaking of which, you got a straw, love?'

'We actually don't serve straws anymore. By order of management,' I said. I nodded towards Trevor, who was in animated conversation with a group of bearded guys. In any other bar, they were the guys who would be edging towards violence now, but in this bar, they were probably discussing structural discrimination, or permaculture.

'Right you are,' the woman said. 'I was in Bali with my kids a few years ago and it was disgusting, the plastic. My daughter was worried about all the marine life dying.'

'It's a big problem,' I said.

'Do you have any kids?'

As a journalist, I had always been affronted when personal questions were asked of me. I considered myself the only person entitled to make inquiries. It was equal parts amazing and appalling, the licence you could take just by calling yourself a reporter. You could ask anything of anyone, steam people open like clams, pop them like corn kernels. I had only ever given up personal information as a way of establishing intimacy with a source, or an interview subject. Once you shared something of your own story, people tended to relax better into telling theirs. But as a barmaid, I was getting used to talking more about myself. The movies and the scenes painted in Frank Sinatra songs were true – solo drinkers were often sad. They wanted to talk.

'A daughter. Four,' I said.

'Just the one?'

'Yep.'

'Plans for a second?'

I got this question a lot, usually from older ladies who were grandmothers, or wished they were. People never seemed to think one child was enough. I had a standard response for this, one that banished the small ghosts of the parallel life. 'Got my hands full as it is.' I smiled at the woman, who had drained her drink. 'Another?'

'Oh, yes please. It's New Year's Eve, after all.'

I made her another, with a generous pour. I set the drink down and the woman took it and held it up, her gel nails like claws around the tumbler.

'Cheers,' she said, and she opened her throat to down the lot, all in one go. 'Another, please.'

She set her glass down with a slam. The fingernails, painted a dark red, drummed the counter. I had completed my responsible service of alcohol certificate but I did not want to have to ever enforce its teachings. Generally Jessica or Trevor dealt with the messier drunks, and we had few of those because of the kind of small, boutique bar we were. Every week or so a man came into the bar wearing a 'This is what a feminist looks like' T-shirt.

'Do you want to maybe slow down?' I asked her. 'I could get you a glass of wine?'

'I just want the Bacardi. I don't want to slow down. I want to speed this night up. Get to next year.'

I relented. It was New Year's Eve – who was I to tell anyone not to get drunk? I fixed her another but made the pour shorter this time, just a puddle on top of the Coke.

'I've had an annus horribilis, you might say. Isn't that what the Queen called it?'

'I believe so,' I said.

'Trouble touches everyone, I suppose.'

'It does.'

I waited a moment. I wondered if I could be bothered knowing more. I knew well when someone wanted to talk. I looked around the bar – it was humming along towards midnight. The crowd had thinned a little with people heading to see fireworks, or off to parties, and service seemed under control.

'I'm sorry you had a bad year,' I told the woman.

Her head ducked low to meet her drink, and I saw the vulnerable scalp that peeked through the blonde highlights.

'My daughter died,' said the woman. She looked up, her eyes shining. 'I think you know her, actually. Knew her.'

I had a feeling like I was falling, as happens sometimes in dreams, where you wake suddenly on impact. I kept still and waited.

'Tracey was her name. Tracey Doran. You're Suzy Hamilton, aren't you?'

'I am.'

'My girl was special.'

The woman's eyes were glittering now, and I wondered if she was going to shout at me, or glass me. My heart threw itself against my ribcage.

'What are you doing here?' I asked her. 'What do you want me to say?'

'A little fucking *sorry* would be nice,' the woman hissed. Then she seemed to remember herself, and drew herself up straight, and clutched her diamante purse. She was nervous, I could see. Sweat shone on her face.

'But you probably don't feel sorry,' she continued. 'People like you just trample things and don't care.'

'I never meant to trample your daughter,' I said. I spoke as evenly as I could. 'I was just doing my job.'

Panic snaked in my chest. I looked around for a rescue. Trevor was still talking to the bearded people, Jessica was making up what looked like a tequila sunrise, placing the maraschino cherries carefully, like pretty baubles. She always took great pride.

'What job? You don't have your job anymore,' said the woman. She flashed her pretty smile.

'You're right, I resigned.'

'You were carrying on with your boss. I read all about it online.'

I realised with cold certainty that this woman knew everything there was to know about me, as made available from public sources.

'Anyway, I'll have that drink now, thanks love.'

Because I didn't know what else to do, I made her another Bacardi and Coke. I felt the woman's eyes on me as I poured the liquor into the tumbler. I placed it in front of her.

'I think you should finish this drink and then you should leave,' I said.

Trevor, detaching himself from the beards, ambled over, squeezing Jessica on the shoulders as he passed her – she was placing the cocktail umbrella – and stood behind me.

'Everything all right here, Suze?' he said. His good cheer was reaching its highest pitch as midnight drew near.

'Yes. Everything is fine.'

'I was just going, actually,' said the woman. She tipped her head back and opened her throat to her drink, keeping eye contact with me as she did. She replaced the glass and gathered her purse, and raised her bulk off the stool with the exaggerated dignity of the half-drunk.

'Actually, I think I'll keep this.' She took the glass, tucked it into the top of her purse, and walked out.

I could see, as she went, that she was wearing those orthopaedic shoes which have curved soles and are supposed to mimic the footfall of the Masai warrior. Tracey Doran's mother, round, squat and pinkish, could not have been less like a Masai warrior. Trevor and I watched her go, fluttering leopard print. She was quickly engulfed by the stream of people on the footpath outside.

'Did that lady just steal a glass?' Trevor asked.

'I believe she did.'

'Do you know her?'

'No,' I said. 'I don't.'

Stunned, I looked around the room. The bearded boys were standing arm-to-arm like comrades, their arms laced around each other. In the corner, there was an arguing couple, her face pinched with irritation, him bending his arm to swill his schooner glass. She was wearing a red dress and tasselled earrings which twitched as she admonished him. He put his hand out to stroke her cheek, and she softened. The recipient of Jessica's tequila sunrise was cheers-ing her companion, a tall girl in a denim jumpsuit with intricately braided hair. She took a maraschino cherry from her girlfriend's drink and popped it into her own mouth. Jessica had opened champagne and was pressing a flute of it into my hand, and Pete had abandoned his reggae-synth-crooning to count backwards to midnight.

'Ten! Nine! Eight!' bellowed the bar.

Jessica looped an arm around my waist.

'Seven! Six! Five!'

I leaned into her soft strength.

'Four! Three Two!'

Trevor was grinning at us all, surveying his bar like a proud father.

'One! Happy New Year!'

Someone produced streamers, which flailed brightly across the room. Someone else lit sparklers which were waved around. Their light was a nonsense calligraphy written on the bar's dim atmosphere. In my ear's middle distance, the boom of the fireworks could be heard, a low rumble like a waking volcano. Pete began a version of 'Auld Lang Syne', rendered in hip-hop form, with querulous, lingering, Stevie Wonder vocals. The new year claimed us.

*

I helped clean up and close, and by the time I got home, it was around 4 am. I took my clothes and shoes off and left them in a puddle on the floor. I got into bed naked. It was hot and I was too tired to put anything on, too tired to even brush my teeth or remove my makeup. My feet were swollen, and I could feel a pulse throbbing in them as I lay flat. And then, because it was New Year's Eve – New Year's Day, actually – and I was a masochist, I took out my phone and scrolled through my photo app, the one that kept all my Maddy pictures in the cloud, where they could be safe. I scrolled back and back, reverse-marching through time, from first steps to first words and back into the belly of it – the baby's first few months, when everything she did was a miracle which deserved chronicling and jubilant praise, when the crown of her head fit into the crook of my neck like a necessary part.

Where are people made?

I found a video and pressed play. It was from when Maddy was about six months old, and we had given her her first taste of solid food, although as Charlie had pointed out, that was a misnomer. I pureed some sweet potato, lovingly massaging out the lumps. We had jammed Maddy in her little moulded plastic seat, the one she grew out of in about five minutes because her legs became so sausage-like. In the video, I offered her the spoon and Maddy looked at it suspiciously, then, as I moved it closer to her mouth, she grew alarmed. Her eyes widened and she wheeled her arms like Charlie Chaplin, straining to avoid the spoon coming at her, but unable to move because she was so fatly wedged into the seat. I thought it was funny, and in the video I laughed. But Charlie saw the anxiety in Maddy's face and put his hand on her little leg.

'It's okay,' he said softly. 'Really, it's okay.'

To watch that now, I reflected, you would think that Charlie was the good parent.

CHAPTER SEVEN

That, actually, was the terrible thing, but also the good thing. It was the thing that was so confounding. He was a great parent. He cooed and changed nappies, he patted and caressed, he sang her nonsense songs and stood over her while she slept, like a magpie guarding its nest. He was convinced of Maddy's precocious genius.

'Look, she is turning the pages!' he said when Maddy, aged two months, had reached out to bat the book she was being read. 'She knows when I've finished a page.' Another time, later, just before he left for good, Charlie convinced himself she could write. He swore to me that she had marked the shape of an 'M' on a piece of paper, that she knew it was her first initial. I did not think our toddler was literate, but it was obvious she loved her father. She flapped her arms for him like an enthusiastic bird. He made up names for her – Madlet, Madigan Brown, cuddlecup, sausage. It was nauseating, we agreed. We used to lie in bed together and flick through photos of our girl. We showered her in love and accessories. We bought baby gyms and bouncers, swingers and rockers, board books and jangle toys and basketfuls of teddies. The teddies formed a community – Charlie sat them all in a row along a shelf in Maddy's bedroom, like furry judges on a bench. He animated them while I changed Maddy's nappy, making her laugh, a sort of gurgle-chirrup noise which, to our ears, was a rendition of pure mirth. We bought a mirror to affix to her back-facing car seat, so we could see her face from the front seat while driving. She hated the car seat, at first, and cried ragefully when in it, so all the mirror offered was a circle of contorted pink outrage, an angry strawberry. I wanted to take it out because it distressed me too much to see the crying as well as hear it. Charlie said she would settle down soon enough, and she did, and the mirror became another communication tool – you could glance in it while driving, and see the burst of a smile reflected back at you. Her eyes were bright, like her dad's, and they took in everything.

Charlie bathed Maddy in affection. He didn't touch me. I knew we were cooked when he burst in on me changing, in our bedroom one day, trying to harness myself into a nursing bra, and he made an anguished noise and said 'Sorry!' and closed the door again. This, from a guy whose every square inch I had once, not so long ago, traced with my tongue. A strange, deadened politeness fell over us. Neither of us would take the last piece of chocolate at night, and each would insist the other take the first shower in the morning. When he wasn't being nasty, Charlie used this sort of exaggerated consideration like a shield. Faced with a joint decision, he said 'No really, it's up to you', or 'You decide, I don't mind', which came to infuriate me, this casualness, as though none of these choices – where to go for dinner, where we would live when our lease expired, what we should do for a holiday over summer – were of any interest to him. He was just coasting along with me until he could find an out.

The out came along soon enough. He made sure of it.

*

After that, I kept thinking that I saw Tracey Doran's mother. I would catch sight of a blonde head in my peripheral vision, and turn swiftly to see another, different late-middle-aged lady, with highlighted hair and aggressively sensible shoes. At the beach, on New Year's Day, my eye was snagged by the breeze-billow of a leopard-print kaftan, but the woman squiring it around was, on inspection, a Balmoral matriarch with the tightened face and designer sandals of her set. I wished I knew the mother's name. Was she a Mrs Doran? In the articles after Tracey's death, which I had tried mostly not to read, little was said about her family. Her friends were the ones to pay tribute, cluttering up Instagram feeds with visions of the balloons set free at her memorial, yellow, because it was Tracey's favourite colour. Her pets attended the memorial, I knew that. The disconsolate dog was forced to wear a yellow bow on its collar. Once again I wondered what had happened to the dog and the cat. Perhaps Tracey's mother had taken them.

The Little Friend closed for a week following New Year's, when Trevor took his family to the South Coast, where he had a holiday home and probably, I imagined, lovely late-night sex with his wife, after their children were in bed and the sound of the waves rose to meet their sighs. My parents rented a house at Avoca Beach, every year, for the first two weeks of January. They used to take a designer four-bedroom place, built on elegant stilts and clad in bangalay wood, designed to fade and scar with the weather. But my dad lost all their money in the late-noughties, in a series of bad investment decisions which had to do with the sub-prime crisis and his exposure to US markets. Everything he could, he had put in Beverley's name, a sacrifice which worsened her martyr complex. They managed to save the Californian bungalow on the top of the hill at Vaucluse. But there was little else. I knew my parents would have to live on the aged pension when my dad retired, something my mother would have thought unfathomable when she married him out of university. Simon, the long-haired medicine student in corduroys, and Beverley, beautiful in a way that distracted people when they talked with her, determined to live up to the high expectations she had of herself. Beverley was adopted, given away by her teen mother and taken in by a family of Christians in Brisbane. Her adoptive family was large and kind, although they were motivated more by Christian duty than love. Beverley told me that she always felt like an alien among them. I never met her adoptive parents; they died before I was born. My mother seemed to retain little attachment to them, and rarely spoke of them.

'I hated the way they ate,' she told me, one evening when she smoked her cigarette in the kitchen. 'Their jaws all clicking. Their mouths made a *moist* sound I couldn't stand. I used to watch them all gobbling away at dinnertime and just know I was different. I wasn't meant to be there.'

She was clever, and she won a scholarship to Sydney University, where Simon had ambled after school, on the track worn by his own father, a doctor, a track which had not accounted for a collision with a smashingly gorgeous arts student who liked to believe she was going to be an actress. He saw her play Viola at the opening night of the student dramatic society's version of *The Twelfth Night*. Because it was the seventies, the play had been adapted to incorporate a Marxist world view, with the Duke Orsino recast as a capitalist factory owner. It was mid-July, and colder than Beverley, a Queenslander, could bear. There was a party after the show. A few hours after the curtain went down, Beverley stood with Simon outside the theatre, in a campus wind tunnel, and she moved towards the shelter of his corduroy jacket, and they shared their first kiss. By Christmas, she was pregnant with me, and they married quickly. Beverley never finished her degree, because it was a few years 'before women's lib really took off', she told me, and once you got pregnant back then, you were expected to retire from public forums, more or less. I had once accepted this, but I no longer did. I came to believe that my mother dropped out of university through relief and lack of interest, and that it had nothing at all to do with the patriarchy. Married life was her destination.

But Beverley's problem had always been that her intelligence out-stripped her imagination, so after a few years, when she got bored and very angry, she didn't know why. That was right around the time I was Maddy's age now, the age when a child wakes up. I woke to a mother enraged by her entrapment but too proud to commence any career in which her gifts were not immediately recognised and lauded. As long as I had been alive, my mother had not worked outside the home. She had tried on many different jobs, like hats, testing their effect before discarding them. Photographer – too difficult. Receptionist – too lowly. Teacher – the diploma would take up too much time, and she was so busy, with me, and the house, and everything. I breathed relief on behalf of my mother's would-have-been students. She probably would have made them line up every morning and checked their teeth (that's what she did to me), or cried when their marks did not meet her expectations (that's what she did to me). So Beverley renovated for about a decade, and then switched to entertaining, which she treated like a blood sport. When her husband, the hapless, happy Simon, had lost all their money, her kinetic fury, previously trapped in the house and her family, erupted outwards. She had put all her eggs in her husband's basket, and then the bottom fell out, so she kicked it into the dust. She began to rail against politicians and corporates, against men in power and the women who abetted them. I was pretty sure my mother voted for the Greens now. That was a lonely position for a Vaucluse-dwelling housewife, a woman who had, not so long ago, been sponsored for membership of the yacht club (they had been forced to withdraw their application when they lost the money and any prospect of a boat).

So they only took a cottage in Avoca now. They were not really poor, but that was not a conversation you could have with Beverley.

There was nothing to keep me and Maddy in the city. A few days into January, when I felt a little less sad, I packed some bags and drove my daughter up the Pacific Highway, through the flick-and-shadow of the eucalypts, past the expansive sigh where the road opens up to the Hawkesbury, past the exit for Gosford. We wound around the green hill towards Avoca, and over its top, where the view exploded into the full glory of the Australian beach in summer, the hard slant of the sun revealing the blue and frill of the waves.

'The beach is closed,' trilled Beverley, as soon as we swung in the door. And then, to Maddy: 'Hello, my darling! Come and tell Grandma everything.'

'Jellyfish,' said my dad. 'The buggers are back. Onshore wind.'

My parents were sitting at the kitchen table in the humble cottage, which was really just a normal, unrenovated beach house. Beverley thought poverty and despair lay in laminate floors and veneer benchtops. They were playing cards.

'That's disappointing,' I said, bending to kiss my parents, my mother first. 'But we won't let it bother us too much. Maddy's in it for the sand, anyway. All we need is a bucket and a spade.'

'Does the beach have jelly, Mummy?' Maddy wanted to know.

'No darling, it has jellyfish,' Beverley said. 'Great big jellyfish that will sting you!'

'Mum,' I said. And then, because I knew it would piss her off: 'Beverley.'

Maddy had lately developed some fears and strange fancies. She thought *The Cat in the Hat* was menacing. She squealed when I opened the hatch to the attic one day, climbing up the fold-down ladder to put away the boxes of notepads I retrieved from my office desk. She had become inconsolable, believing her mother swallowed by a doomy hole. Sometimes, she twitched and shouted in her sleep, and I wondered who she was warding off.

'Tomorrow we can make sandcastles and eat ice cream, and Grandpa will take you to the rockpools in the afternoon,' I said. 'Won't you, Dad?'

'I will,' he said, although, as it turned out, every day of our stay, he was too drunk by afternoon to do anything but sleep, so Beverley and I took Maddy instead, to poke around the small limpid worlds cupped into the beach's rocky northern headland.

Instead of being scared off the beach, Maddy came to associate it with jelly in some way, and she loved jelly. The jellyfish cleared after the first couple of days, anyway, when the wind changed, but we kept calling it the Jelly Beach, and we passed a pleasant week padding around it. In the mornings we rose early, and my mother would make coffee (fresh, in the gleaming silver of the pot she had brought from Sydney) and my father, sleep-addled, and with the lines of the bedsheets folded into his cheeks, would do the crossword, or attempt it, while leaving the more difficult clues to his wife. Beverley was much cleverer than he was. This was an undisputed fact in our small family. Her merit was supreme, and innate, and no amount of industry from my father would overcome it. This was an accommodation Dad and Beverley had made early in their marriage, when they cut their expectations to meet what they found in each other. Maddy sat in her grandpa's lap, because she adored him, and she placed her fingers on his fingers as he drew the letters into the black boxes of the crossword. She knew her letters.

'We need a B here, little bug,' Dad would say, breathing yesterday's whisky onto her sleep-damp head.

'I can do B,' she would reply, and she would furl her small hand around his, and together, they would draw a 'B'. Then, the four of us would walk the few streets to the beach, past the designer house where we were supposed to be staying, and Beverley would always point out some flaw in it – it was ageing badly, it needed repair, the furnishings had been looking tired anyway.

'Maybe they updated the furnishings,' I said, one morning, quite innocently, but I knew immediately that was wrong, and it was a full hour before my mother recovered enough to speak to me directly. My mother had a special gift for the manipulation of silence.

I had told my parents a cagey and ultimately untruthful story about why I had quit my job. I said airily I had been feeling creatively unsatisfied, and then propped myself up with some semi-truths about how the industry was flailing anyway and it was time to think about the second phase of my career. Dad responded that he wanted me to do what made me happy, and I thought that was true enough. Beverley wanted to know if I was going back to the law. She had looked at me flintily. Beverley surely knew what had happened at the paper – she had a Twitter account on which she followed countless journalists. She must have come across the *Media Watchers* story detailing her daughter's disgrace. But she didn't say anything about it. Beverley always held the line by withholding, and not for the first time, I pondered whether that's why I had ended up with a man like Charlie, who offered the promise of great love but always welched on it, a man who shrouded his own need by turning on those who loved him, by telling them – by telling me – that he despised me, that he thought me pathetic, ugly and low; a man who forgot, or misplaced, in his war on me, the capacious needs of our daughter.

After the morning trip to the beach, we would walk up the bush track and back to the house, where my dad, still lucid, would make us a breakfast of pancakes adorned with summer fruits – everything Beverley could find at the markets – mangoes and raspberries, papayas, figs, blueberries. There was no maple syrup but we did have a portable speaker, and therefore Frank Sinatra. After pancakes and a shower, Beverley would always need some bit or piece from the market – gorgonzola or pomegranate molasses or cos lettuce for the Greek salad. She maintained an elegant table, even if the table itself happened to be built of cheap pine, as the cottage's was. Maddy liked to help her grandma, and Beverley had her trotting through the small market, squeezing avocados and smell-testing lemons. Maddy liked to take guardianship of the lightweight groceries, particularly the ham. She loved ham. One day, when Beverley was fishing in her wallet at the till, a small photograph fell out. It was of me, aged about ten, wearing a romper suit I was too old for, and squinting into the sun. Maddy clutched at it.

'That's me when I'm big!' she said, delighted.

When we got home from the market, we prepared lunch, and Dad would announce it was time for a drink, because it was holidays after all, and Beverley's face would pinch but nothing would be said, because nothing ever had been and there was no point starting now.

When I left home and grew into adulthood, and realised slowly what my father was, and put a name to it, I made accommodations. I knew of other fathers who raged and shouted. Some womanised, others said unforgivable things, things they didn't remember, but which sat, forever after, on the throat of the person, the sober person, who did remember.

My father didn't do any of that. He just got sozzled every lunchtime and fell asleep by mid-afternoon, if he could, and then perked up for dinner, where he could serve his own thirst under the shroud of serving drinks to his family. He was what they called functional. The alcohol helped him segue out of situations. Through it, he was able to leave, without moving, and without rancour. He could absent himself without causing any bother. It was a style of life management I thought had its merits. I dipped into it myself, from time to time.

Afternoons were for the rockpools, just me and Maddy and Beverley, in shorts and bare feet, dinking nets and buckets and phones to take pictures of Maddy skittering from rock to rock. She crouched on her haunches next to the rockpools and peered into them like a seer. She announced shells and crabs, seaweed and starfish. She could never understand why the crabs ran from her, and would try to woo them back, sometimes with songs she made up. Maddy's attempt at the word 'anemone' made the whole trip worthwhile, my unchangeable and faulty parents notwithstanding

*

On our last night, I pinched one of my mother's cigarettes, even though I could have simply asked for one. I plucked it from my mother's packet on the kitchen bench, mild as a professional pickpocket, while Beverley's back was turned, doing the washing up. That was another thing Beverley hated about this beach house – no dishwasher. She said this was a human rights abuse. I helped my mother clean the kitchen, then I swung out the flyscreen door and wound down to the beach, which was illuminated by a gibbous moon and a bright blanket of stars. I took off my shoes and dug my feet into the sand, which was still warm from the day's heat.

I thought of the last time I had walked this beach alone. Charlie and I had taken what was known as a 'babymoon' up here, just weeks before Maddy's birth. The birth would end up quite a violent event for me – thankfully not for her – but I was ignorant of everything my future offered when we set off for the babymoon. I thought it might be the fix we needed. A babymoon is marketed as a blissful, tummy-stroking holiday, during which the couple takes walks on the beach and sleeps in. They enjoy each other's company for the last time as a childless couple. They hold hands. By contrast, our babymoon had been a wretched weekend of reflux and insomnia (mine) and sullen withdrawal and smartphone immersion (Charlie's). Its low point was when I discovered he had a photo-sharing app on his phone, the one where the photo 'explodes' after 30 seconds, leaving no apparent trace (a lie, of course – on the internet everything is traceable, yet another melancholy fact I would soon discover). I said to Charlie that I thought this app was used for sexting. He said it was just something for messing around with his friends. We argued, and I left the house – I did a lot of dramatic walk-outs in those days, to little or no effect – and waddled the beach on my own.

Now, here I was again. Alone. But at least I was free now. I lit up, the match flare a small signal in the dark. I thought about that night, and how much I had feared being alone, and left, with my baby, but how, when it happened, the loss was absorbed into my life quite easily, considering, and I was able to bunch up my love for Charlie and put it away. I'd had many realisations in the last few years, but the most liberating was the discovery that my own sorrow didn't matter. It was a small thing, relatively, so easily lost in the world's great thrum. After a while, it became light enough to carry around, and I had thought: *This is how it is now, and sometimes I can forget that it's there at all.*

But for Tracey Doran's mum, there was no folding up of her sorrow. It saturated her, it filled her up, she overflowed with it. It was what the French called *insupportable* – no structure could be built, within the self, to support it, to contain it, or prop it up, or to stop it from growing and spilling and combusting towards those who deserved it, like me, and probably plenty who didn't. No wonder she stole glasses from bars. The universe had stolen her child. Her whole life had narrowed to one goal: she must shriek the injustice.

The next morning, we packed up and drove south to Sydney. I had a tan across my shoulders and a constellation of what were either new freckles, or sun spots, on my nose. Maddy had a shell collection, and a new pet crab, which my dad had sealed into a bag of saline water for her, a marine captive with no option to leave her. She sang to it all the way home.

CHAPTER EIGHT

A couple of weeks passed in the belly of the Sydney summer. The humidity had a hostile edge and the middle of the day was so brutal with heat it wasn't possible to go out in it. Maddy's preschool was on a break, and so I worked nights but spent the days with my daughter. We went to beaches and museums, I convened playdates, remembered to bring snacks, and we baked cookies and collaborated on a giant puzzle of the tree mice family, so big it dominated the kitchen table. Once it was completed, Maddy did not want a single piece of it touched. She did not believe in the ephemeral nature of art. So we just ate over the top of it, our Weet-Bix bowls placed on whiskers and tiny clawed paws. Money worries edged my mind. My biography ghostwriting had hit a dry patch. I needed the world of business and public service corporatese to spark back into gear and call upon my translation skills. I sent out emails casting for work, but got back out-of-office replies.

Early one evening, Maddy and I went into Hyde Park, where the Sydney Festival was on, populated by women in halter-neck tops and men in ironic T-shirts, and some families there for the early shift. I watched the people going to the grown-up shows, disappearing into a dark tent for a cabaret or a gig.

How I longed to sit back and accept the luxury of someone else entertaining me, just for a while. I felt a sternum-jab of jealousy for those single mothers who got every second weekend off, to drink, have sex, to walk home at their own pace and sleep in alone. Instead, Maddy pattered along beside me, her little hand a damp caress held in my own palm. We met up with Vic, who was working over summer and came straight from the office. He queued for rosé while Maddy and I acquired boxes of noodles for our dinner. We sat on the grass in front of a large stage where a children's entertainer was dressed as a clown, performing kids' songs with a hip-hop back-beat. He included some call-and-response stuff. The kids were lapping it up.

'Is he doing "Yo mama" jokes for the under-fives?' said Victor, handing me a glass of pink.

'I believe so.'

'Perfect target market, I suppose,' Victor said.

Maddy was perched between my legs, transfixed. Occasionally she voiced responses to the hip-hop clown's questions. The hip-hop clown, who was situated about 20 metres away on a high stage, could definitely not hear her.

'So, how's work?' I asked. It was a question with many undercurrents. I didn't exactly miss work yet, because I was still aggrieved, and because my departure still had the aura of a holiday about it. It hadn't yet become a lifestyle.

'Dull,' said Vic. 'Curtis and I are pretty much the only grown-ups working over the Christmas dead zone.'

'How is Curtis?'

'Sad, I think. Her ex has taken the kids back to Adelaide for the holidays so she stinks of loneliness. And cigarettes.'

'She's started smoking again?'

'Of course she has.'

Vic chatted for a while about his love life. He was cycling through various men on various dating apps. His main problem, he said, was that everyone in the scene had become very *genre*, and he was neither twink nor bear.

'Doesn't that make you a wolf?' I asked.

'Mostly it makes me tired.'

We reclined under giant eucalypts and breathed hot malty air and watched a giant rat scuttle through an open bin at the back of a stall selling Vietnamese street food. Sydney was so verdantly alive, despite the deadening heat. Every piece of land that wasn't concreted over, sprouted something. Animals and insects multiplied. Every crevice of it held life. I knew that Victor worked over the Christmas period because he didn't like going home for it, and the 24-hourliness of the newspaper business gave him a ready excuse not to. The last time he had gone home for Christmas, several years ago, his father had got blackly drunk over lunch, and his mother hid the gin, which, Victor said, made everything completely unbearable. His father had called him a 'mincer' and Victor had resolved never to go again. 'All his homophobic slurs date from the seventies,' Vic said. 'It's embarrassing for everyone involved.' *See*, I thought, *my father was not like that.* He was a gentle, drunken lamb, who could not possibly harm anyone, as long as you didn't let him drive. I supposed I came from the last generation which expected so little of their fathers.

'How is your man?' Vic asked, after a pause. 'What is his name again? Tim? Robert?'

'Tom.'

'How is Tom?'

'There is no Tom,' I said.

'Oh. What happened to Tom?'

'Tom learned of his cuckolding.'

'Ah. Your boss-banging.'

'My upwardly mobile sex life.'

We laughed, throwing our throats up to the sky, where the bats were crossing the pinked dusk in formation, winged Rorschach blots.

'That is a shame though,' said Victor. 'About Tom.'

'Nah, he was too young anyway,' I replied. 'I'm an old lady now. I have arthritis in my knee. I see other people my age and I think they look old. I saw a photo of myself the other day and thought, *Who is that lady with the thick waist and the uncertain chin?*'

'You don't have a thick waist. Your chin is certain,' Vic said. 'And fuck "too young".'

I placed my hands over Maddy's ears and widened my eyes at him.

'Sorry. I mean, to hell with "too young".'

Maddy wasn't listening anyway. She was chanting along to the hip-hop clown's distant song. It was something about riding in a rainbow plane – suitably creepy.

'Victor?' I asked. I felt loosened by the wine.

'Hmm?'

'Do you think I'm a bad person?'

'No,' he said. 'I think perhaps you're acting out. I think most people spend their lives acting out, one way or another.' He paused to take a pink sip. 'So don't beat yourself up.'

'What if I can never get over it?'

'Get over what? Charlie, you mean, or – what happened with Tracey Doran was not –'

'I know. Not my fault,' I said.

'You don't have to get over it,' he said. 'The idea that anyone gets over anything is bullshit. It's an Oprah-ism. It's a stupid idea plucked from positive psychology.' And then, more quietly: 'I hate positive psychology.'

'Well that's not very hopeful,' I told him.

'I don't think we get over things. But I think we can learn to get out from under them. And when you do, you relax in your skin a little bit and you're vibin' again.'

'Vibin'?'

'Yes, *vibing*.'

At that moment the hip-hop clown leapt off the stage and advanced towards the cluster of children gathered to watch him, his face a white mask of grotesque mirth. Maddy screamed in horror, and flung herself onto my chest in a wrestler's grapple.

'Why do we give children clowns?' said Vic. 'Do we hate children so much?'

We took that as our cue to get ice cream, one scoop each, different flavours, and three mini-spoons, so we could share it.

*

January ambled towards its midpoint, preschool was blessedly resumed, and I began a new push to get more writing work, to fill my days. I eventually got something from a charity which promoted literacy in disadvantaged communities. The charity's literacy push did not extend to being able to formulate readable sentences in brochure form, so they outsourced that to me, and they paid well, even with the discount I gave them for being a not-for-profit. I was running out of money, and my car registration was due in early February.

One night at the bar, about three weeks after the New Year's Eve apparition of Tracey Doran's mother and her diamante purse, I received a phone call. It was her. She apologised. She said she had been drinking too much that night, it was a tough time of year.

'I've been drinking too much all round,' she said. 'I'm going to come in again. But this time I won't drink so much, and we can talk.'

'I don't know what there is to talk about,' I said.

'I want to talk about my daughter.'

'I didn't know your daughter.'

'I know you didn't,' Tracey's mother said, with heat in her voice. 'What you wrote – it wasn't her. That wasn't her.'

'It wasn't supposed to be a biography.'

'But it ended up one, didn't it.'

I sighed. She waited.

'What is it that you want?' I asked her.

'To talk.'

I took a pause. Jessica was across the bar, mixing something blue for a waiting redhead, and ignoring Pete's attempts to flirt with her. I felt ancient as a Wollemi pine. What was I doing here?

'If you don't say yes,' said Tracey Doran's mother, 'I will come into your bar every night and sit up at the bench and drink until you do.'

Banquo at the hipster bar, I thought.

'What is your name?' I asked. 'You never told me your name.'

'Jan,' she said. 'Jan Doran.'

Of course it was Jan. There were a million Jans in late middle age across Queensland. Jans manning tuckshops and firing the starter gun at school carnivals and easing ageing parents into chairs and sifting through their belongings when they died; Jans who had double garages, and husbands who rarely spoke; Jans who had sons who left them, and daughters who depended on them too much; Jans who worked in accountants' offices and in school receptions, who did everything and asked for nothing. Jans who shopped at Kmart and maybe, on special occasions, at Sussan, who did Weight Watchers and then gave up, and then, in the new year, signed up again. Jans kept things afloat. The energy of Jans across the nation powered towns, communities, families. Nobody ever noticed the Jans. I had known several but never really paid attention to them. Not until one of them walked into my bar and demanded that I look at her, and speak to her, and listen to her, and see her.

'All right,' I told her. 'Let's meet.'

*

There was some evidence to support the hypothesis that Jan Doran was crazy, or experiencing some sort of episode, depressive or otherwise. On balance, I thought it best we meet in public. So we arranged to meet the next day at a spot on the Glebe foreshore, private enough that we could talk properly, but not so private that any attempts at murder or maiming would go unnoticed by the passing public. I arrived first, and fiddled with my phone for a while before giving up and staring out into the morning glare of the sun on the water. I had a deadline the next day for the literacy charity brochure. I had a bad feeling Maddy had early-stage nits – she had been scratching her scalp, and this was not my first rodeo. I knew what that meant. I was mentally preparing myself for the harrowing task of fine-tooth combing my daughter's hair. Last time, Maddy's scalp had bled. I needed to scout for more freelance work, and at some point, think about finding a proper job, one that didn't involve serving popcorn to 20-year-olds, or untangling the prose of other people. In the middle distance I saw Jan, who was wearing sensible trousers and another animal-print shirt, zebra this time. Her gait was distinctive. She rolled on her feet because of the Masai warrior shoes, an effect which made her look like she was floating, almost. I wasn't sure whether to wave. I settled on a brief gesture, which alerted Jan to my presence without representing much of a welcome. Jan rolled up to me and sat next to me, heavily, breathing fast. She exuded a damp, loamy heat. It was 9 am and the temperature was probably already 26 degrees or so, plus humidity. She turned to look at me and flashed her pretty smile. She rustled in her handbag, a large, cheerfully floral, cotton-canvas thing this time, and produced a small flask, which was beaded with condensation on its exterior.

'Iced tea?' Jan said, offering it to me.

I declined.

'Don't mind if I do,' Jan said, and took a swig. 'Doctor says I'm prone to dehydration and bad blood sugar, so this is me killing two birds with one stone.'

I wasn't sure of the ins and outs of hypo- versus hyperglycaemia, but I thought perhaps Jan had the wrong end of the stick with the iced tea. She panted, and we waited until her panting slowed and she was better able to speak.

'So here we are,' Jan said.

'Yes,' I said. I felt stiff, and guilty, and angry, although I wasn't sure why. 'Here we are.'

'I wanted to tell you about my girl,' Jan said. 'Those things you wrote about her weren't right. And you know that. You told stories about her.'

'I wrote a story about her,' I said. 'That's what journalists do. We write stories.'

'But you're not a journalist,' said Jan, with satisfaction.

'Okay, you got me,' I said. 'I am no longer a journalist. I still write, though.'

I sounded defensive. I wasn't sure why I cared what Jan thought of me, why I wanted Jan to understand that just because my work wasn't being seen anymore, didn't make me any less a writer. I was, after all, still writing for a living. It was just that my writing was now of no consequence.

'Listen –' I began.

'No. No. *No!*' cried Jan, suddenly animated. She shifted her weight on the park bench and turned to face me. I could see that many of the veins on her nose had burst, a small estuary. 'I won't listen! I'm finished *listening* to you people. Tracey wanted to be just like you, you know?'

'Like me, how?'

'She wanted to be a writer, and important, and noticed.'

'She wanted to be a celebrity, you mean?' I replied. 'She achieved that.' Immediately, I felt cruel. But Jan didn't seem to have noticed the slight.

'She was pretty, and I always knew that part of things would mean trouble,' she said to me. 'But she wanted to be known for her brains. She had real brains. You could see it from when she was tiny.'

I stayed silent. The white flash of a cockatoo flew over us. We were sitting in the dappled shade of a yellow box gum.

'Cat got your tongue, now?' she asked me.

'I don't know what you want me to say.'

'Well you can stop by saying that,' she said. '*I don't know what you want me to say.*'

'Okay,' I started. 'Well –'

'Just listen!' Jan snapped. 'Don't say anything.'

'But you keep asking –'

'Just bloody listen.'

I sat very still. Out on the harbour a kayaker made his lonely way towards the shore, striking the water with his paddle. The cockatoos fought overhead. Loud cicada song added to the day's atmosphere.

'You made Tracey seem silly, and a liar, and like she was a no-good person, who was only out for herself, just wanting to get clicks and likes, and all that.'

'Well,' I said. 'She did court a big following. She had a lot of social media success. And she was smart. She parlayed it.'

I was trying to say things that were true but not hurtful.

'*Parlayed*,' Jan mocked me again. 'Parlayed! That's exactly the kind of word she wanted to use. Just wanted to be able to throw *parlayed* into conversation like it was no big deal.'

'You talk like Tracey had no chances in life.'

'She did go to university,' said Jan, stonily. 'She had to drop out. She had a problem. We weren't supposed to call it a breakdown, the doctor said that was old-fashioned. Unhelpful. She got real stressed and skinny and she copied another girl's essay, and that was it for her.'

I wondered why no one I had interviewed for the story had mentioned a plagiarism scandal. It would have been good detail.

'Tracey was troubled,' I said. 'From when she was young. Younger, I mean.'

'It's a wonderful word, "troubled",' said Jan. 'Hides all manner of sins, doesn't it? Because who doesn't have troubles? We are all troubled. Or maybe you don't.'

'Don't what?'

'Have troubles.'

She looked at me sharply. I looked away.

'I want to know why you did this story,' she demanded.

Jan talked in circles, doubling around like a dragonfly, then returned swiftly to land on her point.

'I was given a tip-off,' I replied. 'I checked it out. It stacked up. Your daughter was a well-known public figure who had … apparently acted fraudulently. It was therefore a good story.'

'Capital B, capital S!' Jan bellowed. She laughed cheerlessly, her bulk shimmying on the bench beside me. 'You wrote it cos you thought it would make you famous, too. Famous with all your media people. You thought you could steal my daughter's story and win awards and all that palaver. You thought you could exploit her, just like she exploited her cancer.'

'But she didn't really have —'

'Just admit it.'

'Tell me one thing I wrote that wasn't —'

'Just admit it.'

I closed my eyes for a moment. 'Okay, I admit it. I did,' I said. 'If you want to look at it like that. I knew it would be a good story. Your daughter was very well known. It didn't hurt that she was pretty, and so beloved by her fans. I knew it would be a big story, and yes. I enjoyed that feeling.'

There was a lull, and for a moment the morning was filled only by the conflict between the cockatoos.

'You're a single mother, aren't you?' said Jan. She was off on another circle. I wondered how she knew that. It didn't really matter.

'Yes,' I said.

'Do you feel angry?'

'No, I feel lucky,' I said. 'Lucky I've got her.'

'Capital B, capital S,' said Jan, but sadly, quietly, this time.

'It's not bullshit,' I said. 'It's true. I do feel lucky. Every day.'

'I'm sure you do, honey,' said Jan. 'But you're kidding me if you tell me you don't feel angry. I know a fellow traveller when I see one.'

'I have to go soon,' I told her. 'I have work to do.'

The humidity was becoming too much, a wall of thick atmosphere you had to breathe through. Clouds were stacking on top of each other across the sun. The sky felt too low.

'You wrote a bunch of facts, sure,' said Jan. 'But you sure as shit didn't write the truth about my daughter. You just wrote a story.'

'I really have to go now.' There were two loads of washing to do, and nit shampoo to buy, and dinner to sort out, and suddenly, urgently, I wanted to be in the cool dark of my bedroom, shaded by the giant fig tree, just sitting on my bed and remembering, quietly, that my troubles didn't matter much. I couldn't think properly through the heat and the squawk and hustle of the birds.

'I'll walk with you,' said Jan, and she picked herself up, and as I waited for her to pass in front of me, I could see the indentation from the bench planks ghosted on the large bottom of this strange, admirable woman. Jan glanced above her, into the boughs of the yellow box gums, which were still shaking with the exertions of the birds.

'Bloody cockies,' she said, and we walked back to the road together.

*

In the days afterwards, it was as though Jan Doran had touched something off in me, had placed a spell on my head, either a curse or a gift; as though Jan had crumbled a small piece of brick and now a wall was falling down. My anger arrived. It was a brilliant, multivalent anger, a fury so pure and strong that I found myself enjoying it. It pushed me forward, it had me striding instead of walking, and in my mind's eye, my hair flew behind me like a flare, and I moved with new purpose. I felt angry, so angry, that it was me who sat down with Maddy that night, as Maddy squirmed and cried, and pulled the malevolent metal prongs of the nit comb through her hair. Angry that I had to hurt my daughter in order to help her. I felt angry the next morning, when Maddy accidentally smashed her favourite bowl, and the cereal it contained, fell, with a sludge and a spray, onto the kitchen floor and the table legs, across Maddy's fresh clothes, and across the wall. Fury surged as I knelt on the floor to clean it up. I felt anger as I sat at my desk, and worked through the near-impenetrable prose of the literacy charity, their mangled vowels and dangling modifiers and the way they turned verbs into nouns when they shouldn't have. Righteous irritation saw me write my way through, killing the obfuscation of meaning, trying to scythe through the words and fashion them into something readable. I felt rage for the other mothers at preschool pick-up, with their blunt fringes and their organic shoes, shoes that looked like they'd been foraged from the feet of a scarecrow. Why did these women allow themselves to become this whey-faced, this ordinary? I was probably whey-faced too, and I was certainly ordinary, and this made me angry too. I felt irritability surge again, later, when Maddy wanted one more book, and then another book, and I shouted at my daughter that I was tired of reading stories and that *Mummies need a rest too!*, and Maddy cried, and I comforted her half-heartedly, but in truth, I didn't really care too much for my daughter's tears, because I was too angry. I discovered that anger was the very best way to keep empathy at bay, that anger gave you clarity, and the black-and-white sense that there were right things to do, and wrong things. It helped you surge down the path you had chosen, without looking back. Anger gave you certitude. Anger made you blind. No wonder Charlie had stayed so angry for so long. Anger made you right. Anger, it turned out, could be lovely.

*

It didn't last. It washed away as suddenly as it had surged up, and I was left with my old feelings, exposed like a dry reef. My mother called me. They were back from the coast, and she wanted to know if I had accidentally taken her Turkish towel home, the cornflower blue one with the white fringing. Really, I knew my mother was ringing to check whether I was looking for a job and if so, what kind of job.

'I can speak to Jacob Telig,' she said. 'He's a partner at Mellon and Madison. Or David Keller, at Hunter Thompson.'

'There's a firm called Hunter Thompson?' I asked, sniggering.

'Yes. What's funny about that?'

Of course Beverley didn't know who Hunter S. Thompson was. Her forays into counterculture had ended with the communist production of *The Twelfth Night* at Sydney University, 1976.

'Do they serve their subpoenas by firing them into the air with a giant cannon?' I asked, purely for my own amusement.

'I don't know what you're talking about,' Beverley said. 'I'm only saying, I know some people down at the club, some people we have dinner with. I mean, we know lots of lawyers.'

'I know you do. I don't want to go back to law, Beverley,' I said. 'There's not even anything to go back to. I was never a proper lawyer. I'm not about to go and get admitted as a solicitor at age 39. Or age 40.'

'Well, what are you going to do, then?'

'I'm a reporter. I am a writer. I guess I'll write,' I said.

'You're a reporter who has no route to publication.'

'You're right. It's a Zen koan. If the writer goes unpublished, is she really a writer?'

'Stop being clever,' Beverley snapped. 'You have a daughter to support. Do you think that's a Zen koan?'

'No, I don't,' I said, and sighed. I wished I could muster some anger now. 'I have things under control for now.'

'All right,' said Beverley, her voice full of grudge. She paused. 'Please keep an eye out for my towel.'

CHAPTER NINE

I often thought about the concept of infant amnesia, the fact that babies don't remember anything, or rather, the fact that adults don't remember anything from when they were babies. I had seen it mentioned in one of my baby books. The book said no psychologist or scientist could explain it. Everyone agreed that kids woke up at the age of two or three, and started laying down their first memories in the frontal cortex of the brain. I often looked at Maddy now, and thought, will you remember this? Or maybe you will remember this? My own earliest memories were fragmentary and unreliable, some of them pleasant – a new puppy, an ice cream with my dad, the excitement of swimming in a neighbour's pool. Others, I was sure I had stored because the events took place in an atmosphere of strong adult emotion, confusing to me as a child. A Christmas morning where my father was in a red towelling robe, and my mother was furious. The clink of bottles thrown into a garbage bin. The thrill of my presents cruelled by the silence between my parents. Now, whenever I had big emotions myself, I looked at Maddy and wondered if she was laying down a memory. I wondered if Maddy already had some stored up, from before, when the atmosphere around her baby head was swirling with adult emotion. I wondered if Maddy had imprinted some things from that earlier time, things she wouldn't remember, but she would keep anyway, in some deeper, unconscious part of herself, the part that made you act the way you acted when you were an adult, without understanding why. Maybe that's where all our stories about ourselves started, in the dark of unknown memory.

*

For example, would Maddy remember this? She was around one year old, and I planned our days around her nap and the various nourishments she needed to take. What did I do with her then? I walked her through streets in her stroller. We went to cafés and parks. I tried to amuse her with plastic toys of different sizes and colours. I looked at her, I thought about who she would become. I thought about who I was, now, with a cheerful baby and a husband who turned his back to me in bed.

In those days, with Charlie still around, we were living in a flat in the inner city, a flat which was too small and cramped. I spent all day there and I often felt the walls pressing in on me. Charlie didn't, and he said I was complaining too much, and nothing would ever be good enough for me. Charlie was now working for one of the big consulting firms, and he was part of the great human press that left offices at 6 pm and got on trains or buses or motorways, and arrived home to babies and wives, at 7 pm. Once, I had greeted him with wine and stories about my day. Now, I greeted him with an upturned cheek, for him to perfunctorily kiss, and silence. On this particular night, the buzzer on the flat rang. I was partway through feeding Maddy, so the buzzer exasperated me. I was annoyed at Charlie for forgetting his keys. I buzzed him in without speaking. There was a knock at the door, and I rose, awkwardly, with Maddy hanging off me, fussing over the disruption. I opened the door and saw, on the landing, not Charlie, but an unknown person, a woman – a young woman. She had a sheen of beauty and health. She had long brown hair, which had been carefully tonged into curls. She looked like she belonged on a reality television show, one of those shows where a whole bouquet of pleasantly beautiful women was presented to one man, for him to choose between. This girl would not be the winner, probably, but she would make it to the final three before being sent away with a tear in her eye for the camera. She wore a happy, expectant expression which fell, on seeing me, like a heavy stone from a great height: me, with a baby unhappily clamped to my hip.

'Can I help –'

'Oh my god I am so soo –'

'I'm not –'

'I must totally have the wrong house –'

And she apologised, profusely, and her face reddened, and she was gone. I didn't think too much of it, until Charlie didn't come home that night, and all attempts to reach him on his mobile were futile, and Maddy seemed to sense something was wrong because she picked that night to cry into the night, long and squalling, her face puckering in rage or anguish, and she wouldn't stop. I was terrified something was wrong with Charlie, and after several hours of Maddy crying for no apparent reason, I had to put her down, carefully, in her cot, and walk away for a few minutes, because I felt like something deep and strong and dark was leaching up through my skin, something close to panic, or despair, and it was not something I wanted around her. That night I understood why people throw babies at walls. I did not throw my baby at the wall, but I did leave her – in my mind, anyway. I stayed present physically, and rocked the baby back and forth and patted and soothed her, but in my mind, I went as far away from her as

I could. I left her for the beach in Thailand. I cycled through fields of golden wheat in the south of France. I went to a party in Venice and strolled through the San Marco square, which, in my imagination, I had completely emptied of people, so it was all mine. At about 5 am, Maddy dropped into sleep, and Charlie came home. He looked unshaven and unslept.

'Where have you been?' I wailed at him.

'I had a work function on last night,' he lied, casually. 'Sorry, my phone died. We had a nightcap at Steve's, so I crashed on his couch.'

I was flummoxed. I said he had never told me he was going out. This was the first I knew about a work function.

'Bullshit,' he said. 'I told you about it last week. You have baby brain, you silly bitch.'

He walked past me, not looking at me, to the bathroom, closing the door heavily, so that Maddy woke up. She began to cry and I felt dread rise in my throat. I heard the shower turn on. It was around that time I began to realise what kind of marriage I was in.

*

A few days after our meeting under the cockatoos, I was leaving the house one morning, with Maddy in tow, when I saw a flash of colour across the road, and there was Jan Doran, leaning against a Moreton Bay fig, wearing a blouse of coloured spots that were designed to mimic the pelt of some jungle animal. Cheetah? Leopard?

'Yoo-hoo!' she cried, flapping her arms, and she rolled across the road on her orthopaedic shoes. Alarmed, I told Maddy to go back inside, and shuffled her back through the rusted iron gate and indoors. I half-shut the front door on her. Maddy protested. I turned back to see Jan at my gate, leaning one hand on it, casual as you like, as though she was a neighbour about to bring in the paper for me. She could move fast on her rolling shoes. Her face was open and she looked happy.

'Is that your little one? Maddy, isn't it?'

I couldn't remember if I had told Jan my daughter's name. I was pretty sure I hadn't.

'Please don't come to my house,' I said, with urgency. 'It's an invasion of privacy. How did you even get my address?'

'How did you get my daughter's?' Jan asked, with a broad smile.

'I can see what you are doing,' I said. 'But you should tread carefully.'

'Take a chill pill! I was just in the area. Truly. I'm staying just up the road from you.' Jan pointed towards a block of flats which stood on a hill behind Tree Park, not more than 300 metres from my place. 'It's an Airbnb,' she said.

'Are you in Sydney for long?'

'I'm not sure yet,' Jan said. 'I'm here because I want you to do something for me.'

I felt exasperated. And tired. On the other side of the door, Maddy was hammering her little fists and shouting. She was outraged, and rightfully.

'And what can I do for you, Jan?' I asked.

'I want you to write my daughter's story. The real one.'

'Will you stop sending me those packages?'

I crossed my arms and leaned against my front door. It was large and red, and had a letterbox slot the size of a decent hardback novel. Maddy was shouting through it.

'Let me OUT,' she cried. 'I wanna get *OUT*.'

Jan opened her mouth to speak, but I cut across her, irritated: 'I don't write for the paper anymore, Jan. I'm not a journalist anymore. I don't have an outlet,' I said. 'Do you understand? I've quit.'

'I looked on your website,' she said. 'About your writing. It says you do ghostwriting. Biographies of people. I want you to do one of those biographies for her. I will hire you properly.'

It would be a job, she said. 'And I reckon you need one of those.'

*

It turned out that Jan Doran, a woman who had grown up poor in Sydney's south-west, living in a weatherboard post-war kit-home with her widowed father and her sister, and leaving school at 15 to train as a nurse so she could contribute to her family – it turned out the death of her daughter had made Jan very rich. There was the Queenslander, a pastel wooden box on stilts, that her daughter had bought from the advance on her book, and which Jan had moved into after her daughter's death. At first it was just to look after the pets, but once probate went through, it would become permanent, and Jan would give up her rental at Broadbeach on the Gold Coast, and move into her daughter's silent house, importing her entire collection of crystals and fairy cards there. I didn't know what fairy cards were, exactly, but by now I had enough of a sense of Jan Doran to know not to ask, because Jan would most certainly have told me, and fulsomely. Jan Doran's conversation, I discovered, was torrential, the chatter of a sociable extrovert who had spent too long behind the cloaked windows of grief. Now it was time to draw open the curtains, and when she did, there I was, blinking in the sunlight.

There had been the house, with its photogenic kitchen, but also, because Tracey was no fool, she had negotiated a higher-than-usual royalties ratio, and strangely, her book kept selling, even after its author had been discredited, and when Tracey died Jan had inherited a sum of cash from her daughter which she invested in shares. She chose organic food businesses and pet food companies, in honour of her daughter's passions. Jan found herself an unlikely late-life share trader. She began to read the financial papers. She borrowed a few books on day trading from the Southport library, where the other late-middle-aged ladies came to take out erotic romances, and read the newspapers in peace in the morning, to keep abreast of things. Jan Doran told me what she wanted, now that she had enough money to indulge her wants – and what else were riches for? She wanted her daughter's life story told properly, with equal weight given to all of her 28 years. She wanted Tracey's achievements marked. Her successes duly lauded. She wanted her good qualities documented, and her beauty, both inner and outer, to be admired.

'Why me?' I asked. 'Surely I'm the last person you want to be writing about your daughter?'

Jan Doran's logic was quite simple. 'You're the only writer I know,' she said. 'And you owe me.'

*

As I approached the dairy aisle, a familiar set of shoulders presented itself to me, broad and tall, among the yoghurt and the custards, with a faint stoop around the neck. From this familiar figure, its back turned to me, a hand reached out to acquire milk. It was Tom, and for a moment I luxuriated in the feeling of knowingness I had about the back of his neck, the place where his dark hairline edged towards the nape. I had kissed that spot.

'Hello, you,' I said, and Tom turned around to face me.

'Well well,' he said, smiling. 'If it isn't my old friend. Writer of stories. Appreciator of art.'

'Actually, I quit,' I said. 'I quit my job.'

'I heard that.'

I wondered briefly how he had heard, before settling on Betty. Betty no doubt channelled some information, some general news, from Ruby Street back to her coworker. I wondered if Tom asked after me, or if Betty just blurted it out to an indifferent Tom.

'How's your work going? The portraits?'

'Yeah, good.' He ran his hands through his hair. 'I'm going to be exhibiting some of the pieces, actually, at a gallery over in Paddington.'

'That's so great!' I said. I was showing more enthusiasm for his art than I ever had while we had been together. Or rather, while we had been sleeping together. 'This is still the Roman god stuff, right?'

'Right,' said Tom. 'Greek, actually. But whatever.' In his hands he held a litre of milk, which was perspiring in the heat. 'How is Maddy?'

'Oh, she's great. She finally learned to scoot.'

'Yeah right,' he said, noncommittal. I felt foolish for thinking he would care.

'Anyway, I'm just here for a few things,' I said, stating the obvious, looking down into my basket, laden sadly with toilet rolls and frozen peas. 'I'll let you go.'

I scurried off to the tinned vegetables where I cowered for a while, cursing myself. When I thought the coast was clear, I filled my basket with yoghurt, fishfingers, tampons, and walked to the till. The young woman working it was small and freckled, and wore a face of disdain. She rang up the groceries, and announced their price: $42.55. Inwardly I admonished myself for shopping at the expensive mini-mart several times a week, instead of being organised and going for bigger, less frequent shops at the cut-price supermarket one suburb over. The Park Mothers were always talking about the Wednesday specials at that supermarket. I presented my card to the checkout girl, only to have the card declined. I was waiting for some freelance income that was supposed to land that day but hadn't, obviously. I presented a second and different card, but then realised I couldn't remember the PIN number attached to it. I had no way of paying for my groceries.

'Oh god. I'm so sorry,' I told the freckled girl. 'I think I'm going to have to come back later.'

The freckled girl was silent. She shot me a dead glance.

'I can't seem to remember the PIN for this card.'

Still she stood impassive, offering no relief. Blood filled my head.

'Here, I'll put it on mine.' It was Tom, behind me, proffering his own card. 'We can't have Maddy going without her fishfingers.'

My embarrassment was acute, and I told Tom I would pay him back, immediately. I would transfer the money over to his account, as soon as I got home. But Tom said, actually, he quite liked the idea of me being indebted to him, and I couldn't tell if he was joking, or needling me, or what.

*

There was very little way of establishing the bona fides of Jan Doran, a woman with a bent for restorative justice and jungle prints. Jan Doran had picked me, either for reasons of vengeance or perversity, as the person she wanted to write her daughter's memoirs. Was that the correct term? Surely not – there could be no remembering from a dead person. It was more of a life story, or a biography, as Jan described it, and she offered the use of original texts – diaries, family photographs, letters to and from Tracey Doran, and access to her extensive social media archive. Some material I had already, of course, because she had sent it to me via her anonymous packages. The mission was ultimately impossible. I had not read all of the philosophy books that littered the floor of Tom's bedroom. But I knew enough to know there was no capturing a person, no fitting them on the page or anywhere. I believed that other people were essentially unknowable, and not in a nice way. Not for a minute would I presume to describe another person, to pin them down like a trophy butterfly. That was never what I had sought to do professionally; professionally, I had only ever sought to chase stories, to report facts faithfully. Never to sculpt a person in three dimensions. And if I had no experience in it as a reporter, then I was utterly incompetent in it as a person – I had thought Charlie was one person, I thought I had him sculpted in my mind, fixed, and he had turned into someone else entirely. Or not, even. He had been that person all along and I hadn't seen him. What kind of observer of humanity could I claim to be? I wasn't even sure I believed in the notion of fixed identity anyway, because who was I now? I was a woman who had lost half her fixity when she became a mother (because we all do, no matter how hard we try to pretend we don't), and the other half of it when I lost the only thing that tethered me to a world where I mattered – my job. But then, I thought, maybe that's the point: I was no longer a reporter. I was a casual barmaid, and a freelance hack who was about to embark on writing the annual report of AgriFutures Australia. I had yet to learn what an agrifuture was. I strongly suspected that, even after reading the thousands of words of background material sent by the agency, I still would not understand what an agrifuture was. I would make it up somewhere along the way, and the meaning would be eked out from behind a cloak of words. How hard could it be to sketch out the meaning of Tracey Doran's life from a patchwork of diaries, mother's testimony, Instagram posts and old photographs? I was no biographer, sure, and I was no historian. But surely I could do this, for Jan Doran. This is what I told myself. I couldn't take money from her, that was not something that I could countenance. And time spent writing up a story about Tracey would be time taken from other projects, projects that paid money. I knew I could not work behind the bar of the Little Friend forever, who did I think I was, doing it at all? I was mother to a four-year-old. I needed a job that was respectable and paid proper, child-supporting money. In other words, I could not afford to take this job, to spend time – who knew how much time? – with Jan Doran, as she fluttered around in leopard print, expunging her grief over her fraudster daughter. And yet, I needed to expunge something too – my guilt. So I took the job.

CHAPTER TEN

I laid down some ground rules: we would meet at Jan's Airbnb, a little 1960s flat up the road from me, near the old tramsheds that had been converted into what Tom described as a hipster mall. We would meet during business hours, and Jan agreed not to come again to my place unannounced. It wasn't that I didn't trust her, I told Jan, it was just that I thought it best we treat the task like professionals. That was a lie, it was absolutely that I didn't trust her. What kind of person just showed up like Jan Doran had showed up at the Little Friend on New Year's Eve? I asked this of myself, rhetorically, without considering the logical answer: I did. I had done it myself, countless times, while chasing stories and trying to nail down interviews with elusive subjects. Showing up unannounced was something journalists did frequently, and remorselessly.

Over the next few weeks, I met Jan in the mornings. I kept the afternoons for my AgriFutures annual report, when I was less sharp, and the heat fuzzed through the French doors of my bedroom and made my bare skin so damp it stuck to the seat of my chair when I stood up to stretch. In the evenings, I continued to work at the bar, with Jessica feeding me illicit cocktails when she could, often the ones spiked with caffeine, because I was exhausted. More and more my dinner consisted of the bar's free popcorn. Pete's strange music haunted my dreams, and I occasionally nightmared about Jan's face turning up somewhere it shouldn't, like at the foot of my bed, or behind a shower curtain.

The Airbnb flat was small, a three-room lightbox composed entirely of windows on one side. It had a living room with a small kitchen adjoining it, and a bedroom with a small bathroom adjoining that. It looked out onto expansive views of the western end of Tree Park, and water. My place had glimpses of harbour but this place had an eyeful. It was owned and occupied by a pensioner who was visiting grandchildren interstate, Jan said, and every time I walked into it I was struck by the simplicity of this woman's life. It was enviable. She had a small shelf of books – romances, popular history and historical fiction. She was a quilter, it seemed, and the whole place was lit up with the coloured diamonds and squares of her creations, which were laid across every chair and sofa. She had a crossword table with a column of pens set into a high cup, and a strong light to illuminate them. She had one built-in wardrobe full of clothes and another for linen. She had a small tea table which could fold out to accommodate about four people, and it was there that Jan and I sat, on our first morning, and came to terms about what we were doing and how we would do it.

'Okay,' I said. 'So.'

I had come with a pen, a notepad, a phone and no real idea what was expected of me. I laid pen, notepad and phone on the table.

'Do you want me to work chronologically? From birth to – onwards?'

'Yes, I think so,' said Jan. 'That seems like a nice way to do it.'

'And how long do you want it to be?'

'Just like one of your other biographies, of the old folks. How long are they?'

'About 30,000 words, give or take.'

'Sounds spot on.'

'But you want me to write about the good things, the nice stuff?'

'Yes. We can focus on the nicer parts of her journey. It doesn't have to be the whole thing,' said Jan. 'Just, like, a highlights reel.'

I decided, early on, that I would approach it like any other story, except that I would edit the information differently this time. It would be part obituary, and part reminiscence, only I would try to downplay the conflict, the dark patches, and notably, the cause of death. I could be a gun for hire. I could ghostwrite for a ghost. I could maybe, even, seek to assuage my own guilt by building a monument, however small, to the person I had helped put in the ground. I could repay the debt, and convince myself that I no longer owed anything to anyone.

I turned on my Dictaphone. It felt good to be working again.

*

'Not everybody likes their babies straight away, do they?'

It was our second meeting. Jan was sitting on the velveteen sofa, her figure ensconced in a zebra-print garment which hovered between blouse and shift. She had taken well to the role of interviewee. She was frank, although every now and then she leaned forward to touch my knee and say, in a low voice, 'This is off the record, love.' I felt Jan must have seen this in a movie, or read it in a book.

'I think some women take a while to bond, yes,' I said, neutrally.

'Did you?' Jan asked me.

'We are not here to talk about me. Tell me about you. Tell me about Tracey's birth.'

'Well the truth is, it was difficult,' she said. 'And the doctor cut me, you know.'

Jan went silent, which was unusual.

'Are you talking about an – Do you mean a –' I had two attempts before I could truly summon myself. 'Did the doctors have to give you an episiotomy?'

'Yes. One of those. Except, not had to. They didn't have to,' said Jan. 'When I had my hysterectomy done, years later, the surgeon told me the doc, the original doc, had botched it. If he hadn't cut me like that, I think things might have been better. I was in so much pain. I couldn't walk for ages. It meant I couldn't, you know, bond.'

I too had been somewhat undone by childbirth, and shocked by the violence of it, violence written off as necessary by everyone except those experiencing it. I thought of the lactation class I had attended in the hospital just after Maddy's birth. It had been like a veterans' meeting, every single woman in there blasted in body and mind, holding a bundle of human need. One of the women had been given an episiotomy and when the class finished, she tried gingerly to stand up. She found that she couldn't make it to vertical. She asked for help, but the nurse, a blunt-faced old woman who treated us like inmates, told her no. For health and safety reasons, she said. I still remembered the look on the new mother's face.

'It is a brutal operation,' I said to Jan.

'She was fat as a spring lamb, and had the most beautiful golden hair,' Jan said. 'Lovely curls against her scalp. I did feel pride in her. The nurses said she was the most beautiful baby they'd seen in there all week.'

'And you were living on the Gold Coast then?'

'No, Lismore. Terry had a butcher's shop there.'

Terry was Tracey's father. Jan's ex–husband. That was about all I knew.

'So you took Tracey home to Lismore?' I asked.

'Never marry a butcher,' said Jan.

'I will try to avoid it.'

'Did you get married?'

'I did.'

'What happened with you?'

'I don't really want to talk about it.'

'Coy, aren't you. You journalists,' said Jan, and she rustled her zebra print around the couch in apparent irritation.

I waited. Jan was absolutely the kind of person who needed to fill up gaps in conversation.

'Terry was jealous, and he was right to be actually, because I started carrying on with someone when Tracey was about two,' she said. 'Local accountant. I loved him. Terry found out about it, went bloody berserk.'

'What did he do?'

'You know what I fancy?' asked Jan. She stroked her knees and stood up. 'I just had a real fancy for a Honey Jumble. Do you want a Honey Jumble, love?'

I said sure, I'd take a Honey Jumble.

Jan made me a cup of tea, strong and sweet, and we stood in the kitchen, talking of other things, dunking biscuits into our mugs. After that, Jan said it was time for me to go.

'I'm going to the theatre tonight,' she said. '*Mamma Mia*, in town.'

I said I had heard it was fabulous.

'It is. I've already seen it. Me and Tracey went to see it at the Lyric, in Brisbane, last year. She danced in the aisles,' Jan said.

She looked up at me with an unreadable expression. Then she took my cup from my hand, even though I had only drunk half my tea. She slammed it into the sink and began the washing up. Her arms moved vigorously.

'Well, we should put that in the piece,' I said, lamely.

I collected my things and swung my bag onto my shoulder. I told Jan I would see her tomorrow. I let myself out and walked the short distance home. I thought about the afternoon I had ahead, of loading the dishwasher and putting on laundry and sending out CVs to apply for public relations jobs I didn't want. I tried not to think about the thing that edged my mind – Tracey Doran and her mother at a musical, smiling into the dark, with Tracey moved to her feet by ABBA.

*

The next morning, Jan texted me and said she wanted to take the day off.

Heading to the zoo with my cousin! read the message.

I took the opportunity to work on the AgriFutures job. I caught the train into the city and went to the State Library, mostly because it was air-conditioned and Sydney was sweltering through a week of temperatures in the mid- to upper 30s. The humidity was deadening in those weeks. I woke exhausted and swam through each day as though I was working against a current. Sleep was difficult, and every night I had to make the choice between closing the French doors to the balcony, and losing all hopes of a breeze, and opening them, knowing the mosquitoes would come in, swiping their siren past my ear, murdering my sleep.

AgriFutures, it turned out, was the government agency that subsidised research and development for rural industry. They sponsored the annual Rural Women's Awards and aside from the annual report, I had to write the booklet that would be handed out on the awards night. I wrote 500-word bios of each of the nominees. They had all done wonderful, community-building things, like helping drought victims and starting small businesses to build much-needed farm infrastructure. One hand-reared orphaned marsupials. I chewed my pen and looked up at the giant dome of the library, and thought about how little I had contributed to humanity. Journalists liked to boast about being the fourth estate, and about the social impact of their stories. Everyone wanted their reporting to have consequences: the resignation of a minister, a law change, the announcement of a Royal Commission. I had written stories like this. I had written about immigrant women, victims of domestic violence who had been kicked off visas because they had to leave their husbands, their sponsors, who were beating them. I had written about abuse within juvenile prisons. I had written about the lies of politicians and the cant of priests. Consequences: my last story had resulted in the ultimate consequence. And now it felt like that had leached all the meaning out of all the work that had gone before it.

CHAPTER 11

I turned up the next day at Jan's flat, rang the buzzer and walked up the steps, a small exertion that immediately gave me the sweats. When Jan swung open the door, she looked pink. Her forehead was already filmed with sweat, and damp patches spotted the underarms of her blouse. Today she had on a Ken Done shirt, printed with cockatoos. Her capacious bosom was covered in yellow crests. It created a cheerful effect.

'Hot enough for you?' she hooted. I walked in. The flat was not air-conditioned but it was in a double-brick building and it was high up, so it caught some breeze from the water.

'I like your shirt,' I said.

'I bought it at the zoo yesterday,' said Jan. 'Went a little nuts in the souvenir shop. Did you know that giraffes have blue tongues? I had no idea.'

As she spoke, she flapped around the room, patting pillows and shifting books. She had a pile of photographs on a low table. On the top, I could see a young Tracey, angelically blonde, staring at the camera in the way that toddlers sometimes do, with real belligerence, like they are about to headbutt you.

'I got you something,' said Jan. She came to rest on a Lazyboy recliner. It was big, and Jan was short, and her feet didn't quite touch the ground, they only toed it lightly.

'You really shouldn't have done that,' I said. I was irritated. As a journalist I had always been suspicious of gifts. People often used them to manipulate.

'Well don't worry, because it's not really for you,' Jan said. 'It's for Maddy.'

On her lap she held a small plastic bag with the zoo's logo on it. She patted it with her palm, and I felt obliged to walk over to get it. As I took it Jan smiled up at me. It was a warm smile but it was edged with something else, too. It was a T-shirt, with the words *Life is a zoo!* printed across it, and a collection of baby animals, koalas, kangaroos, monkeys, in cartoon-form, crowded together. It was a size 5. It was sweet.

'It's a little too big,' said Jan.

'That's okay,' I said. 'Maddy will grow into it.'

'Yes, she will. She will grow bigger,' said Jan. 'And older.'

She looked directly at me with a stare similar to the one her dead daughter had in her toddler photo.

'She will,' I said. I folded up the T-shirt. 'Shall we get started?'

'Let's.'

I took out my notebook and placed my Dictaphone on the table. I generally took notes even when I was recording. It occupied me, and it diffused the intensity of one-on-one interviews. I wrote the date on the top of the page. I hovered the tip of my pen, its end mangled from chewing, above my notepad.

'Last time you were telling me about Tracey as a baby,' I said. 'Let's go back to that.'

*

'Ever filleted a pig?' Jan asked. She had been speaking for nearly two hours without break. At one point, I had stopped her to clear space on the digital Dictaphone so I could record more talking. To make room for Jan, I erased a recording of an interview with the head of correctional services department, and one of a prime minister's press conference. Both recordings were only a few months old, but they felt as though they belonged to another life, which they did. I would not need them again. Anyway, the prime minister had changed since that press conference, and now they had a new man, who was essentially the same man in the same suit, with slightly different glasses. This new prime minister had once made a pass at me, when he had been in opposition, and drunk. I had seen him on the television a few nights ago, brandishing his wife at a cricket event.

Over the recording of the old prime minister and the department head, went the voice of Jan, describing Tracey's early childhood. The Lismore butcher shop, Tracey's first year, Jan's gradual physical recovery keeping pace with her growing bond to her daughter, who she dressed in white bootees and bonnets like a Victorian baby. During the daytime, she loved to take Tracey shopping and drink in the praise of the other shoppers, mostly other women and retirees, who congratulated her on the beauty of her baby. 'I was like a celebrity, she was that gorgeous,' said Jan. 'At parties she got passed around like a plate of lamingtons.'

Then, when Tracey was only six months old, the conception of her baby brother, Mike. 'Can you imagine?' she asked me. I couldn't. Jan told me it had taken her years to get pregnant with Tracey, that Terry had 'almost given up' on her, and now, like buses arriving, two babies under two, and this part had really not been easy, especially not put together with a volatile husband and a shredded vagina, in a regional area of New South Wales poorly served by gynaecological professionals. 'Imagine,' she said to me, 'if half the blokes in Australia had to walk around with their willies blasted open, wetting themselves every time they had a laugh. And doctors told them it was just all part of the process. Natural. If it happened to blokes there would be a Royal Commission.' And then, checking herself, 'Listen to me, I sound like Gloria bloody Steinem.'

Despite (or perhaps because of?) Jan's shredded vagina, she had an affair, when Tracey was two and Mike was one. Jan had trained as a nurse, but Terry wanted her with him at the shop, so she put the kids in daycare and helped at the till and did the accounts. When Jan had to consult the local accountant, Alan, over a tax issue, she found romance over the ledger book – it was almost like a Danielle Steel, she said, except Alan drove a Mazda and lived with his elderly mother. Alan was tender and bookish, and stood in great contrast to Jan's husband, who did not read, and who was never tender, only sentimental, in a needy, cloying way, after he had hurt her and was feeling guilty. Her romance with Alan was short-lived and 'crazy' she said, carrying with it far more risk than reward. 'We didn't do much, you know, physically,' she told me. 'Sometimes we would go to the movies together, him going in first, and me going in ten minutes after, and then we'd sit together in the dark, just holding hands.' They saw *Point Break* together, and Alan gave Jan his handkerchief when she got weepy. There was 'a bit of messing around in cars', and one full day together, when they visited a local historical museum in a heritage Federation house. Jan spent the hours imagining they lived there. The whole thing only lasted a few months before Terry found out. Jan glossed over the details of his reaction. I didn't press.

'I've never filleted a pig, no,' I told her. I shifted my weight on the velveteen couch. I was learning that conversations with Jan were like this. They swirled around in a psychedelic way. They jumped from subject to subject. You might start with a story about Tracey's school days, and end in a discussion of lobster trawling, or an explanation of meridians.

'As a butcher's wife, you learn how to fillet a pig. Even if you've never done it, you learn,' said Jan.

'So you're saying you have filleted a pig? I don't understand,' I said.

'That's unimportant,' Jan replied. 'What I'm getting at is that after all the knife-work and blood I had seen at the butcher shop, why did I get so het up about Tracey's birth? Everyone knows there will be blood.'

'Had anyone told you what to expect?' I asked. 'I mean, did you go to birthing classes or anything?' I stretched my legs onto an ottoman.

'They had birthing classes. It was the 1990s. I mean, it was Lismore, but we had friggin' birth classes,' said Jan, with some heat. I found it hard to tell what would make her angry.

'But they just told you to breathe, which is about as stupid a piece of advice as possible, don't you think?' Jan said. 'Breathing is the one thing the body can do on its own. It's all the other stuff you need help with.'

'I think it's different when it happens to you, though,' I said. 'Don't you think?' I felt tentative. I was conscious of not giving Jan too much to work with in terms of my own backstory. I was trying to be guarded, and careful, because as much as I found myself liking Jan – she had stickability, and wit, and a rare candour – I needed to remind myself that this was someone who had sent me disturbing packages of her daughter's personal effects after her death, and someone who knew things about my personal circumstances that I had never imparted to her. This was a stranger. A possibly unhinged, grief-struck stranger, who had good reason to blame me for the death of her child.

'How so?' said Jan. She had reclined the Lazyboy chair so she was on a tilt, talking up at the ceiling. She snapped it back now, working the chair's lever with prosecutorial precision. She looked at me.

'I mean, you can be used to blood, and gore,' I said. 'But that doesn't prepare you for the shock of it happening to *you*. You know, being the person actually supplying the gore. Nothing could.'

'The shock of being the subject, you mean?' said Jan.

'Yeah.'

'Yes. That is really life's biggest shock, isn't it,' said Jan. 'When things happen to *you*.'

*

I had brought lunch. I found some willow ware plates in the old lady's cupboards, and laid them out on the table. I extracted cheese from plastic film. I sliced a baguette. I made a quick salad of heirloom tomatoes, olive oil and basil. I laid figs, strawberries and a single mango in a bowl. If Beverley had served this lunch she would have expected praise for its simple elegance.

'Is there any meat?' asked Jan. She descended heavily into a chair. We were sitting at the small foldable table next to the window and a small breeze skiffed Jan's hair, making it stand upright for a second.

'No, sorry,' I said. 'I almost bought some prosciutto. Sorry.'

'Of course you did,' said Jan, in a low voice. She heaved herself out of the chair and padded to the fridge. She returned with a slab of sliced devon and a bottle of tomato sauce.

'Tracey was raised on devon and tomato sauce sandwiches,' said Jan. 'Pass us that fancy bread.'

Jan put away three devon and tomato sauce sandwiches, and started on the strawberries. I picked at the cheese but the day was too hot. I took the mango and started filleting it with a paring knife.

'So where's Maddy's father, then?' said Jan.

I cut off one of the mango's cheeks, and laid it, curved side down, on a plate. I started scoring the flesh in a grid. Three lines horizontal, three vertical. The mango flesh gleamed like it had just been slicked with paint.

'Why do you want to know that?' I said.

'Why don't you want to tell me?' said Jan.

'It's not that.' It was exactly that.

'Well why the big secret. You know all about me,' said Jan.

I felt the shuddery coldness come on, the feeling I often got when I thought about Charlie, or The Incident, which I knew was ridiculous, because by any calculus, I should be over it by now. I should have absorbed it into my past experience, synthesised it like a plant does the light, and done something, anything with it, anything other than what I was doing now, plainly, which was still wearing it on my skin.

'It's not a long conversation,' I said. 'He's gone. I don't know where he is.'

'What do you mean, you don't know where he is?'

I pushed the mango cheek so it was convex. It offered up its cubes of flesh.

'He left about two years ago. He didn't say where he was going. I think he might be in London. He had a British passport,' I said. 'Mango?'

'I'll take a mango cheek,' said Jan. She put it straight to her mouth. Mango juice ran over her chin.

'He sends me child support,' I said. I felt defensive now. Lots of fathers didn't do that. It showed he was still connected, still cared. The automatic credit to my account each week, stamped with his account number, was evidence of his love for Maddy. It also served as proof of life.

'Crikey,' said Jan. She reached across and patted my hand. I could feel the mango on her fingers. We sat in quiet for a

159

moment, before she returned to her mango, gnawing at it until the skin was rubbed raw of flesh. Then she wiped her hands and face with a napkin. She did this with great ceremony, like she was a chef on a competitive cooking show, and she was about to give a verdict.

'Stickiest possible fruit,' she said.

CHAPTER 12

Later, at home, when Maddy refused to eat dinner, I flew into a rage, of the kind I rarely had, where I shouted and stormed at her. It was a chicken casserole with hidden vegetables. This was something I had learned from the Park Mothers – to hide grated vegetables in all meals. It was a small motherly trick that marked you out as organised and correct. I had my reservations about the Park Mothers but I was determined that Maddy get the requisite vitamin intake. She had other ideas.

'It has green bits,' said Maddy. 'I don' like it.' She pushed the bowl away in a petulant jab.

'You do like it,' I said, which is what mothers always say. It's always the wrong thing to say. It is extremely irritating to be told what you like.

'I *don'*!' she cried, and broke away from her seat. She tottered to the fridge and opened it to self-select her dinner. At that, I lost control.

'Mummy is the boss of the fridge!' I shouted.

Once you have to assert power verbally, you have lost it. This applies to all areas of life, including politics and war, but is particularly true with children. Parenting is many things, and one of the main things it is, is a masterclass in the nature of authority and power. Both are very hard to maintain, in my

161

experience. They are an edifice that must be built and then constantly guarded. Predictably, Maddy told me that *ackshully*, she was the boss of the fridge. I had a brief ideation of pushing her, touching her in some way to make her comply with my will. These flashes came now and then. I never acted on them. I never discussed them with any other parent, or even with Vic, who probably would have understood, or at least not judged me for them. In contemporary middle-class parenting, nothing was more taboo than hitting your children, and thinking about doing it, no matter how hypothetically, would surely constitute a thought crime. Instead of touching Maddy, I stormed off, shouting, 'Fine!'

I left the room and stomped upstairs to my bedroom, slamming the door. Inside, I sat on the bed and let tears drip onto my chin. I had to get Maddy fed and bathed and into her pyjamas for Betty, who would read her a story and put her to bed, while I went out to do a shift at the Little Friend. I had overshot a deadline for the AgriFutures work, and had used the excuse of my daughter being sick to buy more time, a lie that would surely bite me in some karmic way before too long. I was worried about the car registration, and the insurance was up for renewal too. The savings account I kept for Maddy, which was marked out for her long-off future, was the only fattish account I had left. Everything else had been stripped. I was also worried about how long we would be able to stay at Ruby Street – my mother had mentioned something about New Zealand cousins, who said they had some sort of claim over the place. They wanted to cash in on the market while it was still high. Without cheap rent, our life would fall apart quickly. I pictured us above a shop on Parramatta Road, racketed by exhaust dust and motorbike noise, or in a dank shoebox where Maddy would get chest infections and I would get depressed. Not for the first time I wondered how anyone lived in Sydney.

I needed to get a good job, but I had never finished my degree and I had left my last job, if not under a cloud, then in highly idiosyncratic circumstances that were easily Google-able. I had no discernible skills beyond an ability to ask questions, and the ability to take in information and synthesise it into coherent language. Into a narrative. But I was no longer sure that was much of a skill set at all, and Maddy needed swimming lessons, and wanted to learn ballet, mostly because the girl mouse in her family of tree mice was a ballerina, but still the desire was there and it was real, and I really, really didn't want to be the mother who had to squib on ballet lessons for her four-year-old because she had been fired for screwing her boss.

There was a small knock at the door. I sighed and looked out onto the fig tree, which seemed to loom larger every day, encroaching on the balcony like a bony man with insidious fingers. I needed to ring the council about that tree.

'Mummy?' came a small voice.

My anger went out like a tide.

'Yes, darling,' I said. I got up and went to the door, opening it to see Maddy, chastened, with a ring of crumbs around her mouth that told me she had been into the biscuits. I hugged her, slinking my face into the chubby border between her chin and her neck.

'I am sorry, Mummy,' she said, with the earnestness of a judge. My love for her surged up, but it was flecked with guilt, because she had nothing to be sorry for, and I had everything.

*

Here was the funny thing about the guilt I carried over Tracey's death. I tried to distance myself from it, I tried to adopt the pose of those who cared about me, who told me it wasn't my fault. I didn't force those pills down the throat of the honey-haired girl. I didn't pour her the final glass of vodka with which she washed them down. I did my job, and I didn't think about the consequences of it. How could I have known? In ancient societies, there was no guilt, in the sense of something that sat in the individual conscience. There was only retribution and punishment, which was meted out by the community. This was cruel, sure, but it was also simple. It transferred the need to take action, the burden of the original infraction, onto the person who had been the victim of it. Once upon a time, Jan would have been able to kill me or hurt me, or hurt one of mine, in vengeance. That would have been purer, in a way, than me carrying my guilt around the streets of Sydney, like a tramp with a bindle. The guilt was unpleasant, and it made me unhappy. But here was the thing, the true thing: I wasn't unused to it. I was a mother. We spend our lives sitting in guilt. In some of us, our guilt becomes so bound up with our experience of mothering that we cosset and nurture it. We love it and feed it, just as we do our babies themselves.

*

Later, at the bar, I found Jessica was rostered on to work too, and Pete had been hired to warble his hip-hop reggae fusion in the background while the drinkers bobbed their heads to it. They were wearing ironic shell jackets and inscrutable looks. During set breaks, Pete shovelled popcorn into his mouth. Ever since New Year's Eve, whenever Jessica was working she always made sure to give him a bowl that was at least 50 per cent unpopped kernels. Jessica said Pete would be incapable of locating a clitoris on a biological diagram, let alone on a live woman. She said he was '100 per cent an incel', which was a man who was involuntarily celibate. In recent times these men had apparently banded together in an online community where they railed against women and strategised about ways to subjugate them. If getting no sex was a political position, I was more radical than I thought. I hadn't had sex in about six weeks, and I missed it. Some nights I masturbated in bed, after my shift at the Little Friend, as a way of calming myself down before sleep. I never thought of Tom, probably because Tom treated me with tenderness, and I didn't feel I deserved much tenderness, and certainly not from him. I had not seen Tom since bumping into him at the supermarket. I had texted him asking for his bank details so I could return the money I borrowed, but he never replied. Eventually I stuffed the cash in an envelope and left it at his café. I wrote a note, so it didn't look like a drug deal. I spent a long time labouring over what to write before settling on 'Thank you'. One day soon after, I was thumbing through the local paper, which was the only media I could bring myself to read, and I found a small profile on him, a local aspiring artist, and his upcoming exhibition of his Greek mythology works. The article called him 'impressively built' and 'lavishly talented'. I flicked my eyes to the byline and saw it was a female name. Hating myself, I Googled the journalist and found she was reasonably pretty, in a blunt-fringed, undergraduate ingénue kind of way. She had misspelt the word 'satyr'. Tom was quoted as saying that most of his works depicted male gods, but he had one short series on harpies, whom he described as 'foul, scavenging bird-women who steal food'. I thought about the contents of my shopping basket that day at the supermarket – fishfingers, toilet rolls, tampons – and felt with cold certainty that whatever sexual desire he might once have had for me died then.

It was a Thursday night but it was quiet in the bar. It was the end of January and everyone was partied out, or perhaps they were all at the Sydney Festival, watching acts far better than Pete's. I served a couple on what seemed like an obvious first date, probably a Tinder date, because they greeted each other hesitantly, and he kept shooting glances up at her as she spoke, as if to confirm her identity against whatever persona she had projected online. She was talking too much from nerves, but he didn't seem to mind. We had a solo drinker up at the bar, who Jess was tending to, and a pair of older ladies wearing pointedly interesting necklaces, who looked like they had wandered in after the theatre. They wanted an obscure kind of whisky that was too precious to display at the bar, so I went to the storeroom to look for it. My feet ached and I was so tired I felt disassociated from myself, in a way that was mildly pleasant, like I was drunk, or a bit high. I found the whisky, which was aged and Tasmanian, and brought it back to the bar. Sitting up at it, when I returned, was Jan, dressed as though she was on her way to a nightclub. She wore a heavy sweep of dark eye makeup and what appeared to be false eyelashes, teamed with a sleeveless top depicting the Sydney Opera House in diamantes. She had been shopping again, it seemed. She was alone.

'Yoo-hoo!' she called. 'Just in for a nightcap.'

I was not pleased to see her. I worried that Jan had no concept of boundaries; that her grief, and the personal spillage it had occasioned, meant that she had lost track of where she ended and other people began. Her loneliness, which she papered over with cheer and bustle, was like a magnetic force sucking other people in. I didn't want to be sucked in. I had enough problems of my own.

'Bundy and Coke, please,' she said.

I served the theatre women their whiskey and poured her drink. 'How was your night?' I asked, not really wanting to know.

'Oh fabulous. I went to see *Jersey Boys* down at the Capitol. Do you like musicals? There are two types of people in this world, people who don't like musicals and people who just love musicals. Guess which I am!' She took a sip of her drink. 'Which are you?'

'I'm not a huge fan.'

'Doesn't surprise me,' she said, inscrutably, and I resisted the urge to ask her why.

'Actually,' she said, putting down her drink. 'I forgot to tell you something today.' She fluttered her eyes. They were thick with black lashes that looked like spiders, or the legs of an upturned beetle. She looked at me sideways, quizzically, as though she was withholding something big, something I really would want to know, if I knew what was good for me. It was irritating.

'Jan,' I said. 'I'm at work. Let's keep our stuff to our sessions.' It was a lame attempt. Jan was going to talk, no matter what my feelings were.

'We talked about Tracey's birth today, and all that,' she said.

I sighed. I did a quick survey of the room. Pete was on a set break, eating popcorn and watching Jessica. Jessica was making something green and complicated for the date couple. The theatre ladies were sipping their whisky and having earnest conversation. I didn't really want anyone at the Little Friend to know what I was doing in my mornings with Jan. I had relayed scant details about my former career to Jess and my boss Trevor. They knew I had been a journalist, but I had told them I was 'taking a break from the industry', as though I was a touring rock star who needed time out to restore herself creatively. I didn't know if they bought it, or if they had heard about my disgrace. I didn't have such big tickets on myself to assume that they would. Jan followed my eyes as I scanned the room, and seemed to intuit my anxieties.

'I'll just tell you this quickly, and then pop off,' she said. 'When Tracey was little, very small, like a few weeks old, I left her for one night.'

She looked at me squarely, gauging my reaction.

'Actually it was two nights,' she said. And then, 'Oh golly, all right, it was a week. One evening, she was sleeping and her dad was on the settee watching *Today Tonight* and I told him I was just popping to the shops for ciggies.'

'Yes?' I was listening now.

'And I did get the ciggies, but after I got them, I just kept walking, and I walked around for a long time. I walked to a caravan park down by the water, and I booked in. Ended up staying a few days.'

'What did you do?' I asked. 'Like, what did you do during the daytime?'

'I smoked cigarettes and I read a Danielle Steel. Something about a buccaneer. I just escaped, I guess. My boobs were leaking everywhere.'

She paused to sip her drink delicately, as though it was tea and we were at a lawn party.

She continued. 'It was like I was able to block her out. Every day I stayed away it felt more like I could just keep staying away, just sort of *extend* the holiday, you know. It was like one of those lies you tell, that gets bigger and bigger, but you feel sort of paralysed, like it's gotten bigger than you. I guess that's what Tracey felt, later on.'

'But you went back.'

'Yes. I felt so bad after. I thought Terry would be furious. I thought he would knock me sideways. Maybe that's why I stayed away so long. But actually he didn't. He was so grateful, he cried. Because he thought I had left for good.' She paused for another sip, except this time she missed her mouth a little. 'And that was the one time I did deserve a slap!' she hooted.

'Newborns are terrifying,' I said. 'I think every mother has fantasised about doing what you did.'

Jan appeared to consider this deeply before shaking her head. Her rhinestone earrings shook prettily. 'I'm not sure she ever forgave me for that. It was like, she knew somehow, and she never quite forgave me.'

Jan drained her drink. She got up to leave, but this time she didn't pocket the empty glass.

'Will you put that in?' she said. 'To what you're writing, I mean.'

'Not if you don't want me to,' I said. 'It's up to you. It's your story.'

CHAPTER 13

When I arrived home several hours later, Betty was asleep on the couch, and this time she had a boy draped over her. He was also asleep, but on top of her, like a suffocating pet. On waking them, I ascertained that he was her boyfriend, and they had been doing homework together, although I saw no evidence of books or pens. Maybe teenagers studied entirely in the digital realm these days. On Snapchat.

'Your Aunty Jan came by,' Betty said. She stood up and uncrumpled herself. The boyfriend stood next to her, mute. 'She just wanted to drop off some cookies for Maddy. She was on her way out to the theatre.'

'She did what?'

Betty looked startled.

'She just dropped in quickly. Maddy was asleep. She didn't wake her or anything.'

I was seized with something dark and irrational, and I ran upstairs to Maddy's room, pushing open the door. She was still there, her small face illuminated purple by her butterfly night lamp, her skin shiny and damp, her features even more cherubic when loosed by sleep. I took her thumb out of her mouth, and smoothed the covers over her chest.

Betty came up the stairs behind me. 'Should I not have let her in? She said she was your aunt.'

'She's not my aunt. She's just someone I'm writing about. It's okay.'

I paid Betty from my tips, but it had been a slow night, so I had to use coins from Maddy's piggybank to top up. That was a humiliating moment – upturning my small daughter's Peppa Pig moneybox to scrounge for money. *A foul scavenging bird-woman.* Betty looked away in politeness while her boyfriend watched me in silence, apparently fascinated, like I was a rare species of bat or something. As I let them out the front door, into the dark, fig-shaded night, I could see his fly was undone.

*

That night I had trouble sleeping. I resolved to have a talk with Jan about boundaries. I had learned a lot about boundaries in the therapy I had post-Incident. Counsellors loved boundaries. They loved talking about them and imposing them. I had been so emotionally needy back then that I used to ask my counsellor, a thin woman who wore a lot of brooches, whether I was doing the right thing. I treated her more like a priest than a sounding board. It was as though motherhood, with its thunderclap of real responsibility, had rendered me more infantile than ever. I wanted someone to tell me what to do. 'I've left him,' I would say. 'I am not going back.' And then I would pause, hoping she would fill the space, before going on: 'I feel like that's the right thing to do. Is that the right thing to do?'

My counsellor, whose name was Kathleen Wong, withheld judgement and approval. She had hair that behaved itself beautifully, falling like vertical curtains on either side of her open face. She always held her knees together when she sat, and she wrote notes silently using a fountain pen. At the end of our sessions, I had to resist an impulse to jump over the coffee table between us and rip the notepad from her hands. I felt that only by reading her notes would I find out what she really thought, and that might give me some basis to act. Kathleen never told me what to do, but she coached me on boundaries, on asserting them and policing them. I read all the material she gave me and did about 80 per cent of the homework she assigned me, which mostly involved forming sentences which began with 'I' statements. You were not supposed to make accusations or assertions about the person you were arguing with. You were supposed to just talk about your own feelings, and then discuss, in neutral terms, the effect the person was having on you.

After Charlie left the country, and effectively renounced his fatherhood, it all seemed pointless anyway. I was worried about the cost of the sessions – Kathleen Wong had rooms in Vaucluse (she was recommended by a friend of my mother's) and her Sphinx-like counsel did not come cheap. I ended our therapeutic relationship like a weasel, by repeatedly cancelling appointments, and eventually, never rescheduling. I was unable to assert even the most basic of my desires to my counsellor. And I never found out what she had written about me in her notes.

I decided to send Jan an email detailing my boundaries. I typed out a few sentences on my phone.

Hi Jan, I would appreciate it if you could let me know before dropping in to my house like you did last night. I'm also confused as to why you didn't mention it when you came to the bar later in the evening.

And then, as an afterthought: *While we're working on the piece about Tracey, I think it's better we confine our interactions to your place.*

It was hard even to write Tracey's name without feeling a shuddering thump of guilt, like a quickened heartbeat. Jan shot back an email within five minutes. She was probably one of those women who shopped online late into the night.

As you wish! Didn't mean to overstep! Ps. Your little one is scrummy. Pps. See you tomorrow as usual? I have bought extra Tim Tams.

I still wasn't able to sleep. My anxiety only grew more nebulous. My insomniac thoughts roved wildly between all the things that could happen to Maddy – from illness and injury, to the various forms of psychological damage I was almost certainly inflicting on her – to my financial situation and the dread of the flat above Parramatta Road. The fig tree swayed and creaked outside my window, and occasionally a possum rustled in it. The fluorescence of a streetlight projected through its branches and filled the room with pale light. It felt like I was the only person alive, and at around 3 am I got up to go to the bathroom and looked in on Maddy just to assure myself I wasn't. Back in bed, loneliness descended like a chill on my bones and I couldn't stop thinking about Charlie. The way he ran across the road to meet me on our first date, eager and loose-limbed. The look on his face when we learned I was pregnant, lit up like he had just opened a gift that delighted him. The fury on his face when I discovered, on his phone, the photograph of his girlfriend's vulva. It was pink, hairless and pretty, and unlike mine, it had not been undone by childbirth. I crushed thoughts of the vulva, and Charlie, with a light attempt at job-seeking, via an app on my phone, and I discovered there were various media advisor roles at government departments that I might be suited to, and several at not-for-profits with salaries which would have me hovering over the poverty line, once you factored in daycare fees. Discouraged, I fell to Googling Tom's name, eventually ending up on the website of the gallery hosting his exhibition. It was opening in a week. The gallery blurb called his works 'touched with notes of the epic' and 'an exploration of the symbiosis between the mythical and the modern'. The artist photo they had of him threw me into a pit of longing and self-loathing that lasted until about 4 am. Attempts to masturbate successfully failed. I realised I needed to have sex at the soonest opportunity, preferably with someone I didn't know very well.

*

The next day I felt predictably wretched, like I had a hangover without having enjoyed any of the fun that went into creating it. Maddy roved into my bed at about 5.30 am, the back of her hair frizzed up like the pelt of a feral cat. As I bent my body around hers, I calculated the extra time it would take to comb out the matted part. We lay together, still, for a little oasis minute. I took one of her soft, flat feet and tucked it into my palm as I cradled her. I felt the creep of calm that comes before restful sleep, only to have it shattered by the imposition of my alarm, which sounded at 7 am.

Maddy was becoming increasingly difficult to shoehorn into the schedule of preschool every morning. It was as though she knew I was only marginally employed now, and sensed she was being ripped off in some way, when I dropped her off, that I was breaking a compact. This morning, it was as though Maddy had quietly formulated a purpose while we were lying together so peacefully, and was now intent on making it as difficult as possible to get out the door. I had a meeting with Jan at 9 am, and after our session, I had to get home and finish the AgriFutures copy, which was shamefully overdue. As I served Maddy breakfast at the kitchen table, she began a campaign for 'treats', breaking into stropping tears when I said children were not allowed to have treats for breakfast. She cycled through foot-stomping, whingeing, petulant shouting and snivelling breakdown. She kept saying, over and over, 'I want treats, I want treats.'

After about five minutes, I felt I would go wild with anger and despair. She sat at her booster seat, her head collapsed on her arms in pretty melodrama, and wailed. I stood at the kitchen window and tried to catch hold of a calm inner part of myself, but as I looked out past the broken deck, at the backyard which was the scene of my tragic, second-trimester wedding, I wondered, in a way that felt bone-deep, but also totally detached from me, how I had made it precisely to this moment.

Maddy seemed to sense the wave of dangerous feeling that was beaming off me. She moved from demands to an attempt to bargain with me, as though I was death. 'Just one treat, Mummy,' she was sniffling. 'I only want one treat.' More sniffling. '*Pleeeeeeeease*, Mummy.' She seemed genuinely distressed now, as though she had lost perspective on what it was she had originally wanted, and was unmoored, feeling a global sense of sadness and despair. I knew how she felt.

I gathered myself to say something nice, something soothing and motherly, the kind of thing that the Park Mothers would say – empathising with the child while providing the reassurance of a strong parental boundary around the issue of treats at breakfast. Then, without acknowledging to myself that I was doing it, I picked up the basil plant from the window sill, the one I had successfully grown, and had started using in cooking. I felt sure the Park Mothers would have cultivated fresh herbs quite casually like this, on their window sills and porches. I took the basil plant and I raised it above my head, deliberately, like I was semaphoring to land a plane. I used all the force I had in my shoulders to ram it heavily onto the linoleum floor, and it shattered as predictably as you might imagine, with chunks of terracotta vomiting in all directions, and the dirt oozing from the broken shards of it, like black blood. My anger had broken loose. Maddy's face was a caricature of shock, her mouth a pink oval and her eyes spread wide like a Kewpie doll's. I feared I had crossed some sort of line. I saw that fear reflected in my daughter's rounded features. But instead of crying more, and harder, as I would have predicted, she was silent. Coldly, I removed her from her chair, and we walked around the shattered pot like it was dog's mess. I would deal with it later.

*

Jan was true to her word regarding the Tim Tams. As I entered the flat that morning there was a packet of them open on the table, which was spread with a bold floral oilcloth. Jan had set up a couple of plates to go with the biscuits, and a teapot, which was encased in a sort of crocheted teapot-coat, but I was so tired I couldn't remember the correct word for it.

'Just in time for elevenses!' she carolled, and I sat down as she poured me a cup and doled out a Tim Tam. I had smashed crockery and psychologically scarred my daughter that morning, possibly for life, but I hadn't eaten breakfast. I set upon the biscuit with real hunger, dipping it into my tea to moisten it. Jan told me she was on a diet, so she wouldn't be partaking.

'It's my blood sugar again,' she said. 'Doc says it's up. Wants me to go low GI. But my cousin says to go keto. She says keto is the go-to.'

'What is keto?' I said reflexively, and then, thinking better of it, I shut down Jan's attempts to explain ketosis through the intellectual filter of the article her cousin had read on it in *Woman's Day*.

'It's about starving the body's cells of glucose,' she was saying. 'It's about tricking them into thinking they are starving.'

I told Jan I had a deadline to meet that afternoon and we should get to it. I set my Dictaphone onto the table in an attempt at declaring a professional boundary.

'Of course, of course,' said Jan. She folded her hands into her lap compliantly. 'Where were we?'

'I think we'd just got past Alan the accountant.' I checked my notes. 'Tracey is about five years old, and her brother is three.'

Inwardly, I despaired at how little progress we had made. We still had two decades of Tracey's life to cover. Trying to discover the daughter through the mother was to find one story nestled inside the life of another. I struggled not to give in to the existential futility of trying to nail down a person's life. What was a life? An accumulation of observable deeds, public acts, milestones and biographical detail? Or was it entirely interior, the sum of moments like I had that morning, looking out of a lunar landscape of sweet gum pods and feeling alienated from all the most observable parts of myself? Journalism had not prepared me for such questions. I was not equipped to deal with them on a Tuesday morning, as I ploughed a chocolate biscuit into my mouth and ached with fatigue. I looked across at Jan. She seemed distracted. She was fussing around with the teaspoons and readjusting the coat on the teapot. I closed my eyes briefly. The relief from the light felt cool and rejuvenating, like drinking a glass of water.

'Perhaps I will have one, after all,' she said. 'One can't hurt. Just to get the juices flowing.' She picked up a biscuit and took a strong bite out of it.

I opened my eyes and looked at Jan. She had her own eyes closed in a small moment of private pleasure. I remembered the word I needed: tea-cosy.

*

A few hours later I left Jan's place and headed home to finish the AgriFutures job. I needed to write about ten more bios of notable rural women, including one who had started her own business making kangaroo sausages. The sausages had been picked up and promoted by a celebrity personal trainer from Bondi Beach who recommended them on his Instagram, and the business had taken off. The woman who ran it was ruddy-cheeked and strong-looking. She looked like she would be able to wrestle an eastern grey if necessary. Another of the finalists had devoted herself to Indigenous literacy and local river bio-restoration work. Yet another ran a drop-in counselling service for men who were depressed because of the drought. They were all good lives. I needed to write 500 words on each of them. The problem was that by mid-afternoon I was so tired I felt sedated. My left eyelid twitched like it was attached to a fishing line. I had an urge to put my head down, so strong it was like craving a drug. Short of actual drugs of the illicit kind, I needed caffeine.

I walked up the street and decided to chance Tom's café. It had the best coffee and opened late, I knew. He usually worked morning shifts because he liked to photograph in afternoon light, and play basketball at Tree Park. He had used to, anyway. But I walked in and there he was, wearing a black apron over faded blue jeans and a white T-shirt. He had his back to me and was pulling at the levers of the coffee machine. I could see a spot where his T-shirt had worn away around the pointy part of his shoulder blade. A small round hole showed a window of his flesh. I thought about putting my forefinger through it, laying a fingerprint on his back. He turned around. He had sallow circles under his eyes but it only made him more attractive, like he was a consumptive poet, or the denizen of a nightclub famous in the seventies. He always looked so beautifully undone. I reminded myself that his feelings for me now lay on a spectrum between contempt, pity and dislike.

'Hi, Suzy,' he said. 'How's tricks?'

I said tricks was good, and stared at him dumbly for a few beats before ordering a double-shot coffee.

'Heavy artillery,' he said. 'Big night planned?'

'Oh yes,' I said. 'I'm going clubbing.'

'Sounds wild.'

'Who knows. I may end up at a factory rave in a light industrial suburb.'

'Do they still have those? I went to one once,' he said. 'Getting home afterwards was problematic.'

'Raves are not always well serviced by public transport.'

I wasn't sure what we were talking about. The café was empty except for the two of us. Tom turned around to steam the milk. I gloried in the intimacy of being in a room with just him in it. He poured the milk from a stainless steel jug into my cup, and fixed a lid on it. I wondered, pathetically, if he had crafted any sort of pattern in the milk froth, into which I could read an emotional message. I paid him.

'I'm solvent again!' I said, cheerily. This was a partial lie. I wanted to extend the time I was with him. I had a quick realisation that I was lonely. It was a sudden thought that sparked for a moment like a lit filigree, before receding again. It explained a lot.

'Good to hear,' he said.

'I read the article about your show,' I blurted. 'It sounds great. The journalist said it had touches of the epic. Or something.'

'That journalist was about 90 per cent stupid,' Tom said. 'But thanks.'

I took a sip of my latte and looked at Tom but he didn't meet my eye. He ran a cloth over the polished chrome of the coffee machine.

'Do you want to come to the opening?' he said.

'Oh no,' I said. 'Seriously, you don't have to.'

'No problem. I understand.'

'No, I mean, I'd love to. I just don't want you to think you have –'

'It's fine,' he said. 'I don't think that.'

'Don't think what?' I had lost track of things.

'I don't think anything,' he said.

I smiled. 'Will there be canapés?'

'Don't be ridiculous. Canapés are the enemy of art.'

'Low blood sugar is the enemy of art,' I said. 'In my experience. It's true that my artistic experience is limited.'

'So eat beforehand,' he said.

CHAPTER 14

The next day Tom sent me the invitation to his show, which was called *Modern Myths*. The blurb contained an explanation of his work. Apparently it reflected 'the complexity of the ancient world view transposed into modern settings'. The whole thing read like the sort of studied meaninglessness I would write for the AgriFutures brochure. I wasn't sure what it meant. I knew Tom's photographs were beautiful, full of blue light and shadow. I liked the way his subjects avoided the gaze of the camera. You couldn't tell if they were shy, or proud.

I told myself that going to an opening was something that a friend should do for another friend, and Tom and I were friends. I had never apologised to him for humiliating him with the Ben thing. While it was going on, I had been able to compartmentalise it. I told myself an apology didn't feel necessary because it felt unreal, like something that only existed in my imagination. Apologising for it would have been like apologising for a thought that floated across my mind, or an idea I considered privately for a minute before rejecting. I hated the word 'affair', with its connotations of ghastly lingerie and asymmetrical love. We had not had an affair, we had had sex. But whatever I called it privately, when it became public, and when I saw the horror of it reflected in Beano's eyes, the shame had been real. The shame seemed an accurate reflection of the truth about myself. And once I knew that, I had to surmise that Tom might have felt humiliated. I didn't know what story he had told himself about what happened between us.

Sometimes I wondered how Ben was doing. I knew he had been appointed a partner at a crisis management firm in the city. I had seen the announcement on Twitter, which I scrolled through in masochistic moments. I still got the occasional message from a troll calling me a slut, a husband-stealing whore or a bitch, but overall the abuse was winding down as I faded from people's memories. I wondered if Ben got those messages too. If he did, he showed no trace of it in the photograph accompanying the announcement. His gaze was direct, like a man in a mugshot. I thought about Beano too, from time to time.

I finished the AgriFutures copy and emailed it off. I had summarised the lives of all the good rural women in 500-word bios. There had been ten lives to compress, at 80 cents a word. I had made them seem full and worthy. I sent my invoice straight away and put out a silent prayer for prompt payment. When it came through, the money would cover car insurance and a couple of weeks of preschool fees. Beyond that, I needed to get a well-paying full-time job soon.

That afternoon I had a session with Jan. I'd had a good sleep and I felt well rested. I walked along Ruby Street, shaded by a row of figs. My limbs felt spongy and light. Diamonds of sun projected through the leaves and onto my hair and my hands. The air was so warm it felt like something alive. It seemed as though the world only consisted of the air on skin and my muscles taking me for a walk. The air reminded me of the summer when I had been pregnant. Charlie and I had gone on a holiday down the coast. I was edging towards the end of the second trimester and the pregnancy was starting to feel less fictional. I was definitely on an irreversible trajectory. Charlie had already started drinking quite heavily by then, but he could hold his alcohol and I noticed it only barely, like something you see in the corner of your eye, and pull up for review only later, when it becomes relevant and you want to focus on it. We stayed in a weatherboard cottage in a non-salubrious part of Jervis Bay, where people had couches on their front porches and battered Holdens in their driveways. One backyard on our street had a goat in it. The local shops had a bottleshop, a mini-mart and a bait shop. Charlie cooked a barbecue for us most nights. He always made a big show of giving me the well-cooked meat.

Later, when I was trying to find things to hold on to, I would cite this memory to myself, as proof that he had loved me, after all: he took basic precautions against infecting me with listeria. Another time, he saw me struggling with my shoelaces, and kneeled on the floor to do them up for me. He treated me with care throughout the holiday, as though I was something valuable. But his care seemed faraway, and lacking in intimacy, as though he was my valet and I was his aristocrat – unable to accomplish basic tasks for myself, like getting up from a low chair under my own steam.

By then I was used to Charlie not desiring me, but on that holiday he touched me more; he would stroke my arm across the dinner table or quietly take my hand while we were walking into town. Once, he placed his hand on my bare knee while I was driving us home from the local pub after dinner there. I spent the whole drive wishing he would walk his fingers higher up, to the centre of me. I told myself that he still loved me, and sometimes I caught him looking at me intently, as though he was about to say something, or as though he had just noticed me for the first time. I told myself that was love. He was paying me attention, and if the attention was distracted, or if he was preoccupied, then who was I to complain? I had no insight into other people's relationships, but surely they all contained private corners of misery, invisible oceans of longing, places where one person's inability met another person's naked need, and a hole started wearing away. That was life. That was the life I was about to bring a baby into.

On our last night I woke and Charlie wasn't in bed beside me. He often watched cricket late. I walked into the living room. The doors to the verandah were open to the night, bringing the soft air in. Charlie was motionless on the couch, his muscular legs slack in shorts, the green of the cricket pitch reflected on his face. The room was filled with the soft rhythm of the commentary. To me cricket was like another language. I didn't understand it at all but I was alive to the emotion of it. I could tell when something dramatic had happened. Charlie was lying in a midden of empty beer cans. There was also an empty wine bottle and a tea mug filled with red wine. I felt a flash of irritation – could he not even be bothered using a wineglass? Thinking he was asleep, I picked up the remote and turned the cricket off. The match erased itself. The screen went black.

'Oi,' said Charlie, rousing, and I knew from the thickness of his voice, and the use of that word – *Oi* – that he was drunk. I realised, too, that I had walked into a new atmosphere, that something had been building around him as I lay sleeping.

'I was fucking watching that. Turn it back on,' he said, and then, as I did, he added, quietly: 'Fuck, you're useless.'

When he spoke to me like this, I always knew before it arrived. It is hard to explain how I did, but it has something to do with having an alcoholic parent. There were reams of literature on it and even a name for it: codependency. It was mostly a bad thing, codependency, but it did make you alive to small changes in your environment. And that was a sort of superpower, really. After a while, particularly after he left, I started to see Charlie in a different way. He thought he had power over me, and he did, a lot of it. But the real power he wanted was over himself. He drank and womanised to chase pleasure, in an effort to avoid suffering, but these things only brought more of it on him. He used his props to try to get over things, but they only trapped him further, and he ended up under them, bodily, wholly. None of this stopped me loving him. It made me love him more.

*

'No biscuits today,' announced Jan, as she opened the door. 'I'm on a diet. A real diet this time.'

'Okay,' I said.

Jan seemed in a black mood. She was even wearing black, a demure mumu-esque garment with no print or embellishment.

'The doctor says the pre-diabetes is going to be diabetes sometime soon,' she said. 'So I have decided to go on a juice cleanse. There's a recipe in Tracey's book.'

This Organic Life lay on the tea table, carefully open like a sacred parchment, on a page detailing a green smoothie recipe. The recipe contained kale, acai powder and matcha tea. It was accompanied by a picture of Tracey, wearing a muslin top and perching next to a bowl of tropical fruits which shone like Christmas baubles. She had her head tilted at an angle, the same angle at which all young women now tilted their heads when being photographed. Seeing her, I felt a stab of guilt that felt like voltage. I was alive and Tracey wasn't.

Jan fussed around the kitchen. Piles of spinach lay all over the benches, and stacks of Tupperware containers with chopped-up fruits in them – pineapple, apple, peach. She loaded the contents of various containers into a blender and turned it on, filling the room with noise. She fed stalks of spinach into the blender's mouth. The blender ate them and subsumed them into the green soup. Finally, she poured the green liquid into a tall glass and drank it steadily, as she stood barefoot in the kitchen. She drank it like it was a task, and when she finished she had a green moustache.

'Tea?' she asked, more brightly now.

I said yes, and she put the kettle on. As she waited for it to boil she moved through the kitchen clearing up and rinsing things. When she sprang open the rubbish bin with her foot, I saw that it was piled high with chip packets, squeezed-out bottles of tomato sauce, Paddle Pop wrappers, and a small mountain of Tim Tams, all covered in a red viscous liquid that looked like dishwashing detergent. Jan made a builder's tea for me and a green tea for herself. We sat down at the card table. Tracey's face was between us like a reproach.

'Do you mind if I just close this book up?' I asked, as I set out my Dictaphone and notepad.

'Not at all. It's like looking at a ghost, isn't it.'

Jan's affect was flat. Her eyes looked sunken and the usual chubbiness of her cheeks had flagged. Today she looked merely jowly.

'Is everything okay?' I asked her.

'Not bloody really, no,' she said.

She was dunking the teabag in and out of her tea mug, causing droplets of hot water to land all over the tablecloth. I moved my Dictaphone.

'Today is Tracey's birthday. Twenty-nine.'

The dread surged again and I closed my eyes. 'Ah,' I said. 'Are you sure you want to do this today?'

'Yes. It's best we move quickly on. I don't think we're even at her tenth birthday yet. Where were we? Where are we?'

I checked my notes. 'We are at her ninth birthday, after you've separated from Terry. You described Tracey as a "happy-go-lucky little girl who liked unicorns and colouring in". You said she liked to collect tadpoles from the local creek but always returned them after they grew into frogs.'

I checked Jan's expression. Nothing.

I kept reading. 'Tracey excelled at writing stories. She begged you to paint her nails pink, just like yours. She was obsessed with Polly Pocket, which you encouraged, because you thought Polly was less slutty than Barbie,' I said.

'Don't put that in,' Jan said. 'The thing about Barbie being a slut.'

I made a note and continued. 'Tracey had a collection of porcelain bunnies which she took to her father's place one day but they never came back. She cried about it for days but wouldn't tell you what happened.'

'Let's leave that out.'

'The porcelain bunny collection?'

'Yes, that bit. I would like this to be a positive story,' Jan said. She looked up at me over the doily tablecloth. 'We can leave things out. Everyone leaves things out, don't they. When they tell things.'

'Absolutely. All writers edit,' I said. 'They edit for –'

'Oh edit, *edit*!' Jan spat. 'That's another one of your fancy words.'

She danced the teabag around angrily before swinging it out of the cup and landing it with a splatter on the tablecloth. It began to form a greenish stain. She seemed to have veered into anger again. I felt a surge of it myself. 'Edit' was hardly a fancy word.

Jan gave me a hard look. 'You left out things,' she said. 'When you wrote about her.'

I sighed. Suddenly my bones were heavy. Inside me I held an ocean of fatigue. It sloshed around against my skin. 'I wrote a story about Tracey that was accurate. People had been taken in by your daughter,' I said. 'They needed to know –'

'You left things out,' she said. 'You lied by omission.'

This phrase did not sound like Jan. I wondered if she had picked it up in a late-night crime drama. I knew she watched those sorts of shows when she couldn't sleep, which was most nights.

'We can write whatever kind of story you want,' I said, trying to move things forward.

Jan looked up at me. Her eyes, which I had never looked into before, seemed deep and alive. They held an intelligence that many people in her life, it seemed, had missed. Jan, with her fussing about Tim Tams and her love of *Mamma Mia* and novelty T-shirts, her belief in meridians and her surprising view, relayed to me during one of the mornings we spent together, that September 11 was an inside job.

'I want a good story,' she said. 'I want a story that comforts me.'

CHAPTER 15

Tracey Doran was clinging to my skin as I got ready to go out to Tom's opening. Betty was busy, so I asked my mother to come over and look after Maddy. She hated driving at night, but she came. I could hear her in the kitchen as I applied my makeup in the bathroom upstairs. I was trying to do a cat's-eye flick with my eyeliner. Downstairs, my mother was drilling Maddy on her letters.

'B-A-B-Y,' she was saying. 'What does that say, Maddy?'

Maddy's response was muffled and difficult to determine, but it didn't sound like the correct one.

'No, darling,' said my mother, her voice edging upwards. 'Come on. You know this one.'

It was hot, still 28 degrees and humid even though the sun was sinking. I ditched my ankle-grazing jeans and wore a black linen dress and Roman sandals. I knew all the girls at the opening would be wearing clothes that were deliberately shapeless, because they believed the rejection of sexiness was a political stance. Those same girls would be the ones posting Instagram shots of Tom's show later, and telegraphing their identity to the world that way. I realised I felt hostility for these girls, whoever they were, because I worried that Tom was sleeping with one of them. I accomplished the cat's eye, and I went downstairs.

'Maddy has been reading to me,' Beverley announced.

She was wearing an apron, even though there was no cooking required in preparing Maddy's dinner, only microwaving, which Beverley considered vulgar. Underneath she wore an immaculate white shirt, the collar up, and an expensive gold chain at her neck, teamed with black pedal pushers and leather loafers. She looked like she had just stepped off a yacht. She turned around as the microwave pinged.

'But I can't read, Mummy.' Maddy looked at me, confused.

'You will soon, darling,' I said, and leaned down to put my cheek next to hers for a moment. One of my mothering books said that well-attached children always return to their mothers after exploring for a while. The book said this was the children 'filling their cup'. But often I felt that it was me, not Maddy, who needed her cup filled.

*

The barmaid had a nose-ring and a T-shirt which read 'Eat the Rich'. I was not rich, so I was safe. I took my glass of wine. As Tom had promised, it was warmish, and served in plastic, but at least it was a goblet, not a cup. I wondered on what basis was glassware withheld at openings like this. Perhaps they expected riots one day, or hoped for them, as an anarchic appreciation of the art. I grasped my goblet and moved around the gallery. It was whitewashed and had uneven floors. I scanned the crowd for Tom but couldn't see him. The room was filling hotly with people who looked mostly to be in their thirties, the men with their trouser legs too short – Vic called this the 'potato farmer look'. Some of them carried eco-friendly shopping bags with slogans on them. The women wore the deliberately repellent sacks I had predicted. I admired how they managed to be so gamine in their sacks. These women all looked like they were meant to be thin, and didn't have to put so much effort into it as I did. Their limbs were neat and firm and didn't take up space unnecessarily. There were also older people in the crowd, collectors and critics, I guessed, bearded men and bespectacled women. I recognised the art critic from my old paper, Stefan, a bald man who used hand gestures a lot. He was peering at a work depicting one of Tom's basketball buddies. I recognised this guy from Tom's place, and from the park — he often took off his shirt and tucked it into the back of his shorts while he was playing, with the kind of male nonchalance I held in awe. He was shirtless in Tom's photograph, and magnificently so. I had only ever heard him called Boggo, which I assumed was not his real name.

'Suzy!' Stefan cocked his head towards me and shouted across the crowd. 'How the devil are you?'

Stefan talked like a character from a P.G. Wodehouse novel. I realised I should have removed myself from his sightline while I had the chance. It was too late now, and I walked over to him, urging my facial muscles into a smile. He turned from me to the work, admiring it.

'Quite marvellously magnificent, isn't it?'

Boggo, I saw now, was clutching a plastic wine bladder, held above him in a classical pose. Behind him, a bony girl was hunched over what looked like a crack pipe. Somehow, she was lit by a cloud of thundery blue-black, and Boggo, in the foreground, was illuminated in a strong white light that made him hyperreal.

'He's Dionysus,' Stefan said. He looked enthralled. 'It's witty and sublime. Yet utterly prosaic at the same time. Magic.'

I guessed Tom was going to get a good review from Stefan, and I felt a complex series of emotions. I realised, suddenly, I didn't want Tom taken away from working at the café up the road and playing basketball in Tree Park. I wanted him to stay where he was, even if I didn't get to see him so much anymore. That feeling was followed by the strong realisation that other people's lives were moving on, and mine was stuck, my identity now fixed in time on the internet, which was forever. As if to underline this point, Stefan turned from Tom's photograph to examine me.

'It's a surprise to see you here,' he said. 'Do you know the artist?'

I wanted to say: *Yes, I do know him, in the sense that we used to fuck.* But I realised Stefan would know about Ben and had probably come to our conversation with preconceptions about my sexual availability that I didn't want to reinforce.

'He lives near me,' I replied, lamely. 'We're friends.'

'He's a talent. If you know him, might I suggest you buy one of his pieces. Trust me, his work is about to get expensive.'

It had never occurred to me to ask Tom for anything, but now I wished I had. When we began seeing each other, Tom had taken pictures of me with an old SLR camera he took down from the wonky bookshelf in his room. He did all his proper work with a digital camera that was black and exquisite, like a miniature panther, and which he kept in a small metal safe. He kept the shabby SLR lying around his room, stocked with real film ordered in bulk from the internet. 'It's just for tooling around,' he said, and although I hated having my photo taken, I loved the capture and delay of the old-school film cameras. You didn't know exactly what you were doing when you took the picture, and you didn't know what you would end up with.

To me, that seemed a better approximation of the creative process than the Tracey Doran school of photography, where pictures were posed and immediately manipulated, amended to become something other, something beyond the artist and her subject. Those pictures obscured reality rather than depicting it. The artist and the subject were usually one and the same, anyway, locked in a narcissistic gaze. I liked being under Tom's gaze, being seen in that way, even if I didn't want to look at the results. He had a way of engaging me in conversation about something – a book usually, asking me question after question, as though he really wanted my thoughts, and then as I spoke he would raise the camera from his waist to his eyes and snap it quickly. He made the gesture seem innocuous, like he was brushing away a fly or pushing a curl out of his eyeline. He never got me to pose. He must have taken dozens of shots of me with my mouth open. That's if he ever had the film developed, which I doubted. For him taking pictures like that was just a reflex.

The barmaid who urged us to devour the rich sauntered past with a half-full bottle of chardonnay, and Stefan grabbed her hungrily, asking for a refill. I got one too. We stood together beneath Boggo's image. I wished fervently that someone else would come along quickly to rescue me from the conversation I was about to have.

'So … how is life treating you?' Stefan began. 'How is life after …'

'The apocalypse?'

'I was going to say journalism. How is life after journalism.'

'Oh,' I said. I felt defeated. 'Well I'm still working. I'm still writing.'

'Well, good for you, old girl,' Stefan said. 'What are you working on? A book of memoirs?'

He rolled the 'r'.

'I think there is a market for that sort of thing,' he continued. 'People, you know, who have been –'

'Shamed.'

'Tested in the court of public opinion, I was going to say.'

'No,' I said. 'I'm helping someone else with theirs, actually. I am writing biography.' I coughed thinly as I told my light lie. 'I'm doing a bit of longform biography work. That kind of thing.'

Stefan looked me over like I was a dull painting. 'How interesting.'

*

I found more warm wine and extracted myself from Stefan with as much politeness as I could muster. There, in the corner, I saw Boggo, who was wearing a hoodie and a pair of long shorts, skater shoes with socks that he had pulled up to a half-mast position on his shins, and a baseball cap featuring the logo of a team I couldn't name. Boggo was staring intently at a photograph of a greyhound trainer. The man held his dog's lead taut. The dog stared proudly out towards the camera, its pigeon-chest held high. The photograph was taken on a time lapse and the dog must have moved around during the session, which had the effect of giving it several heads. The photograph was called *Cerberus*. I made a mental note to Google that later. I didn't know what the picture meant, but it felt mystical and remote. I stood next to Boggo and introduced myself, even though we had met once before, when he had come to Tom's house to pick up a bicycle pump. I had been sipping tea and reading a newspaper at the kitchen table, wearing an old T-shirt of Tom's, and we had been briefly introduced, but I doubted Boggo remembered that. Tom said Boggo spent 90 per cent of his waking life stoned, and the other ten per cent seeking marijuana.

'Yo,' Boggo said. One look into his eyes confirmed that he had smoked pot very recently. 'I remember you. Suzy. You're Tom's girl.'

'Not really his girl,' I said.

'No. Not since you went and fucked your boss.' Boggo giggled girlishly, as though this was very funny. I sipped some

194

warm wine as I tried to assimilate this comment. Why would Boggo think I was Tom's girl? Why would Boggo know about the incident with Ben? I must have looked a certain way because Boggo seemed to remember himself. He straightened his back and took off his hat, revealing a cap of symmetrical black hair. He looked at me. His eyes were suspended in a blood-red cloud. Underneath the engorged blood vessels, they appeared to be a hazel-green colour. He smiled, and revealed dimples, which were appealing.

'Sorry. I'm being a dick. It's none of my business,' he said. 'You've got a little girl, right?'

'I do. Her name is Maddy.'

'I remember her from the park. My name is Abdel, by the way. With an "e" not a "u".'

'I like the portrait Tom did of you. You look very … regal.'

As I spoke, I caught a glimpse of the artist, finally, over Abdel's shoulder. He was talking to Stefan, or rather Stefan was talking to him, waving his arms around in ecstasy, as though he was trying to amuse and impress Tom. It struck me quickly that this show, which was magnificent and interesting – and sensitive, so sensitive – this show would make Tom's reputation. He would stand in many more rooms like this one, holding bad wine (maybe the wine would get better, though) and taking in the praise of important people, all with his head bent and a curl flung over his eye in defence. Tom glanced up briefly and met my eye, before looking down again, to absorb Stefan's gesticulations.

'Yeah, it's sick.' Abdel was looking at me now, intently.

Sick, I knew, in this context, was a good thing. I swayed slightly and realised I was a little drunk. I cursed the artistic absence of canapés. I would have taken beer nuts at this point, or popcorn.

'Oop,' said Abdel, as he grabbed my arm to steady me. 'There we go.'

'I haven't eaten today.'

'Yeah, it looks like it,' he said. And then, taking his hand away: 'Have you seen yours?'

'Seen my what?'

'Your photographs?'

'I don't have any photographs.' I was confused and I felt hot. The aftertaste of the wine was unpleasant in my mouth.

'No, not your photographs, I don't mean.'

I looked at him blankly.

'I mean Tom's photographs of you,' he said. 'They're over there – in the harpy room.'

That didn't sound good.

*

The harpy room was blessedly small, a sort of anteroom adjoining the main gallery space, so inconsequential I supposed a lot of people might have missed it, thinking it belonged to a different exhibition. In it were the most beautiful works of all, Tom's female portraits. I had thought he only used men as his subjects, but as soon as I saw these pieces I realised how silly I had been to assume that just because the male portraits were the ones I had seen, that they were the only ones he did.

Tom seemed to be the perfect observer of femininity, revealing his subjects as both soft and strong. His male subjects were depicted in superhero poses, standing abreast of things, lit from above, hyperreal and titanic. They faced the camera, but looked far out beyond it, as though their eyes were fixed on something other, something on the horizon which was loftier and more important than what was here. But the women looked down, their gazes held inward and away. They were working, all at different tasks – one plucked chickens on a production line, another bent over a market garden, one sat at a computer with her face glowing from its light. I wondered how Tom found all these women and marvelled again at my own ignorance of him, this man I had been sleeping with for a good part of the previous year, and yet who had this life of which I knew nothing, a life in which he sourced photography subjects from other worlds, and rendered them with such care. A couple of other women were tending to children, one in a squalid room on a mattress, the stained walls hung with Disney characters cut from magazines. Another woman, a better dressed woman, dabbed at her child's face, as the child stood ready in a feathered dance costume, waiting for a performance. All the women were doing something, not being something. All their faces were obscured and they were unposed. The pieces were simply called *Harpy 1* and *Harpy 2* and so on, up to eight. I followed the portraits around the walls of the small room, walking slowly as though picking my way through a maze.

On the last wall were the pictures of me. I was Harpy 8. In one, I was plaiting Maddy's hair. The photograph was taken from the back and you couldn't see either of our faces, but I recognised myself, and the navy dress shirt I was wearing. I was ready for work, with my own hair done, slicked back and businesslike, off my face. Maddy was, for once, compliant, and the camera trained on my fingers, bent and working. You couldn't see my face, but you could see my nose in an oblique profile. Maddy was wearing white, and with her braided hair, she somehow looked like a Grecian nymph, or a cherub making a cameo in a Renaissance rendition of a Greek myth. I remembered that one night, about six months ago, Tom had stayed over at my place, a rare occurrence that I almost never allowed. In the morning, I woke him minutes before Maddy stormed into my room, and kicked him out on the street with his backpack. He responded by knocking at the door and pretending he was passing by, that he had just decided to drop in for breakfast. Informality came naturally to him. Maddy was delighted, and I had no option but to invite him in. He was still warm from my bed. He had his camera with him and snapped some shots while I was getting Maddy ready at the kitchen table. What he took, I never imagined would end up here, in this white-walled room.

The last picture was also of me, but only me, and in it I was asleep, my features slackened in a way that almost made me unrecognisable to myself. I was wrapped in a sheet and the light was so shadowed and low that the resolution blurred in a cinematic way. My head lay to one side and I looked blank, and peaceful, and alone. I also looked beautiful; even through the lens of my self-criticism I could see that. Tom had made me beautiful.

*

A week after the show's opening, I read Stefan's review of it in the paper, the only time I had picked it up since I had been effectively sacked from it. Stefan had all sorts of adjectives for Tom's work, and he used the word 'luminous' twice. He said the works combined the mystery of Bill Henson with the clear-eyed realism of a war photographer. He reserved his most special praise for the *Harpy* series, which he said 're-imagined the harpy as a transformative figure, a figure of industry and an agent of change, as a feminist and a fighter, not a scold'. I didn't know about that. I read up a little about harpies and discovered they were portrayed almost universally badly in literature, particularly by Dante in his 'Inferno', where he had them lurking in the infernal wood, in the seventh circle of hell. That was the worst spot, the place where the suicides went to burn and suffer. The harpies tormented the suicides – did Tom know that when he depicted me as one? Would he be that cruel in the pursuit of his art?

But other classical writers, the more obscure ones, had depicted the harpies as beautiful, the heraldic personification of the great storm winds of the ancient world. I could live with being a storm wind. In the days after I saw Tom's portraits, I was struck dumb by the potency of his version of me, a version that had nothing to do with how I saw myself. He had taken me and made me something else, something other. He had changed me entirely. I never gave him permission to take my photograph, still less to use it in a public exhibition. But I knew from my own work that no one owns their public image, that the world can steal it away from you, without permission or warning. So I was less angry, in the end, than I was awestruck. Tom had taken something from me but he had given me something too – another version of myself to assess, and consider.

*

But all of that was on reflection, later. At the time, I stood dumbly in front of myself. Tom came up behind me. I didn't need to turn around to know it was him. He asked me if I liked the pictures.

'I think they're extremely surprising,' I said, turning.

He had dressed up – he was wearing a faded denim shirt with black jeans and his usual trainers. His hair was cut short and his curls glistened close to his head. He was desirable in a way that hurt.

'I should have told you,' he said.

'But you didn't.'

'I was worried you would say no. I know how much you hate photographs of yourself.'

'I should be angry,' I said. 'I mean, I am angry.' I tried to work my way up to something, some form of rage, or something which at least edged towards irritation, but I had nothing. Maybe anger was a finite resource, and I had used mine up. I was drunk and had no heart for a fight.

'They're great, Tom. They're really good.'

'You say that like you're disappointed, or something.'

'I'm disappointed in myself.'

'Why would you say that?'

'I have never apologised to you,' I said.

'There's really no need.'

'There is.'

'There's not. Are you drunk? Do I need to feed you?'

I felt a surge of happiness at the implied possessiveness of this inquiry.

'You said canapés were the enemy of art, remember?'

'Yes, but burgers aren't. Burgers and art get along very well.'

'Where are the burgers?' I looked around, hoping for a white-gloved waiter to spring out from the harpies, brandishing a double cheeseburger. Maybe some fries in his other hand.

'No burgers here, but a bunch of us are going out after. You should come.'

Tom made his excuses and left me to mingle, and I sauntered out of the harpy room, my room, back into the main gallery space. It was full of people, and unbearably hot and cacophonously loud. The ceilings were high and the room was naked, the way all galleries and even restaurants were now, with not even a kilim on the floor. I was waiting patiently for the day when soft furnishings would make a comeback. I made my way to a trestle table where a water jug stood among a sea of used plastic goblets. I couldn't find a clean one, so I swilled the last of my warm wine and poured water into my own goblet. This gave me wine-flavoured water but it was better than nothing.

'Suze!' Jessica, my fellow barmaid, advanced across the room to me. I was surprised to see her – I didn't know she was friends with Tom. She was wearing a bodiced dress with polka dots on it. It nipped in at the waist and had buttons down its entire front. Looking at her, you couldn't help but think about undoing her. Her tattoos glowed against the pearl of her skin. We chatted for a minute about work. Jessica said that last night during her shift at the Little Friend, Pete had followed her into the yard on her break, offered her a light and asked her out.

'Wow. Nice one, Pete. I never thought he'd screw up the courage,' I said.

'He didn't really. He asked if I had seen his Facebook request. Apparently he had sent me an invitation to some concert on Facebook. I told him I never check Facebook.'

'Is that how millennials do it now?' I asked. 'Is Pete a millennial?'

'I don't know. But after he said that, I checked Facebook, and had a poke around his profile, and I was right. He is a men's rights guy. He Facebook-liked the official page of that Stirling Kirk dude. Along with a whole bunch of Harry Potter fan fiction.'

Stirling Kirk was an internet celebrity and pop psychologist who had written a bestselling manual on how to be a man. I only knew about it because Tom had bought a copy, out of interest, and tossed it aside, literally to the floor of his room, in disgust. I remembered he had called it 'pseudo-Jungian bullshit', and I had made a mental note to Google the main beliefs of Jung. I was often dismayed by my own ignorance.

'My misogynist radar is failsafe,' Jessica was saying. 'I'm telling you, you should run your next boyfriend by me.'

'Maybe I will,' I said. I sipped more wine-water. 'I'm intrigued. Is that all Pete did? Ask if you had seen his Facebook request? I thought Stirling Kirk urged his followers to toughen up.'

'He does. He calls them weasels. Hey, do you want to go outside for a smoke?'

Generally speaking I only smoked when I was drunk, so I said yes. I also needed some air. We stepped through the crowd to the street. The gallery door led directly onto a small laneway with little through-traffic. Opposite us was a large skip which spilled Christmas decorations. The arm from a Santa suit, trimmed with white fake fur, dropped from its opening. It looked as though Santa had been murdered, and his body hastily disposed there. Jessica lit a cigarette in her own mouth and passed it to me. The butt was indented with the sexy loop of her lipstick. I took a drag and coughed lightly.

'What was the concert Pete invited you to?' I asked.

'It was some kinda Appalachian banjo band. Not my thing,' Jessica said.

'How did you get out of it? What did you say?'

'He put me on the spot, which pissed me off. Later I messaged him on Facebook to tell him I was seeing someone else.'

'Poor Pete.'

We stood in silence for a moment. I took another drag and contemplated Pete, with his strange music and his bony, feline energy. He seemed to be trying to construct an identity for himself, and a girlfriend like Jessica was part of his vision. She was striking and laughed easily. She had a gap in her front teeth which made me think of the Wife of Bath. She had something about her, something I could most closely describe as certitude, which made you want to be around her. I could see why Pete, who was all edges and precariousness, would want a piece of that.

'Anyway, obviously don't tell Pete I told you,' said Jessica. She dropped her cigarette from her pretty mouth and ground it into the cobblestones underfoot. She was wearing cork-heeled shoes. She looked like a gorgeous punk who had detoured onto the set of an Elvis movie. 'He might have a crack at you next. Are you seeing anyone?'

'No.'

At that moment Boggo stepped out from the hustle of the gallery and joined us in the back lane. He was ploughing frantically through the pockets of his shorts while humming to himself. I couldn't work out if his shorts were skate shorts or board shorts, but I was confident they had been purchased at an urban streetwear shop that catered to teenage boys. I estimated Boggo was in his late-twenties. I wondered what he did for a living, or if he even had one.

'Fuck me,' he said. 'It's hot in there.' He pulled a small, crumpled joint from his pocket and smoothed it lovingly against his shirt. Jessica looked on with approval. I glanced around to see if there was anyone else on the street, but it was empty.

I had a short vision, shadowed by guilt and longing, of Maddy asleep. It was 9 pm and by now she would probably have worked her way into a horizontal position across the bed. She squirmed in her sleep, her legs stretching outwards like the hands of a clock. By midnight she would be upside down, her feet on the pillow. I wondered how often the Park Mothers smoked outside galleries, how often they left their children with their mothers so they could mingle with the likes of Boggo. I had a flash of the parallel life, where Charlie was waiting for me at home, reading in bed. I would stand in front of the mirror and talk to his reflection, telling him about the evening. I would take off my makeup, my earrings, one by one, and sit down in front of him, my head bent forward like a supplicant, while he unhooked my necklace and the back of my dress. I added this flash to the list of the things in my life that never happened.

'There we are,' Boggo said with some satisfaction, as he righted the joint. He lit it and passed it to Jessica. 'Will you do the honours, milady?'

'Thanks, Ab,' Jessica said, and I realised she knew Boggo too.

Jessica took a toke and passed the joint to me. I felt furtive – the last time I had smoked pot had been pre-Maddy, with Charlie. We had been on a beach holiday with some friends not long after we met. I smoked too much and felt sick, and dizzy, and I ended the night in a darkened tent, convinced the people outside it – our friends – thought I was embarrassing and stupid. The next day Charlie stroked my head as I lay, sheepish, in his lap. 'You greened out, Suze,' he said, and he took me home, and I thrilled with his care of me, because it had only been a few months, and already I knew how much I loved him. I knew, even early on, that I would have taken off my skin and handed it to him, had he asked.

Now Charlie was gone, no one knew where, or at least I didn't, and it was a bizarre and embarrassing thing not to know the whereabouts of your baby-daddy, most unusual in middle-class circles like mine. I had tried out various versions of the story, whenever people asked. 'He's overseas', or 'He's not involved in our daughter's life right now', and 'He travels a lot for work'. But none had the urgency or the righteous, simple anger of the way it was put by the generations of women before me to whom it had also happened: he shot through. I took the joint and inhaled cautiously. My mother could always sleep over on the couch. I texted her to tell her I might be home late, and then I switched my phone to flight mode, so no one could bother me.

*

It turned out Boggo worked at the trots, as a sort of bookie-cum-dogsbody. 'Pun intended,' he said, and he emitted that girlish laugh again, and then he adjusted his expression to a serious one as he took the last of the joint in his mouth, narrowed his eyes and sucked on it carefully and with earnest application. He looked like a glass-blowing artisan, working in reverse. Just as he finished it, the door swung open, and Tom appeared, poking his head around the side of the door in a comical way, like a Marx brother. He laughed when he saw us.

'Who are you corrupting here, Bog?' he said.

'The girls. Your girls,' said Boggo. My head felt sticky, jammy, but also light. I wanted to object to being called a girl, but my mouth was non-operational.

Jessica turned to Tom. 'When can we go have food? Have you done everything you need to do?'

I watched them, wondering at the casual familiarity that seemed to exist between them. Then Tom stepped into the laneway and put his arm over Jessica's shoulder. She looked up at him and kissed him, enthusiastically, on the mouth.

'I'm all done,' he said. 'I'm ready to go, babe.'

Tom had once called me babe and I had told him immediately, and firmly, that I hated it. He never called me babe again. Tom was very respectful like that.

But Jessica didn't seem to mind at all.

*

Sometime later, we were in a subterranean bar stashed adjacent to the CBD, somewhere in the inner city, Surry Hills or Darlinghurst perhaps. Tom had chosen it because they served absinthe, or at least the watered-down version of absinthe that the bar owners had a licence to import. These sorts of bars seemed to be doing well in Sydney that summer – what were essentially gimmick bars for the bourgeois set. They served Mexican food that was meant to mimic street food but in an upscale way; or they served gin only, or they were tequila bars, or burrata bars, where the only thing on the menu was a milky knot of Italian cheese dusted with Ibizan salt. I didn't really go to these sorts of places anymore, but I read about them in my mother's cosmopolitan food magazines, and I remembered fondly the days I used to go to them, before Maddy was born, when Charlie and I explored the city like eager tourists.

The fact of Tom-and-Jessica, or Jessica-and-Tom, was new information that hit me with a surprising force, but I knew the full impact was delayed by the weed, and the wine, and that was a comfortable feeling. It was like a concussion – the true damage would not emerge until later, when I was in the privacy of my own home. We sat around the table of a booth as a woman appeared in front of us with an absinthe fountain. The boys were on one side and the girls on the other. I was directly opposite Boggo, whose eyes had become so obscure they were notional. I wondered if Tom and Jessica's feet were touching under the table, but retained enough self-respect not to look. The fountain was glass and polished silver – it looked like a crystal castle from one of Maddy's storybooks. A nude *art nouveau* lady rendered in silver reached up to hold the glass bowl which held the absinthe.

'Artemis,' Tom said, looking at me.

'I'll take your word for it,' I said, not looking back.

The waitress placed a glass tumbler in front of each of us, and lay an intricately wrought silver spoon across the top of it. Each glass held a cube of sugar, and because I was still pretty high, I noticed each glinting crystal and thought about its minuteness compared to other, larger things, like sperm whales, and space and time. With a flourish in her elbow, the waitress gave each of the taps a turn so that the alcohol began to drip slowly, deliberately, out of the fountain, down past Artemis, through the slotted spoon and onto the sugar lump, which began to erode with the pressure of each droplet. The process was fascinating to watch. It was the slowest thing I could remember witnessing in a very long time. I had an epiphany about how slowness was powerful, and relaxing, and curved my mouth into a smile, which for some reason made Boggo giggle again, this time quite ecstatically. When it became clear our drinks wouldn't be ready for some time, Jessica and Abdel decided to head outside to have another smoke. Boggo pulled another crumpled, paper-rolled stick from his pocket. I wondered why he didn't get some sort of hard receptacle to store his joints in. I guessed his ability to forward plan was limited. I moved aside to let Jessica out of the booth and as she passed me, I felt the squish and heave of her buttocks against my bones. I tried, but couldn't remember, why I had chased thinness for so long.

'So,' said Tom, once we were alone. He was sitting diagonally from me across the table, and it felt off-kilter, as though we were both solo travellers in a bus station, waiting on opposite seats and trying not to make eye contact. He shifted over slightly towards me, as though to bridge the gap. 'Tell me the truth,' he said. 'Are you mad?'

'About what, in particular?' I replied. 'That you used my image without permission, or that you are dating my friend and didn't tell me?' My plan to treat Tom with silent hauteur had already gone awry.

'Are you joking?' he said. 'I can't tell if you're joking.'

I didn't respond. I toggled my silver spoon around a bit. I tried to soak every corner of the sugar cube evenly.

'I don't even know where to start with that,' he said.

'Any place will do.'

'Okay. You never wanted to date me, or to be my girlfriend.'

'How would you know? You never asked.'

'I worked it out right around the time I read a few dozen Twitter posts about you fucking your boss.'

'Nice.'

'I don't even care about that,' he said. 'I wouldn't care.'

'So we are having this conversation because …?' I snagged a little rip-tide of anger. It felt good. It was like stepping from a stuffy room into air so cold it caught at the back of your throat.

'Because I want to know why you tell yourself these stories.'

'Now I don't know what you're talking about,' I said. 'You're the one who's spent the last few months apparently working on depicting me as a harpy. For fuck's sake.'

And because I was still high, and therefore a little bit outside myself, I was suddenly struck by the extremely obscure and bespoke nature of this argument. No other two people in the mass of the global population could possibly be having, at this moment, a dispute about the fairness of being artistically depicted as a Greek monster/goddess with a bad reputation. I laughed, and the table, which was unsteady, jiggled, rattling the absinthe fountain and glasses. Everything tinkled, lightly, like fairy laughter, as though we were already in an absinthe fugue.

'What's funny?' Tom looked belligerent in a way I had never seen him.

'It's just a very specific argument we're having.' I gathered myself. 'Tell me, what are these stories I tell myself?'

'That you are some sort of roving, I dunno, lone ranger. That you can just take what you want from people but never need anything from them.' He paused. 'That your ex is coming back.'

'I don't –'

'Don't what?' Boggo and Jessica were at the table, carrying a skunky scent with them. This time I shuffled over so I was facing Tom. Jessica seemed freshly filled with some sort of joy, and she leaned across me to give Tom an explosive kiss on the mouth. He closed his eyes to receive it and I felt iridescent with jealousy, but the still-stoned part of me was detached and only mildly interested in this feeling. Another part of me, the remnants of my super-ego, perhaps, wondered what I was doing here at all, and how I was going to feel about myself the next day. Jan's face appeared in my mind's eye. I had a session with her tomorrow – how would I face her Honey Jumbles and her yoo-hoos?

'Let's play a game,' said Boggo.

'Oooh, goody,' said Jessica.

'Hang on, first we need to drink these fuckers,' said Boggo.

The taps had stopped dripping and all our glasses held an inch of cloudy liquid, sitting on top of a collapsed pile of saturated sugar. I added some water to mine. The waitress had told us to sip slowly. Boggo tipped his head back and opened his throat to swallow the drink in one go. After some coughing he righted himself, ordered a beer, and explained we would play what he called a 'Mafia' version of 'I never ever' where the person who was volunteering the thing they had never done, could lie, and if the others picked the lie, the liar had to perform a dare.

'But how will we know if the liar is just doubling down on their lie to avoid doing a dare?' I said.

'They have to be honest about that bit,' said Boggo. 'Them's the rules.'

'The whole game is based on honesty, you dolts,' said Jess. 'No one knows what you've done but you. That's the premise.'

It was a game that made little sense, but then nothing about this evening did. I looked at Tom, who was staring intently at his absinthe, stirring it and adjusting water levels in it, as though it was a magic potion. I said I would start.

'I've never ever danced the polka.'

No one drank.

'Boring as fuck, man,' said Boggo. 'I'll go. I've never ever shoplifted – gah! Just kidding, course I have.'

Everyone drank except for me.

'Oh come on, seriously, Suze? Not even, like, a pair of earrings, or a CD or something?' Jessica asked me.

'I have a strict moral code.'

Tom snorted. 'Your turn, Jess.'

'I've never ever … played a Justin Bieber song on my Spotify.'

I drank. 'I like that song about it being too late to say sorry,' I said.

'Tom,' said Boggo, nodding to him.

'I've never ever had a one-night stand,' Tom said.

'Oh come ON, man,' said Boggo, and he took several swigs of his European beer. Jessica and I both sipped of our absinthe. It burned the back of my throat and then the aniseed re-presented itself in my nasal passage somehow, which made me sneeze. Tom did not drink to this one. He put his hands in a priestly fold on the tabletop.

'Tom,' I said. 'You've never had a one-night stand? I absolutely do not believe that. I call bullshit, or whatever it is you're supposed to do here. Boggo?'

'Tom, Suze's callin' you a liar here, man. You are honour-bound to respond truthfully now,' said Boggo.

'It's the truth. I've only ever gone to bed with girls I've known for a bit,' said Tom. Jessica watched his face intently, presumably for lying signs.

'I absolutely and 100 per cent do not believe you,' I said. 'I believe you to be lying.'

'Well, you are 100 per cent wrong.'

'You need to confess and we will give you a dare,' I said. 'Boggo? You be umpire.'

'Tomboy, on your honour and your mother's life, are you telling the truth?'

'Yes I am,' Tom said. He took a sip of his absinthe. 'I'm drinking that because I want to, not because I'm lying, by the way.'

'Yeah right,' I said.

'Not everyone is as sexually liberated as you, Suze,' he said, and when he said it, I had a horrible feeling, like a balloon in my chest had just deflated, and air was leaching out of me soundlessly, and in a way that was unnoticeable to anyone but myself. I checked my phone for the time. It was 1 am. I thought about Maddy's face on my face in the morning, the damp marsupial snuffle of her nose, waking me up.

'Tommy has sworn on his mother's life and the case is closed,' said Boggo. 'That means it's your turn again, my man.'

'Oh man, I don't know,' said Tom. 'I'm losing interest here. I've never ever … I dunno. Killed someone.'

I picked up my absinthe glass and drank it down, all of it, mechanically, like it was medicine. Boggo, Tom and Jessica all watched me, their faces full of anxious curiosity, like I was an acrobat making a jump they weren't sure I would land. I put the glass down and pushed out past Jessica, the bones of my hip colliding with the dinky table on the way out, causing more glass tinklage, and a light bruise that would show up later on my skin, like a surprising tattoo I'd got while loaded.

*

I took a cab home. I had a feeling of clarity as I rode in it, the window wound down and the freshness of a breeze on my face as we streaked through city streets, through the pulse of the city's fluorescent streetlights to the shadowed streets of Glebe, where the houses were dark and everyone was asleep except me and the driver, who was listening to a talkback session on male loneliness. The announcer said men often grew isolated following divorce and family breakdown, and the cabbie, white-haired and jowly like a disappointed dog, nodded his head as he turned on the indicator to swerve into Ruby Street.

When I entered the house, under the menacing canopy of the fig, which rustled with possums as I passed, I knew, on some sort of level that was either electromagnetic or psychic, or perhaps, I hoped to think, deeply maternal, that no one was home. This instinct was followed by the certain knowledge that something was wrong, and it was something to do with Maddy. I stalked through the house. There was no Beverley on the couch. I ran upstairs and walked into Maddy's room – on her bed lay the imprint of her, but no her. My own room was empty. I realised with a jolt of horror that I had been non-contactable for the last four hours or so, and grappled with my phone to switch it back on. Agonising seconds later it pinged, and pinged, and pinged, with text messages and notifications of voicemail messages. The most recent one, I saw, was from Tom, but I ignored it, scrolling straight to my mother's name: *Maddy is in the hospital. Prince of Wales. You need to come right away.* It was followed by a series of other messages which just repeated a question, like a drill of shame: *Where are you? Where are you? Where are you?*

CHAPTER 16

The same taxi driver took me back, across and over the city, to the hospital where my daughter lay sick. He was only a block away when he got the call, and if he was surprised, he didn't look it. When I jumped in the back, with smoke clinging to my hair and my makeup sliding off my face like fading stage paint, he simply said: 'Prince of Wales', with a heavy sense of duty in his voice, like he was announcing a regret. He drove fast and silent through empty streets, and when he ran a red on Oxford Street I felt a swell of gratitude in my chest so strong it brought forth a sob. The hospital reception was starkly lit and populated only by a few listless families awaiting triage, their children either overly stimulated and jumping about, or lying still as dolls in their mothers' arms. The walls were decorated with the buoyantly cheerful imagery of childhood: friendly giraffes and building blocks featuring numbers, a mural obviously daubed by children, probably patients. I wondered how many were dead now.

The reception nurse was picking at her fingernails when I arrived, breathless, to ask where I could find Maddy. She looked up and told me the floor, and she must have seen something needy in my face because she asked one of the passing orderlies to show me the way. When I found Maddy, she was asleep, her little body aloft on a high white raft. She was hooked up to a breathing monitor and various tubes were attached to her. My whole body crested with relief to see her, and I made a bargain with whichever god was on offer, all of them, any of them, to hold and protect her, to make her better, to do whatever it took to keep her safe. These gods could take whatever they needed from me to do it, including my life, or another person's life. I thought of the last time she had been in hospital, for her birth, and how I had waited several seconds between the moment they lifted her from me, and the moment I heard her cry; and how the word happiness didn't really cover the feeling of hearing that sound, robust and heart-punching, the sound of arrival and strength of life. We needed a new word for that feeling, one that encompassed the thunderclap joy of hearing the cry, and the sweet, sad knowing of all that would follow it, the glorious travel and pain of the life that has just been set off like a fat gold watch, as the poet wrote.

My mother, whose face I had been afraid of, as a secondary fear to what might have happened to Maddy, turned to me with only gentle things written in her expression. I lay my head next to Maddy's and grasped her little hand. It took every effort I had not to pick her up and envelop her. I wanted to stash her back into my own body.

'Don't wake her,' Beverley said. 'She's been crying for you and she only just dropped off.'

Maddy's chest rose and fell with a sticky rattle, the sound like a heavy milkshake drawn up through a straw. My mother put her hand on my shoulder as I collapsed on my daughter. I stayed with Maddy like that for a long time, watching her breathe, and at some point the sun pointed through the blinds in the window and the hospital seemed to click into gear — soft-soled nurses padded in, looking at charts and checking drip levels. They wrote things down in biros they had strung around their necks like charms. The nail-picking nurse from reception came in to us with a bright 'Good morning!' She took a device from her pocket and hovered it over Maddy's forehead. It beeped. She checked it, and said: 'Her temp is down. That's good,' and Maddy began to stir into life, her thumb shifting in her mouth. Her little eyes wavered and then clicked open. When she spoke, her voice was croaky and low, like a singer in a cocktail bar, or a smoker. When she spoke it was the most joyous sound possible, and an unbearable reproach.

'Mummy,' she said, and she flung her arms around my neck, grabbing me like I was a life raft.

*

'I need my stickers,' Maddy was saying. 'I *need* them.'

It was the following day and Maddy was awake, and mostly better, although the rattle of her chest was still present, and it gave me shudders every time I heard it. It seemed as though the essential parts of her, lungs and blood vessels and bronchioles, parts I had formed within myself and never given much thought to, had grown suddenly contentious and unreliable.

'Which stickers, little bug?' My father was visiting, along with Beverley. They had arrived mid-morning, bringing cake and toys and fresh clothes for me. At lunchtime my father announced he had 'better source some lunch', and when Beverley said no need, that she had packed sandwiches and fruit, he said he needed to move the car, and when Beverley said it was fine, the hospital had three hours' free parking, he said finally that he would go and buy Maddy one of those magazines she liked. The pink ones, he said. We understood what he really wanted to do, but my mother must have been in a sadistic mood, or a playful one. He came back with the bittersweet smell of liquor on his breath, carrying a *Care Bears* magazine, which was full of rainbows and stickers. The bears' catchphrase was about the magic of friendship, and my dad read to Maddy from the magazine, in an earnest voice, like a newsreader. She was enthralled.

'Are these bears related to the three little ones?' he asked Maddy.

'No, Grandpa,' she said. 'Those are different bears.'

'Hang on, are these bears related to Fozzie Bear? The Bear Under the Stairs? Paddington Bear?'

'No, Grandpa.'

'I can't keep track of all the bears.' He shook his head sadly.

It was croup, only croup, and it had come on quickly, Beverley said. After she had gone to sleep herself she heard a barking cough from Maddy's room. At first, she said, she thought it was the possums doing something abominable. Then she heard the high-pitched, supernatural sound Maddy was making on the intake of her breath. They called it stridor, I learned, and it was terrifically scary. Maddy had also had a temperature, which was coming off now, and very possibly, asthma, which the doctors were waiting to confirm. Charlie was asthmatic and I had been waiting for it to develop in Maddy, watching for it closely, wondering if this part of him would be one of the parts he left behind with us.

I called Jan and told her Maddy was ill, and that I wouldn't be able to make our session that day, and Jan's voice trembled and broke and I could hear the thickness of her tears down the phone and her words shook as she said, 'Oh jeepers creepers,' and I thought of all the things I had that I didn't deserve, with Maddy being top of the list, and Jan's compassion for me, in a crisis of my motherhood, running a close second. I told her Maddy would be fine, and was due to be discharged in a couple of days. I would be able to finish off the piece about Tracey soon, I said, although maybe a little later than planned.

'I'm so sorry, Jan,' I said as I stood in the corner of Maddy's hospital room and watched as my daughter placed a line of unicorn stickers up my father's arm.

'It's all right, duck,' Jan said. 'It's quite all right.'

CHAPTER 17

We stayed in the hospital for two nights, and on the second night, as I sat in a chair and watched Maddy sleep, I heard my phone ping with the sound of an email landing. It was from Tom. In the subject heading, he had written: 'Cities of Refuge'.

So I was reading the Hebrew Bible, he wrote. *Yeah, I know. It's for my next project. Anyway, I found this for you: Joshua 20.*

He included a link. I clicked on it and read the passage. It told how God had instructed Joshua to tell the Israelites to designate cities of refuge for people who have accidentally killed someone. The city elders were commanded to allow such killers entry and make them welcome, and protect them from any blood avengers who might come in pursuit. Because, the Bible said, these fugitives had killed unintentionally, and without malicious forethought. The killers had to stand trial, and then they had to wait until the high priest of the city died. Only then could the killer go back to his home village, and be free. The next passage named the cities. I whispered the names out loud, a rollcall of Arabic and Persian respirations, like Hebron and Kadesh and Shechem.

I wrote back to Tom.

All of these cities are located in the Middle East. Long way from Glebe.

He must have been online because he wrote back immediately.

Don't be so literal, Hamilton.

And who can I sub in for a high priest? I replied. I didn't want the conversation to end.

Someone very old and/or very sick. All the better to release you sooner.

As I was trying to think of something witty to write, back, another email came in from Tom.

Are you okay? I texted you after the other night but you didn't write back.

Maddy's been sick, I replied.

I looked over at her, her eyelids fluttering with sleep, her thumb falling from her mouth as her muscles relaxed.

Is it bad? What can I do?

She's okay, and nothing.

There was no point getting into it with Tom. I didn't doubt the sincerity of his offer but I didn't want to be that person – a woman with no man, who prevailed upon a man who belonged to another woman. A woman who depended on the kindness of strangers. I thought about Jess – luscious, ardent, strong – and realised she was right for Tom in ways that I wasn't. I logged off my emails. Reflexively I opened Twitter, and saw in my mentions that in the last few days I had been called a slut, a whore, a bitch and a dirty slag. I deleted my account.

Cities of refuge for those who had committed moral injury. Release from culpability by the death of a high priest. It was a nice idea. A death for a death, a blood debt. All cultures had some version of the same thing, and in the modern age, we had updated it to include internet shaming, which was as impervious to reason as it was to feeling.

*

'It was a bad business, the business with the chicken,' Jan was saying. 'I think that was where the trouble started.'

We had made it to age 12. Tracey had just started high school, but Jan seemed stuck at this point, as though she feared going further and discovering Tracey as an adult, in her complexity and darkness.

'You forget things, don't you? It's all such a blur,' she said, and nibbled an almond. She said the almonds were activated, and I agreed this was a good thing, even though I didn't know what it meant. The doctor had warned her again about her blood sugar, and had given her a small device to check it at home. She pricked herself with it after eating, and it gave her a verdict on the glycaemic impact of the meal.

'Blimey,' she would say. 'And here I was thinking corn was good for you,' or, once, quietly: 'How does it know about the bread?'

I wondered how much food Jan was sneaking.

'Try latching onto something specific,' I said. 'What were her best subjects?'

'English, always English,' she replied. 'And drama. No surprises there.'

'Did she have any teachers she particularly liked, or bonded with?'

'It's hard for me to know,' Jan said.

'Did she do any after-school activities?' I asked.

'I worked nights during that time. Nursing. As far as I know, she and her brother went home straight from school. They watched TV and did their homework, that sort of thing.'

'Lots of girls that age have obsessions,' I said. 'Like, collecting a certain kind of toy, or ponies, or playing a sport. Was there anything like that, anything she was nuts about?'

'She liked chickens.'

'Come again?'

'Chickens,' Jan said. 'She read a book someone gave her, a neighbour of ours in Broadbeach, a woman who was a Hare Krishna. This woman had fallen in love with a Hare Krishna so she was right into it. They used to dance around at the bus stop and I'd say g'day on my way to work just to scandalise the neighbours. Everyone shunned them, you know, said they were hippies and into drugs. But I could see they were just seekers. And who isn't seeking something, I say.'

Jan looked up at me before continuing.

'Anyway, Tracey read that book and then she went vego, then the whole hog. 'Scuse the pun.'

She gave a small snort and an almond fleck dislodged from her mouth cavity and flew towards me, landing on the Dictaphone between us.

'Tina,' she said.

'Tina was the chicken?'

'No Tina was the Hare Krishna,' Jan said. 'Tracey used to go to her flat when I was at work. She liked the incense and the clothes I think. She would come home with these terrible books, all these pictures in them, pictures in soft colours but of awful things, of sex and all the Hindu gods, you know. I wondered if it was suitable. Religion is so violent, isn't it?'

I nodded, noncommittal.

'Anyway,' Jan continued. 'One day she comes home with a book about animal welfare. About chickens. She says battery hens are oppressed. This book has all sorts of horrors in it, you know, about the chicks having their beaks cut off, and all of them being crammed into cages that are stacked on top of each other like blocks of Lego. She said the faeces drips down through the cages. I still think about that sometimes. She was dreadfully upset about the chickens, crying at the kitchen table. I was always exhausted when I got home from the hospital. Too tired to care about chickens.'

'Tracey had a lot of compassion,' I said.

'Yes, but it was like a tap she couldn't turn off. You can't live like that. She was just devastated about those chickens. She said the boy chickens were taken at birth and suffocated, or they were ground up for meat while still alive. It was only the girl chickens who were useful, to be mothers. She said as a feminist she could no longer eat eggs. Which was news to me. I didn't raise her to be a feminist! Not that there's anything wrong with that.'

She looked at me to see if I was offended. She continued.

'And the eggs – well, if I couldn't feed her eggs and I couldn't feed her chicken, I was pretty stuck. I still fed her pancakes though. It took her a long time to realise they had eggs in them. When she found out she was furious with me.'

'Do you think that's where Tracey started becoming interested in … ethical eating?' I asked.

'I suppose so. She turned into a real little evangelist about the chickens. Then one weekend, she and her brother went with their dad to a local fete, you know the sort of thing, and they were selling baby chicks. So of course her father bought her one, to torture me. He dropped them back on Sunday and there Tracey was, with a bloody live chick. Said she was going to raise it free range, give it a good life. She said her dad had helped her name it.'

'What was the name?' I asked.

'Kiev,' said Jan. 'Terry is a sick bastard.'

'What happened to the chicken?'

'I found a coop for it; of course Terry hadn't thought of that. He just dumped it with me. I found a coop and the chicken, Kiev, lived for about a week.' She went silent for a moment, apparently lost in memory. 'I think he was happy for that week.'

'What happened to Kiev?'

'I got home one day from an early shift, while Tracey was still at school, thanks be. I only had Mikey with me. We walked in to the kitchen. The cat had Kiev in her jaws. Kiev was dead as a dodo. The cat was all smeared with feathers and blood.'

'Oh.'

'Dreadful mess,' Jan said. 'Do you want a Tim Tam? I've been so good for days and I fancy one.'

'Not for me, thanks.'

Jan heaved herself up and rustled around the kitchen. She came back with a plate of biscuits. I reached for one and nibbled it.

'Anyway, I cleaned up all the chicken gore and when Tracey came home I told her Kiev had just left. I tried to make it sound like he had just freed himself and was off having a nice life somewhere, you know? In a good chicken place.'

'Did she ever find out the truth?'

'Yes, Mikey blabbed it, of course.'

'And?'

'She was inconsolable. She said she had brought suffering on Kiev and it was all her fault. She said she could never look at Binky — that was the cat — in the same way again. She went vegan after that, which was a bloody nightmare. She started losing weight and ... it was then that the sex stuff started. It was a tricky time.'

'Do you want to talk about that at all?'

'No.'

'Okay.'

I munched my Tim Tam and let the silence between us be.

*

Following The Incident, and after Maddy and I had moved into Uncle Sam's place, I had gone through a period where I worried about everything. There was never a time when I was not worrying. Instead of providing respite, sleep made it worse – my night-times were tense with anxiety dreams. The worries had been global and untethered, catapulting in a hundred different directions, like a brood of baby chicks scattered by the arrival of a cat. My counsellor, Kathleen Wong who talked about boundaries, said I should do something about the things I could control, and practise detachment over the things I could not. One big worry was financial stability. It haunted me that Maddy might grow up in lesser circumstances than I had enjoyed as a child. Unlike me, she would not live in a stable home that her parents owned. She did not have a functional backyard. What about all the educational opportunities she should have? When I was 16 I had gone on a student exchange to France and was French-kissed by a boy named Christophe, who drove a Citroën and told me *Tu me rends complètement fou*. I returned home fluent in French. I wanted those kinds of opportunities for Maddy. I wanted her life to have scope and freedom and adventure. I decided that, even if Maddy could not enjoy financial stability as a child, she would have some as an adult. She had time on her side, and I would harness its power, along with the magic of compound interest, to set her up as an adult. Since then I had put away a small amount every fortnight, and invested it in an indexed fund. Maddy was now a thousandaire several times over. When I checked my bank balance in the week after she was discharged from hospital, I realised she had more money than me. The car registration was overdue, as was the insurance bill. Taking a week off working, and searching for work, to care for Maddy, had put me behind. I logged onto my internet banking and transferred some money from the box marked 'Maddy' into my transaction account. Of all the reasons I had to believe I was a bad person, this was the one that made me feel the worst.

*

After Maddy came home, and she was back at daycare, her breathing normal, I felt differently towards her. She seemed less safe, as though she had something coiled in her, something unknown to me and unknowable, and it could come back at any time. This new feeling had to do with Charlie in some way, and the parallel life, and the not knowing when he was coming back, or whether he was. She had his asthma. What else did she have? It felt like a scare waiting to happen, not knowing what parts of him would surface next. And yet I wanted to know, too. I wanted to see where he would show up, in her. I had emailed him, letting him know that Maddy had been sick, that she had been in the hospital. He didn't respond.

*

My sessions with Jan were drawing to a close, and I spent the next few days transcribing tapes and drafting the story – the true story of Tracey Doran. I would write it straight, with little embellishment, but focusing on the positive pieces of her story – her beauty, her success, the fact that she was beloved. Who could understand another person's life? I could put some parts of it together, like threading beads onto a string. Different parts of it would spark light for different people. Most of a person's life would remain obscure to everyone except the person inhabiting it. Tom liked to say people were their actions, and quoted Jean-Paul Sartre, from one of the books on the floor of his room. He said Sartre said that man built himself from his actions. That there was no predetermined essence of a person. I thought about this a lot after I was internet-shamed and sacked. My actions added up to someone terrible. One night I Googled Sartre. I read that he had attempted to turn down a Nobel Prize, which seemed on-brand for someone who rejected bourgeois values. I was happy to learn he later rejected a lot of the views he expressed in that book about essence and existence. He wished he had never published them. I wasn't sure what that said about Sartre's essence, beyond the fact that we all have regrets, and we would all like to change the past.

CHAPTER 18

I had a job interview. It was for a position in a small public relations consultancy, one which specialised in government relations and crisis management, which I supposed I had some experience in. Beverley was overjoyed. She lent me clothes to wear, because she said that I needed to look expensive. She looked the firm up on the internet and quoted approvingly from its client list, reading out, over the phone, the companies it dealt with where she and my father knew people. 'You'll put your hair up, won't you darling?' she said, and: 'Do either your lips or your eyes, but not both.' Beverley liked things to be discreet, elegant. For Beverley it was important to look as though you hadn't put too much thought in, even though she always did. The interview was in the late afternoon and I didn't know what time it would finish, so she said she would pick up Maddy from daycare and bring her back to Ruby Street for dinner. She said she would bring champagne 'just in case'. I told her she was getting ahead of herself, but her enthusiasm infected me and I began to think about what it might be like to travel on a bus in a suit, to be the sort of woman who kept several pairs of heels at work for important meetings, and who had an expense account and shopped at boutiques. Who might consider buying herself a handbag bauble. The sort of woman who was behind the doors that I had spent my journalistic career knocking on. Perhaps there would be more dignity in that, more dignity in being inside, not outside, and trying to put a good spin on stories, rather than trying to force awful things out into the daylight. Maybe it would be nice to help keep things hidden, or at least small, rather than trying to make things large and show them to the world, bloated and ungainly.

I caught the train into town and walked with some difficulty to the consultancy's offices. I had on a pair of heels Beverley had insisted on buying for me. They were black patent-leather pumps with a pointed toe, and they made walking much more arduous than it needed to be. The foyer of the building flashed with glass and steel, and great urns of flowers were placed throughout it like offerings to an invisible corporate god. There were several sets of elevators, organised into rows. I found my way to a touchscreen, which asked me to enter the number of the floor I was seeking. I did, and the toneless voice of a woman robot told me another number. It took me several attempts, and an intervention from a security guard, before I realised that the robot was telling me the number of the lift that had been assigned to convey me to my chosen floor. I jolted with inertia as the lift pulled me upwards, and I wondered at this system, which seemed like the most intricate way possible to make sure none of the building's employees were kept waiting for a moment longer than was necessary. I worried about the level of efficiency that might be required of me at this job.

I was greeted by a young man with an unreadable expression who asked me to sit and wait, and it was a moment before I realised he was the receptionist. This seemed modern, and was encouraging. I sat on a leather couch and waited. The couch was too deep to lean back on and it was too minimalist to have armrests, so I was forced into a strictly upright sitting position, which felt professional, like I was already partway to becoming the person I would need to be to work at a place like this. Perhaps everything in the building was designed with that in mind – the efficient lift, the curated flower urns, the way that every single office here was a glass box, its contents fully observable. It crafted the people it needed. I sat with my knees held together looking out at the expansive view of glittering blue harbour; from such a height the yachts looked like slow-moving insects making curlicue trails. A woman approached me.

'You must be Suzy,' she said. Her voice was high and gentle, and she wore a trouser suit of some exquisite material that lounged softly over her body. She was small, and her cheekbones pointed outwards from her face like a cat's. Her skin was translucent and she had let her hair go silver even though she looked young, in an ageless sort of way. Her hair was swept backwards from her face and fastened with a barrette at the nape of her neck.

'I'm Olivia. We are ready to see you,' she said. 'We're in the boardroom, which I know is a little intimidating. But all the other meeting rooms were booked out.'

Olivia led me down a corridor and into a large room with a long blond wood table in it. The walls were mostly glass, giving an eastern view of the harbour, the water snaking out towards the Heads. On the southern wall was an exquisite Aboriginal dot painting. I guessed it was from the Western Desert, which was surely the antithesis of this air-conditioned place, which was cool, dustless, and clean as bones. Olivia indicated a chair for me to sit in, facing the view, which dazzled me. She introduced me to two men in dark suits. They were silhouetted against the view, like figures standing in front of a lit-up movie screen. They had interchangeable male Bible names, they were John and Mark, or Luke and Peter. As soon as Olivia introduced them I forgot which was which, and then I forgot the names altogether. Both the men, and Olivia too, made a point of using my name a lot, tacked onto the end of a statement or a question. I guessed this was a technique they used with clients to make them feel individually appreciated. It was probably something they taught in the MBA course these people had doubtlessly completed. I didn't know why I was being so snobby about MBAs. After all I had no degree, a fact which must have been a glaring void in my CV, of which each of my three interviewers had a copy, neatly laid in front of them.

'So,' said Luke, or Peter. 'You want to come and work at Rafter & Robinson.'

I hadn't factored in being asked to lie so early on. Wanting did not come into it, of course, but I knew this was a dance I needed to step.

'Yes,' I said. 'I feel that … after years of journalism, I have decided I want to work on the other side, I guess.'

'See how the sausage is made!' boomed the other one – John, or Mark. He guffawed as though this was very funny. 'So to speak.'

I wasn't sure this was the correct analogy but I nodded.

'Your CV is interesting,' said Olivia. She observed me coolly, like I was an object that had nothing to do with her, but had somehow crossed her line of vision. 'You've won some journalism awards, I see.'

'I have,' I said.

John, or Peter, the man who had made the joke about sausages, said that they needed someone with my kind of inside experience. Their clients needed them to work their web of contacts, to put out information, but also to glean it themselves. This was done, he said, through a combination of soft power and hard power.

'We try to mostly use soft, of course,' he said, with another guffaw. 'But sometimes we need to go hard.'

I had no real idea what he meant but I guessed he was probably talking about the kinds of things I had always been on alert for as a journalist – the plying of misinformation, backgrounding as a way of influencing the story, the levering of favours, using personal relationships as currency. All these things were manipulations I had used. Always in service of the story though, or so I told myself. Perhaps I had used them in service of other things too. Perhaps I had used them in service of my ego. I wondered if they knew about the circumstances of my leaving my former employer, and if they cared. Occasionally I Googled myself to see what came up, and the gossip item published about me and Ben was still high on the search results. One look at my Twitter mentions would be enough to turn off any potential employers, surely. The words the trolls used, the medievalisms like 'whore' and 'harlot', the modernisms like 'ho' and 'skank', the evergreen punch of 'slut'. Surely no professional firm would want that sort of thing associated with its name.

Olivia regarded me.

'We know about the circumstances of your departure from *The Tribune*,' she said. She was exquisitely beautiful, like the queen from a fantasy film franchise, the sort of queen who was in command, but just imperilled enough to inspire the heroes to take up arms for her. 'If that's something that is bothering you,' she added, and she examined me for signs that it did.

The two men, Peter and Paul, looked down at the papers they had before them, my CV, which contained no mention of my internet shaming, or the death of Tracey Doran. The truth lay in the gaps.

Olivia seemed to be laying down a challenge, or testing me in some way. I sensed she was daring me to prostrate myself, to issue a *mea culpa*, to explain how I had examined myself and subsequently changed as a person, to use words like 'regrettable' and phrases like 'lapse of judgement'. She was testing me to see if I would do all that, I sensed, but I also felt she would be disappointed if I did. Many months ago I had realised that all public shamings were the same – the times might have changed but the pattern hadn't. The moves never altered. The best act of resistance was to not dance along, to stay silent in the noise, to make no move at all, just to make the necessary accommodations within yourself to absorb the shame and move on. It didn't matter what amount of effort needed to be expended doing this, only that the effort was invisible to others. I looked up at the frames of Olivia and the two biblical men, darkened against the lightbox of Sydney Harbour, which was rendered glittering and exclusive by the sheer height from which I saw it.

'My mother always told me to never apologise and to never explain,' I said.

*

It was around the time of Tracey's 15th birthday, Jan said, that she realised her daughter had an awesome capacity for lying. Jan was working shifts at the hospital, and her memory of those years was fragmented by the gigantic fatigue that was with her constantly, like a mournful companion animal that was always silently present. The fatigue was a fog which made the most obvious things obscure – like the fact that her daughter was drifting further away into some fantastic alternative reality, and that her son, now 13, was getting into drugs.

'But that's another story,' Jan said.

She looked tired today. Her face seemed naked, somehow, exposed in a way that should have been private.

I was preoccupied and didn't really want to be there. That morning I had missed a call from Uncle Sam, who left a message asking I come and see him. He said it was about the house. His exact words were 'arrangements for the house' and the formulation worried me. Anxious, I called Beverley. She said the New Zealand cousins were asking pressing questions about Ruby Street. Sam had been the sole bachelor brother of six siblings, including my dad's dad, and the cousins said he had bought the terrace with money borrowed from their father. I asked my mother if I should be worried.

'I don't know, darling,' she said, 'is the honest answer.'

She was rushing out to a Vinyasa yoga class so she didn't have a lot of time. They were doing headstands today.

'I've been working up to it for weeks,' she said.

Beverley said it was crass to discuss it, but it all depended on how long Sam lived. No one knew what was in his will, of course. And so many people challenged wills these days, anyway, she said.

'No one respects the dead anymore. And you know what Kiwis are like.'

I said I didn't.

'Litigious, darling,' she said. 'Terribly litigious.'

In front of me now, Jan adjusted her bulk in her easy chair. She looked so sad that I asked if she really wanted to do this.

'Yes,' she said firmly. 'Today is the day. I want to get it all out. I want you to get it all down.'

I set my Dictaphone down between us, on a table that was covered in doilies. I folded my hands on my knees and listened.

There was, Jan said, no way of ever knowing who a teenager was, or what she wanted, from the world, or herself, let alone from you. Jan said that was one of the great horrors of motherhood, that your baby forged you in her neediness, she started life attached to you, and then grew into a toddler who wanted to be attached to you, and then into a child with needs that were even more complicated. Why do we pretend we are not weighed down by it, she said. Why do we pretend we don't crave the weightlessness of before?

'But it's all happening when you're so busy with work and laying on food, and making sure you have everything in the house, schoolbooks and lunches and money in an envelope for swimming lessons, and new shoelaces and all the rest.'

She had a theory, she said. By the time they're teens, they've seen you do so much unpaid labour, so much making of lunches and bending down to clean up, and driving them about and so much wiping – oh! when she thought of all the wiping – of faces and bottoms, of countertops and floors – of shirt fronts and trouser legs. Embarrassed wiping, reflexive wiping, apologetic wiping, furious wiping, doleful wiping. They've seen you do so much of this drudge work that, unconsciously at least, they must think of us, their mothers, as their slaves. And the arrival of this knowledge comes at the same time, for a teenage girl, that she wants independence, and craves the creation of an identity that is striking, and pure in its difference from all that went before. She wants to define herself away from you, and in you she sees someone defined only in her relationship to others, namely, her.

'It's no wonder they hate us,' Jan said. 'I know you think it won't happen to you. You can't see how it's possible now. But it will.'

I thought of Maddy and the way she curled into me while she slept, the way she reached out soundlessly in the night, to place my hand on her belly, or to bring my head closer to hers. It did seem impossible that we would one day rupture. But like many impossible things, I had no doubt it could happen.

'So, anyway,' Jan continued. 'Tracey took to hating me overnight, it felt. On her 15th birthday she woke up and she hated me. She started making jibes about my weight. I would shout at her and tell her she sounded just like her dad. That was one of his things. He always told me I was fat.'

'What do you mean?' I asked. 'Even after you separated?'

'Oh yes. He was much worse after we separated. Used to come in when he picked up the kids and pick through my cupboards, tell me I shouldn't be eating this, or that, or tell me I was feeding the kids wrong.

'Sometimes he would be in there when I came home from work at lunchtime, sitting up at the kitchen table with his boots on it, filthy, asking what I was cooking them for dinner that night.'

'But you were separated,' I said. 'How did he get in?'

'Oh, he would take Tracey's key. He would say he needed to pick up one of their school books, or that they had forgotten their swimming gear or something. There was always a reason.'

'Why didn't you tell him to get out?' I asked.

Jan seemed to think that was very funny. She looked at me as though trying to ascertain if I was serious and then let out a few whoops. Her belly jiggled pleasantly beneath her clothes.

'That wouldn't have worked out well,' she said. 'Terry's brother was a cop. His brother-in-law was too. Family of bloody cops and butchers.'

'Did he threaten you?'

'No, not after the shotgun thing. Even back then, I think he knew that wasn't something the cops could ignore, if he carried on like that. So he knew he could get in trouble from that sort of thing.'

'What shotgun thing?'

'I didn't tell you about that?'

'No. Definitely you didn't.'

'Ah,' said Jan.

*

Jan had been able to extract herself from Lismore, and her marriage to Terry, during a brief period when he had fallen in love with someone else, a female apprentice at his shop. The apprentice was 20, and extremely able, both at her job and in other, sexual respects, Jan said. Jan noticed a change in her husband, who left her alone 'in the bedroom', she said, and seemed brighter, more optimistic, more inclined to let pass the sort of infringements he would normally police, like overcooked peas (Jan was a terrible cook, he said) or undercooked chops (Terry liked his well done). She had noticed the pleasant change in her husband and put it all together when she saw them together in the shop one day.

'It was something about the way he handed her the tenderiser when she asked for it,' Jan said. 'She was doing up some schnitzels. He had a gentleness to him that I hadn't seen since we were courting. And I just knew.'

She confirmed it the old-fashioned way, through spying, and realised her husband and his lover were meeting at night at the scout hall near their house, which stood empty apart from meetings of the scouts and the local train enthusiasts on Monday and Wednesday nights respectively. They made love on an old couch next to the kitchenette. Often Terry brought along a six-pack of beer, and sometimes, a small transistor radio which he tuned to the local soft rock station.

Instead of being jealous or devastated, Jan nearly collapsed with relief. It was all she could do not to turn cartwheels in the street outside their brick bungalow. She began to plot her escape. She waited until the school holidays, and told Terry she would take the children to her mother's place in Surfers Paradise for a few weeks. He said he thought that seemed like a good idea. Terry made sure she had a full tank of petrol and packed the car for them. She remembered watching him as he stood in his Stubbies and singlet, in the carport, waving them off, his underarm hair a shag of black against the pale muscle of his arm.

'I have never been gladder to say goodbye,' Jan said. 'I knew we weren't going back.'

On the drive north, Tracey and her brother had been quiet and peaceful. They watched the world outside the car windows and seemed happier to breathe a new atmosphere. Once they arrived at her mother's, Jan kept extending the holiday. She would call Terry once every few days, although often he was out, and she would have to try him the next day, at the butcher shop, which suited well because he could never talk for long there. He always sounded cheerful, and sometimes she heard the high voice of the apprentice, Terry's girlfriend, in the background, as she served a customer. One day she got a call from a Lismore neighbour who told Jan she had seen a young woman come and go from Jan's house. This was all Jan needed – she rang Terry and told him she wouldn't be coming home and that he could visit the children whenever he liked. A friend of her mum's found her a nursing job, she rented the top floor of an old duplex in Broadbeach, and she and the kids settled into their new life.

'Oh golly, was it ever fine,' said Jan. 'I loved it. I felt so free. The kids got bikes and surfboards and roamed as wild as they wanted. Made a whole bunch of new friends. I made friends too, real ones, and I started going to calisthenics and listening to Carole King. The sea would breeze in through my windows and I started to think, you know, this was life, this was closer to how I wanted things to be for me. For us.'

Maybe things would be better for me and Maddy in Queensland, I thought, fleetingly, with a warm breeze and cheap housing.

'Anyway this is about me,' said Jan. 'We're supposed to be talking about Tracey. How did we get onto this?'

'You were telling me about Tracey as an adolescent,' I prompted her. 'She turned against you and started criticising you like Terry did.'

Jan said their peace was broken when Terry broke up with his girlfriend, or his girlfriend broke up with him, and he turned his focus back to her. She said it filled her with dread. He sold up the shop and moved up the coast, near them. She felt uneasy about it, but what could she do? She couldn't control where he moved to. He started seeing the kids more, and using them to get to her. They should have dinner as a family, he said, for the kids. He invented excuses to come to the house. He said he had a dream she was seeing someone else. Was she seeing someone else? He was at the shops, did she need milk? He thought she should go to Mikey's soccer games every Saturday, even when it was his turn to have the kids and she had a weekend off. It was better for Mikey that way. Terry turned his gaze back to her; she became his object again, watched.

'Tracey begged us to get back together. Their dad would cry, you know, when he dropped them back after a weekend. Said he was so lonely on his own, that I had thrown him out of his own family. At first Tracey would try to get us back together. Later, she gave up and just resented me.'

Jan said Tracey must have known about the violence. She had watched so many arguments as a child, her little face a moon in the dark of her bedroom doorway, as Terry roved the house, blustering and blaring at Jan.

'And then there was the shotgun thing,' Jan said.

'When did the shotgun thing happen?' I asked. 'What is the shotgun thing? You talk about it as though I should know.'

'I told you about it already.'

'No, you didn't.'

Jan was circling around again, doubling back through time, leap-frogging important parts of the story.

'I'll tell you that another day. It was around the time he killed Tracey's chicken. Kiev.'

'Wait,' I said. 'You told me the cat killed the chicken.'

'No, I didn't,' Jan said. 'That's what I told the kids.'

'That's what you told me. Sitting in the chair you're in now. Just the other day,' I said. 'That the cat killed the chicken.'

Jan sighed. She seemed irritated. I was baffled. How much of what she had told me was true?

'I think it was one of those things where you tell a lie for so long it becomes the truth. In your mind. But no, Terry definitely killed that chicken. He did it quite deliberately.'

By this time it was late afternoon and in the window behind Jan the jacarandas flared softly in the slanted sun. Jan had been speaking for hours, and I was no closer to the truth, to the detail about Tracey as a 15-year-old that would help me fill in the last decade of her life, the decade where she turned from a happy girl into a pathological liar, and a grifter who invented her own cancer to fleece people. Instead, every session, I knew a bit more about Jan. Inside the story of every mother was the story of the daughter, nestling like a Russian doll. I left to go pick up Maddy. The preschool would fine you if you showed up late.

*

The next day as I was crossing Glebe Point Road with Maddy latched to my hand, taking her to preschool, I saw Tom and Jess walking on the other side of the street. She was leaning into his shoulder and he pressed his arm around her to tuck his palm flat into the back pocket of her jeans. I remembered times he tried to take my hand as we walked together outside, and I remember dropping it. I wasn't really into public displays of affection. I told him that because I wanted to believe it for myself. I watched them looking so happy and normal and in communion with each other, and I backed into a hydrangea bush, to breaststroke silently for a moment in an ocean of regret. Maddy asked me what I was doing and said loudly that she wanted to go to preschool now. Not for the first time, I reflected on the pitilessness of children when it came to the adult emotion that surrounded them, baffling them.

*

Later that night, I sat up in my room, working at my computer. Another freelance job had come through, this time from an old contact who was now working in the beauty industry. I was writing some piecemeal copy about lipsticks for a makeup-testing website. It was fantastically easy. You just needed to find different ways to say that this or that lipstick would make you more fuckable, which, for insecure women, is the same as being lovable. I guessed that insecure women would be over-represented in the readership of a lipstick website. The work was poorly paid – only 75 cents a word, but it was easily done while I was half asleep and half tipsy, which I was that night. I sat at my desk and looked out towards the fig, which rustled with intent every so often as a breeze shivered through it. I had bought some contraption to plug into the electrical sockets to ward off mosquitoes. It oozed a silent chemical which seemed to kill them, or keep them away. As I wrote a few pars on Blood Diamond (I called it luscious and pearlescent, definitely a Date Night shade), my email inbox pinged. It was from Jan, entitled: 'Okay this is it'.

*

Hi Suze. The truth is it's easier to write this stuff down. I hope this helps fill in some blanks for you.

The shotgun thing.

This happened after we moved away, up to Broadbeach. It had been years and Terry still wouldn't sign the divorce papers and it was getting to the stage where I needed him to because the family welfare payment it was dependent on me being a single parent. I needed the money and the government welfare people started asking questions, asking for proof I was on my own. Terry said he had got into hunting and had bought a shotgun. He used to take the kids out on his weekends with them, which horrified Tracey of course because you know how much she loved animals. It used to terrify her, but Mikey loved it. Anyway, there was some trouble with the gun, god knows what, and Terry brought the thing over to our place. Said he needed to hide it. I said no of course but he insisted, and he made a scene in front of the kids, and I eventually said okay. He put it in a cupboard, high up.

One day I come home after work, with the kids, and I'm exhausted, you know. I'm putting in 12-hour shifts at the hospital just trying to cover our bills. I knew you couldn't push Terry but I was getting sick of it, him coming over all the time. I needed some space from him. Boundaries, that's what they call it. He needed to sign those papers and he just wouldn't. So I come home, and there he is at the kitchen table, with the gun out, shining it up with a cloth. He's got a little bottle of oil next to him and he is stroking this thing like it's his pet or something. I said, Terry what are you doing here? Put that thing away, I said. He said he needed to clean it, or it would seize up and become useless and all that money would be wasted. He said it was the one thing he really loved and I wouldn't understand, because I didn't know how to take care of precious things. Never had, he said. (He was probably right there, ha, but not for want of trying.) I decided to let it go and I started getting the dinner on. The kids went off to watch TV and he is just sitting there, watching me, slicking oil and more oil onto this bloody gun, while I'm faffing around making the chips and eggs, or whatever. He says to me – Make me one more dinner. I say, what? He says – Make me one more dinner as my wife, and I'll sign those papers you want so much. I thought okay, fine. He said he wanted chops and I had some chops there so I set about cooking them. I am at the stove, working away, and he is just sitting there, not talking. The telly is on in the next room. I turn around, and he has got the gun up, cocked, it's pointing at me. He is squinting through the viewfinder thing (I don't know a thing about guns, and happy to keep it that way). I got a real fright and I squealed a bit. He laughs, says, relax Jan, it's not loaded. I'm just doing a bit of target practice here, he says, and god knows your arse makes a big enough target. Here we go, I thought, but I kept getting the dinner on, just thinking, please God, let him be true to his word. I have the papers in my bedroom, ready for him to sign. I just need to give him chops. Chops and then I'm free. He sits at the table with his gun cocked and ready, with me in its sights, and follows me around as I get tea. I just tried to stay calm, ignore him, because I know he is wanting to get a rise out of me. This is him squeezing out his last little bit of power, I knew. Let him squeeze, I thought, let him have one last squeeze before he lets me go. I call the kids in to eat and Terry puts the gun down. And they rattle in, they just want to bolt down their food and get back to Home and Away, or whatever. Honestly if Terry wasn't there, they would have been eating in front of the TV, that's what we did most nights, but I knew Terry would not like that so I kept it from him.

Anyway Terry starts picking at the kids, their table manners, gives Mikey a cuff over the back of the head, he's really coming down on them, and they're not used to it anymore because I let them go a bit free. I can see he's testing me, waiting for me to cut in and tell him to back off. This was always a fine line with him – he wanted me to make myself a target by telling him off. So how much do you let him pick at the kids before you step in? Cos you know once you step in he's got you in his hands and it's gonna escalate from there and be worse for everyone, not least the kids. So that was always a balance I was doing in my head, and I'd be the first to say I got it wrong many times and let him hit the kids or shame them for small things. But this night I was fed up, I was tired and I was so angry, just furious, you know, that he wouldn't just let me go. I was filled with this real sense of outrage that I had to give, give, give to this bastard and he was like a genie's lamp with all this need he had – he just kept replenishing. So I told him to leave the kids alone. I told them they could take their plates to the sink, and then go back to the TV. He said, no, stay here. The kids freeze. They can hear something in his voice. Your mother wants me to sign the divorce papers, he says. What do you think about that? I said, Terry, leave them out of it. Then he looks at the kids, who are sort of looking down, hang-dog, you know, just looking at the floor, and he reaches out to touch their faces, and strokes their cheeks, and he says, real gentle: I can sign the papers, if it's what your mother wants. Or, he says, I can go get the cartridges for this gun and blow her fucking brains out. Tonight. It's your choice, he tells them.

Now I'm scared and I'm trying to think if he has the thing loaded, I am trying to think if I noticed if there were cartridges in the barrel. I think, surely not, surely not. Mikey starts blubbing straight away, he looks up at me and he is stricken with fear, and that face I will take to my grave. But Tracey is calm. She looks straight up at him. She sort of tilts her chin a bit, and her voice is steady when she talks. You don't have any cartridges, Dad, she says. Yes I fucking well do, he says back, and you can go and get them for me. They're in the cupboard.

No Dad, she says, I gave them away. And she starts to tell a story, a story about how her friend Tim is in the gun club at school, and he was here the other day, and he needed cartridges for his shooting trip to Caboolture, and how she gave him the cartridges because she knew Terry wouldn't mind. She fills in all sorts of detail, and really tells it, you know, so we all get distracted. Sorry Dad, she says, and butter wouldn't melt. She is looking straight at him with her blue eyes, she doesn't blink, she doesn't flinch. There are no cartridges here, she says. All of a sudden, Terry's mood changes, and he looks at me and says, go get those fucking papers now. I go get them, he signs them, and then he kisses the kids and leaves.

I lodged them the next day, and something lifts off me like I've been swimming underwater with weights around my ankles, for years. Finally I can swim up to the surface and let my face feel the sun! After Terry left, I looked in the cupboard, and there was a full box of shotgun cartridges in there. Tracey didn't have a friend called Tim. She made all that up. She spun him a tale, to protect me. And that's what I hold onto. Even if that's where the lying started. It turned bad, later, but she started doing it for a good reason. That's comfort, a bit anyway, and these days I will take all I can get.

Hope that helps.

A bit all over the shop but there it is.

Love, Jan

P.S. kisses to that scrummy child of yours

*

I looked out into the rustle of the fig and thought about Maddy, asleep in the next room, and how pure our shared world was; that was the upside, really, of being a one-child, single-parent unit. There was no one else to mediate your relationship or meddle in it, no one else's feelings to consider, no one else's experience to intersect with, or opinions to contend with, or loyalties to divide with. It meant, I hoped, that nothing subterranean would develop in Maddy, the way it had in Tracey. But I also knew that close observance of someone, having them in your sightline all the time, was no guarantee you were seeing them straight. There were lacunas that could form under even the most tranquil of waters, sightless. Intimacy was no guarantor of transparency. If Charlie had taught me anything, it was that.

I closed my emails, ignoring one from Tom, asking how I was, and finished off the lipstick copy. I lost myself in breathy description of a pink lip being just the thing for the spring races. I had never been to the spring races, but it didn't matter. All writing is a kind of lying.

CHAPTER 19

It was around this time that the money started to really crunch – there were daycare fees. There was a big electricity bill. There was an overdue tax bill from last year's undisclosed freelance income, and in early February, my car blew up, quite literally, when the radiator busted on Parramatta Road in 40-degree heat. That had been a very, very bad day, one of those days when I joined Maddy in her tears, and then my tears became so plentiful that she got frightened and we switched roles, with her patting my back and telling me to stop crying. If it had just been me, I would have replaced the car with a Korean tinbox, but Maddy's gruesome death in the torn metal of a car crash was one of my fiercest late-night anxieties. I would not have her safety compromised by our (relative) poverty. So I spent a chunk of money on a new, second-hand, car. That was about the sum of my payout, with a little left over in case something even more terrible happened. Something like, say, eviction. I hadn't visited Uncle Sam in over a month, and one afternoon I drove over, in the new car, to the eastern suburbs, to visit the uncle whose house we lived in. I needed to find a delicate way to ask him what our future was, whether we would be evicted when he died. In my conversations with Jan, I was becoming an expert in skirting death, circling it and nodding to it but never looking it in the eye. And although Sam didn't seem to be actively dying at this moment, it was an eventuality that would be forced on him sooner rather than later.

Sam's self-contained unit was small but elegant, lined with books, and carpeted with Persian rugs that overlapped, like a wealthy mosaic. They made the room warm and offset the various pieces of medical equipment that were scattered through it, and the institutional touches, like the guardrails next to the toilet, and the emergency button in the shower. Sam was 87 and fit, but his age meant he communicated with death quite easily; it segued in and out of his life casually, like a neighbour popping his head over the fence, or a dog whose barking was a frequent background noise.

'How's my girl?' Sam asked, as soon as I arrived. He walked with a cane now, and it took him a long time to answer the door.

He meant Maddy.

'Delightful. She would be very cross to know I was here without her,' I said.

'That child is you at the same age. The very same.'

Uncle Sam always said this. My mother said Maddy and I were the only things he was ever sentimental over. Although he was mostly lucid, Sam was losing his memory; it was fraying at the edges like one of his worn rugs. He looked the same as he ever had, with a high forehead and a Roman nose, and a slick of white hair which was surprisingly robust for anyone so old. But like all very old white people, he looked as though he had been leached of colour, gradually denuded of any pigment – his hair was white, his skin pallid, his eyes, once a fierce, Tyrolean blue, were pale. It was as though he was literally fading. Beverley called Uncle Sam 'one of the last great bachelors', and she romanticised him as the sort of man who eschewed nuptial commitment for a life of books and work and gentlemanly leisure pursuits, perhaps interrupted by the occasional discreet affair. It never seemed to occur to her that the affair might not be with a woman. Beverley had a way of omitting certain facts from her field of vision, things that didn't fit or that were awkward in some way, and I had never shared with her the discovery of Uncle Sam's startling pornography cache. She read the newspapers every day, both broadsheets, she was educated and informed, and, apparently, now a Greens voter. So therefore she was theoretically on board with LGBTQI rights. But she was also steeped in the values of the 1950s, and valued appearances. I also suspected her female vanity meant she had trouble truly believing in homosexuality. Whenever it came up in general conversation, she always said mysteriously that some men went through 'phases'.

As a child, Uncle Sam had been a consistent and gentle presence for me. He appeared for dinners and lunches; he brought wine and always a book for me, never wrapped, because these books weren't presents per se, nothing so frivolous as that. They were my literary and moral education. Either Uncle Sam had a good secretary, or he had a perfect instinct for what little girls liked – he brought me *Milly-Molly-Mandy* and *Anne of Green Gables*, countless Enid Blyton novels, *Seven Little Australians* and then, one glorious birthday, he produced a hardcover copy of *Little Women*, and I gulped it down over the course of a thrilling week. Sam was one of those adults who seems to have access to a personal reserve of amusement, a private treasure of mirth which he chose not to share. He chuckled and twinkled and smiled at things my mother said, and I liked to watch him at the dining table with other grown-ups, not saying much but listening intently, and always finding something to quietly smile about. He would catch my eye and wink, and for a moment I was let in, and the world narrowed to a conspiracy of us.

Sometimes Sam spoke about his work as a divorce lawyer, a family lawyer. Some clients he could never call at home, and others ended conversations abruptly when their husbands came through the front door, talking loudly and falsely as they pretended he was a plumber, or a nuisance call, and rung off quickly. There were the women who paid in cash because the chequebook was policed, and the women desperate for their husbands to have an affair, so they could sue him for it. Those women dangled pretty neighbours and sexy colleagues and sometimes even luscious friends beneath the noses of their imperious husbands, hoping one would catch his interest, and shift his eye onto anything but them. Everything changed when the Whitlam government legislated for no-fault divorce, and the floodgates opened. If you wanted any incontrovertible proof of the many ways in which the institution of marriage didn't serve women, Uncle Sam said, you just needed to come to the waiting room of his Macquarie Street office on any day in 1976. He called it 'the miserable exodus'.

What had they thought of him, this urbane, laconic, tall man who was handsome and kind, and who served them with quiet ease, setting himself between them and their angry, needy, caterwauling husbands? Sam sponged up all the masculine mess and protected his clients from the threats and warnings of the men who had promised to have and hold them. At least one or two of these desperate women must have fallen in love with him, I always figured. Just like his friend Gina, for whose death I gave condolences now.

'Thank you, darling,' he said. 'She was a lovely girl, very lively. I thought she would outlast me, without doubt. It is a most peculiar position to be in, watching friend after friend die off. Very strange thing. Makes me feel a poetic figure, sometimes.'

'How so?' I asked. Conversations with Uncle Sam were always interesting. His aversion to small talk was long-standing and had nothing to do with his time running out.

'You become a silent keeper of so many things,' he said. 'Small details of a person, things that will never be replicated, a quirk of DNA and circumstance and environment and whatever else is it that contributes to a person's originality. Every person has a collection of things that make them totally unique. And when that person goes, you become the receptacle of that originality. Tea?'

I said yes, and offered to make it, but Sam waved me down.

'Let me be useful for once. Nurse Cherry tells me not to sit for too long, for my circulation. So here I go. Just give me a minute.'

He began the process of standing up from his chair, which started with him stretching his bony legs outwards, and jerking his brogued feet sharply backwards, to create enough momentum to rock the chair and swing himself up. With a balletic leap, his legs crouched and his arms held out, he landed upright.

He gave a hoot of delight. 'It's like launching a ship!'

He put on the kettle and arranged a couple of china teacups on a tray, pretty as flowers that had just opened in the sun.

'So what was unique about Gina?' I asked as we waited.

'Ah.' He doled out tea into the pot, measuring it carefully.

'Lots of things. She had been in the land army during the war when she was just a young woman, fixing tractors out in western New South Wales. She told me she had an affair while she was there, with the son of a Chinese market gardener. Never told anyone about that, she said. The resulting child was adopted out and she met him again when he was 50, and living in Chatswood with his pet schnauzer. He didn't want to see her again after they met. Terribly sad. Said she always wondered if she had been someone else, would he have wanted a relationship with her? She felt she deserved the rejection.'

'That is sad,' I said. I thought about how it must feel to leave a child, the impossibility of living easily with having done it.

Sam poured the water into the teapot and stood facing me while it steeped.

'Yes. But she was an excellent mechanic and she never felt sorry for herself. She read a lot of short stories because she said these days if she started a novel she was never sure she would be around to finish it. She would come in here and sit with me and we'd listen to the radio and chat a little, reading, or sometimes she would knit. Nurse Cherry has a huge collection of children, countless numbers of them, and they all walk around the hot streets of Manila in hats made by Gina.'

Sam lifted the lid of the teapot and peeked into it.

'Her tummy would grumble dreadfully,' he continued. 'She said it was something to do with the bowel surgery she had. Around 11.30 it would start up. Her tummy would moan and gurgle like an angry baby.'

Sam poured the tea out, as expertly as a Japanese hostess, and brought the tray over to where I was sitting. He eased himself back down into his chair, which he managed with a combination of dexterity and luck.

'I miss her dreadfully,' he said. 'Very intimate thing, a tummy rumble.'

'Cheers to Gina,' I said, and raised my teacup.

'Here's to her memory,' Sam said, and clinked my cup.

'And to your memory of her.'

We sat in silence for a minute. I listened to the constellation of small noises in the atmosphere around us – the rattle of a tea trolley in the hallway, the soft knock and professional cheer of the nurse asking for permission to enter the neighbouring apartment, the snarl of a motorbike taking off in the street outside. I wondered briefly what happened to the estate of a person like Gina. Did she leave her assets to the child that she gave up, the baby who needed her, who grew into the man who didn't want her? It was a way of loving him from the grave. My mind was on succession, and I tried to think of ways to bring up the Glebe terrace, and our residence in it, residence which Beverley seemed to think was threatened by the distant malice of the New Zealand cousins, with their claim.

'A lot of people get silly about wills,' said Sam, as though he could sense the turn of my mind. 'That's the other thing you see when you live as long as me. Nothing worse than seeing grown children fighting over the money of a parent.'

'I guess a lot of it is about favour,' I said, neutrally. 'Everybody wants their parents' favour, even adults. It's only natural.'

'Yes, but fully developed adults don't expect money to solve the problems of their childhood.'

I thought that plenty of adults did, actually, fully developed or not, but I kept the thought inside my head. I wondered if he was going to bring up the subject of the house. I swallowed.

'Uncle Sam, I —' I began. As I spoke, a firm knock sounded on the door and Nurse Cherry announced herself. The knock was a formality, a courtesy. In a place like this, a failure to respond would not result in the knocker going away.

'Mid-morning meds!' she trilled as she entered. Nurse Cherry was small and firm-skinned, with hips that bloomed wonderfully from a waist I could have encircled with my hands.

'Mr Hamilton is my favourite client in this place,' she told me.

'Meet my grand-niece, Suzy,' Uncle Sam said. 'Suzy, this is Cherry, my favourite nurse.'

'Well, all the other nurses are terrible bitches,' said Cherry. I couldn't tell if she was joking. 'So. No big compliment. Still, I'll take it.'

'Cherry is very frank,' Sam said to me. 'That's why I like her.'

Cherry fluttered around Sam. She extracted a thermometer from a top pocket and unfurled a blood pressure cuff like a ribbon. She cast her eyes skywards as she listened through the stethoscope, and we fell silent.

'Blood pressure is good. Good. Mr Hamilton is also my best patient,' she said.

'I'm not sick. I'm just old.'

'Old body, young heart,' Cherry said, and she disconnected him from the blood pressure cuff and doled out a handful of pills, which fell like pebbles into the kidney bowl she held out. 'Take.'

Sam swallowed them one by one, chased by a glass of something yellow which Cherry gave him.

'These keep me on the road,' he said to me, and then turned to Cherry.

'You know our Suzy is a renowned journalist,' he told her. 'A writer.'

'Ohhhhh.' Cherry turned to me, fixing me with her sharp eyes. 'You write for the newspaper?'

'Yes,' I said. 'I mean, I used to. I am on a break. I'm a writer now, more than a journalist.' I wasn't sure how much Sam knew, how much Beverley had passed on.

Cherry was patting herself down, distracted, and seemed to have lost interest in the conversation.

'My glasses. I lose my glasses all the time, sometimes I think I'm losing memory because I'm around all the old croakers,' she said.

I looked at Sam to see if he was offended, but he only laughed.

'They're around your neck,' he said.

Cherry clucked at herself.

'Goodbye to you, Suzy writer,' she said. 'And Mr Hamilton, I will see you at midday meds.'

She soft-shoed over to the door and closed it with a decisive click.

'Cherry often makes my day,' said Sam, looking after her. 'She's a card. She has dreadful things to say about the Chinese. But she does make me laugh. She only gets to see her children twice a year.'

He looked at me with a smile. 'But today, you are my highlight,' he said.

'Uncle Sam,' I tried again. Guilt engulfed me. He thought I was here to see him, to talk to him, not to ask about my inheritance.

'Yes, darling?'

I changed tack. 'You know I quit the paper, right? I am not a journo anymore.'

'Yes, your mother briefed me,' he said. 'It doesn't matter a jot to me. I couldn't be prouder of you and I have the clippings to prove it.'

'You keep my articles?'

'Yes, of course. It's become something of a hobby for me,' he said. 'I thought one day you might need a record of all your work, although of course everything is online now.'

'Do you have it here?'

He gestured towards a shelf, and I walked over and pulled down a large, hardback scrapbook. Inside was the sum of my working life, my writing life, carefully pasted in sequential order, and painstakingly notated. There were early news reports from my brief stint on police rounds, there were colour stories and weather stories, political profiles and soft profiles of artists and scientists that had been conducted over lunch. There were investigations into politicians' travel expenses and an exclusive interview with a jihadi bride who had realised, somewhat belatedly, the awful ramifications of her nuptial choices, and wanted back into Australia. That one I won an award for. The bride was still in a refugee camp on the Syrian border.

'Do you want to take it, dear? You may as well.'

I turned over the pages, thumbing the yellowing newsprint and regarding my photo-bylines, which aged as I turned through the book.

'Nah,' I said. 'You hang onto it.'

I couldn't bring up Ruby Street. It seemed wrong to talk to Sam so openly about his death. The only way we exist in the world is by staving off thoughts of the death of the ones we love. Death is only bearable in the never-never, when it hasn't happened near you, and you have played no part in its cause.

'The truth is I left the paper under a cloud,' I told Sam. 'It's been hard to think about. Everything I lost.'

'Beverley told me about the girl,' Sam said. 'Do you need me to say it? Because it is true: that wasn't your fault.'

'There was another thing I did, too,' I said. 'That I wasn't proud of.'

By now, Sam seemed a little frayed, and his eyelids were dipping like a junkie's. He seemed to have forgotten he wanted to talk to me about Ruby Street. His pills were kicking in. I gathered my things and told him I would visit again soon. He held out his hand to me, its back a patchwork of pearly skin grafts, with blue veins so close to the surface his skin looked flimsy as cellophane. It was remarkable to think he had lived for the better part of a century. Now he had an email address and a Filipina nurse who sent electronic money to her faraway children, practical love that travelled through the synapses and byways of the internet to clothe them and feed them in real time.

Sam grasped my hand with surprising strength, and pulled me down to him so he could talk softly in my ear. 'I'll tell you another thing from the great height of 87 years old,' he said. 'Shame is very ageing. And it is very heavy.'

PART THREE

CHAPTER 20

Pete was going through a hip-hop phase. It was unfortunate for everyone involved, but mostly for us, the staff of the Little Friend, because the patrons could leave, but we were stuck, for the duration of our shift, like the passengers of a strange cruise ship. Pete was, at least, reaching for the old-school, nineties stuff, although what he did to it was a travesty, adding guitars and his idiosyncratic vocal style and sometimes even a bongo drum. None of it was okay, but I needed the money and had little choice. I thought about George Orwell's cogitations on just how boring (relative) poverty was, and agreed, and also wished I had an inheritance to fall back on, like he did. In the weeks after I visited Uncle Sam, I picked up more shifts and took on more copywriting. A friend of a friend needed posts written for an accountancy blog, work which was nose-bleedingly boring but which paid reasonably well and was easily done.

Since her email about her ex and the shotgun, Jan had gone mysteriously off-grid. She wrote again and said she needed to take a week to travel back to Queensland and tie up loose ends, and see Mikey, who had just come out of a rehab clinic and needed help settling back into society. Jan said he would live at 'the house', by which she meant Tracey's house, and they could bring the pets back home (they had been staying with a cousin but had grown depressed, Jan said) so Mikey could take care of them. *What do they call it? Pet therapy? It's good for people recovering from things*, she wrote in her email. *Like equine therapy but with dogs. And there is the silly cat too.* Jan had never liked the cat, which was one of those fluffy white ones which looked like a cartoon cloud, or a marshmallow with eyes. Jan sometimes spoke ruefully about how young it was, barely graduated from kittenhood, and how much it would outlive her dead daughter. The dog, she liked. She didn't begrudge him his life.

One rainy night Tom came into the bar to wait for Jessica to finish her shift.

'Hey!' he said to me. 'I was hoping you'd be here.'

'Hey,' I said, with less enthusiasm. I was tired as hell. I knew I looked it. Lately the quality of my skin seemed to be rapidly deteriorating, as though it had independently decided to gallop towards 40, to meet this milestone sooner than scheduled. I suspected this was the result of years of sleep deprivation, and I allowed myself a small, silent curse of Charlie. Where was he now? On a yacht? In a ditch? On a balcony somewhere, surveying an unbroken horizon? *Wherever you are*, I thought, *I curse you and I curse your freedom.* I wished upon him some sort of chronic problem, something which would not kill him but which would bring him near-constant discomfort, like psoriasis, or a bowel issue.

'Drink?' I asked Tom. Jess was with Pete on the other side of the room, helping him untangle a complex structure of cords. When I glanced over I could see Pete's face, drinking in the dip and pillow of Jess's breasts as she bent over in front of him.

'I'll take a beer. Pale ale.'

'Hipster or non-hipster?'

'Give me one from the largest commercial brewery possible.'

'We only stock local. Here, this one is non-vegan, at least.'

'Beer can be vegan?'

'Yes. Normal beer uses pigs' guts in the brewing process. Or something.'

As I pushed his beer across the bar to meet his hand, he looked into my face and asked how I was. I said I was fine, because there was no point saying otherwise, and no time, anyway, to explain the ways in which I wasn't. Jessica came up behind Tom and wrapped her arms around him, kissing him on the cheek. This gesture caused me pain.

She looked up, and straight into my eyes. 'Thanks for looking after him, Suze,' she said, and I couldn't work out if there was an edge to her voice or if that was just a projection of my guilt. Perhaps she saw, somehow, that I held my body differently when he walked in, or maybe, being in love with Tom, she recognised a fellow traveller. Or thought she did. Jess whispered something in Tom's ear that I couldn't catch and I moved off to serve a group of students who had just walked in.

It was an all-male crew and they looked like college boys, the type who had stepped straight from a boys' private school to one of the private men's colleges that still defended their hazing rituals. I had grown up with these boys and I was wise to the ways they sought to make men of themselves by resting their identities on an institution. When they got to uni, they grew their hair and sometimes during summer they walked the campus barefoot, in a display of what they thought was liberation, but which only reinforced the appearance of their entitlement. They knew the university lawns would be bindi-free, just as their lives had been.

'Miss!' one of them called me over. 'A round here, please.'

He made a swirling gesture with his hand, to indicate the group. They were all interchangeable, and had longish hair, a nod to bohemia, but they couldn't quite commit to it: the only ones not wearing rugby jerseys were wearing polo shirts instead. They probably complained about being broke in the days before their allowance landed in their bank accounts, and made a show of eating cheap at the discount pasta and noodle joints on King Street. Vic called these kinds of dudes the nouveau pauvre. *I see you, guy*, I thought as I walked over. *I know you.*

'A round of what?'

'Beer, obviously,' he said.

His face was already flushed with alcohol, and he was blond in a sandy way. His hair was charmingly mussed, like it had just been ruffled by the hand of an indulgent headmaster.

'Obviously,' I said. 'We have many different kinds of it. Would you like to choose one?'

'You choose for me,' he said. 'You look like a woman of good taste.'

If he was flirting with me, that was okay. I looked down the bar. Jessica had resumed her spot behind the counter, but was facing Tom, talking to him. She looked at him like she was hungry and he was a snack. She said something that made him laugh and I watched his chin tilt upwards to reveal a slope of vulnerable neck. I served the college boys five schooners of the most expensive of the boutique beers we stocked. Trevor would be happy with me. I tapped the sandy-haired boy on the shoulder – he had his back to me – and told him the price. Without turning, he flipped a credit card from his wallet and told me to start a tab. As they sipped their over-priced beer, I could hear them talking about a girl they knew. The sandy blond said she was a philosophy major and one of his friends said philosophy students were 'like fuckable versions of feminists'. It was just as well I was serving them, not Jess. She would have tipped a bowl of popcorn over their heads. I remembered the popcorn and took a couple of bowls over to them. I thought the sandy blond said, 'Thanks, toots,' as I walked away, but I couldn't be sure.

Down the other end of the bar, Jess was leaning in close to Tom. I looked around for something to do. It was a Friday night but the rain was keeping people away – apart from Tom and the college boys, there was only a smattering of patrons. These included an obvious Tinder date couple, the girl stroking her long plait nervously, like it was a treasured pet; and a couple of gay guys who had settled into themselves, and into their coupledom, so much that they resembled each other. I wiped a few tables and cleared some empties, surveyed the bar for more customers and then, finding none, I withdrew my paperback from its crevice beside the cash register, and leaned against the bar to read it. It was Somerset Maugham, *The Razor's Edge*. Tom had lent it to me months and months ago. 'The main character is kind of a ball-ache,' he told me. 'But if you discounted great books for this reason, you would read no great books.' Two chapters in, I agreed with Tom's assessment, but mostly I was in it for the locations – the protagonist, eschewing all committed ties or responsible relationships, snaked through Europe and attended great parties. He was doing things I couldn't. He was dedicated to a life of the mind, but he was able to resurface every so often, for coq au vin and a glass of burgundy at a good restaurant. I thought I, too, could be committed to a life of the mind, under such conditions.

'Maugham, eh?' said the sandy blond. He had separated from his friends to order another round. He seemed the chief silverback of the group, either appointed or self-nominated.

'I'm a literature major,' he said, winking, as though he was letting me in on a naughty secret.

'I didn't think they taught Maugham at university anymore,' I said. 'I thought he was out of fashion.'

'He's not on the syllabus,' he replied. 'But I tend not to stick to syllabi.' Another wink.

I had a flash-forward to him, older, as a barrister, or maybe head of equities at one of the banks. He would be the kind of man who called other men 'champ'.

'I see. Another round?' I asked.

'Hit us up.'

In the absence of instruction otherwise, I poured five more glasses of the criminally expensive vegan beer. The next half-hour passed peaceably, with me reading intermittent stretches of my book – here the guy was in Paris, oh look, now he was back in London – as the sandy blond came back, and back again for more beers, making chit-chat while he waited for them. His name was Oliver, he said, and I had been right about his living on campus, although he said he was a 'student adviser', which seemed to mean he acted as some sort of hall monitor who was also a mentor. He was a few years older than the other undergrads, and he got a better room. He told me he was working his way through 'the Greats' by which he meant all those big-name American man-authors who write about women as though they have fantasised about them a lot but never met one, much less communed with one. Oliver said he was a 'paragraph guy'.

'They talk about the first-page test, but for me, it's the first paragraph,' he explained. 'If they don't get me then, they don't get me.'

'What a shame for the greats of literature,' I said. 'Some of those guys don't really heat up until paragraph two. Or three, even.'

Jess was knocking off at ten. She had offered to stay until close but I insisted she leave early. I said I would close up, because I needed to not be around her and Tom, as soon as was practicable. At about ten to ten, a man in Lycra walked in to the bar, the tight fluorescent green skin of it glistening with raindrops. His cycling shoes made a clacking sound that could be heard over Pete's folk rendition of 'Fuck tha Police'. In his hand the cyclist held a large envelope.

'Suzy Hamilton?' he called. He looked between me and Jess, trying to judge which one of us suited the name better.

'That's me,' I said, surprised.

'I have a package for you.'

He handed it to me and exited, clacking on his heels, pausing to shake himself at the door, like a wet horse, before heading into the night.

'What is it?' said Jess. 'Who the fuck is sending you mail at ten o'clock on a Friday night?'

I didn't know, and I pretended to myself that there could be lots of people who would do so, that it wasn't so unusual. Perhaps I had ordered something online, maybe when I was drunk one night and writing the lipstick copy, and I had forgotten I ordered it, and now it had turned up and was being redirected to my place of employment.

This reasoning, such as it was, made no sense because no one was at my home to redirect mail. Maddy was having a sleepover with Beverley. She would have been asleep for several hours by now. Her legs would be on her pillow and the air around her head would be hot, and scented like her – biscuity. Jess looked on as I opened the package. I tore one side of it and carefully tipped its contents onto the counter. Out rattled five or six objects, white and pearlescent as miniature dice. They were teeth, baby teeth, by the looks. I felt an unpleasant rocking in my bowels. I rummaged for a note, half expecting the envelope to snatch my hand off its wrist. It was painstakingly addressed, and politely worded, as ever.

Dear Ms Hamilton,

Have you forgotten Tracey yet? These are her teeth, as many of them as I still have. Tracey didn't believe in the tooth fairy, from when she was young she knew it was bollocks, but she played along to please us, and to get the money. There are pieces of her everywhere. For me there are, anyway. I thought you should have some more pieces of her too. I thought you might be interested.

'What the fuck … ?' Jess picked up one of the teeth from the counter, and turned it over in her hand.

'Don't,' I said. 'It's just some nutjob from when I was working at the paper. All journos attract them sooner or later. We used to call it Crazy Mail.'

'But why are they still sending this stuff?' she asked. 'You don't work at the paper anymore. You're not a journalist anymore.'

'You're expecting logic from a person who has none,' I told her, shortly.

I told Jess she should go, that she and Tom should have a nightcap somewhere that wasn't here. It was fine, I reassured her. The bar had cleared out, it was only the college boys left, and they were easily handled. She gathered her purse and Tom put his hand at the small of her back. He turned and gave me a small salute as he left, before ducking his chin against the rain and passing into the night.

I looked at the teeth on the counter, reproaching me. Maddy hadn't lost any teeth yet but we had already had plenty of discussions about the tooth fairy. Maddy had wanted to know when she would lose her teeth. I said she would lose them when she was seven, which was far enough in the future as to seem fictional to her. I don't think she really believed in the future anyway. She didn't need to because I was taking care of it, just like I took care of everything else. I had a blue treasure box of Maddy's things: her hospital newborn's ID band, its loop cut, the nurse's handwriting on it fading, a lock of fairy-soft hair from her first haircut, several of her abstract drawings – lately she was going through a psychedelic lollipop period, in which she drew swirling lollipops in rows, like she was planting a candy garden. The box had baby clothes I couldn't bear to part with – a woollen hat that cupped her head like a gumnut, a little pink baby dress with matching britches that fitted over her nappy-padded bottom, and a photo of me, Maddy and Charlie taken at a wedding, when she was tiny, only about three months old. In it she is wearing a white embroidered smock-dress I bought her on the internet, and she looks like a baby angered by her own christening. I am looking at her and Charlie is looking at the camera, squinting hard as though he's trying to see through it. It is the only photo I have of our small family before it divided, like cancerous cells. I figured Maddy may want it one day. Into that same treasure box, I expected I would place Maddy's teeth as they fell from her mouth, which was wet and red like a cat's.

But this, now, was too much. Why was Jan sending me more genetic material from her dead daughter? I felt some anger, this time experienced as a tingling and a head-thumping, although that may have been dehydration and fatigue – depthless, heavy, ankle-grabbing fatigue. I glanced over at the college boys, who were deep in conversation and seemingly at the midpoint of their latest schooner cycle. I picked out my purse from beneath the bar and plucked my phone from it. A text from Tom lit on the screen: *Good to see you*, and a smiley face that only served to annoy me. He used to send me the kissy emoji, or the face with throbbing-heart eyes.

I called Jan. It was late but she was an insomniac.

'Hello? This is late for you, Suzy Q.'

'I'm working tonight. Listen,' I said.

'I'm *a-listening*!' Jan sounded very chipper. In the background I could hear music. Dolly Parton was yelping about Jolene, to the raucous accompaniment of several other female voices.

'We're having a little party,' said Jan, breathing heavily into the receiver. 'A sort of a wake, I guess you could say. Some of

Tracey's friends are here, and my cousins. As you know, they are my only family.'

I didn't know that, but Jan often lost track of what she had and hadn't told me. I guessed this had to do with her lack of boundaries – if she wasn't sure where she ended and other people began, it made sense that she attributed knowledge to them that actually belonged in her own consciousness.

'That's nice,' I said. 'I won't take a minute here.'

'Always got time for you, Suzy-girl. Just gimme a minute while I move myself somewhere nice and quiet.'

I heard her walk closer to Dolly's voice and then it faded again. She puffed into the phone and a door closed.

'I'm alone now. What's up?'

'I just got your package. At work. At 10 pm on a Friday night.'

'You did? What package now, darl?'

'Is there more than one package? The teeth.'

'Whose teeth? What teeth?'

'Tracey's teeth.'

'They gave you Tracey's teeth?' she said, her voice rising. 'Why? Why are her teeth with you? Why would they take her teeth off her?'

'It's her baby teeth,' I said.

I turned my back to the bar and cupped the phone to try to shield out Pete's music – which I vaguely recognised as an a capella version of 'Brown Skin Lady' by Black Star. This was getting ridiculous.

'How do you have her baby teeth?' Jan spoke low now. A sob choked her voice.

'What do you mean, how? You sent them to me, that's how.'

'I don't have Tracey's baby teeth. I thought they were lost!' Jan shrieked, so loud now I held the phone away from my ear.

'I looked for them. I looked everywhere! I think her dad took them. After he signed those papers, he took boxes of things from the Broadbeach house, he just came while I was out and took things, cleared me out like he was a debt collector and I was in hock to him. He did the same after Tracey died, he just went to her house and took stuff, before I could get in there to stop him. I didn't care about most of it, but I cared about the kids' stuff, you know, awards and swimming carnival medals and all that stuff you keep. The baby teeth were in there somewhere, I kept 'em locked in a little box like they were jewels. Are you telling me you have them?'

'Yes. I mean ...' I looked down at the teeth, gleaming innocent against the black bar, with faint ridges running through them, their gum-side edges spiky and naked-looking. 'The note says they are Tracey's teeth. I suppose they could be anyone's.'

'I need to see those teeth!' she shouted. 'I'll know. Send me a picture! Quickly!'

I told Jan to hang on while I opened the camera app and took a photograph. I sent it. I could hear her clucking down the phone, like a chicken.

'I know those teeth,' she said. Her voice was firm. 'I *know* those teeth. They're Tracey's teeth.'

My mind was moving now, moving through all the packages, the lock of hair and the pet certificate and the book of Plath's poems.

'Jan, you need to tell me,' I said. 'Just be straight-up. Is it you who sent those packages, all the packages?'

'What packages?'

'For months now, since Tracey's ... since I wrote the story, I've got things in the mail. First it was at work, at *The Tribune*, I mean, and now it's here, at the bar. They're Tracey's things. Her personal effects, books and even a lock of her hair.'

Silence.

'You have my baby's hair?'

'Well yes,' I said. 'But I don't want it. You can have it.'

'I made it,' she said. 'I made that hair. *I grew it in me!*' Jan was breathing fast now, and getting upset again. 'If you have her things, you need to give them back!'

'I will.'

I glanced over at Oliver. He was looking at me, a look that was quite naked in its intent, veiled though it was by his drunkenness. I turned my back and burrowed my face into the phone.

'Jan, I have kept all Tracey's things,' I said. I was trying to be soothing, like a Lifeline counsellor, or a kind cop. 'They're yours, for when you come back. I will keep them safe. But you need to think now. If you haven't been sending me all this stuff, who has?'

'It's Terry,' she said. Her voice was calm now. Grim. 'It's that sick bastard Terry.'

*

I was mid-pour when Oliver approached the bar.

'I see you,' he said, and for a minute I thought he was talking about my thoughts, or my soul, that everything I was feeling on the inside was in fact written on the outside. Then I realised he was just referring to the gin I was rolling from its bottle into a tumbler. Top-shelf stuff, laced with juniper. I had cut a cucumber slice for the glass, something my father had taught me.

'Busted,' I said. 'We're closing up soon. You and your little buddies are getting cut off, I'm afraid.'

'My little buddies? Do you mean that literally? Or are you saying we are sophomoric?' he said. He stood back and waited for me to be impressed with this term, or perhaps baffled by it. 'Are you usually this rude to your customers?'

'We call you people patrons,' I replied. 'And I don't think I'm being rude. Am I?'

I held the gin to my mouth and sipped, to test its levels against the tonic, and then, satisfied with the mix, I took a good gulletful of it. I had learned some things while working as a barmaid. A drinks waitress. A hospitality professional. Someone whom guys like this, guys who had barely double the half-degree that I had, could patronise with impunity. Beverley, whose frustrated ambitions saw their outlet in me, had told me, when I was little, that I had more talent in my little finger than all the kids in my class put together. I used to look at my little finger, waggle it, and wonder at its hidden properties. Now both fingers were clutched around a gin and tonic, gripping it like it was a warm mug.

'You certainly have a lot of sass,' Oliver said. At that moment one of his friends, or charges, hooted loudly at something one of the other polo shirts had said. Perhaps it was another joke about feminists. As he did so, one of his nostrils emitted a clear stream of beer, and he coughed and snorted like an upset horse. His friends fell about in hilarity.

'Look,' said Oliver. 'Entre nous, they are a little juvenile. I find them wearing too, after more than a couple of hours of their company.'

He snaked a hand across the bar towards me. I looked at it like it was an object, not a living thing that was attached to a person. He withdrew it.

'What are you doing after you close up, then?'

'Going home,' I said.

'How about a nightcap with me first? I can walk you home. It's late to be walking alone.'

As I considered this proposal, the gin flushed through me pleasantly, and I felt myself physically relax, expanding softly outwards like a belly uncinched from a tight belt. I returned Oliver's credit card to him. I rang up the bill for his tab, which came to an unspeakable amount, and tucked it into a discreet leather folder. When he passed it back to me, it contained his credit card, for the bill, and two crisp $50 dollar notes, for me. He had already walked away, back to round up his friends, before I could object to the money, and I would be lying if I pretended this wasn't part of the reason I went home with him after powering down the lights and locking up, skipping all pretence of a nightcap because he didn't need to be any more drunk, and I preferred my sex sober. He led me across Parramatta Road, over a lawn as vast and still as a green sea, and into a sandstone building which he accessed with a swipe card. In his room, which was small but had impressive campus views, he performed all sorts of ministrations on me, far more sweetly than I would have deemed him capable of. He gave me what I needed, which was the blankness only sex can bring. Afterwards he fell asleep, promptly, like he was working to an invisible stopwatch. I looked at him for a while. I thought about how watching someone sleep was far more intimate than any of the other things we had just done in his bed. I thought about how Tom had photographed me in this state, a tender violation. Oliver did not walk me home, but I didn't blame him for it. I crept down the corridor and was able to exit the building when some drunk college boys clattered in, one leaning on the other for support. As they passed me I caught the scent of vomit, which one of them had splayed down his shirt like a bib. I kept my head down, knowing that eye contact sometimes brings trouble with it.

Once outside, I crossed back over the green sea and gloried in the softness of the air. The rain had stopped and the world was washed. It was past midnight, and this was about the only time of the day that the air cooled to a point that was pleasant. I walked across Victoria Park, sticking to the fluorescent-lit paths, and I stopped at the Broadway crossing, which was quiet except for the occasional sweep of a car driving past on the wet road. As I waited, I sensed a person beside me. I looked up and saw the figure of a man, tall and heavy-set, and covered in a raincoat, one of those stupendous yellow raincoats that fishermen wear in American movies, with a hood which had a built-in cap. He reached his hand out to me, quick as a whip, and instinctively, I jumped back.

'Steady on, love,' came a voice from beneath the hood. The hand pressed the button for the pedestrian crossing. A moment later, the lights changed and the button whirred into action with a squeak, announcing with high-pitched beeps that we were safe to cross. The green man lit up. For Maddy, I called the green man the green person. It pissed me off how maleness was promoted as the norm, as though the green man represented all the men in the world, so free to walk and stalk it, without commitments, like Charlie, or the man in my Maugham novel; and without fear, like this man beside me now. I took off in front of him, quickening my pace as I started down Glebe Point Road, sticking to the illuminated footpath lining the shuttered shopfront. I passed the Little Friend, tucked up for the night like a sleeping child. I glanced across the road and saw the man in the raincoat walking in parallel with me. I wasn't particularly worried about him, but I felt a flicker of annoyance that his presence meant I should probably prioritise guarding myself against risk, however remote, over enjoying my walk in the soft midnight. I walked faster and put my head down, down along Glebe Point Road, past the grocer and the new champagne-and-pedicure parlour – soon there would be a macaron boutique, or a high-end donut store, and the neighbourhood really would be shot. I walked on as the shops segued into the residential part of the road, winding down the hill, past the shabby terraces that still belonged to the Anglican church, and past the glitzy ones that had been bought and done up, and which reacted with sensor lights when I walked past, illuminating doors painted in gleaming black or red, and front gardens planted with tasteful hydrangeas. I wished, acutely, that Maddy was home so I could go into her, and smooth her covers and put my face next to her cheek. When I watched her sleep at night, I loved her in a different way, in a way that was unavailable to me during the day. Across the road, the raincoated man trudged on, seemingly oblivious to me but still there, mirroring me. Soon I would have to cross the road myself, to get to my home. I rounded the corner into Ruby Street with its sentinel-lines of fig trees. I was sober. The effects of my sole gin and tonic had long worn off, but I was so tired I felt dizzy, even slightly high. I hesitated a little before an internal voice told me to take command of myself, and I crossed the road to home. I cast my eyes up and down the street as I did, and saw no one. As I reached my gate and opened it, the man in the raincoat appeared suddenly, to my left, walking along the pavement towards my house. Alarm strobed through my gut. I quickly stepped in front of him and through the gate. I banged it shut.

'G'night, love,' he said, and walked on. He must be a shift worker, I thought. Or perhaps just a regular insomniac. I walked into the empty house and put myself to bed.

CHAPTER 21

A few days later, Jan came back from Queensland, her décolletage reddened with sunburn, armed with a new store of kaftan-like garments that she unspooled, day to day, like she was choreographing a fashion parade at a Floridian mall. For the first time, I invited her to my place, while I was having a rare day off. I had just submitted electronic reams of prose for the accountancy blog, words that were just this side of meaningless. If I had had more energy, I would have puzzled over how I could earn money by writing thousands of words of technocratic blather, adverb-dense copy that I was certain no one would read, which served only to window-dress a website, to clad it in a shawl of professionalism. I was filling up space on the internet, which was boundless. I tried not to feel as though my life, at this point, had no point. There was always Maddy. I had sent her off to preschool that morning equipped with an item for 'news'. Every week the children had to present to the class for 'news', choosing an item, or an experience, to describe and share with their peers. This morning Maddy had chosen Cupcake Girl, a favoured doll with iridescent pink hair and star-shaped freckles on her snub nose. I doubted if Cupcake Girl was sufficiently newsworthy, and then reminded myself that few other toys turned themselves into cupcakes. Cupcake

Girl had transformative power, and I envied her that. Through the changes of the last few months, my life had transformed, but not into anything particularly good, like a cupcake.

As luck would have it, Jan brought cupcakes with her when she appeared at the front door, her pleasant bulk shimmering underneath a sea-green garment which was sprinkled with sequins and faux-pearls.

'They're gluten-free, sugar-free, fully organic and superfood-enhanced,' she said as she walked down the hall into the living room. 'They're made with stevia and beetroot for natural sweetness. And chia seeds. They're dusted with nasturtium, um, dust. They're healthy. They're from a recipe in Tracey's book.'

I thanked her and ushered her into the kitchen. Over the last few months, now that I was spending more time at home, I had relaxed into this space. I was cooking more, well-balanced meals with secret vegetables folded into them for the benefit of Maddy's health. I was proud of these meals. She hadn't eaten 2 Minute Noodles in months. I was doing my job. I replaced the basil plant I had smashed in maternal rage, and I partnered it with some thyme, and one day, a pot of parsley, so it was like I had a little herb family, and that added to our sense of cosiness. At some point, I realised, I had to stop living like everything was contingent, like our small family, our duo, was unreal in some way, that we were living in black and white until Charlie came back and turned us colour again.

Jan splayed herself into one of the wooden chairs at the round kitchen table. 'Note to self,' she said, puffing. 'Never fly Onejet again! You have to pay for a pillow, and the hosties are stingy with the roasted almonds. *And* with the beer nuts.'

'How was your trip?'

'Oh good, good,' she said. 'Mikey is staying in the house, and he says he's quit for good this time. Tracey paid for his rehab out of what she left us. Left me. I like to think of it that way, that she paid for it. She didn't leave Mikey anything directly, because she knew he'd only spend it on drugs. And she cut her dad out. So it's just left to me and the pets. The poor pets have been terribly sad without her. Except the cat. The cat has no feelings that I can tell.'

I put a mug of tea in front of her, and the cupcakes she had brought, on a plate. They looked damp and unnaturally red. But Jan didn't reach for them.

'I want to see Tracey's things. The things that were sent to you.'

I had them ready in the box where I had placed them, carefully, like they were explosive – the book of poems with her thumbprint, the hair, the vaccination certificate for the dog, and the most recent mail, the tiny, vulnerable teeth. Jan took them each, one by one, and caressed them silently. The faux-pearls and the sequins covering her began to tremble and it was a moment before I realised what was happening. Jan was crying. This was not something I had seen before.

'It makes it so real,' she whispered. 'Her *gone-ness*.'

I turned several sets of words over in my mind and rejected each for their inadequacy. I rocked from foot to foot. I started to say something and stopped. In the end, I walked over to her and patted my hand flimsily on the soft round of her shoulder. Jan had her head down and I could see a translucent spool of mucus dripping long from her nose. Glad to offer some practical help, I grabbed the tissues. Jan took them silently and then blew her nose, loudly and long, as though in the blowing she could get rid of something she needed to be free from.

*

Later, when she was calmer, Jan told me that Terry and Tracey had been estranged when she died – he had worked out her lying long before anyone else had. Jan said that it takes one to know one. She had always been worried that both her kids might get something from Terry, inherit his cruelty, or the insecurity that made him cruel. She said Tracey got Terry's gift for lying, 'although who knows if that was nature or nurture,' she said, and her face looked like a sad moon. Terry came to the funeral and was a wreck, Jan said. He blamed himself, and trailed Jan around, weeping like a giant ghost. He made a scene and told Jan that she had been his one true love, that he had never loved any other woman like he'd loved her. 'I should hope bloody not,' Jan said to me. 'If what he did was love, leave me out of it!'

'He was just telling a story,' she said. 'More for his own benefit than mine. He wanted to pretend we were a grand love affair.'

Jan said she had 'left it late' to marry, and by the time she was in her 30s she had behind her plenty of bad experience with men. She thought men like Terry were 'the only kind going', and at least he wanted to commit to her, she said. 'I couldn't imagine any other life, but Tracey could. That's what made me so proud of her, even after everything,' she said. 'Say what you like about her, she had imagination. She had *vision*.'

After the funeral, Terry had contacted Jan to ask about Tracey's will – typical, she said – and when she told him there was nothing in it for him, he melted away. Or so she thought.

'Now I find out he's been sending you these things. I don't know what he's playing at,' Jan said. 'He's trying to get your attention, I guess. He always needed to hold the attention of someone, that man. Another thing Tracey inherited.'

Jan had settled on the couch now, in the front room with the bay window, and the sun through the fig tree cast kaleidoscope shapes onto the rug. The shapes trembled and changed as the tree's branches swayed. I sat opposite her, eating a beetroot cupcake. It was surprisingly good.

Jan stayed until the sun moved west and sank through the fence. She told me about the last few years of Tracey's life, how Tracey dropped out of university after one of her professors had run her essay – 'it was on Janey Austen, I think, or one of the Shakespeares – through plagiarism software, and discovered that Tracey had taken large tracts of it from an American website that dealt in academic essays on the classics. Tracey was careful – she changed American spellings to Australian ones, and she pieced together the stolen parts with paragraphs of her own. All stories are part-stolen, but this was academe. They cracked down hard on this stuff. They made an example of her.

Around this time, Jan said, there were rumours about Tracey's promiscuity. She was running around with all sorts of bad types and taking risks with it, Jan said. She worried Tracey might catch something, or get pregnant. She worried Tracey was into drugs, or dabbling. She tried to see Tracey. She felt that only by laying eyes on her child would she know if she was all right, by putting a hand on each shoulder and looking her girl straight in the face. But Tracey didn't answer phone calls and only responded to one text message out of every ten. She always wrote back cheerfully, saying she was 'SO busy rn!!!! Talk later, ILY'. Jan had to Google the acronyms to find out what they meant.

Was it always so hard to reach your own child? When Tracey was a little girl, she shadowed and copied her mother, mirroring her intonation and even parroting her turns of phrase. When Tracey was small, Jan knew her little body's every inch, she had so much access to it. Back then she could close her eyes and feel, in her mind's eye somehow, what it was like to press the back of her hand against Tracey's cheek, or run her arm around her back and place a forefinger under the strum of her little toes. Now her girl had grown up and away, and even if she squinted hard, the mother couldn't quite make the daughter out. The mother lived her life – there was another child to manage, a child from whom she could have done with a bit more distance, frankly, from time to time, a child who seemed never to want to grow up at all, much less grow away.

Jan was still nursing but her knees were giving out and her superannuation was barely enough to buy a new car. She had always wanted to go to southern Spain, to Barcelona and Seville and Granada. Ever since she saw an ABC documentary on the Moorish invasion she had been fascinated, and she had a vision of herself walking through the gardens of the Alhambra with Roman sandals on her feet and a sunset flaming on the horizon. Maybe a cold beer waiting for her at a tapas bar afterwards. She bought a guidebook and planned things meticulously. Jan said she knew the leather sandals were a fantasy – her bunions were too bad, after all those years of nursing – but she was determined to go to that place she held in her mind, even if she had to do it in orthotics. She had to do this travel while she was still working, while she could still take on extra shifts and increase her income that way. Even then it would take years to save enough. So she worked more and when she wasn't working, she was tired.

It wasn't as though her daughter was at the back of her mind, no, she was front, always front, every mother knows that your children are with you always. Even when they leave you, you keep them. One time she showed up unannounced at Tracey's share house in Brisbane. The lawn was unmown and there was children's furniture on the front porch, ugly-coloured plastic stuff that was falling apart. A guy with scratches on his face had answered the door and said Tracey wasn't home. He didn't invite her in. Jan hoped Tracey would come to her when she needed her mother, and sometimes Tracey did come to the house, driving down from Brisbane to Jan's Queenslander at Broadbeach. Jan had left the kids' rooms as they were, as though they had just popped to the shops for a minute, because when she was alone in the house, she liked to pretend that was the case. Occasionally she would finish a shift and come home to a house that she sensed wasn't empty, and she would look in Tracey's room and there she was, her daughter with hair the colour of maple syrup, curled up asleep under her blue tie-dye doona, the one she had bought at the markets in Byron Bay on a day trip they had taken, just the two of them. Tracey would rouse, eventually, and Jan would feed her the food of her childhood – crumbed lamb chops and mashed potato with gravy, or sausages and sweet corn and peas with mint. Simple stuff, cooked properly. Food that Tracey would later call 'toxic' and 'chemical' and refer to disparagingly in her blog posts about free radicals and cell rejuvenation.

'I thought maybe she was depressed,' Jan said. 'And then she announced she was popping off to the ashram.'

I had not known there was an ashram.

'How did she pay for that?' I asked.

'I don't know and I don't want to know,' said Jan. 'I mean, they don't cost much, do they, ashrams? You're not eating much when you're meditating all day, and monks tend to be vegetarians in my experience – not that I've known too many, I'll admit. Even vegan, some of them.'

'How long was she there for?' I asked.

'Seven months. She was in Kerala,' said Jan. She pronounced the name of the Indian state icily, like it was the name of a disgraced child. 'I had hoped to visit her, but they said no visitors. She told me before she went that they did periods of silence, you know how they do, it's called something started with a V.'

'Vippassana,' I said.

'That's it,' she confirmed. 'Good luck with that, monks! I thought. Good luck keeping my daughter from chatting while she's supposed to be seeking enlightenment, or raking sand, or whatever it is they do.'

'I think it's the Japanese Buddhists who rake sand,' I said.

'Oh yes, you're right,' said Jan. 'The Zen lot.'

Jan didn't hear from Tracey for about a month, and then one night, her phone rang, very late, startling her from her sleep like a conch call from another world, and dread surged through her.

'No one ever wants to be called at that hour. The phone holds all sorts of terrors after midnight.'

But it was Tracey. The line was bad, and she was whispering into the phone.

'Mum,' she said, her voice a hiss. 'I haven't heard a human speak in six days. I don't know whether I'm bored or crazy or what. I just need to hear a voice.'

So Jan had sat for half an hour with her back against the dry wall that the phone was affixed to, and she had chatted to her daughter, about the hospital and her patients, and what Mikey was up to, and about the crop of Tracey's high school friends she had seen down at the club last Saturday. Jenny was pregnant. Hilary had gone plump. Derrick was still a dickhead. She poured words into her daughter's ear until the line broke up, and Tracey went back, Jan supposed, to her efforts to be silent, and at peace. Jan went to sleep wondering why people who go on journeys of spiritual growth had to be so selfish about it. She didn't hear from her daughter for another six months, when she got a reverse-charges call from Tracey. She was at Sydney airport. She asked her mother if she could transfer some money to her account for a bus fare. Tracey was coming home.

CHAPTER 22

The next day, after I deposited Maddy at preschool, I stood
in front of the mirror in my bathroom, the fig letting through
strong fistfuls of morning light, conducting a full examination
of my neck, and wondering about its lapsing elasticity. I tried to
relax my face and turn my eyes to the ground, and then whip
them back up to the mirror's surface, to catch myself unawares,
and see myself as other people saw me. We can never own
our own image, it belongs to the world, just as the things that
happen to us don't really belong to us either. Everything is
connected, and no experience could be cordoned off.

The keeping of secrets was an attempt to hoard experience,
I thought, but look how well that had worked out for Tracey
Doran. I'd stolen her secrets and exploited them for a story.
I had told myself it was in the public interest, and it was,
there was a strong public interest argument for outing Tracey
and her lies about having cancer, and her organic food-cure.
I hadn't even had to make this argument myself. I had quoted
oncologists and public health experts, cancer survivors and
patient advocates who had made it for me. Tracey's claims
could have caused deaths. Instead, it was Tracey's death that
had been caused. In explaining the eggshell-skull principle, my
Torts teacher had used the analogy of the driver who rear-ends

a car with a Ming vase in its boot. The driver has to pay the damages, all of it. He even has to pay for the bits of damage he couldn't possibly foresee. You take the applicant as you find them. Tracey was a Ming vase. I was a vandal. It didn't matter what my intentions had been. It didn't matter what lay in the burrow of my heart. It was my 40th birthday in a few months, and my neck was becoming infirm, but at least the neck was intact, still sucking down breath and reliably expelling it again, to mingle with the rest of the world's air. My phone rang. I had changed the ring tones Tom had put on there. Now my phone chirruped like an electronic pet. Maddy had received one of those at her last birthday – a hamster – but had killed it so many times through neglect that I ended up putting it away.

'Hello?'

'Suzy?' It was a female voice. 'Olivia,' she said. She repeated the name of the boutique public relations consultancy where I had attended the job interview under the gaze of two men whose names were still obscure, and a Western Desert dot painting.

'We'd like to offer you the job,' Olivia said. 'We think you're the best qualified and you impressed us in the interview. Your on-ground media expertise would fill a lack in our collective skills base.'

I was very surprised. I had gone to that interview as a form of exercise, like an invalid who heaves herself off the chaise longue to take a walk every so often. I did it to stop my muscles from atrophying into full-blown, long-term unemployment. Not for a minute did I think it would lead me to its natural consequence – a job. A job with a fine salary and superannuation, sick leave and holiday pay and perhaps, even, an expense account for lunches in the city, at restaurants with round cloth-covered tables and waiters who asked you which kind of water you would like, as though the possibilities were endless. With money, and some sort of forward movement, maybe the possibilities were endless. At the very least, they would widen. A job like this could bring things with it – freedom from anxiety, the very best swimming lessons, the certainty that my credit card would never again bounce at the local supermarket as the checkout chick clouded the air with her disgust of me. Without thinking about it much, I said yes. Olivia named a starting date two weeks hence, and a time the following week for me to come into the office again, 'to discuss terms', she said. I noted it down on the back of one of Maddy's preschool paintings – another rendition of lollipops, multiple and multi-coloured, some of her boldest work yet.

*

The first call I made was to Beverley, who hollered like a game show host when she got the news.

'See, darling, this is worthy of you!' she said. She was delighted. She called my father over to tell him. 'What's the name of the firm again? I'm just going to Google it. Simon, open up the computer.'

She wanted to know if I would get my own office. I said I didn't know. She wanted to know what the salary was. I said I didn't know, but that it would have to be better than a journalist's.

'Well, you're off out of that now,' she said. 'You can put all that unpleasantness behind you.'

I put down the phone and thought about the next call I should make. I should call Jan, and let her know that we needed to wrap up our project. I had started a draft of Tracey's story and had made copious notes. Jan had told me enough to be able to fashion most of a story. I had the basics down on Tracey's life up until the last year and a half, which, I knew from my previous journalistic research, was when she announced her cancer diagnosis and began blogging about it. That part of Tracey's story, the last part, would begin a precipitous slide towards her death, and neither of us were ready, yet, to cast off into those waters. I texted Vic to tell him I had a new job, and he texted back: *Going to the dark side?!? Good for you. Drink soon? On you obvs.* Then he went quiet. He was probably busy with a story. I had a thought about Charlie, about how we might have celebrated a new job, a well-paid and objectively good job, in the parallel life. I started thinking about a wine bar in the city, or a restaurant table by the harbour somewhere, but then the fact of Charlie's absence, of his abandonment, reared and I felt pathetic, then angry. Wherever he was, he wasn't thinking about us. I thought about telling Tom, but I had an instinct he wouldn't like me taking this job. He always said I was a good writer. He thought I should write books. He once said he would want to read any book that I wrote.

*

It was early evening. I had a night off work and I was reclining on my couch like a tired lizard. I summoned the stupidest show I could find on the TV. It was called *Love Shack*. A group of 20 contestants were assigned their 'one true love' by a panel of experts. The twist was that none of them was told who their one true love was, so they had to shag their way around each other until they found the person they believed was their match. The show's action took place inside a large compound on a tropical island. It was diabolical, although the premise was not too dissimilar to the plot of *A Midsummer Night's Dream*, I thought. My phone rang, and a voice told me Sam was having an episode of some kind. A 'possible cardiac event'. I asked for Cherry, but Cherry wasn't there, the voice said. Cherry was on leave. She was probably visiting her children in the Philippines, taking over some money for them, and I had a brief vision of her arriving at an airport terminal, a small troupe of children, in a von Trapp-family range of sizes and ages, flinging themselves upon her like darts at a dartboard. I drove across town to the eastern suburbs hospital where Sam had been taken. It happened to be the same one where my mother had taken Maddy on that awful night a few weeks ago, when I had been out getting high while my daughter had struggled to breathe.

Sam was in the emergency department. I said his name to the concierge and a tired woman in hospital scrubs walked past me and gestured down the hall. I found him on a gurney in a ward with two other patients, both of whom were asleep, or unconscious, in such a resounding way that I would have thought they were dead, but for the activity of the machines they were hooked up to. The machines showed various signs of life – beeps, lights, flashing numbers. Uncle Sam was the only patient awake. He seemed small in his hospital robe. The robe was short-sleeved, and the flesh of his arms was puckered and frail-looking, like the skin of a de-feathered bird. He was propped up on his bed, which had been elevated to sit him at a 45-degree angle. He had a notepad resting on his knees and was scribbling in it. As I entered, he looked up.

'Darling,' he said. 'They shouldn't have called you. Turns out it's only my gallbladder. It's coming out first thing in the morning. I'm sorry to have worried you. What did you do with Maddy?'

Betty had been unavailable at short notice, and Beverley and my father were not picking up their phones. They often went to the movies in the early evening, and in any case my dad treated his mobile like a precious resource, only turning it on when he wanted to make a call himself. In the end, I had called Jan, who flapped over in a jiffy, sitting herself down on the couch in my lieu. She would just watch a bit of *Love Shack*, she said. 'Don't worry about me.'

'Maddy's fine,' I said to Sam. 'Tell me what happened to you.'

Sam had been in his pyjamas early, about 6 pm. He said he liked to prepare for bed well in advance, because at his age sleep could often catch you by surprise, and at his age, he didn't like surprises of any kind. He had been watching the weather report on television. The weatherman predicted heat, endless heat which only varied in its type, humid or dry, but never in the unrelenting nature of its hotness. As he looked at a panel of sun icons with numbers next to them which ranged between the high 30s and the low 40s, Sam ate a biscuit, and was assaulted with pain which striped through him like a fast cat. It started high, in his chest cavity, and he thought about the ordinariness of a death by heart attack, and yet there was nothing ordinary about this feeling, this pain which was now working its way downwards towards his stomach and finally, settling itself with a punch in his abdomen, where it met with nausea. He began to vomit, and pressed the assistance button which was positioned in a discreet spot next to his reclining chair. A wealthy person's ageing, infirmity and eventual death is attended by service personnel, even if it is ultimately endured alone, just like a poor person's. Three nurses and one on-call doctor were soon crowding the room, and a concierge called an ambulance. Sam's pain was eased in the ambulance by a woman with long hair and firm hands who reminded him of his sister, long dead. He was confused by the fast pace of events, and by the pain which continued to fill him like electricity in a light bulb, so strong and alive that he felt he must be pulsating with it, that there must be some evidence of it on the outside of him, something visual like a force-field, or an aura. And then this woman appeared, a face above him from his past, kindly inquiring what his name was and could he tell her what year it was. 'We used to ask people who the Prime Minister was,' she said as she laced a tourniquet around his arm, and eased a needle into him with calm authority. 'We don't anymore, for obvious reasons.' He had been determined to show off, and supply the name of the current prime minister anyway, Sam said, but his speech wasn't working well and Emily – his sister, his paramedic, this woman – told him to stop talking and rest. He didn't want to rest, he said, he wanted to live, but his surroundings grew vague and his consciousness melted to nothing as the drugs iced through his veins.

'I woke up in an examination room, groggy. That's when I knew I hadn't died. Wonderful feeling, incidentally. Anyway, they ran a few tests and turns out it's only my gallbladder. They can take it out tomorrow, keyhole surgery, and I'll be home in two days.'

Sam really was a marvel, calmly dismissive of the idea of death, still able to seek and find pleasure, in the crossword, in Cherry's company, in news of Maddy's escapades, in Mahler's Fifth and in the songs of Otis Redding. I wonder what he thought about as his life neared its end. Did he still lament its losses? Did he still feel exhilaration? Did he remember love with tenderness or was he angry that he never got more of it for himself, even though he gave so much of it out?

'Suzy, darling,' Sam said now. 'I'm absolutely desperate for a piss here. Be a dear and call the orderly, will you?'

*

I took my time on the drive home, flushed with relief that Sam was all right, and that Maddy was all right, and strangely euphoric that I had jagged a few hours out of the house in the evening. Usually I was either working, or chained to my home with an invisible thread which led to Maddy, asleep in her bed and unleaveable. Perhaps the to-be-discussed terms of the new job would allow for some sort of nanny, or a proper, non-teenage babysitter whom I could entrust with preschool pick-ups and complicated tasks like bathing and bedtime, someone who had completed high school and didn't have a boyfriend who hung off her like a surly chimpanzee. Perhaps the new job would open the door a crack, and allow in a chink of light, illuminate a path forward to a good life of breakfasts in a sunny kitchen, heels in my handbag for the daily commute, calendars marked in advance with holidays and birthdays and swimming lessons and plans, all sorts of plans. Maybe the new job, the money of it, the security of it, would give me and Maddy some space, some blessed room. Right now the only space I got, it felt, was the few seconds' walk around the back of the car to the driver's side, after strapping Maddy into her seat. Or the summer nights, after Maddy was in bed, when I rolled the bins out from the side of the house and onto the street, and looked up, catching a piece of the evening sky before returning to my place inside.

I called Jan to tell her I was coming home. She picked up on the third ring.

'Hello, chook,' she said breathlessly, as though she had been running. I told her that Sam was all right, and that I was on my way. She seemed to sense my light mood.

'It's only nine o'clock,' she said. 'Why don't you stay out a while? I am fine here. Just watching *Love Shack*. They're playing the episodes back to back. There are more love triangles here than a Danielle Steel. All the girls have these swimsuits which go up their bottoms now. Have you noticed that?'

'I think it's the Brazilian style,' I said. 'It's in vogue.'

'Looks uncomfy. Although I cannot deny the quality of the bottoms themselves,' Jan said. 'All is quiet here, love. Not a peep. You take a few hours if you need it.'

A small gift of time. Something prized above all other riches. A valuable resource, not to be squandered. I called Tom.

*

I swept from east to west in my newish car, and drove through the just-darkened streets to Tom's place. He lived in a terrace up the road from us. I could never keep track of its occupants. They seemed to change constantly. At one point there had been a minor actress, who became less minor when she landed a role in one of the long-running soaps. She abandoned her theatrical pretensions and moved to Melbourne for the show. I often wondered if Tom had slept with her. At some other stage, one of the upstairs rooms had housed a puppeteer who never paid rent on time, and there were often students – students of engineering, medicine, feminist studies, international studies, economic theory, economics. Back when Tom and I had been sleeping together, seeing each other, I had met them late at night, usually when I was coming to see him, or exchanged awkward, overly polite greetings with them as I nudged past them in a hallway, on my way to the bathroom. Tom was the unofficial *paterfamilias* of this constantly fragmenting group. He had the best room, at the front of the house, big, with high ceilings and a balcony which stretched along its flank. The balcony sloped slightly, outwards and downwards, tipping itself towards the street below. It was excellent for sitting on, on summer evenings like this, and that's what Tom was doing when I pulled up outside. He had a beer resting on his knee and a paperback in his hand. I got out of the car and stood for a moment with my hands folded on its roof, looking up at him.

'There she is,' he called down. 'The door is open. Come up. Grab a beer on the way if you want.'

I walked through the house, which was empty. Somewhere a radio was playing. Karen Carpenter was singing to the man she wanted to be close to. I walked up the stairs, which creaked, and into Tom's room. It was more or less as I had last seen it, with a few additions. There was a chest of drawers, solid timber, mid-century in style, that didn't look foraged, and on its surface were a few gleaming pieces of feminine stuff. A makeup compact, a small dish bearing earrings, and a bottle of Comme des Garçons perfume. Tom's books, which were usually strewn across the floor like autumn leaves, were stacked in rows next to the wall, and there was a piece from his exhibition leaning against the far wall, opposite the bed, framed but not hung. It was the Cerberus/greyhound that Boggo had liked so much. I walked out to join Tom on the balcony. He got up and kissed my cheek, and then told me to take his chair, because it was more comfortable. He sat on a rickety dining chair opposite me. He took my beer and opened it for me.

'Service,' I said.

'Some habits die hard.'

We looked at each other for a moment, and for me it seemed as though there was an affinity of feeling between us, which neither of us wanted to break by talking. Being in solitude with Tom felt like a surprise present. I wanted to sit with it in my lap for a moment before opening it.

'So –' I said, just as he started to speak.

'You go.'

'No, you go.'

'So you kept the Cerberus,' I said.

'I did. Everything sold, I was really lucky. But there were one or two pieces I couldn't part with. And I figured it was time I put something on my own walls.'

'Or leaned something against your own walls.'

'Yes. To actually hang a picture would be tempting fate, wouldn't it? It's a big commitment.'

'Indeed. And your generation hates commitment.'

Irritation flickered across Tom's face. I had noticed that he hated to be reminded of the age gap between us, as though it undermined him in some important way. I don't know why I did it. I suppose it was to put some distance between us.

'Although I notice you have committed to having perfume on your chest of drawers,' I said.

'Well,' said Tom, taking a swig of his beer. 'It just appeared there. You could have put any number of things on my chest of drawers while we were dating, and I wouldn't have minded.'

'So to speak.'

Tom laughed. I felt a cheap surge of happiness that I could still make him do that.

'So what is with the visit? To what do I owe the pleasure?'

'Oh, I was just passing by,' I said. 'In the neighbourhood.'

'Who's with Maddy?'

I told him that it was complicated, that the babysitter was the mother of the young woman who died after I wrote the story about her. That we had become friends, sort of. Tom listened to the anecdote and said nothing. He was very good at listening, and when I spoke he alternated between looking at my face and looking down into the throat of his beer, as though he could absorb what I was saying better if he concentrated his gaze on one point. I ended up telling him the whole story, of how I had received packages in the mail from someone who knew Tracey, and how Jan had appeared in my life one night, and I assumed the packages were from her, and she asked me to write an account of Tracey's life and although it might seem like a strange thing to do, I said yes.

'I don't think it's strange,' Tom said. 'I think it's nice. Like a form of atonement.'

When he said that word, atonement, it felt like some pressure had been released, like the shapeless, heavy thing that had been sitting on my chest these last few months had shifted its weight for a minute, allowing me to fill my lungs with air. I had never spoken to anyone about my guilt, about the cold certainty that lived in me that I had caused Tracey's death. It was a fact I woke to every day now, as steady and dependable as my obligation to get out of bed and make Maddy's breakfast, dress her, and send her off to preschool so I could make some money to keep the cycle going. I had never told anyone how the guilt was a sort of antimatter to joy, how it leached ordinary pleasures of colour.

'I know you feel guilty,' Tom said. He reached out and tapped his foot, giant in basketball boots, against my foot, less giant, in leather sandals. 'You shouldn't.'

I took a slug of my beer. 'Have you heard of the "but for test"? It's a test for causation they use in negligence law. In tort law.'

'No, but I think I can see where this is going.'

'You like Latin, right?'

'Well I'm into the Greeks mostly, but sure.'

'It's called the Sine Qua Non rule. But for X, would Y have happened? It establishes a simple chain of causation. It's lasted as a test for culpability for hundreds of years.'

'But you —'

'But for the story I wrote exposing Tracey Doran, she would not have killed herself.'

'You don't know that.'

'I think any court would rule that.'

'Life is not a court, Suzy!' Tom said. 'No one is passing judgement on you except yourself.'

Somewhere a fruit bat screeched.

'It's not the only thing I feel guilty for,' I said. 'I should never have slept with my boss. With Ben. It was wrong, obviously, because he was married, and that's another chain of causation I've probably kicked off, the end of his marriage.'

'If his wife dumped him, I think he also had something to do with it,' Tom said quietly. His expression had changed. He looked down at his hands and it seemed he was accessing a private bank of pain.

'I told myself I didn't owe his wife anything,' I said. 'Now I've changed my mind about that. I think we're all much more connected than that. But I did have an obligation to you.'

Tom said nothing. I could hear the dinking noise of a bicycle and I looked down to see the figure of a teenage girl, bony and insubstantial, riding past on the street. The air was still and her hair surged behind her like a flare, her legs working quickly, as though she was trying to speed up to the point where she could take flight. These days I often found myself looking at young girls with great tenderness, thinking about how Maddy would one day be one – a jumble of self-consciousness and need and foalish limbs. A fragile, strong thing. It was like the inverse feeling to nostalgia, like a tender longing for something that hasn't happened yet.

We fell to talking about other things. I asked Tom what he was reading and he picked up the paperback, and flipped it over so I could see the cover.

'*Jane Eyre!*' I said. 'I love that book.'

'I'm trying to do the classics,' he said. 'You know, educate myself.'

'Maybe it will inspire your next exhibition,' I replied. 'You could do a whole series on orphans. Or on governesses. Or on women who live in attics. To complement your harpies.'

'Governesses are cool,' Tom said. 'I wish I'd had one.'

'So do you like the book?'

'I do,' Tom said. He shifted his weight on his chair and went to get up. 'Do you want a vodka? I fancy a vodka.'

'Sure.' I watched as Tom walked past me. His limbs stretched in a way I always found enthralling. There was something athletic about his legs which made them look sprung, enthusiastic. I heard him descend the creaky staircase and ascend it again, and I took a minute to glory in the warmth of the air on my neck and legs. I felt pleasantly tired, in a relaxed way that loosened my own limbs. I took my sandals off and felt the boards of the balcony under my feet. The wood was worn into smoothness by the steps of unknown people who had walked over it during the life of the building. A frangipani tree dropped flowers on the balcony. They lay there like small white gloves.

'Whatchya thinking about?' Tom appeared at my side with what I assumed was a screwdriver. Small fibres of desiccated orange floated on the surface of the drink.

'I was just contemplating the age of this building and, you know, the cycle of life.' I took a sip. The vodka burned pleasantly in my throat. 'Tell me what you think about *Jane Eyre*.'

Tom took a thoughtful swig of his drink. 'I think it's a near-perfect depiction of loneliness. The intense craving for love. To be loved and understood.'

'It's a story of self-determination!' I said. I felt confident in my take. 'Of the drive to make your own way. You know, to be true to your own north. And how that conflicts with love. Jane loves Rochester but she has to leave him when she realises marrying him would compromise her integrity.'

'And yet she still marries him, right? I haven't got to the end yet, by the way. But I'm pretty sure she marries him.'

'Well I'm not telling you then,' I said, prudishly. I sipped my drink. We were silent for a moment.

'I guess I've never thought about the loneliness aspect,' I said, after a pause. 'To me it seemed like loneliness is Jane's natural state. It's so ingrained in her that she will live alone. That she will have to make her own way without any help. So she doesn't seek love. She doesn't have any expectation of it.'

'She thinks it's not her lot,' Tom said. 'But then she meets a sexy lord.'

'Is Rochester a lord?'

'Yeah, I dunno. Maybe just a generic aristocrat. But there is a class difference. That's important.'

'Yes. Jane only marries him once she's equal to him. She gets rich and he gets hobbled.'

'So they do marry. I knew it.'

'Oops,' I said.

'It's okay. Sometimes I enjoy a story more when I know how it's going to end.'

'I blame the disinhibiting effects of the screwdriver,' I said.

We sipped our drinks in silence as a couple of bats made dark shapes in the still sky over our head.

'Do you ever feel lonely?' I asked him.

Tom looked at me and cocked one eyebrow. 'Wow. Okay. Real talk,' he said. He held his glass up to the streetlight as if to appraise its quality. He drank from it. 'Of course I do,' he said. 'It's part of the human condition. Maybe that sounds like a wank, but it's true. People who expect never to be lonely are just more likely to be lonely. You can't expect life to be happy. You can only hope that it will be fulfilling.'

'True,' I replied. 'But loneliness is on the rise. It's an epidemic. I read an article in *The Atlantic* about it. Therefore it must be so. Social fragmentation caused by social media, the changing nature of families, digital disruption, et cetera.'

'I think probably my generation –' Tom said. 'There you go, do you like that? My generation?' He looked over at me and nodded. 'Members of *my generation* are not very good at being alone. They are so used to performing their lives on social media that they experience no genuine solitude. Solitude in a positive way, I mean. And learning to love the good kind of solitude is a necessary skill if you want to avoid loneliness.'

'Yes. But people on social media always talk about it being a community. When done right, obviously,' I said. 'And surely it's a good thing for people who are already socially isolated. Or mums' groups. I swear mums' groups make up 80 per cent of internet content, and only, like, 20 per cent is porn.'

Tom laughed. 'It's 100 per cent guaranteed that someone in your Facebook mums' group will be awake at 3 am when you're having a dark night of the soul. Are they actually supportive, though? Like, which of those women online is going to come to your house with a meal or, I dunno, give you a shoulder rub, or whatever.'

'Moral support. They give moral support.'

'It's easy to give moral support online. It's often insincere anyway. Don't you think?' Tom replied. 'Just another performative pose. The supportive friend, you know the kind, cheerleading for their contemporaries' successes online. Inside you know they're seething with professional jealousy.'

I thought about Tracey, with her shoutouts and generous hashtagging, how she was always engaging with her followers online, adopting a role of guide, role model, kindly prefect and fun big sister, her positivity so relentless and urgent that it felt hostile, almost; always projecting a bubble-like vision of organic perfection, forever dressed in pastel linens, the light of her photographs over-exposed so her whole world had the retro-charm aura of a seventies Super 8 film. Her online world was edged with gold. Blonde heads haloed with light. Tumbling gardens and perfect kitchens, shelves lined with Bakelite jars in sorbet colours. All that *content*. Yet her interior life was opaque.

'Haven't artists always been like that?' I said. 'Jealous and spiteful?'

'True.'

'People share things online,' I said. 'They connect with each other.' I had absolutely no allegiance to this line of argument, in fact I probably disbelieved it. But I liked to talk with Tom, to toss an idea around like Maddy played with a balloon – chasing it to make sure it never touched the ground.

'That's the major problem. That's what I'm talking about,' Tom said. 'People see a sunset, or a flower, or a pair of girls catfighting on a train, and the first impulse is to take a picture and share it online. Nobody observes things anymore, or savours them, or, heaven forbid, keeps them private, kept special. They share them online. But they're not really sharing. They're claiming. They're claiming the experience as their own. So all experience is cheapened into a form of boast.'

Tom dipped his head back and brushed his hair back from his face. He looked at me. 'Lecture over.'

I smiled back. 'Say what you like about the mothers' groups,' I said. 'And trust me, I do. But they have provided me with excellent advice on the treatment of cracked nipples. Also incontinence. It's a safe space for the incontinent.'

'Well I retract my earlier comments.'

'The incontinent are one of society's most marginalised groups,' I said, and then, after a beat: 'Sorry. Too much information.'

'With you, too much information is never enough.' Tom looked over at me and his dark eyes looked bright and nocturnal, like a friendly marsupial's.

'Tell me what's going on with you,' he said.

'*Welllll*,' I said, stretching my arms above my head. 'As a matter of fact, I've just been offered a new job.'

'That's awesome,' Tom said. 'Where?'

I told him the name of the company. 'They're taking me on as a senior consultant. I'll do media strategy, crisis management, that sort of thing.'

Tom said nothing.

'They're well regarded,' I continued. 'They have a good client list. They do media companies, some of the government agencies. Some of the big banks.'

'But you won't like that,' Tom said. 'Since when do you want to work on that side?'

'Lots of journalists do it,' I said. 'Being a reporter is exhausting. I was tired. That's why I made the mistakes I did. You have all these divided loyalties, between your sources and your readers and yourself. It's exhausting.'

'So now you'll go work for a company that spins for big corporates and mining companies,' he said. 'Good way to eliminate conflicts of interest.'

I looked over at him, astonished by his tone. I had never heard him speak sarcastically before. I responded in kind.

'You understand I have to earn money, right?' I said. 'I have a small daughter to support. We can't all live the entitled fantasy of the artist in his dilapidated share house. I don't want to live on foraged furniture. Does that make me problematic?'

'Is that how you see me?' said Tom. 'Do you really think I'm that basic?'

I knew Tom's mother was a school teacher. I knew his father had left the family when he was small. Unlike Danton and probably most of his contemporaries and competitors, Tom could not really afford to be an artist.

'You're calling me a sellout,' I said. 'It's inherently privileged, not to mention spineless, to judge other people's choices like that. Come back to me when you've got a kid.'

'I thought your Uncle Sam rents your place to you for cheap.'

Tom had met Sam once, last spring, when my uncle had come to Ruby Street for lunch. Afterwards we had walked up to Tom's café for coffee and cake. On the walk back down the hill, Sam had asked what was between me and the handsome waiter. Nothing, I said.

'It's cheap rent which will run out the day he dies, which is statistically likely to happen fairly soon,' I said. 'Much as I hate the thought.'

'So you'll find somewhere else to live,' he said. 'There's a couple of rooms coming up here in April. Mindy has some fellowship in Berlin. Chelsea is moving home to her folks' place to save for a deposit.'

'Jesus.' I felt a surge of contempt for Chelsea, whoever she was. For Mindy, whoever she was, there was jealousy. I had always wanted to go to Berlin.

'Do they have fossil fuel companies on their client list?' Tom asked. 'I bet they do.'

'Oh for goodness sake.' I swallowed the last of my screwdriver. I needed to get home. It had been a mistake to come. Now I was slightly drunk and had to deal with Jan on my couch. She would probably want to discuss *Love Shack* and Brazilian bikinis. I suddenly felt tired in a bone-deep way, so tired it was impossible to imagine a time when I would not be, or remember a time when I had not been.

'You walk around with such a sense of righteous aggrievement, Suzy,' Tom said, flaring in anger in a way that surprised me, even beneath my own anger. 'You act as though your life stopped when your ex left you. He didn't put a spell on you. You're not paralysed.'

'I've got to go,' I said, and I held up my empty glass. 'What should I do with this?'

'Just leave it,' Tom said. He looked morose. His eyebrows creased and as he stood up, he reached out to me, touching my arm as I turned to walk through the open doors to his room. He said my name.

'I have to go,' I said.

As I walked out I caught a glimpse of Tom's closet, a double-doored thing made of chipped plywood, which looked like something that had been in his bedroom since boyhood, and had endured one too many moves since then. It was full of clothes, mostly T-shirts, which had been touchingly placed on coat hangers, like they did at the high-end stores where T-shirts cost upwards of $50. Amid the hang of navy and greys there was a panel of printed colour which I figured was one of Jess's dresses, something with toucans on it. I envied her ability to take up visual space with her prints and her colours and the luxuriant size of her body. She made no apology for herself. She was happy to be looked at, and she accepted the looking quite brazenly. Jess was magnificent, with her toucan-print attitude to life. In my jealousy I wished something on her, something which would take her away from Tom. And then, just past the toucan print, under it, behind it, obstructed by the stem of a squash racquet, I saw my own face, and the splay of my limbs on a mattress. My face was asleep, deeply, like I had been given a narcotic. Tom had not sold *Harpy 8*. He had hung onto it, and then he had shoved it down the back of his wardrobe. Not to share, or to show, but to keep.

CHAPTER 23

Ten minutes later I was back in front of the Ruby Street terrace. The upstairs was dark and the downstairs was lit up like an electrified doll's house. I guessed Jan must still be up. It was half past eleven and *Love Shack* would be over, but I knew that after *Love Shack*, there was a panel show which discussed *Love Shack*, dissecting the various couplings and Shakespearean misunderstandings that had occurred in that week's episode. The panel featured former contestants of the show, who had surprised but otherwise expressionless expressions, and hair extensions as coarse as hemp rope. Discussion was led by a woman from the television network who used to anchor the news. I opened the door and called out to Jan, kicking my shoes off in the hallway and throwing my purse down. I walked past the living room. The *Love Shack* panel discussion – it was called *Love Shack Live*, I remembered now – burbled on the television, but the room was empty. One of the panellists was waggling a finger at another, who was finger-waggling back, and the fallen newsreader was attempting to break up the waggle-off. I called out to Jan but heard nothing. I walked through to the kitchen, which was very still and very quiet, and there she was, sitting at the table, her head just below the breakfast bar where my herbs were lined up, like children in formation. Jan was sitting in a stilted way that sparked an alarm in me, with her hands on her knees and her back straight, like she had been instructed to sit up tall for a photograph, or had been frozen while meditating.

'Jan –' I said, entering the kitchen. 'Why –'

She stayed still as a stroke victim, but her eyes veered wildly around her, like she had locked-in syndrome and was trying to communicate something complex, but without the help of a talking computer. Even for Jan, it was strange behaviour.

'Are you all right?' I said, and as I moved towards her, I heard a footstep behind me on the stairs, and a squinching in my gut told me the answer better than Jan could. No, she was not all right. It was not all right.

'Hello.' A voice behind me. I turned and saw him – a large man, about 60, with shoulders that sloped fleshily downwards to strong biceps, biceps layered in the decades-old fat of the Australian male, a person who has lived his life in contravention of all heart disease warnings about the consumption of meat and alcohol. Right now, though, he looked calm enough, this man in my kitchen. He was wearing a navy shirt I would have called dressy; it was long-sleeved and had two small buttons which kept the collar neat. It was a shirt that would get you into a golf club. Below the shirt, a different personality was on show. He wore a pair of flimsy shorts, from which sprouted the powerful legs of a man who had once played some sort of rugby, either league or union, and whose muscles kept the memory of it. I looked into his face. It was broad, with a strong nose at its centre, shaped like a root vegetable. His eyes were blue and his eyelashes were long, which gave his face a tenderness it didn't otherwise deserve. His hair was darkly golden, just like his daughter's. I recognised him as the man in the raincoat from last week. I didn't need to ask who he was.

'Terry,' said Jan, from behind me. 'Terry is here.'

'And you must be Suzy,' he said. 'Pleased to meet you in the flesh. At last. You're a pretty thing, but too thin for me. I like my women with upholstery. Isn't that right, Jan?'

'Maddy.' The word was a croak. A plea.

'She's safe,' Jan said. She met my eyes and nodded firmly. 'She's asleep.'

'Unlike our daughter, I might say,' said Terry, and he made a dry laughing noise.

'Let me just go see her,' I said, and I made towards the kitchen doorway. Terry, who was standing in it, put his hand silently on the doorframe. His arm crossed it diagonally, like a buttress.

'Go and sit next to my wife, for a minute,' he said, his voice low. 'I come in peace. I'm not going to hurt your girl. I came here to get something that belongs to me.'

I turned and walked to sit next to Jan. My mind was turning quickly through scenarios and outcomes, risks and possibilities. He didn't seem to be armed. Could the two of us overpower him? I knew with utter certainty that I would find a way to kill or maim him before I let him go near Maddy.

'He hasn't hurt her, I swear,' Jan whispered to me as I sat next to her. 'She's asleep. She's not harmed. He took my phone.'

My heart leapt in my chest like a panicked bird. My vision swam. I thought about my phone, which was inaccessible, tucked in my handbag, which was slung over the banister to the staircase. I thought about all the decisions, the small and blind choices, that had brought me to this point. Terry walked forward and stood before us in the kitchen like a malignant obelisk, if an obelisk wore shorts and had varicose veins. He was someone clearly at ease with the behaviour of intimidation, but there was something pronounced and actorly about him too, as though this form of masculinity had not come naturally to him, but he had chosen it, quite consciously, and studied it to get it right. Who was he copying? The men on panel shows about football? The hand-breaking standover guys of mafia B-movies? His own father? He had in him all the striding, owning, bullying men of the world. Watching those men had taught Terry to hone his expression into a weak snarl, and his body into a mass of meat and bone which could move to violence quickly, like a switch had been thrown.

'So,' he said, moving closer to us. 'You girls have become good friends. Jan says you've been spending a lot of time together. Making nice. Getting cosy.'

He took one of the chairs from the table and placed it in the middle of the kitchen's black-and-white chequered linoleum floor, a few yards from us. He spun the chair so its back was facing us, and sat astride it, like he was Liza Minnelli and this was a cabaret. The action strained his flimsy shorts, and from them popped, sideways, a solitary testicle, like a puce-coloured quail egg.

I glanced at Jan, whose expression did a quick dance from amusement to contempt to fear. I felt disgust and pity and hoped it wasn't visible on my face. Jan cleared her throat to speak.

'Turns out Terry has been watching me for about a month,' she said. 'He noticed our meetings, and he recognised you, of course, from the paper. He wanted to know why we've been meeting.'

'Did you tell him?'

'I said together we were working on a project. A way of honouring Tracey.'

'And do you know what I said to that?' Terry interjected. 'I said that she should be ashamed of herself for even speaking to the cunt who killed our daughter.'

The funny thing about Terry at this point, apart from the fact that he had a single nut poking from his shorts like a surprise puppet, was that it was a relief to hear him say that out loud. He was the large and hulking personification of my guilt. He was like a visitation from a classical story, a vengeful god with blunt fingernails, the nose of a boxer, and no underpants. I thought of Jan, dancing around him all those years, trying different strategies not to get hit – staying silent, placating him, avoiding him, appeasing him. She had told me about the liberation of giving up these strategies, which never worked anyway, and giving in to the inevitability of the blow, turning towards it with a full face. I was adrenalised now, fully lit up. I wondered what form his vengeance would take. I waited to find out.

'I have tried to tell Terry,' Jan said. She was keeping her voice even, but she had to work at it. 'That what happened, is nobody's fault. People always blame themselves when this type of tragedy occurs.' She spoke as if she was repeating talking points. 'But the truth is no one killed Tracey. She killed herself.'

A giant tear snuck from one of Terry's blue eyes and plopped on the seat, an inch or two from his exposed testicle.

'I miss my girl,' he said. He sounded like a sulky child.

Jan sighed heavily. 'We all do, Terry.' She paused. 'She was there for a long time before she died, too, you know. A long time when you weren't seeing her. But you didn't seem to be missing her then,' she said. 'Not so much that you would get off your bum to come see her.'

I glanced at Terry, wondering if this would provoke him to anger. It did.

He slammed the heel of his hand on the back of the chair. It was an attempt to be dramatic but the sound was muted and the gesture must have hurt.

'You think I don't regret that now?' he shouted. 'I remember the last talk I had with her. We fought. I told her I knew she was lying and that her Grandma Shirl would be turning in her grave.'

'Grandma Shirl was Terry's mother,' Jan said to me. 'She died of cancer. She had great big knots of it, all through her. Not to speak ill of the dead but she was a real old bitch, Grandma Shirl. The first time I met her she asked me why I had come to her house dressed as a dishcloth. Nobody in her own family liked her.'

'Watch it, Jan!' Terry snarled.

'You know it's true,' Jan said quietly. She tilted her chin upwards in defiance.

'The doctor says I have PTSD,' said Terry. He looked downwards while he massaged his hand, the one he had used to hit the chair.

I glanced at Jan, who looked back at me and gave a quick eye-roll.

'You can get counselling for that,' she said to Terry. 'And drugs. They have drugs for everything now. All tested on rats.'

'My heart is broken,' Terry tried again.

Jan gave a small snort of irritation, well suppressed, so that only I could hear it. 'We are all in pain, Terry,' she said. She spoke slowly. 'Your feelings are your feelings, and not a soul could argue with them. But we don't have to slather our feelings all around the place, do we. Slop them all over other people. There's no sense making others pay for what happened to us.'

'There's a lot of sense making her pay for what happened,' he said, looking at me. 'If she hadn't written her story, Tracey would still be here. And we wouldn't be here. Like, where we are right now. In Sydney.' He paused. 'I fuckin' hate Sydney.'

'You need to leave, Terry,' said Jan. 'Suzy needs to get to bed. I'm tired and my ankles are swollen like buggery. There's no sense to this, whatever it is you think you're doing, and you need to let us go.'

'Who says I'm holding you here?' he said, a smile creeping into his mouth. He had a wide mouth, like it had been stretched sideways with pliers at some point in early life. It opened to reveal a surprisingly white set of teeth. 'You're free to leave, as soon as I have what I want.'

'And what is that?' Jan asked. She sounded tired, like she was struggling not to lose her temper. I recognised the tightness in her voice because it was exactly the way I spoke to Maddy when she asked for one more book, or requested Weet-Bix for breakfast and then cried because she wanted toast.

'Where's that story you've been writing?' Terry asked me.

'It's on my computer,' I said. 'It's only a draft. I haven't written the final version yet.'

'And where's your computer?'

'Upstairs.'

'Let's go get it.'

Terry wanted the story of his daughter. For what? To read it, to take it? He jerked his head to indicate I should stand up, so I did. I walked towards him and he stepped aside from the kitchen doorway, moving his hand with a courtly flourish to let me pass. He followed me, his breathing placing him at a point behind me, too close, as I walked to the staircase and up it. I was hyper-aware of Maddy's warm, biscuit-scented presence in her room. As I walked past her bedroom I glimpsed her, lit in the pink halo of her night light. The rise and fall of her chest told me she was asleep, and unharmed. I walked into my bedroom, where my laptop lay shuttered on the desk near the French doors. I untethered it from its plug, turned and passed it to Terry.

'Ta, love,' he said, as though I had handed him a mug of tea. 'We can go back downstairs now.'

We walked back to the kitchen where Jan was sitting in her place at the table, still with her hands on her knees like a terracotta warrior.

'You all right, chook?' she said to me as we entered.

'She's all right, Jan,' said Terry. 'Don't worry about her.'

Terry used his big hands to open the laptop and stabbed at the On button. The familiar music of the computer rebooting broke the silence of the kitchen. Terry's meaty face shone blue with reflected light. Jan and I exchanged glances.

'Come here, love,' Terry said to me. 'You can drive this thing. Show me the article you've written about my girl.'

Now was not the time for it, but I felt a flash of great irritation because I've always hated people, anyone, reading my copy before it's ready for other eyes. My story on Tracey had a strong beginning, I thought, but was patchy and unfinished. I had large notes to myself strewn throughout the copy, written in caps, like 'INFO IN HERE ABOUT UNI DEGREE' and 'WHAT BREED IS THE DOG??'

But I wanted Terry out of my house, so I opened the document that contained the story, and I stood aside so he could read it. I winced inwardly as he did. Jan and I watched as he scanned it, his long eyelashes twitching. He was silent for a minute or so, completely immersed, and then he shut the laptop with a bang, startling Jan and me. He stood up, flipping his chair backwards so it landed on the linoleum like a shot bird.

'The usual bullshit,' he said. 'I've read plenty of your stuff. I've been following you. Set up a Google alert. Tracey showed me how to do that, back when we were still talking. Your stuff –'

He nodded at me. I felt the adrenaline in my system drop away, and my fatigue returned, deep as the bed of the ocean. I understood then that Terry wanted an audience. He wanted to be heard. He was more interested in his feelings about his daughter's death than he was about his daughter's death. Much less in her life, which I had attempted, probably pathetically, to describe, as a monument of words for her mother.

'Your stuff is full of facts and big words and all the usual bullshit of people who try to make themselves sound smart by using facts and big words,' Terry snarled. 'I know you think you're better than my daughter. I bet you come from a real rich family.'

I looked down. I decided against explaining to Terry my father's entanglement with the sub-prime crisis, his exposure to American debt instruments, and my parents' exclusion, for financial reasons, from membership of the yacht club. I said nothing.

'Yep, knew it,' Terry said. 'Rich bitches like you think you can do whatever you like to other people. I've got one question for you.'

I waited.

'I wanna know why you wrote about my daughter. I've had a good look at the sorts of shit you write about. Kiddy-fiddlers. Rugby players who rape girls stupid enough to get into cars with them. That big-deal celebrity chef who ripped off his workers. Why would you pick on my girl? What harm was she ever doing?'

'I didn't go after Tracey,' I said. 'It wasn't like I was targeting her. I got an email with a tip-off about her. And so I decided to look into it.'

'Who was the email from?' Terry asked. He seemed surprised.

'I don't know.'

Jan, who had been silent for several minutes, let out a strange sound which landed someone between a howl and a snarl. I looked over at her and saw she was shaking, her body shimmering under the swirling pink and purple print of her blouse.

'For the love of fucking Christ, Terry!' Jan shouted. 'Does it matter? Does any of it matter? Will any of this bring her back? You parading around here with your balls out, demanding answers and who knows this and that about the story Suzy wrote? Tracey is gone. Every single thing you're doing is making it worse than it already is.'

Terry looked taken aback. 'I think it does matter, actually,' he said, wounded. 'And my counsellor said I needed closure. That's what I'm trying to get here. A little bloody closure.'

Jan snorted with contempt. 'Good luck with that.'

'Well, thank you, Jan,' said Terry. His demeanour had changed in reaction to her outburst. Now he was polite in an exaggerated way, as though he was the civilised one here. He moved towards the laptop again. 'Do you still have that email? That original one?' he asked me. 'Is it in here?'

I kept meticulous records. The email, I knew, was filed in a folder in my webmail.

'Yes,' I said. I didn't think there was any point, at this point, in lying about that, or anything.

'Let's take a look, shall we,' he said, and he went back to the laptop and opened it again. This time it popped back into life quickly, like a light sleeper who needs to be alert at short notice.

'Terry, don't bother,' said Jan. 'You don't have to sleuth around like you're Sherlock bloody Holmes. I know who sent that email. *I* sent that email.'

'Are you fucking kidding me?' he said, to her. His eyes looked frightened. And then to me: 'Open your email. Show me.'

I took the laptop. The email was easy to find: it was in the folder, just where I had filed it. I opened it. Now that I knew her, I realise it did sound like Jan. I passed the computer back to Terry to read. He did so while swallowing rapidly, his Adam's apple undulating under his skin.

Jan avoided my eyes, and instead looked down at her hands, which were laid in her lap, upturned, like the hands of a postulant.

Then Terry snapped shut the laptop and took a couple of quick steps towards Jan. He stood over her, the computer in his right hand, brandishing it above her like a silver bludgeon. If he brought the laptop down on Jan's skull now, he would crack it in half like a golden bowl. I cried out, but just as I did so, Terry lowered his hand and crumbled in front of Jan like she was an altar. He placed his enormous head on her lap and it shook as he cried into her skirt, great heaving cries that came from someplace deep in him, the same place which bred the violence – a place of need, and fear, and sorrow. Jan remained impassive, her face unreadable. She did not respond at all to Terry's touch and barely seemed aware of it.

After a while she said quietly, 'I thought it might stop her. I thought if she faced some consequences, it might stop her.'

Terry raised his head like a giant hound rousing from a sleep, and climbed to his feet slowly. He took the laptop in his hand, walked to the sink, placed the computer in it, and turned the taps on, hard, so the water splashed back against the crotch of his flimsy shorts. Next to the sink I kept a ceramic urn which held kitchen implements, and from it he extracted a silver meat mallet, which I used to pound the veal fillets I turned into schnitzel for Maddy. He held it high above his head and brought it down hard on the wet laptop, and I heard the dull sound of denting metal, with a sickly high note of broken glass. Jan was slumped forward now, with her chin meeting the rise of her chest. Her breathing had quickened and seemed irregular. I worried about her blood sugar, and her heart. After several strikes on the laptop, Terry turned around from the sink, and I saw the dull glint of the mallet in his hand. Time slowed down as I waited for him to raise it high again, and advance upon us, and through the swim of my fatigue, my nerves tingled with readiness to fight him, to take him on, to find a weapon and force this man away from us.

Terry dropped the mallet. It landed with a dull noise on the lino. All was quiet for a moment as we watched him, and I could hear the rushing of the water in the sink, where Terry had left the taps on. I could hear the chatter of the television as *Love Shack Live* soldiered on in the living room, oblivious to us. Terry didn't look at us again before he walked out of the kitchen, opened the front door and exited the house. I heard the swing and flap of the mail-slot as he closed the door behind him.

*

We waited a minute or two after Terry left. Relief married with my fatigue and I felt light-headed.

'Jan,' I said. I spoke in a whisper.

'Yes, love.'

'My article. About Tracey,' I said. 'I didn't have it backed up. I meant to put it on a thumb drive. I'm an idiot. I'm sorry.'

Jan didn't respond, so I repeated myself. 'I am so, so sorry, Jan.'

As I spoke, a sob escaped from my throat and it seemed to hover in the air between us like a live thing, communicating something unsayable, something I could write thousands of words about but never catch the meaning of so well as this single noise.

'You're right, duck,' Jan said. 'You're all right.'

CHAPTER 24

When Charlie and I were together, before he departed for places unknown, before he left me, or I left him, or we left each other, I had often wondered how we would *end up*. That was the term I thought of, and how I expressed it to him too. 'How do you think we'll end up, you and me?' I had asked him once, when we were in bed, me with a novel, him with his phone, scrolling endlessly down through the screen, his thumb moving lazily but never ceasing, as though he was trying to get to the very bottom of the internet. I wondered what riches that phone held for him, but once I got a taste of what they were, I wish I hadn't wondered.

'Huh?' he said. He kept scrolling.

'Where do you think we'll end up?' I repeated. 'You and me.'

I don't know what I expected him to say, but I think I knew early, even when Maddy had only been a curled, semi-formed vertebrate in my abdomen, more notion than flesh, that one day she would end up strapped to my chest and I would be walking alone with her. I think I asked him this to force the issue, because I had grown so frustrated and lonely that I was hoping he would just leave me. Our relationship had become a game of chicken.

'I don't know,' he said. 'Who can know what might happen? Humans were not meant to mate for life. People only did that back when life expectancies were like, 40.'

Maddy was at that stage about six months old. As this conversation took place, she lay sleeping in her crib beside our bed. She was a perfectly formed baby, like one of those dolls advertised in women's magazines, the ones that are dressed in christening gowns that frill like sea foam, and made to be as lifelike as possible. But unlike those dolls, Maddy would wake up soon enough, and wail for the milk in my swelling breasts. They would hurt if I didn't respond to her needs – that's how painfully interdependent we were. After feeding she would need burping and settling, and at some point during the cycle, Charlie would heave to his feet, clasping his phone in his hand, and a pillow in the other, and stalk out of the room to sleep on the living room couch. This was not a perfect moment to hear about the ephemeral nature of all human connection. He looked over at me and squeezed my hand, as though in consolation.

'Why did you ask me to marry you, then?' I asked.

'Well exactly,' he said, nonsensically. 'I'm here now, aren't I? It's unrealistic to expect one person to be your lover and your soul mate for your whole life.'

He went back to his phone and me to my book, and I didn't say what I was thinking, because his manner left no room for sentimentality. The main thing I'd hoped for, and what I still hoped for, if I was honest, was not a lover or a soul mate – although that would be nice – but someone who would, one day, be an old friend. Someone with whom I could survey the vast sprawl of life and somehow make sense of it.

*

We called the cops, and they arrived with blue strobing lights that ricocheted off the fig tree and the walls of the living room. We turned off *Love Shack Live*, where a girl with pink hair was arguing with a man whose muscles were so big they seemed to impede movement rather than enable it. Jan seemed to be in shock; she was shivering and silent. All my enervation had disappeared again, and I was hyper-alert and strangely euphoric, which I supposed was also a form of shock. I put a blanket around Jan and made her tea. I made her eat a biscuit. When the police arrived, I did all the talking. I spilled the whole story in hurried sentences. There was a male cop and a female cop, and both were young – in their late-twenties, I guessed. The female cop took off her blue hat to reveal a ponytail, slicked back and high on her head, like a cheerleader's. She did most of the questioning, her colleague taking notes in a pad.

After taking the facts from me, the female cop sat down next to Jan and looked at her steadily, and she asked her: 'Does your ex-husband have a history of abuse?'

Jan nodded.

'Would you characterise that abuse as physical, emotional or financial?' asked the lady-cop.

'All of the above, officer.'

They said they would take formal statements from us the following day at the station, and they put out an alert for Terry, who was at large. They said they would drop Jan home. I gave her a long, deep hug and watched her get into the police car. The male cop opened the door for her, and placed a hand above her head to prevent her bumping it as she climbed onto the seat. They drove away in a blue flash. I went upstairs and lay down next to Maddy, who snuffled like a piglet and curved herself into me. I laid my face in her hair. She was curled in the foetal position, mimicking her younger self.

*

They picked Terry up about half an hour later. He was sitting up at the bar at the Little Friend, drinking a vegan lager, his large head propped on the brick of his fist. Jessica was working the bar that night, and she had just called last drinks when she saw the cops walk through the door. Jess hated cops, and she particularly objected to sniffer dogs in bars, which she said was a fascist practice. But these police were not drug cops. They walked up to Terry, and the woman with the high ponytail asked if he was Terry Doran, and he said yes. She placed him under arrest and cautioned him. Jess said it was all very civilised. Terry did not resist.

Down the hill on Ruby Street, I was asleep as Terry got taken away, and I stayed asleep until about 7 am, when I heard the distant, insistent noise of my phone ringing, and I walked heavily down the stairs to retrieve it, wondering if the events of last night had been real. I walked into the kitchen and saw the shards of glass from the laptop screen in the sink. The police had photographed and fingerprinted the computer itself, and taken it away for evidence. I retrieved the phone and answered it. The voice on the other end told me she was a nurse from the hospital where Sam had his operation. The voice said that Sam was dead.

'That's not possible,' I said. I was having trouble understanding what was happening. 'I saw him just last night. It was only his gallbladder.'

'I'm afraid, Ms Hamilton, that your great-uncle suffered a cardiac arrest during the operation,' she said. 'It should have been a routine procedure. But this happens sometimes with older patients. It was very quick and he was under anaesthetic, so he was unaware. I'm very sorry.'

With this phone call, another loss was layered into my life, changing its texture again. I looked around the kitchen, which was normal enough, the herb pots still there, Maddy's booster seat standing empty with its back to me, waiting for her to take her place in it and demand Weet-Bix. Outside, sun landed on the backyard, and inside, the air was pleasantly cool. By now, it was mid–February and it felt like all the world was aching for autumn, for a time when the air wasn't soup and it was possible to sit in the sun without scorching like an insect under a magnifying glass. I would have to tidy up the shattered glass before Maddy came down. I had to call my parents. I would need to find time to go to the police station for that statement. Check in on Jan. A funeral to be arranged. And now, I supposed, looking around my home, the wheels of probate would start to turn and when they stopped, Maddy and I would be put out of this house. I thanked the nurse on the phone. She said there were forms to sign, and I promised to come in later and sign them.

As I hung up I heard the flurried thudding of Maddy's footsteps on the ceiling, pattering down the hall, getting louder as she reached the staircase. *Dunk-dunk-dunk.* One of the many things I loved about Maddy was her resolve that if it was worth walking somewhere, it was worth running there. She always expected the place she was going to would be even better than the one she was coming from. She bounded towards her future. This exuberance was innate and it constantly refreshed itself. Her cheerfulness was invincible. She appeared in the kitchen now, her hair haphazard, like she had just slept off a bender, her voice croaky and her body still flushed from sleep. The life in her was a force-field that followed her when she ran.

'Good morning, Mummy,' she said. 'Who are you torking to on the phone?'

*

We found a place that would do the funeral the following week. Beverley wanted a church service. She said that Sam had been christened Catholic and educated Catholic, all the Hamiltons had, and while, sure, he didn't go in for it much in later life, the Catholics knew how to do these things.

'Why not leave it to them?' she said to me, sitting at her kitchen bench one evening, cigarette in hand. She spoke about the Catholics as though they were good caterers for a cocktail party.

But I said no to the Catholics. Sam had told me about the priest who had been his football coach at the vast sandstone building, the Hogwarts by the harbour, where he had been schooled from ages six to 16. Athletic, inquiring and clever, Sam should have been a Jesuit princeling, perhaps even marked out for the priesthood himself. He might have taken orders, had it not been for Father Dominic, who liked to strip his boys, rugby players, mostly, although he coached a bit of cricket too, and then line them up, naked, and trace the swell of their small, fragile buttocks with a strap he kept in his office. He told them he was checking their form, and he made approving noises about the boys with long legs and high buttocks, Sam told me, even though that wasn't, actually, the ideal rugby physique. Sam told me that one of the boys, a boarder whose parents lived on a remote station in western New South Wales, had become Father Dominic's pet, and was often in his office, and in his bedroom up in the dormitories. Sam felt faint pity for this boy, but mostly relief that his selection by the priest spared the rest of them, and the rest of them shunned the boy, which, in turn, pushed him closer to his priest. When Sam was in his fifties and exchanging pleasantries with a fellow old boy, a barrister he had briefed for a complex custody case, this barrister told him that the boy, of course since become a man like them, had killed himself recently, his wife discovering him in the garage one morning as she brought the bins in.

Sam told me all this when the Royal Commission into institutional child abuse was being held. It had triggered in him a tsunami of guilt and sorrow that he didn't understand, because he had lived his whole life with the subterranean knowledge of what had really happened to that boy, and it had not troubled him much until now. And after all, nothing had ever happened to *him*, to Sam. He told me the guilt was unbearably heavy. He kept being surprised by the pale, pointed face of this boy in his dreams. The traceline of the strap on the buttock. The door closing on the child with the remote parents. I wondered if that experience had been part of the reason why Sam had never come out. Perhaps it had confused him in some way and made his homosexuality a guilty thing, and the shame had stayed with him. I didn't ask and I never found out. After a week or so of distress, Uncle Sam smartened himself up, gave a sum of money to a victims' charity, and wrote a letter to the Royal Commission. Father Dominic was named in the eventual report as a paedophile – he had offended against other boys too, who were still alive to tell. By then he was 20 years dead.

So, no to the Catholics, experts though they were in death. Instead, I insisted we engage a celebrant and have a non-religious service at a crematorium in the northern suburbs, where suburbia gave way to pure bushland, and where Sam could have a plaque in a garden of banksia and flannel flowers.

We met the celebrant in his green-carpeted office one stormy afternoon. His name was Christopher. He wore a polka-dot bow tie. He had a ginger beard, an English accent, and his own YouTube channel. He listened to us earnestly, took notes, and exuded exactly the kind of steady-handedness I wanted.

'Well, darling,' said Beverley, as we walked to the car afterwards. 'He's a little ...' She held her pinky finger up in the air, I presumed, to indicate campness. 'Lovely though. Seems very sensitive,' she said.

Beverley always followed her casual prejudice with vague compliments, as though one cancelled out the other.

After meeting Christopher, Beverley and I drove over to Sam's retirement home, where Cherry unlocked his door for us and we walked through the last room of his long life, touching things tentatively, his death so fresh it felt like prying.

'What are we going to do with all this stuff?' I asked her.

'Well the Kiwis might want some of it,' she said. 'But you should take the rugs, darling. You were his favourite.'

I wandered across one of the carpets now, a golden silk thing that looked like it had been salvaged from an Italian castle. The room was bright, with a northerly aspect, and the armchair still carried the impression of Sam's light weight. His tea set stood on a tray on a side table, and his moccasins were lined up at the threshold to the bathroom, waiting at attention for his step. I had loved my great-uncle in a clear and strong way; there was no complication in it at all. And there was no complication in his adoration of me. No difficulties edging it. Something loosened and I started to cry. Beverley came up behind me and put a hand to my back.

'Oh, darling,' she said. 'My pet.'

I turned around and folded into her. She smelled like lipstick and Issey Miyake. I was assailed with self-pity.

'Sam really made me feel like a good person,' I wept. 'When I was with him, I felt like I was good.'

'You are good,' said my mother. 'I think you're wonderful.'

Her voice quavered and she patted me quickly on the bottom – one, two, three – just as she had done when I was a child, as a cue to tell me she had finished braiding my hair or buttoning my collar, a sign that she had adequately prepared me and I was ready to go out into the world. When

I was a teenager, I saw her preoccupation with appearances, with putting on a face to face the world, as superficial and contemptibly bourgeois. But when I was a little girl, Maddy's age, I had just enjoyed the petting. Now, as a mother myself, I saw Beverley's grooming of me as a system of care.

We broke our embrace and set about sorting and packing Sam's life. In the end it amounted to six crates of books, two of household items and miscellanea, three garbage bags of clothes, an elegant Panama hat, and a box of personal effects which included an old colour Polaroid of a handsome, wiry man who looked to be in his thirties, the sun streaming off him as he sat in a rowboat, on a body of water that I didn't recognise. In the photo, he was laughing at the person behind the camera, his chin tilted upwards, a cigarette leaning from his lips as he held the oars. The set of his body was upward-straining, happy. I asked Beverley who the man was, and she said she didn't know. I kept the photo, because it felt important. I have it still.

*

A week later we turned up at the crematorium, and were greeted by Christopher, smart as a polished brogue, walking the aisle of the function room we had booked, straightening stacks of memorial service booklets, and making notes on his run sheet. His competence was evident in the firmness of his step as he walked from the lectern to the flower display, readjusting the hydrangea. It was forecast to hit 41 degrees. Beverley was wearing a black bouclé skirt-suit and a black silk blouse with an elaborate pussy-bow, which draped just so, like the sail of a felucca boat. I suspected the suit was Chanel. Possibly it was vintage Pucci. My dad was there too, of course, ever the quiet companion to Beverley's busy energy. He was shaven but somehow still managed to look rumpled, even though his suit was expensive and Italian, the creases in the trousers falling in a perfect vertical. The suit had been selected by Beverley and tailored to her specifications, back when he had been working full time. Beverley had requested a morning service, 'because of the heat', she said, but we both knew it was because my father was better in the mornings. If he knew he could look forward to alcohol access at the wake following the service, he would be fine. I wondered if he could remember a time when he hadn't wanted a drink, and whether Beverley had done him a disservice by never issuing him with an ultimatum that forced him to choose between his loves.

At 10 am, people began to arrive. The faces were mostly old and white, like Sam's, and I made a game out of guessing who they were as we greeted them at the door. Former colleague. Former students (Sam had taught Family Law for a few years at Sydney Uni). Former lovers? Mid-stream, Cherry appeared, wearing a simple black dress, nylons and her nursing shoes. 'Your uncle was my favourite,' she whispered, and I asked after her children. 'So naughty!' she cried, beaming a smile, and she took a seat towards the back of the room. The Kiwi cousins came, and my mother introduced me to them, and said I must remember the time we met when I was, what, eight or nine years old? I had no memory of the Kiwis. They were my father's cousins and therefore Sam's nieces, and I tried not to think about what their presence here meant for my security of tenure at Ruby Street. There were three of them – the two nieces, stolid-looking, with the sensible haircuts of golfers or female politicians, and a man who I assumed was one of their sons. He looked to be in his mid-forties and was balding in an uneven way. He surprised me by winking at me as he shook my hand.

We sat at the front, me between my parents, both of whom had a way of breathing I found annoying – Dad's was heavy and tired, Mum's was shallow and irritable. Maddy was at preschool but I wished for a moment she was with me. I wanted the weight of her in my lap, and her small hands in mine.

Christopher stood bright-eyed at the lectern and switched on a smile. 'We are here today to celebrate the life of Sam Hamilton,' he began. 'Distinguished legal practitioner. Gifted pianist. Beloved uncle to Simon, Cynthia and Trudie. Affectionate great-uncle to Suzy and Timothy. And much-loved great-great-uncle to little Maddy.

'Over the course of the service, we will hear from Sam's loved ones about the kind of man he was. But first, I would like to invite Beverley Hamilton to the floor, to recite one of Sam's favourite pieces of prose.'

Christopher indicated to my mother, and she rose gracefully, in full awareness of the eyes of the room, and stepped lightly to the lectern. She placed her spectacles on her nose and announced her reading. It was John Donne. I had chosen it.

'No man is an island,' she read, 'entire of itself. Every man is a piece of the continent, a part of the main. If a clod be washed away by the sea, Europe is the less. As well as if a promontory were. As well as if a manor of thy friend's or of thine own were.'

Here Beverley paused. Her voice wavered prettily. Christopher placed a discreet hand on her shoulder and gave her a firm nod. She continued.

'Any man's death diminishes me, because I am involved in mankind. And therefore never send to know for whom the bell tolls: it tolls for thee.'

Beverley glided back to her seat and I handed her a tissue. She rejected it and extracted a linen handkerchief from her clutch purse, which my dad was holding.

'How's my makeup?' she whispered to me. I leaned over to wipe a black rivulet of mascara from her cheekbone. My mother's cheekbones were famously ravishing. Dad always referred to them affectionately as 'where all the trouble started'. She patted my knee in thanks.

'Thank you Beverley, for that moving reading,' Christopher said. 'How hard it is to read aloud when our hearts are aching with loss. But what comfort these timeless words bring.'

I was beginning to think Christopher was a bit florid.

'Over recent days I have spent many hours with Sam's most cherished people,' he continued. 'They have spoken of a brave, true man with a brilliant legal mind and a wicked sense of humour. Although he never married or had any children of his own, Sam exhibited great interest and curiosity in the young people around him. And of course, throughout his long years of legal service, he helped countless clients at a difficult stage in their lives, offering wise counsel and a steadying presence as they navigated the Kafka-esque maze of our legal system.' Christopher looked particularly pleased with this reference.

'Next I invite Jerry Cohen, a former colleague of Sam's, to speak to us about the professional chapter of his life.'

Beverley had found Jerry Cohen. We had wanted someone who could talk about Sam's professional successes, the gratitude of his clients and the High Court cases he had worked on – clarifying important legal principles on property rights and parental responsibility. Beverley had picked up the phone and worked her eastern suburbs legal contacts, the ones she wished so dearly I would leverage. She had got a list of retired partners of Sam's firm. One of my parents' friends who was a retired judge said Jerry Cohen was the best pick. He and my uncle had been particularly firm friends, apparently.

Jerry Cohen was long-legged, with a wiry form that held the memory of what it must have been in youth – the figure of someone unobtrusively slim and handsome. His hair was thick and slate-grey, combed across his head like sheep's wool. His eyes were bright and intelligent and his voice, when he spoke, had traces of American vowels. He began.

'I first met Sam in 1950 at Sydney University, in a crowded pub where all the girls were wearing circle skirts and the men had sports jackets. I was fresh to the city and he said he knew a jazz club. "Great," I say. "I love jazz." At least I thought that's what he said. Later that night, I find myself in Kings Cross, sittin' at the business end of a bar and looking up at the six-foot long legs of a cabaret girl as she takes one shoe off and rubs her toe in my ear. Sam, next to me, sippin' his drink and laughing like he was fit to crack a rib. Only she wasn't a girl. He hadn't said jazz. He'd said drag.'

My father let out a hoot of delight at this, and slapped his thigh in appreciation. The rest of the room tittered slightly, as though seeking permission to laugh, but unsure if it would be granted. My mother frowned. Standing behind Jerry, Christopher the celebrant smiled in a neutral way.

'That was the beginning of our friendship, which was long, and deeper than many people knew. You hear a lot of bunkum at funerals, but Sam was one of the finest people I have known. He had a fine mind and an even finer sensibility. In some ways he was born too late, because he was a very 19th-century kinda guy. Gentlemanly. But in other ways, he was born too soon, because he never got to enjoy the freedoms that should have been his birthright.'

Beverley cleared her throat and picked at the tufts of her bouclé skirt. My mother with her niceties – she still thought it mattered to the world if a man was gay, and she still thought it mattered even though he was dead. It was all over now. Sam was in a box at the front of the room, which we had covered in flowers and draped with an Afghan rug, one of my uncle's favourites from his travels. Whatever life was, Sam's essential Sam-ness, it was extinguished now. The only thing that could keep him alive was the telling of these stories. Sam in 1950, laughing, pleased with his trick, admiring a fishnet-stretch of leg.

Jerry talked for about ten minutes, cycling through their university days and their admission as lawyers and, later, their companionable time as colleagues in the same firm, the late nights at the office, the lunches at the club, the comfort and counsel Sam gave when Jerry's own marriage dissolved. I felt there was a lot lodged in the gaps here. After Jerry's speech we had more readings: one of the Kiwi cousins with the golfer hair read from the Bible, which was fine – Sam hated religion but he loved Ecclesiastes. *There is a time for everything, and a season for every activity under the heavens.* I spoke briefly about Sam's affection and humour as a grandparent-figure to me. As I talked, Christopher activated a multimedia display which beamed photographs from Sam's life onto the wall behind me. My favourite one was of him with Maddy as a baby, around the two-month mark when she started chucking out smiles. He was holding her, beaming, and they were looking at each other, locked in mutual delight.

After the service was over, Christopher activated a button and an electronic screen moved slowly sideways to shield Sam's coffin from sight, a sort of reverse striptease. From there the coffin was to be conveyed to the human kiln where they crisped the bodies of the ones we loved. We would next see Sam in urn form, and that urn would sit on the mantelpiece at Ruby Street for a long time before I figured out what to do with it. For now, though, there was a great press of people, a criss-cross mumble of *Lovely service* and *He will be so missed* and my mother standing outside with large sunglasses, graciously receiving well-wishes, the Jacqueline Kennedy of the Sydney suburbs. Somewhere in it all, me, hot, and needing a moment, just one moment, to stand alone and absorb the latest, which was the stumbling, sudden reality that I would never hear Sam laugh again, and all the things I had never asked him, would now go unknown. His secrets would be burned in the human crisper, along with him. Person after person was greeting me and I said the expected things as my mind rioted with the need to be alone and not talk to anyone, or be talked at. Then, in front of me: the sloping smile of Jerry Cohen, shaking my hand with his right hand, and covering the top of my hand with his left. I thanked him for his speech.

'No worries,' he said. 'I haven't seen your uncle in nearly 20 years, you know. We fell out.'

I said I hadn't known that, and I was sorry to hear it. I wished I had known Jerry existed while Sam was alive.

'I miss him like hell,' said Jerry, and he left. He didn't come to the wake at my parents' house afterwards.

As the crowd broke up, I saw the familiar, tall lope of Tom, hovering at the sidelines of the function room, next to a giant pot of lilies. He was talking to Cherry, who seemed very taken with him. He met my eye and walked over to me.

'I'm friends with Beverley on Facebook,' he said in explanation.

'How …?'

'She friend-requested me ages ago and I accepted. I didn't want to be rude. Also, I like your mum.'

Beverley was active on Facebook. Unaware of the ironic conventions governing social media, she posted earnest personal updates and used it as a message board for procuring gardening services and other information she could easily have Googled. She got into a lot of political arguments with people in the comments sections of posts. She also used it, I was sure, to shamelessly cyber-stalk. I hoped Tom had his privacy settings locked down.

'She posted a notice about the funeral,' Tom said. 'I thought I would come and just pay my respects. As they say. I'm really sorry, Suzy. Sam had a cool energy.'

'He did,' I replied. 'Hey. Any chance you could give me a ride back? I need not to be in a car with my parents right now.'

Once I was safe behind the solid thunk of the closed door of Tom's Subaru, I relaxed a little. I took off my shoes – the same pointy-toed pumps I had worn to the job interview, which seemed like it had occurred decades ago. I unpinned my hair. I reclined the seat and fiddled with the radio until something good came on. I found 'Cigarettes and Coffee' by Otis Redding. Sam had liked this song. Tom jumped into the driver's seat and put his sunglasses on. This had the effect of increasing his natural attractiveness about sevenfold.

'Hi,' he said, looking at me. 'How are you?'

I smiled at him and he took off. He conveyed me through the great green aisleways of the national park, to the suburban streets where once-lush lawns yellowed in the late-morning sun, and where the driveways were empty. We didn't speak. I didn't tell him about what had happened with Terry. I needed an hour when I wasn't having to absorb the reactions of other people. Somewhere around Artarmon, before we hit the expressway for the Harbour Bridge, which seemed the unofficial threshold to the real world, Tom asked me how my story was going. My story about Tracey.

'I lost it,' I said, only half-lying. 'My computer crashed and I have lost it all.'

Tom was silent for a second. His hands gripped the steering wheel like he was helming a ship. He switched his indicator on to merge onto the freeway and I noticed the small muscles in his forearm tense and relax.

'Give me your passwords,' he said. 'I will have a go at retrieving it. It might be in the cloud.'

CHAPTER 25

A few days later I wandered into the Little Friend to give my notice. I hadn't worked a shift there since Sam died, and I had rung Trevor to ask for a few days off. I had already met up with Olivia from the consultancy group, and we had settled on a salary which would make a significant amount of my problems go away. I had a start date of a week hence, and all I needed now were clothes. Beverley had opinions. She sent me a list of items she said comprised an ideal 'capsule wardrobe'. This was, she said, a concept embraced by the French, who believed a woman should own certain quality 'pieces' as the building blocks of elegance. She listed a black pencil skirt, a well-cut blazer and a pair of high-waisted navy trousers. A crisp white button-up shirt. A silk scarf for a flash of colour at the neck. I realised that if I bought all these things I would look like Beverley, which was probably exactly how I should look if I wanted to be taken seriously in my new job. I pictured myself hosting lunches with my former colleagues, lowering my voice to slip them tips about rivals, discreetly feeding them positive information about our clients, my clients, while I refilled their glasses with Sancerre. Was that how it worked? 'We build relationships,' Olivia had said, in her honey-soft yet crisp way, and I guessed I could do that easily enough with a company credit card and a capsule wardrobe.

But first I had to pay my debt to Jan, and finish the Tracey story, and deliver it to her, to do whatever she liked with it. Tom had taken my passwords and somehow he had found the draft of my story in the cloud, and he had emailed it to me with the subject line 'FOR THE LOVE OF GOD BACK UP YOUR WORK'. I had written back to thank him, asking him if I could buy him dinner to repay the favour. But he said he was busy. *Date night with Jess*, he wrote. Reading this had produced a lump of mortification in my throat which I swallowed down. I stomped on the fingers of my desire, in the hope they would lose their grip and fall away. The cop with the high ponytail had called me and Jan the previous day to tell us Terry had been bailed, but that the police had applied for an order on our behalf which prevented him from coming within 10 kilometres of us or our homes, and from contacting us. Jan said she didn't like knowing he was out, but then, she hated to think of him in jail, too, and so far away from home. 'He's always loved his creature comforts,' she said. 'His toast by the telly and his Friday night footy. I know he seems hard, and I'm sure he can handle himself, but he's a bit of a lamb really.' I said nothing, but marvelled inwardly at how loyal people could be to certain beliefs, no matter how much evidence was thrown up to refute them.

It was early evening when I arrived, and the Little Friend was only a quarter full. Jess was at the bar, wearing a T-shirt that said 'Pussy is God', the words stretched impressively across the glory of her bosom. Pete was in the corner singing a strained version of 'Nuthin' but a G Thang' by Dr Dre. He seemed half-hearted tonight, and his voice was infused with melancholy.

'You looking for Trevor?' said Jess. 'He's ducked out to the mini-mart but he'll be back. Sit. I'll make you a drink.'

She groped around the bar for a shaker and some liquor. With a few sharp movements of her wrist she poured a mojito into a glass and topped it with an origami fold of mint. It tasted cool and fresh, like walking through mist.

'Do you think Pete has heard of cultural appropriation?' I asked her.

'Nope. Or if he has, he doesn't believe in it. He rejects identity politics,' Jess said. 'All culture is world culture. How can you appropriate something that's already yours?' Jess said.

'He brings something to the music that Dre never could.'

'True that,' Jess said, nodding.

I reached for a handful of popcorn. 'I'm taking a new job,' I told her.

'Well, good for you,' she replied. 'So am I. In Melbourne.'

Jess said she had been offered a sommelier's position at one of the city's best restaurants. It was a dream job for her, and she had always wanted to live in Melbourne. She felt she was a Melbourne-y kind of person. I could see Jess at a bar in St Kilda, her hair twisted on top of her head, fending off the attentions of pale men in black jeans.

'What about Tom?' I said.

'He's coming with me.'

*

That night I drank a bottle of cheap chardonnay and wafted around the house like I was haunting it. Beverley had said to expect a call from Uncle Sam's probate lawyer any day. I half-heartedly checked the real estate listings online, noting that we could rent a renovated semi on our new budget. One with a useable backyard, and built-in wardrobes, and full-length mirrors that allowed you to see your whole body all at once, head and toe, and everything in between. These places were all freshly painted and looked like they belonged with families who were different from us.

I lightly stalked Tom on social media, even though I knew it would make me feel worse. It did. What did Tom owe me? Nothing. Did I think he would stay making babycinos forever? Of course he wanted to move to Melbourne. Melbourne was where art occurred. He and Jessica could rent an apartment with high ceilings and read the paper in bed on Saturday mornings. In the evenings they would go to cramped restaurants with their friends and discuss cultural appropriation and identity in art, and why liberalism had failed. They would split the bill. Tom would buy a coat that fit the broad stretch of his shoulders and he would loop an arm around Jess as they walked home through cold streets. Disgusted by myself, I closed down the internet browser on my computer.

My phone rang and I looked around, drunkenly, to locate the noise. I picked up. There was a lag, then a 'Hello? Hello? Hello Suzy,' drifting into my ear with the intimacy of a voice I knew. It was Charlie.

'Oh. Hi,' I said, as though it was a routine call. I estimated I had not spoken to him in nearly two years.

'How are you?'

There was just no way to answer that question so I left it hanging. I felt justified in causing him some discomfort. I suppose that was part of what Tom called my righteous aggrievement. Where was the line between righteous and right? It was subjective.

'What the actual fuck, Charlie?' I said. 'What do you want?'

'Okay then,' he said, catching my attitude. 'How's Maddy?'

How was Maddy? How was the girl? How do you stuff two years of early childhood development into a sentence or so? Maddy was tall for her age, full of mischief, heart-stoppingly cute, achingly sweet up to the point where she turned into a devil, perpetually hungry, always curious, and frequently asking questions I couldn't answer like *What do mermaids eat?* and *Where do the stars go?* and *Where's my daddy?* Just the other day she had asked me whether the wishes you make when you blow a dandelion really come true, because, it seemed, hers hadn't. And I had thought, *What do you wish for, my little heart?*

'Oh, she's fine,' I said, and I realised as I said it that it was true. She was more than fine. She was happy.

'So she is over the croup?'

The croup seemed a life ago.

'I wasn't sure you got that email,' I said. 'You never responded to it. Yes, she recovered fine. She's thriving, even.'

I heard Charlie exhale. In the background to the call I could hear a car alarm wail. I wondered where he was.

'I'm sorry I haven't been in touch,' he said. 'My work has been busy, and I needed things to settle in my mind a bit.'

He spoke as though I knew what work he was doing now, and also as though it was reasonable and normal to take a time-out that lasted years. I supposed he was still working in IT, just somewhere else. It was the kind of job that travelled.

'Okay,' I said. 'Has your mind settled then?'

'A little.'

'And what have you settled on?'

'Look, I know you think I'm an arsehole,' he said, and then dangled a pause as though I might jump in to disagree. After I didn't, he continued: 'Think of it as a vote of confidence in you. I knew Maddy would be fine. I knew how well you'd look after her.'

'Thank you for the vote of confidence,' I said.

'Okay, that came out wrong.' He sighed. 'Jesus, you don't make this easy, Suzy.'

'Maybe it would be easier if you told me what it is that I'm supposed to be making easy,' I said.

'I'm back in Sydney,' he said.

I had not expected that. It was not news I had a firm reaction to, one way or the other. It was like blowing on a dandelion, my thoughts like seeds, flying every which way.

'Good for you,' I said. 'How are you enjoying the summer?'

'It's fine. Listen, I want to see her.'

'Right.'

'Maybe I could come and take her for ice cream, or something.'

How to quell the rage that upsurged with an offer of ice cream? It was roiling and incommensurate. The rank inadequacy of an ice cream proposal made me want to snort contempt. Delinquency ameliorated by treats. The offer was made all the worse by how swiftly I knew Maddy would fall for it. She would love it. Who doesn't love ice cream? We often listened to a *Sesame Street* song about how everyone loves ice cream. She would be shy, of course, but such an outing would make her happy like few things would. And then she would want to come home to me, and describe in lengthy detail the kind of ice cream she had chosen, the kinds of ice creams she had considered but not chosen, and the technique she had deployed to eat the ice cream (cone last, biting tip of cone first, at what point in the ice cream's life cycle the sprinkles had been tackled). I knew Maddy better than she knew herself. I could have finished her sentences if I didn't so enjoy listening to her form them. Who was this guy? He didn't know her.

'Why would I agree to that?' I said.

'Oh, I don't know,' he said, some steel entering his voice. 'Because it would be good for Maddy to see her father?'

'Sure,' I said. 'But would it be good for Maddy to see her father only to have him bugger off again?'

'I didn't bugger off, Suzy,' he said. 'You wanted me gone. You can't be angry with me for taking the hint.'

This was bait I would not take. I left it sitting there between us, like a rank prawn.

'I'm not sure it's in Maddy's best interests,' I said. 'Ice cream.'

'Do you want me to beg?' he said. 'Is this a way for you to have power over me? You need to think about what's best for her.'

I thought about someone like Jess, with her toucan print and her give-no-fucks attitude, and wondered what she might say to something like this. She would put the phone down or make a pithy comment about mansplaining. I was probably within my rights to do either or both of those things. The problem was that Charlie was correct. There was probably no harm in ice cream. I wondered how Maddy would remember it later – a father standing tall in a doorway, emerging from his absence without any prior announcement. Her small hand in his large one, some strangled attempts at preschool-level small talk, Maddy's little heart beating with excitement and something else she would never be able to name. Was there any real risk to it? All ties carried the threat of harm. The bigger the attachment, the bigger the harm. But there was no getting around it, if any of us was truthful, no evading the attachment or the hurt. Even Charlie, the great wanderer, the bolter, the father-ghost, had some attachments, it seemed. Who can say no to ice cream? I said yes to ice cream. We made a time for the following week.

*

When I thought of what went wrong between me and Charlie, I thought of the Hemingway quote about going bankrupt – it happened gradually, then all at once. The gradual part probably began not long after we were dating. For the first few months there was just a haze of love which clung to us like bar-smoke and cast us in an unrealistic glow. Charlie was witty, observant, and apparently delighted by me. The fit of our bodies was nothing short of transformative. We spent a lot of time arguing over who loved who more, and other sickening things. It took me a long time to realise that kind of thing is performative, easy to toss off. True intimacy is grinding when it's not smooth, and it thrives on you shutting up much more than it requires demonstrative ardour.

During that early time we texted each other countless times a day, and if there was a lag of more than say, half an hour, in his response, I dashed myself against the rocks and convinced myself he didn't love me anymore, that his dumping of me was imminent. I would become obsessive, distracted and unable to concentrate. I think I worked myself into this state so I could feel the full power of the Eros-surge when he did, finally, message back. *Sorry! Meeting. During which I couldn't stop thinking about your legs*, or something like that. Our relationship was a seesaw. On the outside it looked equal, like we were partners in play. But in truth, he was the greater weight, and he controlled who was up and who was down.

I thought of that early time as the fog of war. When it cleared, I realised how much Charlie held back from me. He preferred my place to his. There were vast tracts of his past he wouldn't speak about. When I tried to piece together the timeline of his early life, he protested and evaded, and insisted he had never told me certain details I could have sworn he had. People from his past – often women – would appear from time to time. He would say they were very old friends, but they would be people I had never heard anything about before. He built with me a reputation for hopeless scattiness with technology, which we laughed about, seeing as technology was his job. *Oh, but how funny!* He was always losing phones and leaving them behind, dropping them or forgetting to charge them, so they stayed dark for hours, my text messages pinging into a dead space. His slow withdrawal – if you called it that, which I didn't, because he was never really there to begin with – made me pretty crazy. I tried to stay cool, failed, clung, cried. We fought more than was ideal. We broke up for periods and then came back together, like opposite poles on a magnet. I became more and more set on him, the clearer it became he was not firm ground on which to set myself. Gradually, the love that once made me feel light, made me heavy, but I was like the famously boiling frog. Things crept up on me. Love can be like that.

*

Then came the suddenly part: The Incident.

Maddy was conceived on the up part of our separation/ reparation cycle, when we had travelled to Europe together. Maddy formed a focus, a bright point of love which we both looked at, and in the looking, we were together. There were even moments I felt like we were a family, vignettes which I painted into my memory. Walks when Charlie carried the baby in a papoose. Her happy arms flapping, she looked like an insect on a windshield. Mornings when he would take Maddy so I could sleep in, and I would wake to the trill and chortle of her baby babble, and his answers to it. But he was so absent so much, and a baby is not company. He discovered new and pressing duties at the office, came home late, smelled of alcohol. The predictability of it made me hate him, which really meant I hated myself, because I should have foreseen it. He always kept his phone close, guarding it tenderly, like a pet mouse he kept in his pocket. But constant vigilance is nearly impossible in any context, and one evening he lapsed when he left the house to pick up takeaway pizza, and I found the phone wedged between the cushions of the couch as I sat down on it heavily. Maddy was asleep and I wanted to watch the news headlines. Instead I tried out the code I had seen him tap into it, having memorised the pattern of his fingers as they moved over the keypad screen. My distrust and his distance meant I had become expert in surveillance, and like a good intelligence officer, I remained concealed until I found opportunity.

On the phone, I found: the vulva picture, various breast pictures, underpants pictures (the sender and recipient called them 'panties', a word that made me curl my lip), and acres of the sort of words that go with such photographic correspondence. Some of it was surprisingly loving. Charlie had a lot of correspondents, so many that I marvelled at his multi-tasking. There was also online gambling, a lot of it, which was truly surprising and had more real-world consequences than the pictures.

Is there a good way to react to such discoveries? If there is a good way, it was not the way I took. The shock was the most physical experience I'd had since childbirth. I ran through all the usual emotions you might imagine. But one thought overrode all the others, streaming through my brain like a banner behind an aeroplane, riding across the air of my mind: *Fuck this. Absolutely fuck this*, I thought. But relief was threaded through my anguish. Here was a good reason to leave. Here was probable cause. Here, I was able to transfer moral responsibility. I had been in emotional pursuit of Charlie for so long I had never admitted to myself that he wasn't the only one who feared closeness, the terror of being known, the truth about you revealed. We accuse people of what we do ourselves. I had chased and waited for so long. Now I would discover the power of being the one who fled. I bathed in it.

On such moments whole worlds turn. When he returned with a 'Hi, honey!', a margherita and a sad side-salad of rocket and parmesan, I cried and raged. I threw and destroyed an exquisite hand-turned vase Uncle Sam had given us as a wedding present. It was from a specialty potter near Canberra and very expensive. I think in such moments we're playing a role, acting out what we think is expected of us, telling ourselves a story that we can comfort ourselves with later. I told him things that were ugly and low, mostly things I didn't believe but which were designed to maim. I mocked the photos he had been sent, deploying all my sarcasm to humiliate him. I sought to disabuse him of any good notion he might have of himself. Later, I told the wives of his colleagues – some of whom I was friendly with – what he had done. I did this in a tearful way, under the guise of sisterly confidence, but really, I wanted the world to know. I kicked him out, then he came back and I moved out with Maddy. He begged me for forgiveness. I was a wall. He said, if I couldn't manage that, then perhaps I could just soften to tolerance of him? For Maddy's sake? I gave him no quarter, I told him to go, go, go. I relished it – finally I had been given a reason to give up, to stop pursuit and lie down by the side of the road with a heaving chest. Every single time I saw him I reminded him of who he was at his worst. I made him stare into a mirror of his own shame. Who can live with that? No one can. He left.

CHAPTER 26

The next evening I went over to Jan's place for the final time. I had spent the day hauling my piece on Tracey into shape, cutting it and recutting it, adding some words and changing others, adjusting it carefully like a floral arrangement at a wedding. At around 5 pm I walked up to Parramatta Road where there was an Officeworks, and I printed it out. It was about 30 pages, or 16,000 words. I didn't know if it would help Jan. I didn't think my words necessarily had much power.

Perhaps it was solipsistic to think that my original story about Tracey, the exposé, had had the power to kill her. Maybe my guilt was a form of narcissism. Just because we're all connected doesn't make us totally responsible for each other. Or did it? I thought about all the hundreds of thousands of words I had written as a journalist. It was a strange way to make a living, to bring together the words of other people with reported facts and opinions from experts and statements from police, politicians, government agencies and public relations spokespeople (I was about to become one of those), and then ball them all into something you hoped was factual. The result was lumpen and frequently unreliable, even if its components were true. This process was imperfect. But on the whole it was correct, because we can only really create stories by looking at one another. As I left the printing place I swung the door behind me and met the wall of heat and traffic noise outside. I heard someone call my name. I turned around and saw Ben, looking like Heathcliff in a suit, his chest hair tufting from the neckline of his shirt. He was standing in the spot where the sun was going down, and I had to squint as I looked at him.

I smiled. 'Well,' I said. 'Hi.'

'Suzy. You look well.' He paused, and cleared his throat. He was as stiff as ever. We exchanged a little small talk about his new job, then he said: 'I have wanted to contact you many times these past months. I wanted to, but I didn't. For obvious reasons.'

'Oh, it's fine,' I said. It really was fine.

'Everything that happened was my fault,' he said. 'I should never have put you in that position. I was your superior. You were vulnerable. It was wrong of me and I apologise to you.'

'I wasn't vulnerable,' I said, a little too quickly. 'I was needy. It's slightly different. I was needy and I was bored, if I'm honest.'

His square chin sank a little and he looked hurt, which is the reaction I had been seeking, although not consciously. Trying to reclaim power from the men I was involved with was like a muscle memory for me, ingrained in me as the Moro reflex is in a baby. But then I looked up at Ben and saw that he needed to take on the burden of this guilt. Maybe it was his way of atoning for things. Of evening things up. *Okay, then*, I thought. *Let him take it.*

'But thank you, Ben,' I said. 'Thank you for apologising.'

I asked him what he was doing here, at this time. He pointed down the road to a doorway with a colourful painted sign which pictured a woman with a swirling skirt and a man in Cuban heels. Next to them was a basket of fruit. The perspective was off, so the grapes were as big as the man.

'Salsa,' he said. 'Beano is meeting me.'

We said our farewells and did not pretend that we would catch up soon, or stay in touch, or that we hoped to run into each other again. As I walked down Glebe Point Road back to Ruby Street, the sun sloped on the footpath and the air was bathed in rose-gold light, the kind Sydney produces often enough for you to forget the city's flaws. My phone rang, and it was as Beverley had warned – it was Uncle Sam's probate lawyer. But she was not calling to tell me the house had gone to the Kiwi cousins, and that we had four weeks to vacate it. She was calling to tell me the house was now mine.

*

Jan opened the door to her flat with a flourish, like a gay hostess. She seemed in excellent spirits, and her upbeat demeanour was augmented by the yellow dress she wore. A red sash cordoned her waist and two small earrings in the shape of bananas hung from her earlobes. She was barefoot.

'Come in, chook!' she trilled. 'I'm all fluttery. I can't wait to see the finished product.'

I walked through the sitting room of the old lady's apartment, past the settees carefully laid with crochet blankets, past the nest of three small tables next to the easychair. I saw that Jan had a pair of matching suitcases standing to attention next to the couch.

'I'm leaving tomorrow, duck,' she said. 'I have to get back to the pets. The kennel rang and the cat has gone utterly feral, they said. Scratched one of the cat carers. Now the poor woman has got cat-scratch disease. I had to look it up on the internet but it's no joke, I can tell you. And the dog is depressed.'

I handed her the booklet, the manuscript, whatever it was. I had bound it and designed a cover with Tracey on the front.

She looked full of health, like a girl in an advertisement for milk. Jan took it in her hands like it was a sacred document.

'Why did you never tell me it was you who wrote that email?' I asked. 'The tip-off.'

Jan looked down at her daughter's face in two dimensions.

'I was sick with my guilt,' she said. 'It was that email which started it. Which led to all of this.' She swept her hand out in a wild gesture which took in everything – the harbour, the doilies on the coffee table, the two of us.

She sat down on the Lazyboy chair and opened the book. I sat with her while she did, getting up at one point to fix us a cup of tea. Jan only had almond milk in the fridge. It would do. I drank almond milk tea while she read, and I looked around the small flat, with its orderly piles of crossword magazines and its clear line out to harbour blue, and I thought about how nice it must be to be an older lady, washed out of your anger and standing on the other shore of life.

When Jan finished reading, her face was wet and she thanked me. We hugged for a long time and we promised to email each other. A few days later she sent me a selfie she had taken with Tracey's pets. Even the spiteful cat looked like it was smiling.

*

But there was a part of the story I didn't include in the book I gave Jan, because it seemed too tender. It was something Jan had told me late one night, a few weeks earlier, when she had come into the Little Friend around closing and asked for a wine spritzer. She was on her way home from seeing *Anything Goes* at the Opera House.

Jan told me she didn't exactly *know* her daughter had been lying. Not for sure. For all she knew, there had been a cancer. Cancers. Tracey had been vague about appointments and treatment, and she had never wanted her mother to accompany her to the doctor. There had, of course, been no chemotherapy courses or radiotherapy. But Jan saw her daughter ailing, she saw her weight loss, she heard her talk about superfoods and vitamins and the crystal therapy her naturopath had recommended. She was sick with worry for her sick daughter and did what she could for her. If questions came up later, then what was she supposed to do? Demand to see Tracey's specialists? Subpoena her daughter's medical records? She asked me if I'd ever known a liar, a real liar, someone who was practised and convincing in their deception, so sincere and so full of detail that the lies formed an impasse. Yes, I had known someone like that. The lies kept things in and they kept things out. Jan was exhausted.

Tracey said she was in remission. Cured, she said. So Jan had booked her trip to Spain; she was flying to Barcelona, and she was doing overtime to save enough money so she could spend money like a person who didn't have to worry about spending money. And what could she do anyway? If she had suspicions, she said nothing about them.

But then Tracey started getting internet-famous and her fame piqued the interest of various commercial brands, and she got her cookbook contract, and it seemed that even the venerable publishing houses had fallen for what Jan was beginning to see very clearly was a hoax. Jan had spent her working life caring for the ill and injured, she had looked into the eyes of the dying, and she had seen their need, their fear and their anger. She knew what cancer patients endured because she had nursed them. She knew that the only way to fight cancer was to poison it, not meet it with smoothies and massages and meridians. She thought of the children who had lain in her wards over the years, their bones showing through their skin like death was straining to take them over. Their suffering. The religious people who visited the wards and told parents there was grace in this suffering – how badly Jan had wanted to chase these men from the ward with a stick, like they were witches. The parents of these children could become quite mad, Jan knew. They would grasp at anything and hold onto the slimmest of hopes, because it was an impossibility that they should lose a child they had known for so short a time. It was impossible that the bawling, angry, life-lit bundle the doctor had handed to them – just a few minutes ago, it seemed – would be stopped soon, an early cancellation by an unseen hand. What if one of these heartbroken, hope-ridden parents fell for her daughter's hokum? Jan would never forgive herself. She felt she bore some responsibility.

'So one night I drank a whisky and I sat down and wrote you that email,' she told me. 'I liked you ever since you did the thing about the celebrity chef under-paying his workers. Nasty twerp, that man.'

Jan didn't know if anything would come of it. She thought I probably got scores of emails from cranks with strange email addresses (I did). She both hoped and feared I would do something about it. Then one day, when she had just walked through the door of her house at Broadbeach and sat down to take off her shoes, the phone on the wall rang. It was Tracey, tearful, saying 'Mum, I have done something bad. I have made a big mistake.' And what mother doesn't drop everything when she receives this phone call from her child, plaintive and babyish, wanting her to swoop in and act as a maternal shield, to place herself between the child and the consequences the world wants to mete out to her? So Jan, nauseous at the thought of what she had set off, laced her shoes up again, ignoring the painful creak of her bunions, and she went to her daughter. What she found was Tracey in a small heap on her white linen couch, obsessively scrolling through her social media accounts and crying. She made her daughter close off all these devices, and took her onto her deck, where the subtropical tangle of the garden emitted various insect and bird noises that were ordinarily soothing, but which now sounded menacing. She looked into her daughter's face, cupping it with her own hands, and she begged Tracey to tell her everything, to tell her the truth. But Tracey mumbled and obfuscated and made attempts to back down from some lies, while buttressing others. She had been ill, she said, very ill. She had chosen to heal herself with diet and lifestyle and spiritual practice, why was that so hard for people to accept? Yes, said Jan, yes dear, but did the doctors ever say cancer? Did they use the word cancer? It is the word that stops the world. 'It's not that simple, Mum!' Tracey cried, and she talked around and around until the sun sank on the garden and the frogs started in earnest.

They went inside, back to the linen couch, and Jan knew that although her daughter wanted her to make the problem vanish, she couldn't. She was a 62-year-old registered nurse, divorced and afflicted with bunions, with one kid who was a gentle drug addict, and another who was a dangerous fantasist. The house at Broadbeach would not be paid off before her retirement. The house at Broadbeach needed a new roof. Her daughter's book advance had been double her annual wages as a nurse. She had wanted to be a lawyer, but her father had made it clear that further study was not an option for her, she was to work from 15, and she had left school then to train as a nurse. If that was sad, or if that was a waste, then it was one that was as common as dirt among the women she knew. Jan Doran was tired, and she had no power to hold the world back from crashing on her daughter's head. Instead, she held her daughter as she whimpered. She tucked Tracey's head back into her own collarbone, where it still fitted, and stroked her cheek with the back of her hand. She kissed her daughter's gorgeous hair, which was just growing back after its lopping, the hair that was shot through with honey. She breathed in her daughter's scent, of citrus and fresh wood, and for a small half-hour, she found a route back to her girl. Jan blamed herself for leaving that night, she feels a jolt of horror every time she remembers that she did, and she has tried to bend time in her mind, tried to make bargains and threats with forces she doesn't believe in, but nothing can change, now, the fact that Jan released her daughter eventually, patting down the damp spot Tracey had left on her shirt. 'Isn't that what they tell us to do?' she asked me, plaintively, as she relayed this. 'Release our children? What nobody tells you is they never release you.'

Her daughter promised to put her phone away and to go to bed immediately. Jan was tired, and her feet throbbed, and as she let herself out, she made a weary mental note to purchase her travel insurance the next day. She would use one of those cost comparison websites. She lowered herself heavily into her car, and she drove home, her tired eyes blurring the lights on the freeway. She received the phone call the next day while she was mid-shift, assisting at a colonoscopy. She cancelled her trip to Barcelona.

In her mind, she returns every day, every minute, to that place – her daughter's head in the crook of her chin, her hand on the globe of Tracey's cheek. It is a place she can still visit. It is a place where love idles and spreads. It is the best thing she has.

CHAPTER 27

I sat on my bed amid my new capsule wardrobe, the pieces of which were scattered across the quilt like a pile of money bills after someone had thrown them into the air. I had spent the afternoon shopping in the city with Beverley, trotting around after her like a pliant assistant as she plucked silk shirts from hangers and tugged at trouser legs and demanded sewing pins so she could show me what something would look like once it had been tailored properly. I thought it was strange to buy expensive clothes that didn't already fit you well, but it was an article of faith to Beverley that if you had things tailored, you could rely on their elegance forever. In Beverley's world gaining weight or changing shape was not a likelihood worth considering. You simply dieted to prevent that happening. She had also insisted I get a proper fitting for a bra – I was still wearing the no-longer-elasticised lingerie of my pre-Maddy days. The sales assistant who conducted the fitting confirmed what I already knew – I had dropped a cup size since having a baby. 'Don't worry, hun,' she said to me as she rang up my purchases, 'once you're finished having babies, you can fix that up.' She nodded towards my A-cup cleavage as though it was a problem child.

Now I sat surveying my treasures like a pirate king, picking garments up and holding them against my skin. The previous weekend, I had marched to the local hardware store and I had bought a full-length mirror, carrying it home under my arm like I had just looted it. Vic came over and stuck it onto the back of my bedroom door for me while we drank celebratory negronis. Now I could see myself in full. I touched my new clothes and imagined the impression I could create while wearing them. I wanted impenetrable professionalism. Serene civility. The clothes were a costume that would help me shake off my past, available to everyone I met who also had access to Google. It was evening and the branches of the fig swayed lazily in the late-summer light outside the balcony doors. Soon the light would switch from tawny to white, as the streetlights came on. I really had to ring the council about that tree. Now that I owned the house — something that still felt impossible and abstract — I really would have to do something about that tree. Across the room, my phone cheeped in my handbag. I got up to retrieve it and found a message from Tom. He wanted to come over. He had something to tell me.

'I know you're moving to Melbourne,' I said as I opened the door to him ten minutes later. 'I'm sorry to steal your thunder. Jess already told me.'

'Hello to you too,' he said. He laid a kiss on my cheek as he passed me. 'Maddy asleep?'

'She is.'

'Got any booze?'

'Sure.'

I led him into the kitchen and took a bottle of wine from the fridge. We moved into the lounge room. He sank into the low corduroy couch. I placed myself opposite him on an occasional chair.

'You're very far away,' Tom said. He was wearing a faded black T-shirt and jeans that were slightly ripped at the knee, but not in an on-purpose, fashion way. Everything about Tom was artless.

'And you're about to move very far away,' I replied.

'Jess got this opportunity at Franco's restaurant – I'm sure she told you about it. I've applied for a couple of fellowships. If I don't get one, I'll get another café job and work on my next exhibition. It's cheaper to live down there. And it's the spiritual home of the barista.'

'You make a strong case for Melbourne,' I said. 'Almost as if you're trying to convince yourself.'

'There are things I'll miss about Sydney,' he said.

'Such as?'

'The light.'

He crooked his head backwards to take in some wine from his glass and then looked at me with a brazenness that was unlike him. I felt he was willing me to object to his departure, but then I also believed that was a stupid, solipsistic thing to think. Tom had moved on. Soon I would too. Lying on my bed was the capsule wardrobe which would assist me in doing so.

We chatted in a desultory way about various things. I told him the cops had set a court date for Terry's hearing. He had been allowed to go home to Queensland but had to report to the local police station twice a week, and he was still under the order which prevented him from coming near Jan or me. Maddy had come home that week with a painting (more impressionistic lollipops) that bore her name on it, in her own writing. 'She'll be a writer,' said Tom, 'like her mother', and I told him to wash his mouth out.

I told him that Vic had successfully applied for the London correspondent's job, which was wonderful. It was a job I had once wanted, and fancied I would apply for when it next came up, even though I knew, at the same time, that the life of a drop-everything, chase-disaster correspondent was incompatible with single motherhood.

'Good for Vic,' said Tom. 'But London's a dreadful place. Terrible light. Even worse dentistry.'

I asked Tom what his next series was about and he said he wasn't sure but he had been reading about 'aporia', which was this idea that Socrates had, that all the questioning in the world could only lead to uncertainty.

'Aporia sounds a bit difficult to photograph,' I said.

'I have some ideas,' Tom said. 'Give me some credit, Hamilton.'

The conversation ambled to a natural pause.

'Next week I start at the job you disapprove of,' I said. 'I've bought new clothes and everything.'

'I'm sorry about that,' Tom said. 'I have no right to judge you. I don't know what it's like to live in your skin. I know it's not been easy with Maddy.'

'I'm going to try it for a while,' I said. 'I own this house now. Can you believe it?'

'What? How –'

'Uncle Sam –'

'He gave you the house?'

'He left me the house in his will.'

'Ah, Suzy,' said Tom, smiling broadly. 'Now you have the thing that all artists require. The thing that makes humans thrive, and that single mothers almost never get.'

'Money?'

'Related, but much better,' he said. 'Freedom.'

He raised his glass to me and I laughed. I felt light because I realised he was right. I got up and walked to him, clinking my glass to his and sitting down beside him. The sides of our legs touched. To be near him was a surge. I felt high, like I was composed of air. He put his glass down on the wooden coffee table, where it would leave a small faint ring that would stay for years, and which I wouldn't mind about at all. He leaned towards me and kissed me, and after a while we went upstairs to bed and undressed each other on top of the capsule wardrobe.

The next morning I woke later than usual and realised that I had slept deeply. Ordinarily I would kick Tom out before Maddy woke up. It was too late – I could hear the sounds of them in the kitchen floating up the stairs. I pulled on my kimono and went to join them.

'Tom did a sleepover!' Maddy said brightly as I entered the kitchen.

'We're making pancakes,' Tom said.

Both of them wore aprons and were absorbed in the sort of synchronistic flow that characterises long-standing cooking duos – the application of milk in a hollow of flour, the just-so dab of vanilla essence, the satisfying arrival of a pat of butter in a hot pan.

I knew that Tom was right, and that inquiry only led to uncertainty. Life was as uncertain as it was fragile. I thought that the only way to firm things up, to make the ground sure underfoot, was to grasp at life, to reach for it, to run towards it like Maddy did, with the optimistic *dunk-dunk-dunk* of her footfall in the hall. I thought that even if it didn't work – the running-after, the grasping – you still had to make the attempt. I looked up at Tom now, who stood next to my daughter at the kitchen counter. She gleamed with life, she refracted it like light, while Jan's daughter, Tracey, was dead, recoverable only through the stories we told about her. Tom's hand covered Maddy's, steadying her as she whisked the pancake batter.

'Don't go to Melbourne,' I said to him. 'Stay.'

ACKNOWLEDGEMENTS

If it takes a village to raise a child, then it takes a small metropolis to raise a child and a book at the same time. Thank you foremost and forever to my brilliant mother, Judy, for all your support and love. Mum, if both book and baby turned out okay, it's all because of you.

Richard Walsh was the first person to see my early attempts at fiction. He told me I could do it. For that, and much more besides, I will be always grateful. Richard, I think I owe you a lunch. My publisher Catherine Milne was coaxing, sensitive and enthusiastic at all the right moments. Thank you, Catherine, for your precious encouragement and gentle midwifery. Thank you to my brilliant agent, Jeanne Ryckmans, for your unstinting energy and passion about this book.

I finished the draft of this novel while on fellowship at the Katharine Susannah Prichard Writers' Centre in Perth. It was a golden fortnight, and I thank staff at the KSP centre for it.

Thank you to my marvellous Maleys for loving support and a lifetime of good conversation – Dad, Tan, Matt, Imogen, Paul, Grace, Sebby, Cath, Mark and Karen, Natalya and Olivia, and my wonderful grandparents, Yvonne and Barry. Grandma, you taught me more about books than anyone. Grandfather, thank you for always believing in me. Dad, thanks for being an early reader and for always asking when the book would be published, not if. Paul, thank you for always having my back.

Thank you to my lovely friends – so many of you kept me afloat in recent years. Thanks particularly to my darling Ben Wickham, for true love, loyalty and understanding – Ben, I'm neither dead nor gay, but I hope you will read this book. To Julia Baird, for so much, but especially for your incredible generosity of spirit and joie de vivre (and for memories of the plump bottom of University House). To Jordan Baker – you are my favourite conversationalist and stalwart bestie. To Anna Clark and Gab Abromovitz for giving me a home, and a place to write, when I so needed both. To Sarah Oakes, for being my reader – I am forever grateful for the way you lift people up, it is a real gift. Thanks, too, to Dylan Welch, for skydaddy duties and for making me laugh. To Gillian Khaw for encouragement and for loving-yet-tough talk when I needed to move on after failure.

Thank you to my editors and colleagues at the *Sydney Morning Herald* for their support and understanding while I was working on this book – particularly Lisa Davies, James Chessell, Cosima Marriner, Andrew Forbes, Julie Lewis, Steph Peatling, Nick O'Malley and Katrina Strickland. I swear all the newsroom parts are pure fiction!

Last, but never least, to Michael, for your loyalty and love, for being there for E, and for the gift of two weeks in a cottage in Perth to finish this thing. I cannot ever thank you enough for all you've done for me. I love you more than sleep-ins – one day maybe you'll get one of those.